Enthusiastic praise for
WILLIAM LASHNER

"Intrigu... ...omplex read."
...ia Inquirer

"Flawless . . . a gripping thriller."
Orlando Sentinel

"Riveting . . . shocking . . . a dark and eerie tale
with decidedly Gothic overtones. . . . Lashner has
created a true page-turner—complex enough to
keep the reader guessing until the very end."
Chattanooga Free Press

"This guided tour through the lifestyles of the
rich and nasty teems with clever plot twists and
(literally) buried secrets. . . . [Put] Lashner on the
hot list of up-and-coming legal thriller writers."
Publishers Weekly

By William Lashner

FATAL FLAW
VERITAS (BITTER TRUTH)
HOSTILE WITNESS

Coming Soon in Hardcover

PAST DUE

WILLIAM
LASHNER

BITTER
TRUTH

(Originally published as *Veritas*)

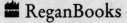 ReganBooks

HarperTorch
An Imprint of HarperCollins*Publishers*

Las

This book was originally published in 1997 as *Veritas* by HarperCollins Publishers.

This is a work of fiction. Names, characters, places, and incidents are products of the author's imagination or are used fictitiously and are not to be construed as real. Any resemblance to actual events, locales, organizations, or persons, living or dead, is entirely coincidental.

HARPERTORCH
An Imprint of HarperCollins*Publishers*
10 East 53rd Street
New York, New York 10022-5299

Copyright © 1997 by William Lashner
ISBN: 0-06-056038-X

First HarperTorch paperback printing: February 2003
First HarperPaperbacks printing: November 1997
First HarperCollins hardcover printing: February 1997

HarperCollins®, HarperTorch™, and ❧™ are trademarks of HarperCollins Publishers Inc.

Printed in the United States of America

Visit HarperTorch on the World Wide Web at
www.harpercollins.com

10 9 8 7 6

11/07
Bet

In memory of my father and partner,
Melvin Lashner,
who knew right from wrong
and lived each day as if it mattered.

A taste for truth at any cost is
a passion which spares nothing.

—ALBERT CAMUS

═══════

BITTER
TRUTH

Part 1

===

AILUROPHOBIA

I know of nothing more despicable and pathetic
than a man who devotes all the hours of the waking day
to the making of money for money's sake.

—JOHN D. ROCKEFELLER

1

En Route to Belize City, Belize

I SUPPOSE EVERY HUNDRED million dollars has its own sordid story and the hundred million I am chasing is no exception.

I am on a TACA International flight to Belize in search of my fortune. Underneath the seat in front of me lies my briefcase and in my briefcase lies all I need, officially, to pick my fortune up and take it home with me. I lift the briefcase onto my lap and open it, carefully pulling out the file folder, and from that folder, with even more care, pulling out the document inside. I like the feel of the smooth copy paper in my hands. I read it covetously, holding it so the nun sitting next to me can't steal a peek. Its text is as short and as evocative as the purest haiku. **"Default judgment is awarded in favor of the plaintiff in the amount of one hundred million dollars."** The document is signed by the judge and stamped in red ink and certified by the Prothonotary of the Court of Common Pleas of the City of Philadelphia and legal in every state of the union and those countries with the appropriate treaties with the United States, a group in which, fortunately, Belize is included. One hundred million dollars, the price of two lives plus punitive damages. I bring the paper to my nose and smell it. I can detect the sweet scent of mint, no, not peppermint, government. One hundred million dollars, of which my fee, as the attorney, is a third.

Think hard on that for a moment; I do, constantly. If I find what I'm hunting it would be like winning the lotto every month for a year. It would be like Ed McMahon coming to my door with his grand prize check not once, not twice, but three times, and I would get it all at once instead of over thirty years. It would be enough money to run for president if I were ever so deranged. Well, maybe not that much, but it is still a hell of a lot of money. And I want it, desperately, passionately, with all my heart and soul. Those who whine that there is no meaning left in American life are blind, for there is fame and there is fortune and, frankly, you can take fame and cram it down your throats. Me, I'll take the money.

For almost a year I've been in search of the assets against which my default judgment will be collected. I've traced them through the Cayman Islands to a bank in Luxembourg to a bank in Switzerland, through Liberia and Beirut and back through the Cayman Islands, from where payments had been wired, repeatedly, to an account at the Belize Bank. From the Belize Bank the funds were immediately withdrawn, in cash. Unlike all the other transfers of funds, the transfers to Belize were neither hidden within the entwining vines of larger transactions nor mathematically encrypted. The owner of the money has grown complacent in his overconfidence or he is sending me an invitation and either way I am heading to Belize, flying down to follow the money until it leads me directly to him. He is a vicious man, violent, deceptive, greedy beyond belief. He has killed without the least hesitation, killed for the basest of reasons. His hands drip with blood and I have no grounds to believe he will not kill again. When I think on his crimes I find it amazing how the possibility of so much money can twist one to act beyond all rationality. I am flying down to Belize to find this man in his tropical asylum so I can serve the judgment personally and start the collection proceedings that will at long last make me rich.

In a voice equally apathetic in Spanish and English we are told that we are beginning our approach to Belize City. I return the document to the briefcase, twist the case's lock, stow it back beneath the seat in front of me. Outside the window I see the teal blue of the Caribbean and then a ragged line of scabrous slicks of land, spread atop the water like foul oil, and then the jungle, green and thick and foreign. Clots of treetops are spotted dark by clouds. For not the first time I feel a doubt rise about my mission. If I were going to Pittsburgh or Bern or Luxembourg City I'd feel more confident, but Belize is a wild, untamed place, a country of hurricanes and rain forests and great Mayan ruins. Anything can happen in Belize.

The nun sitting next to me, habited in white with a black veil and canvas sneakers, puts down her Danielle Steel and smiles reassuringly.

"Have you been to our country before?" she asks with a British accent.

"No," I say.

"It is quite beautiful," she says. "The people are wonderful." She winks. "Keep a hand on your wallet in Belize City, yes? But you will love it, I'm sure. Business or pleasure?"

"Business."

"Of course, I could tell by your suit. It's a bit hot for that. You'll be visiting the barrier reef too, I suppose, they all do, but there's more to Belize than fish. While you are here you must see our rain forests. They are glorious. And the rivers too. You brought insect repellent, I expect."

"I didn't, actually. The bugs are bad?"

"Oh my, yes. The mosquito, well, you know, I'm sure, of the mosquito. The malaria pills they have now work wonders. And the welts from the botlass fly last for days but are not really harmful. Ticks of course and scorpions,

but the worst is the beefworm. It is the larva of the botfly
and it is carried by the mosquito. It comes in with the bite
and lives within your flesh while it grows, grabbing hold of
your skin with pincers and burrowing in. Nasty little para-
site, that. The whole area blows up and is quite painful,
there is a burning sensation, but you mustn't pull it, oh no.
Then you will definitely get an infection. Instead you must
cover the area with glue and tape and suffocate it. The
worm squirms underneath for awhile before it dies and that
is considered painful by some, but the next morning you
can just squeeze the carcass out like toothpaste from a
tube."

I am lost in the possibilities when the plane tilts up,
passes low over a wide jungle river, and slams into the run-
way. "Welcome to the Philip Goldson International
Airport," says the voice over the intercom. "The airport
temperature is ninety-three and humidity is eighty-five percent. Enjoy your stay in Belize."

We depart onto the tarmac. It is oppressively hot, the
Central American sun is brutal. I feel its pressure all over
my body. The air is tropically thick and in its humidity my
suit jacket immediately weighs down with sweat. There is
something on my face. I am confused for a moment before
I realize it is an insect and frantically swipe it away. We
are herded in a line toward customs. To our left is the terminal building, brown as rust, a relic from the fifties, to our
right is a camouflaged military transport, being loaded with
something large I can't identify. A black helicopter circles
overhead. Soldiers rush by in a jeep. Sweat drips from my
temples and down my neck. I shuck off my jacket, but
already my shirt is soaked. I brush a mosquito from my
wrist but not before it bites me. I can almost feel something wiggling beneath the skin.

After we hand our passports over for inspection and
pick up our bags we are sent in lines to wait for the dog. I
sit on my suitcase and pick at the amoebic blob swelling

on my wrist. A German shepherd appears, mangy and fierce. He is straining at his leash. He sniffs first one suitcase, then another, then a backpack. The dog comes up to me and shoves his nose into my crotch. Two policemen laugh.

Even inside the terminal it is hot and the sunlight rushing through the windows is fierce and I feel something dangerous beyond the mosquitoes in the swelter about me. I wonder what the hell I am doing in Belize but then I feel the weight of my briefcase in my hand and remember about the hundred million dollars and its story, a story of betrayal and revenge, of intrigue and sex and revelation, a story of murder and a story of redemption and a story of money most of all. Suddenly I know exactly what I am doing here and why.

2

IT STARTED FOR ME with a routine job in the saddest little room in all of Philadelphia. Crowded with cops and shirt-sleeved lawyers and court clerks and boxes of files, a dusty clothes rack, a computer monitor with plastic wood trim and vacuum tubes like something out of *Popular Mechanics* circa 1954, it was a room heavy with the air of an exhausted bureaucracy. I was sitting alone on the lawyers' bench inside that room, waiting for them to drag my client from the holding cells in the basement. My job that morning was to get him out on a reasonable bail and, considering what he was being charged with, that wasn't going to be easy.

I was in the Roundhouse, Philadelphia Police Headquarters, a circular building constructed in the sixties, all flowing lines, every office a corner office, an architectural marvel bright with egalitarian promise. But the Roundhouse had turned old before its time, worn down by too much misery, too much crime. At the grand entrance on Race Street there was a statue of a cop holding a young boy aloft in his arms, a promise of all the good works envisioned to flow through those doors, except that the entrance on Race Street was now barred and visitors were required to enter through the rear. In through that back entrance, to the right, past the gun permit window, past the bail clerk, through the battered brown doors and up the steps to the benches where a weary public could watch, through a wall of thick Plexiglas, the goings on in the Roundhouse's very own Municipal Court.

"Sit down, ma'am," shouted the bailiff to a young woman who had walked through those doors and was now standing among the benches behind the Plexiglas wall. She was young, thin, a waif with short hair bleached yellow and a black leather jacket. She was either family or friend of one of the defendants, or maybe just whiling away her day, looking for a morning's entertainment. If so, it was bound to be a bit wan. "You can't stand in the back," shouted the bailiff, "you have to sit down," and so she sat.

The defendants were brought into the room in batches of twenty, linked wrist to wrist by steel, and placed in a holding cell, with its own Plexiglas view. You could see them in there, through the Plexiglas, waiting with sullen expectation for their brief time before the bar.

"Sit down, sir," called out the bailiff in what was a steady refrain. "You can't stand back there," and another onlooker dropped onto one of the benches.

"Hakeem Trell," announced the clerk and a young man sauntered a few steps to the large table before the bench that dominated the room.

"Hakeem Trell," said Bail Commissioner Pauling, reading from his file, "also known as Roger Pettibone, also known as Skip Dong." At this last alias Commissioner Pauling looked over the frames of his half-glasses at the young man standing arrogantly before him. There was about Hakeem Trell a.k.a. Roger Pettibone a.k.a. Skip Dong the defiant annoyance of a high school student facing nothing more serious than an afternoon's detention. Where was the anxiety as he faced imprisonment, the trembling fear at the rent in his future? What had we done to these children? My client wasn't in the batch they had just brought up and so I was forced to sit impatiently as Commissioner Pauling preliminarily arraigned Hakeem Trell and then Luis Rodriguez and then Anthony O'Neill and then Jason Lawton and then and then and then, one after another, young kids almost all, mainly minority, primarily poor, or at least dressing that way, all taking it in with a practiced air of hostility. Spend enough time in the Roundhouse's Municipal Court and you begin to feel what it is to be an occupying power.

"Sirs, please sit down, you can't stand back there," shouted the bailiff and two men in the gallery arranged themselves on one of the forward benches, sitting right in front of the young blonde woman, who shifted to a different bench to maintain her view of the proceedings.

I recognized both of the men. I had been expecting them to show, or at least some men like them. One was huge, wearing a shiny warm-up suit, his face permanently cast with the heavy lidded expression of a weightlifter contemplating a difficult squat thrust. I had seen him around, he had grunted at me once. The other was short, thin, looking like a talent scout for a cemetery. He had the face and oily gray hair of a mortician, wearing the same black suit a mortician might wear, clutching a neat little briefcase in his lap. This slick's name was Earl Dante, a minor mob figure I had met a time or two before. His base of operations was a pawnshop, neatly named the Seventh Circle Pawn, on Two Street, south of Washington, just beyond the Mummers Museum, where he made his piranha loans at three points a week and sent out his gap-toothed collectors to muscle in his payments. Dante nodded at me and I contracted the sides of my mouth into an imitation of a smile, hoping no one noticed, before turning back to the goings on in the court.

Commissioner Pauling was staring at me. His gaze drifted up to alight on the mortiferous face of Earl Dante before returning back to my own. I gave a little shrug. The clerk called the next name on his sheet.

In the break between batches, Commissioner Pauling strolled off to what constituted his chambers in the

Roundhouse, no desk of course, or bookshelves filled with West reporters, but a hook for his robe and a sink and an industrial-sized roll of paper to keep his chamberpot clean. I stepped up to the impeccably dressed clerk still at the bench.

"Nice tie, Henry," I said.

"I can't say the same for yours, Mr. Carl," said Henry, shuffling through his files, not deigning to even check out my outfit. "But then I guess you don't got much selection when you buying ties at Woolworth's."

"You'd be surprised," I said. "I'm here for Cressi. Peter Cressi. Some sort of gun problem."

Henry looked through his papers and started nodding. "Yeah, I'd guess trying to buy a hundred and seventy-nine illegally modified automatic assault weapons, three grenade launchers, and a flamethrower from an undercover cop would constitute some sort of gun problem."

"He's a collector."

"Uh huh," said Henry, drawing out his disbelief.

"No, really."

"You don't gots to lie to me, Mr. Carl. You don't see me wearing robes, do you? Your Cressi will be in the next batch. I know what you want, uh huh. I'll get you out of here soon as I can."

"You're a good man, Henry."

"Don't be telling me, be telling my wife."

They brought up the next batch of prisoners, twenty cuffed wrist to wrist, led into the little holding cell behind the bench upon which I uneasily sat. In the middle of the group was Peter Cressi, tall, curly hair flowing long and black behind his ears, broad shoulders, unbelievably handsome. His blue silk shirt, black pants, pointed shiny boots were in stark contrast to the baggy shin-high jeans and hightop sneakers of his new compatriots. As he shuffled through the room he smiled casually at me, as casually as if seeing a neighbor across the street, and I smiled back.

Cressi's gaze drifted up to the benches in the gallery, behind the Plexiglas. When it fell onto Dante's stern face Cressi's features twisted into some sort of fearful reverence.

I didn't like Cressi, actually. There was something ugly and arrogant about him, something uneasy. He was one of those guys who sort of danced while he spoke, as if his bladder was always full to bursting, but you sensed it wasn't his bladder acting up, it was a little organ of evil urging him to go forth and do bad. I didn't like Cressi, but getting the likes of Peter Cressi out of the troubles their little organs of evil got them into was how I now made my living.

I never planned to be a criminal defense attorney, I never planned a lot of things that had happened to my life, like the Soviets never planned for Chernobyl to glow through the long Ukrainian night, but criminal law was what I practiced now. I represented in the American legal system a group of men whose allegiance was not to God and country but to family, not to their natural-born families but to a family with ties that bound so tightly they cut into the flesh. It was a family grown fat and wealthy through selling drugs, pimping women, infiltrating trade unions, and extorting great sums from legitimate industry, from scamming what could be scammed, from loan sharking, from outright thievery, from violence and mayhem and murder. It was the criminal family headed by Enrico Raffaello. I didn't like the work and I didn't like the clients and I didn't like myself while I did the work for the clients. I wanted out, but Enrico Raffaello had once done me the favor of saving my life and so I didn't have much choice anymore.

"All right," said Pauling, back on the bench from his visit to his chambers. "Let's get started."

There were three prisoners in the column of seats beside where I sat, ready to be called to the bar, and the Commissioner was already looking at the first, a young boy with a smirk on his face, when Henry called out Peter Cressi's name.

"Come on up, son," said Pauling to the boy. Henry whispered in the Commissioner's ear. Pauling closed his eyes with exasperation. "Bring out Mr. Cressi," he said.

I stood and slid to the table.

"I assume you're here to represent this miscreant, Mr. Carl," said Pauling as they brought Cressi out from the holding cell.

"This alleged miscreant, yes sir."

When Cressi stood by my side I gave him a stern look of reprobation. He snickered back and did his little dance.

"Mr. Cressi," said Commissioner Pauling, interrupting our charming little moment, "you are hereby charged with one hundred and eighty-three counts of the illegal purchase of firearms in violation of the Pennsylvania Penal Code. You are also charged with conspiracy to commit those offenses. Now I'm going to read you the factual basis for those charges, so you listen up." The commissioner took hold of the police report and started reading. I knew what had happened, I had heard all of it that morning when I was woken by a call to my apartment informing me of Cressi's arrest. The arrest must have been something, Cressi with a Ryder truck, driving out to a warehouse in the Northeast to find waiting for him not the crates of rifles and weapons he had expected but instead a squadron of SWAT cops, guns pointed straight at Peter's handsome face. The cops had been expecting an army, I guess, not just some wiseguy with a rented truck.

"Your Honor, with regard to bail," I said, "Mr. Cressi is a lifelong resident of the city, living at home with his elderly mother, who is dependent on his care." This was one of those lawyer lies. I knew Cressi's mother, she was a spry fifty-year-old bingo fiend, but Peter did make sure she took her hypertension medication every morning. "Mr. Cressi has no intention of fleeing and, as this is not in any way a violent crime, poses no threat to the community. We ask that he be allowed to sign his own bail."

"What was he going to do with those guns, counselor? Aerate his lawn?"

"Mr. Cressi is a collector," I said. I saw Henry shaking in his seat as he fought to stifle his laughter.

"What about the flame-thrower?"

"Would you believe Mr. Cressi was having a problem with roaches?"

The commissioner didn't so much as crack a smile, which was a bad sign. "These weapons are illegal contraband, not allowed to be owned by anyone, even so-called collectors."

"We have a constitutional argument on that, your honor."

"Spare me the Second Amendment, counselor, please. Your client was buying enough guns to wage a war. Three hundred and sixty-six thousand, ten percent cash," said the Commissioner with a quick pound of his gavel.

"Your Honor, I believe that's terribly excessive."

"Two thousand per weapon seems fair to me. I think Mr. Cressi should spend some time in jail. That's all, next case."

"Thank you, Your Honor," I said, fighting to keep all sarcasm out of my voice. I turned to Earl Dante, sitting patiently on the gallery bench behind the Plexiglas, and nodded at him.

Dante gave a look of resigned exasperation, like he would give to a mechanic who has just explained that his car needed an expensive new water pump. Then the loan shark, followed by the hulk in his workout suit, stood and headed out the gallery's doors, taking his briefcase to the waiting bail clerk. As my gaze followed them out I noticed the thin blonde woman in the leather jacket staring at Cressi and me with something more than idle curiosity.

I turned and gave Cressi a complicated series of

instructions. "Keep your mouth shut till you're bailed out, Peter. You got that?"

"What you think, I'm an idiot here?"

"I'm not the one buying guns from cops. Just do as I say and then meet me at my office tomorrow morning so we can figure out where to go from here. And be sure to bring my usual retainer."

"I always do."

"I'll give you that, Peter." I looked back up to the blonde woman who was still watching us. "You know her?" I asked with a flick of my head to the gallery.

He looked up. "Nah, she's not my type, a scrag like that."

"Then if you don't know her and I don't know her, why's she staring?"

He smiled. "When you look and dress like I do, you know, you get used to it."

"That must be it," I said. "I bet you'll look even more dashing in your orange jumpsuit."

Just then a bailiff grabbed Cressi's arm and started leading him back to the holding cell.

"See if you can stay out of trouble until tomorrow morning," I said to him as the Commissioner read out another in his endless list of names.

But Cressi was wrong about in whom the blonde was interested. She was waiting outside the Roundhouse for me. "Mr. Carl?"

"That's right."

"Your office said I could find you here."

"And here I am," I said with a tight smile. It was not a moment poised with promise, her standing before me just then. She was in her mid-twenties, small, her bleached hair hacked to ear's length, as if with a cleaver. Black lipstick, black nail polish, mascara globbed around her eyes like a cry for help. Under her black leather was a blue work shirt, originally the property of some stiff named

Lenny, and a thrift-shop–quality pleated skirt. She had five earrings in her right ear and her left nostril was pierced and she looked like one of those impoverished art students who hang outside the Chinese buy-it-by-the-pound buffet on Chestnut Street. A small black handbag hung low from her shoulder. On the bare ankle above one of her black platform shoes was the tattoo of a rose, and that I noticed it there meant I was checking her out, like men invariably check out every woman they ever meet. Not bad, actually. Cressi was right, she was scrawny, and her face was pinched with apprehension, but there was something there, maybe just youth, but something.

"What can I do for you?" I asked.

She looked around. "Can we, like, talk somewhere?"

"You can walk me to the subway," I said as I headed south to Market Street. I wasn't all that interested in what she had to say. From the look of her I had her figured. She had fished my name out of the Yellow Pages and found I was a criminal attorney and wanted me now to help get her boyfriend out of the stir. Of course he was innocent and wrongfully convicted and of course the trial had been a sham and of course she couldn't pay me right off but if I could only help out from the goodness of my heart she would promise to pay me later. About once a week I got just such a call from a desperate relative or girlfriend trolling for lawyers through the phone book. And what I told each of them I would end up telling her: that nobody does anything from the goodness of his heart and I was no different.

She watched me go and then ran to catch up, doing a hop skip in her platform shoes to keep pace with my stride. "I need your help, Mr. Carl."

"My docket's full right now."

"I'm in serious trouble."

"All my clients are in serious trouble."

"But I'm not like all your clients."

"That's right, my clients have all paid me a retainer for my services. They have bought my loyalty and attention with their cash. Will you be able to pay me a retainer, Ms. . . . ?"

"Shaw. Caroline Shaw. How much?"

"Five thousand for a routine criminal matter."

"This is not routine, I am certain."

"Well in that case it might be more."

"I can pay," she said. "That's not a problem."

I stopped at that. I was expecting an excuse, a promise, a plea, I was not expecting to hear that payment was not a problem. I stopped and turned and took a closer look. Even though she dressed like a waif she held herself regally, her shoulders back, her head high, which was a trick, really, in those ridiculous platform shoes. The eyes within those raccoon bands of mascara were blue and sharply in focus, the eyes of a law student or an accomplished liar. And she spoke better then I would have expected from the outfit. "What do you want me to do for you, Ms. Shaw?"

"I want you to find out who killed my sister."

That was new. I tilted my head. "I thought you said *you* were in trouble?"

"I think I might be next."

"Well that is a problem, and I wish you well. But you should be going to the police. It's their job to investigate murders and protect citizens, my job is to get the murderers off. Good day, Ms. Shaw," I said as I turned and started again to walk south to the subway.

"I told you I'd be willing to pay," she said as she skipped and hopped again to stay with me, her shoes clopping on the cement walk. "Doesn't that matter?"

"That matters a heap," I said as I kept walking, "but signing a check is one thing, having the check clear is entirely another."

"But it will," she said. "And I need your help. I'm scared."

"Go to the police."

"So you're not going to help me?" Her voice had turned pathetic and after it came out she stopped walking beside me. It wasn't tough to keep going, no tougher than passing a homeless beggar without dropping a quarter in her cup. We learn to just walk on in the city, but even as I walked on I could still hear her. "I don't know what I'm going to do if you don't help me. I think whoever killed her is going to kill me next. I'm desperate, Mr. Carl. I carry this but I'm still scared all the time."

I stopped again and, with a feeling of dread, I turned around. She was holding an automatic pistol pointed at my heart.

"Won't you help me, Mr. Carl? Please? You don't know how desperate I am."

The gun had a black dull finish, rakish lines, it was small-bore, sure, but its bore was still large enough to kill a generation's best hope in a hotel ballroom, not to mention a small-time criminal attorney who was nobody's best hope for anything.

I'll say this for her, she knew how to grab my attention.

3

"PUT THE GUN AWAY," I said in my sharpest voice.

"I didn't mean, oh God no, I . . ." Her hand wavered and the barrel drooped as if the gun had gone limp.

"Put the gun away," I said again, and it wasn't as brave as it sounds because the only other options were to run, exposing my back to the .22 slug, or pissing my pants, which no matter how intense the immediate relief makes really an awful mess. And after I told her to put the gun away, told her twice for emphasis, she did just as I said, stuck it right back in her handbag, all of which was unbelievably gratifying for me in a superhero sort of way.

Until she started crying.

"Oh no, now don't do that," I said, "no no don't no."

I stepped toward her as she collapsed in a sitting position to the sidewalk, crying, the thick mascara around her eyes running in lines down her cheek, her nose reddening. She wiped her face with a black leather sleeve, smearing everything.

"Don't cry, please please, it will be all right. We'll go somewhere, we'll talk, just please please stop crying, please."

I couldn't leave her there after that, sitting on the ground like she was, crying black tears that splattered on the cement. In a different era I would have offered to buy her a good stiff drink, but this wasn't a different era, so what I offered to buy her instead was a cappuccino. She let me drag her to a coffee shop a few blocks east. It was a beat little place with old stuffed couches and chairs, a few rickety tables, its back walls filled with shelves of musty used paperbacks. I was drinking a black coffee, decaf actually, since the sight of her gun aimed at my heart had given me enough of a start for the morning. Caroline was sitting across from me at one of the tables, her arms crossed, in front of her the cappuccino, pale, frothy, sprinkled with cinnamon, and completely untouched. Her eyes now were red and smeared and sad. There were a few others in the joint, young and mangy in their slacker outfits, greasy hair and flannel shirts, sandals. Caroline looked right at home. In my blue suit I felt like a narc.

"Do you have a license for that gun?" I asked.

"I suppose I need one, don't I?"

I nodded and took a sip from my mug. "Take some sound legal advice and throw the gun away. I should turn you in, actually, for your own good, though I won't. It goes against my . . ."

"You don't mind if I smoke, do you?" she said, interrupting me mid-sentence, and before I could answer she was already rummaging again in that little black handbag. I must admit I didn't like seeing her hand back inside that bag, but all she brought out this time was a pack of Camel Lights. She managed to light her cigarette with her arms still crossed.

I looked her over again and guessed to myself that she was a clerk in a video store, or a part-time student at Philadelphia Community College, or maybe both. "What is it you do, Caroline?"

"I'm between things at the moment," she said, leaning forward, looking for something on the table. Finding nothing, she tossed her spent match atop the brown sprinkled foam of her cappuccino. I had just spent $2.50 for her liquid ashtray. I assumed she would have preferred the drink.

"Last month I was a photographer. Next month maybe I'll take up tap dancing."

"An unwavering commitment to caprice, I see."

She laughed a laugh so full of rue I felt like I was watching Betty Davis tilt her head back, stretch her white neck. "Exactly. I aspire to live my life like a character in a sitcom, every week a new and perky adventure."

"What's the title of this episode?"

"*Into the Maw*, or maybe *Into the Mall*, because after this I need to go to the Gallery and buy some tampons. Why were you in that stupid little courtroom this morning?"

I took another sip of coffee. "One of my clients attempted to buy one hundred and seventy-nine automatic rifles, three grenade launchers, and a flamethrower from an undercover cop."

"Is he in the mob, this client of yours?"

"There is no mob. It is a figment of the press's imagination."

"Then what was he going to do with all those guns?"

"That's the question, isn't it?"

"I had heard you were a mob lawyer. It's true, isn't it?"

I made an effort to stare at her without blinking as I let the comment slide off me like a glob of phlegm.

Yes, a majority of my clients just happened to be junior associates of Mr. Raffaello, like I said, but I was no house counsel, no mob lawyer. At least not technically. I merely handled their cases after they allegedly committed their alleged crimes, nothing more. And though my clients never flipped, never ratted out the organization that fed them since they were pups, that sustained them, that took care of their families and their futures, though my clients never informed on the family, the decision not to inform was made well before they ever stepped into my office. And was I really representing these men, or was I instead enforcing the promises made to all citizens in the

Constitution of the United States? Wasn't I among the noblest defenders of those sacred rights for which our fore-fathers fought and died? Who among us was doing more to protect liberty, to ensure justice? Who among us was doing more to safeguard the American way of life?

Do I sound defensive?

I was about to explain it all to her but it bored even me by then so all I said was, "I do criminal law. I don't get involved in . . ."

"What's that?" she shouted as she leaped to kneeling on her seat. "What is it? What?"

I stared for a moment into her anxious face, filled with a true terror, before I looked under the table at where her legs had been only an instant before. A cat, brown and ruf-fled, was rubbing its back on the legs of her chair. It looked quite contented as it rubbed.

"It's just a cat," I said.

"Get rid of it."

"It's just a cat," I repeated.

"I hate them, miserable ungrateful little manipulators, with their claws and their teeth and their fur-licking tongues. They eat human flesh, do you know that? It's one of their favorite things. Faint near a cat and it'll chew your face off."

"I don't think so."

"Get rid of it, please please please."

I reached under the table and the cat scurried away from my grasp. I stood up and went after it, herding it to the back of the coffee shop where, behind the bookshelves, was an open bathroom door. When the cat slipped into the bathroom I closed the door behind it.

"What was that all about?" I asked Caroline when I returned to the table.

"I don't like cats," she said as she fiddled with her cigarette.

"I don't especially like cats either, but I don't jump on my seat and go ballistic when I see one."

"I have a little problem with them, that's all."

"With cats?"

"I'm afraid of cats. I'm not the only one. It has a name. Ailurophobia. So what? We're all afraid of something."

I thought on that a bit. She was right of course, we were all afraid of something, and in the scheme of things being afraid of cats was not the worst of fears. My great fear in this life didn't have a name that I knew of. I was afraid of remaining exactly who I was, and that phobia instilled a shiver of fear into every one of my days. Something as simple as a fear of cats would have been a blessing.

"All right, Caroline," I said. "Tell me about your sister."

She took a drag from her cigarette and exhaled in a long white stream. "Well, for one thing, she was murdered."

"Have the police found the killer?"

She reached for her pack of Camel Lights even though the cigarette she had was still lit. "Jackie was hanging from the end of a rope in her apartment. They've concluded that she hung herself."

"The police said that?"

"That's right. The coroner and some troglodyte detective named McDeiss. They closed the case, said it was a suicide. But she didn't."

"Hang herself?"

"She wouldn't."

"Detective McDeiss ruled it a suicide?"

She sighed. "You don't believe me either."

"No, actually," I said. "I've had a few run-ins with McDeiss but he's a pretty good cop. If he said it was a suicide, it's a fair bet your sister killed herself. You may not have thought she was suicidal, that's perfectly natural, but . . ."

"Of course she was suicidal," she said, interrupting me once again. "Jackie read Sylvia Plath as if her poetry were some sort of a road map through adolescence. One of her favorite lines was from a poem called 'Lady Lazarus.' 'Dying is an art, like everything else. I do it exceptionally well.'"

"Then I don't understand your problem."

"Jackie talked of suicide as naturally as others talked of the weather, but she said she'd never hang herself. She was disgusted by the idea of dangling there, aware of the pain, turning as the rope tightened and creaked, the pressure on your neck, on your backbone, hanging there until they cut you down."

"What would have been her way?"

"Pills. Darvon. Two thousand milligrams is fatal. She always had six thousand on hand. Jackie used to joke that she wanted to be prepared if ever a really terrific suicidal urge came along. Besides, in her last couple years she almost seemed happy. It was like she was actually finding the peacefulness she once thought was only for her in death through this New Age church she had joined, finding it through meditation. She had even gotten herself engaged, to an idiot, yes, but still engaged."

"So let's say she was murdered. What do you want me to do about it?"

"Find out who did it."

"I'm just a lawyer," I said. "What you're looking for is a private investigator. Now I have one that I use who is terrific. His name is Morris Kapustin and he's a bit unorthodox, but if anyone can help he can. I can set . . ."

"I don't want him, I want you."

"Why me?"

"What exactly do mob lawyers do, anyway, eat in Italian restaurants and plot?"

"Why me, Caroline?" I stared at her and waited.

She lit her new cigarette from the still-glowing butt of her old one and then crushed the old against the edge of the mug. "Do you think I smoke too much? Everybody thinks

I smoke too much. I used to be cool, now it's like I'm a leper. Old ladies stop me in the street and lecture."

I just stared at her and waited some more and after all the waiting she took a deep drag from her cigarette, exhaled, and said:

"I think a bookie named Jimmy Vigs killed her."

So that was it, why she had chased me, insignificant me, down the street and pulled a gun and collapsed to the cement in black tears, all of which was perfectly designed to gain my attention, if not my sympathy. I knew Jimmy Vigs Dubinsky, sure I did. I had represented him on his last bookmaking charge and gotten him an acquittal too, when I denied he was a gambler, denied it was his ledger that the cops had found, denied it was his handwriting in the ledger despite what the experts said because wink-wink what do experts know, denied the notes in the ledger referred to bets on football games, denied the units mentioned in the ledger notes referred to dollar amounts, and then, after all those sweet denials, I had opened my arms and said with my best boys-will-be-boys voice, "And where's the harm?" It helped that the jury was all men, after I had booted all the women, and that the trial was held in the spring, smack in the middle of March madness, when every one of those men had money in an NCAA pool. So, yes, I knew Jimmy Vigs Dubinsky.

"He's a sometime client, as you obviously know," I said, "so I really don't want to hear anymore. But what I can tell you about Jim Dubinsky is that he's not a killer. I've known him for . . ."

"Then you can clear him."

"Will you stop interrupting me? It's rude and annoying."

She tilted her head at me and smiled, as if provoking me was her intent.

"I don't need to clear Jimmy," I said. "He's not a suspect since the cops ruled your sister's death a suicide."

"I suspect him and I have a gun."

I pursed my lips. "And you'll kill him if I don't take the case, is that it?"

"I'm a desperate woman, Mr. Carl," she said, and there was just the right touch of husky fear in her voice, as if she had prepared the line in advance, repeated it to the mirror over and over until she got it just right.

"Let me guess, just a wild hunch of mine, but before you started playing around with f-stops and film speeds, did you happen to take a stab at acting?"

She smiled. "For a few years, yes. I was actually starring in a film until the financing was pulled."

"And that point the gun, 'Oh-my-God,' collapse into a sobbing heap on the sidewalk thing, that was just part of an act?"

Her smile broadened and there was something sly and inviting in it. "I need your help."

"You made the right decision giving up on the dramatics." I thought for a moment that it might be entertaining to see her go up against Jimmy Vigs with her pop gun, but then thought better of it. And I did like that smile of hers, at least enough to listen. "All right, Caroline, tell me why you think my friend Jimmy killed your sister."

She sighed and inhaled and sprayed a cloud of smoke into the air above my face. "It's my brother Eddie," she said. "He has a gambling problem. He bets too much and he loses too often. From what I understand, he is into this Jimmy Vigs person for a lot of money, too much money. There were threatening calls, there were late-night visits, Eddie's car was vandalized. One of Eddie's arms was broken, in a fall, he said, but no one believed him. Then Jackie died, in what seemed like a suicide but which I know wasn't, and suddenly the threats stopped, the visits were finished, and Eddie's repaired and repainted car maintained its pristine condition. The bookie must have been paid off. If this Jimmy Vigs person had killed Eddie he would have lost everything, but he killed Jackie and that must have scared Eddie into digging up the money and paying. But I heard he's betting again, raising his debt even farther. And if your Jimmy Vigs needs to scare Eddie again I'm the one he'll go after next."

I listened to her, nodding all the while, not believing a word of it. If Jimmy was stiffed he'd threaten, sure, who wouldn't, and maybe break a leg or two, which could be quite painful when done correctly, but that was as far as it would go. Unless, maybe, we were talking big big bucks, but it didn't seem likely that Jim would let it get that high with someone like this girl's brother.

"So what I want," she said, "is for you to find out who killed her and get them to stay away from me. I thought with your connections to this Jimmy Vigs and the mob it would be easy for you."

"I bet you did," I said. "But what if it wasn't Jimmy Vigs?"

"He did it."

"Most victims are killed by someone they know. If she was murdered, maybe it was by a lover or a family member?"

"My family had nothing to do with it," she said sharply.

"Jimmy Dubinsky is not a murderer. The mere fact that your brother owed him money is . . ."

"Then what about this?" she said while she reached into her handbag.

"You did it again, dammit. And I wish you wouldn't keep putting your hand in there."

"Frightened?" She smiled as she pulled out a plastic sandwich bag and dangled it before me.

I took the bag from her and examined it. Inside was a piece of cellophane, a candy wrapper, one end twisted, the other opened and the word "Tosca's" printed on one side. When I saw the printing my throat closed on me.

"I found this lying on her bathroom floor, behind the toilet, when I was cleaning out her apartment," she said.

"So she had been to Tosca's. So what?"

"Jackie was an obsessive cleaner. She wouldn't have just left this lying about. The cops missed it, I guess they don't do toilets, but Jackie surely wouldn't have left it there. And tomato sauce was too acidic for her stomach. She never ate Italian food."

"Then someone else, maybe."

"Exactly. I asked around and Tosca's seems to be some sort of mob hangout."

"So they say."

"I think she was murdered, Mr. Carl, and that the murderer had been to Tosca's and left this and I think you're the one who can find out for me."

I looked at the wrapper and then at Caroline and then back at the wrapper. Maybe I had underestimated the viciousness of Jimmy Vigs Dubinsky, and maybe one of my clients, in collecting for my other client, had left this little calling card from Tosca's at the murder scene.

"And if I find out who did it," I said, "then what?"

"I just want them to leave me alone. If you find out who did it, could you get them to leave me alone?"

"Maybe," I said. "What about the cops?"

"That will be up to you," she said.

I didn't like the idea of this waif rummaging through Tosca's looking for trouble and I figured Enrico Raffaello wouldn't like it much either. If I took the retainer and proved to her, somehow, that her sister actually killed herself, I could save everyone, especially Caroline, a lot of trouble. I took another look at the wrapper in that plastic bag, wondered whose fingerprints might still be found there, and then stuffed it into my jacket pocket where it could do no harm.

"I'll need a retainer of ten thousand dollars," I said.

She smiled, not with gratitude but with victory, as if she knew all along I'd take the case. "I thought it was five thousand."

"I charge one eighty-five an hour plus expenses."

"That seems very high."

"That's my price. And you have to promise to throw that gun away."

She pressed her lips together and thought about it for a moment. "But I want to keep the gun," she said, with a slight pout in her voice. "It keeps me warm."

"Buy a dog."

She thought some more and then reached into her handbag once again and this time what she pulled out was a checkbook, opening it with the practiced air you see in well-dressed women at grocery stores. "Who should I make it out to?"

"Derringer and Carl," I said. "Ten thousand dollars."

"I remember the amount," she said with a laugh as she wrote.

"Is this going to clear?"

She ripped the check from her book and handed it to me. "I hope so."

"Hopes have never paid my rent. When it clears I'll start to work." I looked the check over. It was drawn on the First Mercantile Bank of the Main Line. "Nice bank," I said.

"They gave me a toaster."

"And you'll get rid of the gun?"

"I'll get rid of the gun."

So that was that. I took her number and stuffed the check into my pocket and left her there with a cigarette smoldering between her fingers. I had been retained, sort of, assuming the check cleared, to investigate the mysterious death of Jacqueline Shaw. I had expected it would be a simple case of checking the files and finding a suicide. I didn't know then, couldn't possibly have known, all the crimes and all the hells through which that investigation would lead. But just then, with that check in my hand, I wasn't thinking so much about poor Jacqueline Shaw hanging by her neck from a rope, but instead about Caroline, her sister, and the slyness of her smile.

I took the subway back to Sixteenth Street and walked the rest of the way to my office on Twenty-first. Up the stairs, past the lists of names, through the hallway with all the other offices with which we shared our space, to the three doorways in the rear.

"Any messages, Ellie?" I asked my secretary. She was a young blonde woman with freckles, our most loyal employee as she was our only employee.

She handed me a pile of slips. "Nothing exciting."

"Is there ever?" I said as I nodded sadly and went into my scuff of an office. Marked white walls, files piled in lilting towers, dead flowers drooping like desiccated corpses from a glass vase atop my big brown filing cabinet. Through the single window was a sad view of the decrepit alleyway below. I unlocked the file cabinet and dropped the plastic bag with the Tosca's candy wrapper inside into a file marked "Recent Court Decisions." I closed the drawer and pushed in the cabinet lock and sat at my desk, staring at all the work I needed to do, transcripts to review, briefs to write, discovery to discover. Instead of getting down to work I took the check out of my pocket. Ten thousand dollars. Caroline Shaw. First Mercantile Bank of the Main Line. That was a pretty fancy banking address for a punkette with a post in her nose. I stood and strolled into my partner's office.

She was at her desk, chewing, a pen in one hand and a carrot in the other. Gray-and-white-streaked copies of case opinions, paragraphs highlighted in fluorescent pink, were scattered across her desktop and she stared up at me as if I were a rude interruption.

"What's up, doc?" Beth Derringer said.

"Want to go for a ride?"

"Sure," she said as she snapped a chunk of carrot with her teeth. "What for?"

"Credit check."

4
≡

"WHERE ARE WE OFF TO?" asked Beth, sitting in the passenger seat of my little Mazda as I negotiated the wilds of the Schuylkill Expressway.

Short and sharp-faced, with glossy black hair cut even and fierce, Elizabeth Derringer had been my partner since we both fell out of law school, all except for one short period a few years back when I lost my way in a case, choosing money over honor, and she felt compelled to resign. That was very much like Beth, to pretend that integrity counted for more than cash, and of all the people I ever met in my life who pretended just that same thing, and there have been far too many, she was the best at pulling it off. Beth was smarter than me, wiser than me, a better lawyer all around, but she had an annoying tendency to pursue causes rather then currency, representing cripples thrown off SSI disability rolls, secretaries whose nipples had been tweaked by Neanderthal superiors, deadbeats looking to stave off foreclosure of the family homestead. It was my criminal work that kept us solvent, but I liked to think that Beth's unprofitable good deeds justified my profitable descent into the mire with my bad boy clients. In today's predatory legal world I would have been well advised to jettison her income drag, except I never would. I knew I could trust Beth more deeply than I could trust anyone else in this world, which was not a bad recipe, actually, for a partner and which explained why I hitched my shingle to hers but not why she hitched hers to mine. That I still hadn't figured out.

"I found us a new client," I said. "I want to see if the retainer check clears."

"You smell like a chimney."

"This new client is a bit nervous."

"Why don't you just have Morris do a background check for you?" she said, referring to Morris Kapustin, our usual private detective.

"This isn't big enough yet to bring in Morris."

A brown Chevette cut in front of me on the expressway and I slammed my horn. The guy in the Chevette swung around into a different lane and slowed to give me the finger. I gestured back. He shouted something and I shouted something and we jawed at each other for a few moments, neither hearing a word of what the other was yelling, before he sped away.

"So tell me about the new client. Who is he?"

"*She* is Caroline Shaw. Her sister, one Jacqueline Shaw, killed herself, apparently. Caroline doesn't believe it was a suicide. She suspects one of my clients and wants me to investigate. I'm certain it's nothing more than what it looks like but I figure I can keep her out of trouble if I can convince her. My clients don't like being accused of murder."

"That's rather noble of you."

"She gave us a ten-thousand-dollar retainer."

"I should have figured."

"Even nobility has a price. You know what knighthoods go for these days?"

A maroon van started sliding out of its lane, inching closer and closer to the side of my car. I pressed my horn and accelerated away from the van, braking just in time to avoid a Cadillac, before veering into the center lane.

"It's not the sort of thing you usually take up, Victor. I didn't know you had an investigator's license."

"She paid us a ten-thousand-dollar retainer, Beth. If the check clears, I'll buy a belted raincoat and turn into Philip Marlowe."

The First Mercantile Bank of the Main Line was a surprising choice for Caroline Shaw's checking account. It was a stately white-shoe bank with three discreet offices and a huge estates department to handle the peculiar bequests of the wealthy dead. The bank's jumbo mortgage rates were surprisingly low, the rich watched every penny with a rapaciousness that would stun, but the bank's credit checks were vicious, kicking out all but those with the littlest need for the institution's money. It catered to the very wealthy suburban crowd who didn't want to deal with the hoi polloi when they dug their paws into their piles of gold and laughed. The bank didn't discriminate against the not very rich, of course, but keep just a few hundred dollars in a checking account at the First Mercantile Bank of the Main Line and the fees would wipe out your principal in a breathtakingly short time. Keep a few hundred thousand and your Yves St. Laurent designer checks were complimentary. Wood-paneled offices, tellers in Brooks Brothers suits, personal banking, ads in *The Wall Street Journal* proclaiming the soundness of their investment advice for portfolios of two million dollars or more. Sorry, no, they didn't cash welfare checks at the First Mercantile Bank of the Main Line and the glass door was always locked so that they could bar your entry until they gave you the once-over, as if they were selling diamond tiaras.

Even though I was in a suit, and Beth was in a nice print dress, we had to knock twice and smile gamely before we heard the buzz.

"Yes, can I help you?" said a somberly dressed young man with a thin smile who greeted us as soon as we stepped inside. I guessed he was some sort of a concierge, there to take the rich old ladies' coats and escort them to the tapestry chairs arranged before willing and obsequious personal bankers.

"We need to cash a check," I said.

"Do either of you have an account here?"

I looked around at the portraits of old bankers tacked onto the dark walnut of the walls, gray-haired men in their frock coats staring solemnly down at me with disapproval. Even if I was a Rothschild I don't think I would have felt comfortable in that bank and, believe me, I was no Rothschild.

"No," I said. "No account."

"I'm sorry, sir, but we don't cash checks for those without accounts here." He whispered so as not to embarrass us, which was very considerate of him, considering. "There is a Core States Bank branch down the road a bit, I'm sure they could be of assistance."

"We're being sloughed off," said Beth.

"It's policy, ma'am," said the concierge. "I'm sorry."

"I've been sloughed off by worse places than this," I said. "But still . . ."

The concierge stepped to the side and opened the door graciously for us to leave. "I hope we can be of service another time."

"But the check I wanted to cash," I said in a loud voice, "was drawn on this very bank." And then I raised my voice even louder, not in anger, my tone still kindly, but the voice high enough and the syllables distinct enough so that I could have been heard in the rear of the balcony, had there been one. "You don't mean to say that you won't honor a check drawn on this bank?"

Heads reared, a personal banker stood, an old lady turned slowly to look at me and grabbed tightly to her purse. The concierge put a hand on my forearm, his face registering as much shock as if I had started babbling in Yiddish right there in that gilded tomb of a bank building.

Before he could say anything else a wonderfully dressed older man with nervous hands and razored gray hair was at his side.

"Thank you, James," the older man said, his pale blue eyes fixed on my brown ones. "I'll take it from here." The young concierge bowed and backed away. "Follow me, please."

We walked in a column to a desk in the middle of the bank's dark-carpeted main room and were seated on the tapestry seats of claw-and-ball chairs. Atop the desk was a bronze name plate that read: "Mr. Jeffries." "Now," said the impeccably dressed Jeffries with an impeccably false smile, "you said you wished to cash a check drawn on an account at this bank?"

I reached into my jacket pocket and Jeffries flinched ever so slightly. Not the main man in this bank, I figured, if he was flinching from so minimally an imagined threat. From my jacket I pulled out Caroline Shaw's check, unfolded it, read it once again, and handed it over.

Jeffries's eyes rose in surprise when he examined the check. "And you're Mr. Carl?"

"The very same. Is the check any good?"

There was a computer on his desk and I expected him to make a quick review of the account balance, of which I hoped to grab a peek, but that's not what he did. What he did instead was to simply say, "I'll need identification."

I dug for my wallet and pulled out my driver's license.

"And a credit card."

I pulled that out, too. "So the check is good?"

He examined my license and MasterCard. "If you'll just endorse the check, Mr. Carl."

I signed the back. He compared my signature to the license and the credit card, making some notations beneath my signature on the check.

"And how would you like this paid, Mr. Carl, cash or cashier's check?"

"Cash."

"Are hundreds satisfactory?"

"Perfectly."

"One moment, please," and then with my license and credit card and check he stood and turned and walked out of the room to somewhere in the rear of the building.

"Your Miss Shaw seems to be known in this bank," said Beth.

"Yes, either she has a substantial account or she is a known forger and the police will be out presently."

"Which do you expect?"

"Oh the police," I said. "I have found it is always safest to expect the worst. Anything else is mere accident."

It took a good long time, far too long a time. I waited, first patiently, then impatiently, and then angrily. I was about to stand and make another scene when Jeffries finally returned. Behind him came another man, about my age, handsome enough and tall enough and blond enough so that he seemed as much a part of the bank as the paneling on the walls and the portraits in their gilded frames. I wondered to which eating club at Princeton he had belonged.

As Jeffries sat back down at the desk and fiddled with the paperwork, the blond man stood behind him looking over his shoulder. Jeffries took out an envelope and extracted a thick wad of bills, hundred-dollar bills. Slowly he began to count.

"I didn't know cashing a check was such a production," I said.

The blond man lifted his head and smiled at me. It was a warm, generous smile and completely ungenuine. "We'll have this for you in just a moment, Mr. Carl," he said. "By the way, what kind of business are you in?"

"This and that," I said. "Why do you ask?"

"Our loan department is always on the lookout for clients. We handle the accounts for many lawyers. I was just hoping our business loan department could be of help to your firm."

So that was why they spent so much time in the back, they were checking me out, and he wanted me to know it, too. "I believe our line of credit is presently sufficient," I said. "Miss Derringer is the partner in charge of finances. How are we doing with our loans, Beth?"

"I'm still under my MasterCard limit," said Beth.

"Now you're bragging," I said.

"It helps if you pay more than the minimum each month, Victor."

"Well then, with Beth under her limit, we're sitting pretty for the next month at least."

"How good for you," said the blond man.

Jeffries finished counting the bills. He neatened the pile, tapping it gently first on one side, then another, and proceeded to count it again. There was about Jeffries, as he counted the bills with the blond man behind him, the tense air of a blackjack dealer with the pit boss looking over his shoulder. They were taking quite a bit of care, the two of them, for ten thousand dollars, a pittance to a bank that considered anything under a million small change.

"What type of law is it that you two practice?" asked the blond man.

"Oh this and that," I said.

"No specialty?"

"Not really. We take pretty much whatever comes in the door."

"Do you do any banking work? Sometimes we have work our primary counsel can't handle due to conflicts."

"Is that a fact? And who exactly is your primary counsel?"

"Talbott, Kittredge & Chase."

"Of course it is," I said. Talbott, Kittredge & Chase was the richest, most prestigious, most powerful firm in the city.

"Oh, so they would know of you?"

"Yes," I said. "Very well."

"Then maybe we can do some business after all."

"I don't think so," I said. They had checked me out all right, and it was interesting as hell that they were so interested, but their scouting report was old. I might have gone for the bait one time or another, given much to garner the business of an old and revered client like the First Mercantile Bank of the Main Line, but not anymore. "You see, we once sued Talbott, Kittredge & Chase and won a large settlement. They hate me there, in fact a memo has been circulated to have their lawyers harass me at every turn, so I don't think they'd agree to your giving me any work."

"Well of course," said the blond man, "it's our choice really."

"Thank you for the offer," I said, "but no. We don't really represent banks."

"It's sort of a moral quirk of ours," said Beth. "They're so big and rich and unkind."

"We sue them, of course," I said. "That's always good for a laugh or two, but we don't represent them. We sometimes represent murderers and tax cheats and crack mothers who have deserted their babies, but we will only sink so low. Are you finished counting, Jeffries, or do you think Ben Franklin will start to smile if you keep tickling him like that?"

"Give Mr. Carl his money," said the blond man.

Jeffries put the bills back in the envelope and handed it to me. "Thank you for banking with us, sir."

"My pleasure," I said as I tapped the envelope to my forehead in a salute. "I'm a little surprised though at how much interest you both seem to take in Miss Shaw's affairs. She must be someone very special."

"We take a keen interest in all of our clients' affairs," said the blond man.

"How wonderfully Orwellian. Is there anything about Miss Shaw's situation we should know?"

The blond man stared at me for a moment. "No. Nothing at all. I hope we can be of further service sometime, Mr. Carl."

"I'm sure you do," I said, certain he never wanted to hear from me again.

James, the young concierge, was waiting at the door for us after we left the desk. As soon as we came near he swung the glass door open. "Good day," he said with a nod and a smile.

Beth was already through when I stopped in the door frame. Without turning around, I said, "Thank you, James. By the way, that man standing behind Mr. Jeffries, staring at me with a peculiar distaste right now. Who is he?"

"Oh, that's Mr. Harrington. He is in the trust and estates department," said James.

"With a face like that I bet he's got a load of old lady clients."

"No sir, just the one keeps him busy enough."

"One?" I turned around in surprise. As I had expected, Harrington was still staring bullets at me.

"The Reddmans, sir. He manages the entire Reddman estate."

"Of the Reddman Pickle Reddmans?"

"Exactly, sir," said James as he urged me out the entranceway.

"The Reddmans," I said. "Imagine that."

"Thank you for banking at First Mercantile," said James, just before I heard the click of the glass door's lock behind me.

5

DRIVING BACK INTO TOWN on the Schuylkill Expressway I wasn't fighting my way through the left lanes. I stayed, instead, in the safe slow right and let the buzz of the aggressive traffic slide by. When a white convertible elbowed into my lane, inches from my bumper, as it sped to pass a truck in the center, I didn't so much as tap my horn. I was too busy thinking. One woman was dead, from suicide or murder, I wasn't sure yet which, another was paying me ten thousand dollars to find out, and now, most surprisingly, they both seemed to be Reddmans.

We all know Reddman Foods, we've been consuming its pressure-flavored pickles since we were kids—sweet pickles, sour pickles, kosher dill pickles, fine pickled gherkins. The green and red pickle jar with the founder's stern picture above the name is an icon and the Reddman Pickle has taken its place in the pantheon of American products, alongside Heinz Ketchup and Kellogg's cereal and the Ford motor car and Campbell's soup. The brand names become trademarks, so we forget that there are families behind the names, families whose wealth grows ever more obscene whenever we throw ketchup on the burger, shake out a bowl of cereal, buy ourselves a fragrant new automobile. Or snap a garlic pickle between our teeth. And like Henry Ford and Henry John Heinz and Andrew Carnegie, Claudius Reddman was one of the great men of America's industrial past, earning his fortune in business and his reputation in philanthropy. The Reddman Library at the University of Pennsylvania. The Reddman Wing of the Philadelphia Art Museum. The Reddman Foundation with its prestigious and lucrative Claudius Reddman grants for the most accomplished artists and writers and scholars.

So, it was a Reddman who had pointed a gun at me and then begged me for help, an heir to the great pickle fortune. Why hadn't she told me? Why had she wanted me to think her only a poverty-struck little liar? Well, maybe she was a little liar, but a liar with money was something else again. And I did like that smile.

"What would you do if you were suddenly stinkingly rich?" I asked Beth.

"I don't know, it never crossed my mind."

"Liar," I said. "Of course it crossed your mind. It crosses every American mind. It is our joint national fantasy, the communal American wishing for a fortune that is the very engine of our economic growth."

"Well, when the lottery was at sixty-six million I admit I bought a ticket."

"Only one?"

"All right, ten."

"And what would you have done with all that money?"

"I sort of fantasized about starting a foundation to help public interest law organizations."

"That's noble and pathetic, both."

"And I thought a Porsche would be nice."

"Better," I said. "You'd look good in a Porsche."

"I think so, yes. What about you, Victor? You've thought about this, I suppose."

"Some." A radical understatement. Whole afternoons had been plundered in my fervent imaginings of great wealth acquired and spent.

"So what would you do?"

"The first thing I'd do," I said, "is quit."

"You'd leave the firm?"

"I'd leave the law, I'd leave the city, I'd leave my life. I'd cocoon somewhere hot and thick with coconuts and return as something else completely. I always thought I'd like to paint."

"I didn't know you had any talent."

"I have none whatsoever," I said cheerfully. "But isn't that the point? If I had talent I'd be a slave to it, concerned about producing my oh so important work. Thankfully, I am completely talentless. Maybe I'd go to Long Island and wear Gap khakis and throw paint on canvas like Jackson Pollock and drink like a fish every afternoon."

"You don't drink well."

"You're right, and I've never been to Long Island, but the image is nice. And did I mention the Ferrari? I'd like an F355 Spider in candy-apple red. I hear the babes, they love the Ferrari. Oh hell, who knows, I'd probably be miserable even so, but at least I wouldn't be a lawyer."

"Do you really hate it that much?"

"You see the law as a noble pursuit, as a way to right wrongs. I see it as a somewhat distasteful job that I'm shackled to by my monthly credit card bills. And if I don't get out, and soon," I said, without a hint of humor in my voice, "it's going to kill me."

The car in front of me flashed its rear red lights and the car beside me slowed and I braked to a stop and soon we were just sitting there, all of us, hundreds and hundreds of us, parked in the largest parking lot in the city. The Schuylkill did this every now and then, just stopped, for no apparent reason, as if the King of Commuting, in his headquarters in King of Prussia, simply flicked a switch and turned the highway off. We sat quietly for a few minutes before the horns began. Is there anything so futile in a traffic jam as a horn? *Oh, I'm sorry, I didn't know you were in such a hurry, in that case maybe I'll just ram the car in front of me.*

"I'd like to travel," said Beth. "That's what I would do if I suddenly had too much money."

She had been thinking about it the whole time we had been stuck and that surprised me. For me to mull over all I would do with all the money I wanted was as natural as breathing, but it was not so natural for Beth. Generally she evinced great satisfaction with her life as it was. This was my first indication ever that her satisfaction was waning.

"I never saw the point of traveling," I said. "There's only so many museums you can rush through, so many old churches, until you're sick of it all."

"I'm not talking for just a week to see some museums," said Beth. "I'm talking about taking a few years off and seeing the world." I turned and looked at her. She was staring forward, as if from the prow of a swift ocean liner instead of through the windshield of a car stalled in traffic. "I always thought, as a girl, that there was something out there waiting for me and my purpose in life was to go out and find it. If there is a disappointment in my life it's that I haven't even really searched. I feel like I've been tromping around looking for it in Philadelphia only because the light is better here, when all along I know it's someplace else."

"Where?"

"I don't know."

"What?"

"I don't know. It's stupid, but it's what I'd like to do. And even if it's here in Philadelphia after all, maybe I need to spend time away, shucking off all my old habits and old ways of seeing and learn to look at everything new again, so I can find it. A couple of years in a foreign land is supposed to sharpen your vision."

"At LensCrafters they'll do it for you in less than an hour."

"A safari in Africa. A jungle cruise up the Amazon. A month on a houseboat in India. Nepal. Sometimes I look at a map of Nepal and get chills. Katmandu."

"What kind of toilets do they have in Katmandu? I won't do any of that squatting stuff."

"So if we were suddenly rich, Victor, I think what I'd do is go to Katmandu."

The traffic started to crawl forward. First a foot at a time, then a few feet, then we began a twenty-mile-per-hour jog into the heart of the city. Beth was thinking about Katmandu, I suppose, while I thought about my Gap khakis and my Ferrari. And about Caroline Shaw.

Back in the office I sat at the quiet of my desk and ignored the message slips handed me by Ellie. I thought of things, thought of my neediness and my deprivations and how much I wanted out. I wanted out so desperately it hurt as bad as a lost love. I had to get out, for reasons that haunted half the lawyers in the country and for darker, more sinister reasons that Beth could never know. Everything was against my ever leaving, sure, except for how fiercely I wanted out. I sat and daydreamed about winning the lottery and dripping paint on canvases in the Hamptons with a gin and tonic in my hand and then I stopped daydreaming and thought about the Reddmans.

Guys like me, we don't often brush shoulders with that much money and to accidentally rub up against it, like I did in that bank, does something ugly to us. It's like seeing the most beautiful woman in the world walk by, a woman who makes you ache just to look at her, and knowing that she'll never even glance in your direction, which slips the ache in even deeper. I thought about the Reddmans and all they were born to and I ached. More than anything in this world, I wish I had been born rich. It would have made up for everything. I'd still be ugly, sure, but I'd be rich and ugly. I'd still be weak and dim and tongue-tied with women, but I'd be rich enough for them not to care. I'd no longer be a social misfit, I'd be eccentric. And most of all, I'd no longer be what I was, I'd be something different. I thought about it all and let the pain of my impoverishment wash over me and then I started making calls.

"I don't have time to chitchat," said Detective McDeiss over the phone, after I had tracked him down to the Criminal Justice Building. "You need something from me, you can go through the D.A."

"It's not about an active prosecution," I said. "The case I want to talk about is old and closed. Jacqueline Shaw."

There was a pause and a deep breath. "The heiress."

"I like that word, don't you?"

"Yeah, well, this one hung herself. What could there possibly be left to talk about?"

"I don't know. I just want to get some background. I'm representing the sister."

"Good for you, Carl. It's a step up I guess from your usual low-class grease-bucket clientele. How did you ever hook onto her?"

"She chased me down the street with a gun."

"Tell me about it, you slimeball."

"You free for lunch tomorrow?"

"To talk about Jacqueline Shaw?"

"Exactly. My treat."

"Your treat, huh?" There was a pause while McDeiss reprioritized his day. "You eat Chinese, Carl?"

"I'm Jewish, aren't I?" I said.

"All right then, one o'clock," and he tossed out an address before hanging up. I knew that McDeiss wanted nothing to do with me, disdain dripped thick as oil from his voice, but in the last few years I had learned something about cops and one of the things I had learned was that there was not a cop on the force who would turn down a free lunch, even if it was just a $4.25 luncheon special at some Chinatown dive with fried rice and an egg roll soggy with grease.

Except the address he tossed out was not to some Chinatown dive, it was to Susanna Foo, the fanciest, priciest Chinese restaurant in the city.

6

PETER CRESSI HAD A DARK, Elvisine look that just sort of melted women. He told me so in his own modest way, but he was right. Take the way our secretary, Ellie, reacted after he walked by whenever he walked by. She stared at him as he strutted past, her eyes popping, her mouth agape, and then, when the door was closed, she let out a sort of helpless giggle. He was a tomato for sure, Cressi, Big Boy or beefsteak, one of them, and from my dealings with him I knew him to be just about as smart. He was actually a little brighter than he looked, but then again he'd have to be.

"How's it hanging wit' you, Vic?" he said to me as he sat indolently in the chair across from my desk. "Low?" His dark eyes were partly brooding, partly blank, as if he were angry at something he couldn't quite remember. His lemon tie, delicious and bright against his black shirt, was tied with entirely too much care.

"It's not hanging so terrifically, Pete," I said, shaking my head at him. "Next time you buy an arsenal, try not to purchase it from an undercover cop."

Peter gave me a wink and looked off to the side, bobbing his head up and down as he chuckled at some private little joke. Cressi chuckled a lot, little he-he-he's coming through his Elvis lips. "Who knew?"

"Good answer. That's exactly what we'll tell the jury."

That chuckle again. "Just say I'm a collector."

I opened the file and scanned the police report. "One

hundred and seventy-nine Ruger Mini–14 semiautomatics with folding fiberglass stocks and two hundred kits for illegally modifying said firearms for fully automatic performance."

"That's what you should tell them I was collecting."

"Also three grenade launchers and a flamethrower. A flamethrower, Peter. Jesus. What the hell did you need a flamethrower for?"

"A weenie roast?"

"That's what your trial is going to be unless you sharpen up and get serious. You were also trying to buy twenty thousand rounds of ammunition."

"Me and the guys, like we sometimes target shoot out in the woods."

"What woods are we talking about here, Peter? They got any woods in South Philly I don't know about? Like there's a block just south of Washington they forgot to put a row of crappy houses on, it just slipped their minds?"

"Now you being funny, Vic." His head bobbing, the he-he-he's coming like an underpowered lawn mower. "Upstate, I'm talking. You know, bottles and cans. Maybe next time you want I should ask you along? It's good to keep in training, if you know what I mean. And every now and then a stray bird it lands like a douche bag on the target and then, what do you think, bam, it's just feathers floating."

"Seriously, Pete. Why the guns?"

His eyes darkened. "I'm being serious as a fucking heart attack."

He looked at me and I looked at him and I knew his look was fiercer than mine so I dropped my gaze back to the file. The guys I represented were nice guys generally, respectful, funny, guys to hang around and drink beer with, nice guys except that by and large they were killers. I must admit it didn't take much to be fiercer than me, but still my clients scared me. Which made my current position even more tenuous and doubtful. But still I had a job to do.

"It says here," I said, looking through the file, "that the undercover cop you were buying the weapons from, this Detective Scarpatti, made tapes of certain of your conversations." I looked back up at Cressi, hoping to see something. "Anything we should be worried about?"

"What, you shitting me? Of course we should be worried. They probably got me on tape making the whole deal with that scum-sucking slob."

"I assumed that. What I mean is any surprises, any talk about what you were going to do with the weapons? Any plots against a government building in Oklahoma or specific crimes planned which might cause us any problems? We're not looking at additional conspiracy charges, are we?"

"No, no way. Just the deal."

"How much money are we talking about?"

"In general or specific terms do you want?"

"Always be specific, Pete."

"Ninety-five thou, eight hundred and ten. Scarpatti figured it out with a calculator, the fat bastard. I had more than that when they busted me, you know, for incidentals. He told me cash only."

"No Visa card I guess."

"I'm already over my limit."

"Guys like you and me, Pete, it's congenital."

He chuckled and bobbed and said, "What's that, dirty or something?"

I picked up another piece of paper from the file. It was just a copy of a subpoena, but I wanted to have something to look at so the question would seem offhand. "Where'd you get the cash?"

"You know, just lying around." He-he-he.

I dropped the subpoena and looked up and put on my most annoyed look. I kind of squinted and twisted my lips and pretended I had just eaten a lemon. Then I waited a bit for his chuckling to die down, which, surprisingly, it did. "Maybe you are confused," I said. "Maybe you are color blind. The guy in the blue suit, black shoes, red tie, that's the prosecutor. He wants to put your butt in jail for a decade. My suit is blue and my shoes are black, sure, but look at my tie. It's green."

"Where'd you get that tie anyway, Woolworth's?"

"Why not?"

"You know, Vic, your whole sense of style is in the toilet. Who shines your suits, anyway? And then you got them shoes. You should let me set you up with something new. I know a guy what got some flash suits might change your whole look. You might even get laid, do you some good. They's a little warm is all, but you being a lawyer, what do you care, right?"

"Something wrong with my shoes?"

His sneer lengthened.

"What I'm trying to say is that I'm not the prosecutor here, I'm your lawyer. I'm here to help you. Everything we say in this room is confidential, you know that, it's privileged, and no subpoena on earth can drag it out of me. But I can't defend you properly unless I know the truth."

"I'm not sure what you want I should tell you here, Vic. I thought you lawyers didn't want to know the truth, that it limited what you could do, stopped you from bobbing here and weaving there, turned you from a Muhammad Ali, who was always dancing and sliding, to a Chuckie Wepner, from up there in Bayonne, getting hit like a speed bag, bam-bam-bam, and whose face was a bloody slice of sausage after round two. I thought the gig was that you would get the truth from me once you, like, knew what the best truth it was to tell."

He was right, of course, which made everything a little more difficult. Cressi was an idiot, actually, except in the three things in which he had the most experience, screwing, shooting, and the criminal justice system. "It's different," I told him, "when there's an undercover cop with tapes. When there's an undercover cop with tapes I need to know everything or we're liable to get blasted at trial. So I'm asking you again, and I want you to tell me. Where did you get the money?"

Cressi looked at me for a while, head tilted like a dog that was trying to figure out exactly what he was looking at. Then he shrugged. "I boosted six Mercedes off a lot. Just came in with a carrier I borrowed from a buddy what knew nothing about it, waived around some paperwork, and just took them. Drove them right to Delaware. Some Arab sheik and his sons right now they're probably riding around in circles in the desert, smiling like retards."

"You touch base with Raffaello on that deal?"

"You working for him or you working for me?"

"I'm working for you," I said quickly, "but if you're crossing him I have to know. I'm not going to create a defense for you that gets you out of trouble with the law but gets you dead when you hit the street. I'm trying to watch your back and your front, but you've got to level with me."

Cressi turned his head and started bobbing, but there was no chuckle now. "We gave Raffaello his fifteen percent, sure, soon as the deal was done. It went through Dante, his new number two."

"I thought Calvi was number two?"

"No, no more. There was a shake-up. Calvi's in Florida. For good. Things change. Now it's Dante."

"Dante? I didn't even know he was made."

"Sure he was, under Little Nicky," said Cressi, referring to the boss before the boss before Enrico Raffaello.

"Dante," I repeated, shaking my head. Dante was the loan shark who bailed out Cressi yesterday morning. I had thought him strictly small time, just another street hood paying into the mob because he couldn't count on the police to protect his illegal sharking operation, nothing more. He had moved up fast, Dante. Well, moving and lasting were two different things. I had liked Calvi, an irascible old buzzard with a sense of humor, a vicious smile, and a taste for thick, foul cigars that smelled of burning tires and rancid rum. I had liked Calvi, but he apparently hadn't lasted and I didn't expect Dante to last either.

"What about the guns?" I asked. "Did you touch base there too?"

"Nah, it was just kind of a hustle for a while. I didn't think the guy could deliver, so I was going to play it out and see. I had a buyer, but I wasn't sure of the seller."

"Who was the buyer?"

"This group of wackos up in Allentown. Aryan bullshit, shaved heads and ratty trailers and target practice getting ready for the holy race war."

"Who set it up?"

"I did."

"Who else?"

"It was my gig, like, completely. Met this broad who took me to one of the meetings. Tits like cantaloupes, you know ripe ones like you get on Ninth Street. She talked about a retreat and I thought it was going to be hot. I thought an orgy or something. Turned out to be this militia-Nazi-bullshit-crap. I drilled her anyway. Then this tall, weird-looking geek started talking about guns and we set it up."

"Just you? You were solo on this?"

"That's what I said."

He looked away and bobbed and his Adam's apple bobbed too.

"All right," I said. "That's all for now. We have your preliminary hearing next week. We're scheduled for ten, you get here nine-thirty and we'll walk over together."

"You don't want to prepare me or nothing?"

"You're going to sit next to me and not say a word and when I am done you're going to leave with me. You think we need more preparation?"

"I think I can handle that."

"I think maybe you can too. Tell me one thing more, Pete. You know Jimmy Vigs Dubinsky?"

"The bookie, sure. I done some favors for him."

"You ever known him to whack someone who stiffs him?"

"Who, Jimmy? Nah, he's a sweetheart. He cuts them off is all. Besides, you know, you can't clip nobody without the boss's approval. That's like bottom line."

"And he doesn't approve much."

"Are you kidding, you got to go to New York nowadays to get any kind of good experience. Up there it still rocks."

"Thanks, that's what I figured," I said as I walked him out of my office into the hallway. Beth just happened to be at Ellie's desk, talking about something oh-so-important as Peter walked by. They were both polite enough to hold their giggles until he was out of earshot.

"You too, huh, Beth?" I said, looking through a stack of mail on Ellie's desk. "Well forget it, ladies. He likes women with cantaloupe breasts and empty minds."

"Don't you all?" said Beth.

"Come to think of it," I said. "I'm going to step out for a cup of coffee. I'll be right back. Anyone want anything?"

"Diet Coke," said Beth. I nodded.

Down the hallway, past the accountant's office and the architect's office and the design firm that shared our office space, out the door, down the stairs, out to Twenty-first Street. I walked a few blocks to the Wawa convenience store and bought a cup of coffee in blue cardboard and a Diet Coke, which I stuck in my pocket. Out on the street, with my coffee in my hand, I looked both ways. Nothing. I walked a few more blocks and turned around. Nothing. Then I found a phone booth and put the coffee on the aluminum shelf. I dropped in a quarter and dialed and waited for the ringing to end.

"Tosca's," said a voice.

"Let me talk to table nine," I said.

"One'a moment. I see if it available."

About a minute later I heard a familiar voice, older and softer, peppered with an Old World accent. "Table nine," it said.

"He says he got the money by stealing six cars off a Mercedes-Benz lot. He said he got you your share through Dante."

"Go on."

"He says he was going to resell the guns to some white supremacist group out in Allentown for a big profit."

"You believe him?"

"He says he was on his own. I don't think he whacks off on his own."

"I don't think so neither. He ever had a bright idea it'd be beginner's luck. You find out who he was with."

"And then we're even and I'm through, right?"

"It's so hard to quantify human relationships, don't you think?"

"I hate this."

"Life is hard."

There was a firm click. I stood in the phone booth and tried to take a sip of the coffee but my hand was shaking so much it spilled on my pants. I cursed loudly and shook my pants leg and wondered at how I had made such a mess of everything.

7

"IT'S THE ASIAN RADISH that makes this dish truly memorable," said Detective McDeiss as he skillfully manipulated the bamboo chopsticks with his thick fingers. On the little plate before him, tastefully garnished, were two tiny cakes, lightly fried. *Hundred Corner Crab Cakes with Daikon Radish and Tomato Pineapple Salsa ($10.00).* "The Asian radish is subtler than your basic American radish, with a sweet and mild flavor when cooked, like a delicate turnip. The pineapple salsa is a nice touch, though a little harsh for my preference, but it's the radish that adds that touch of excitement to the fresh crab. I detect a hint of ginger too, which is entirely appropriate."

"I'm glad you're enjoying yourself," I said.

"Oh, I am. It's not too often I get to eat at so fine an establishment. More wine?"

"No thank you," I said. "But please, help yourself." The last was a bit gratuitous, as the detective was already pouring himself another glass from the bottle. *Pouilly Fuissé 1983 ($48.00).*

"Normally, of course, I wouldn't drink at lunch, but being as the trial was recessed for the day and I'm off shift, I figure, why not?"

"Why not indeed?"

McDeiss was a big man, tall and broad, with the stomach of a football lineman ten years gone from the game. He dressed rather badly, a garish jacket over a short-sleeve shirt, a wide tie with indifferent stripes choking his thick neck. His bulbous face held a closed arrogant expression that seemed to refute any possibility of an inner life but the thick lines in his forehead rose with a cultured joy as he tasted his crab, his lips tightened, his shoulders seemed to sway with a swooning delight. Just my luck, I figured, offering to buy lunch for the only five star gourmand on the force. Susanna Foo was elegantly decorated with fresh flowers and mirrors and gold-flocked wallpaper; no Formica tables, no cheap plastic chopsticks, everything first class, including the prices, which made me flinch as I saw the wine drain down his substantial gullet. Even though I fully intended to bill Caroline for expenses, I was still fronting our lunch money.

"We were talking about Jacqueline Shaw," I said. "Your investigation."

He finished the last of his crab cakes, closed his eyes in appreciation, and reached again for his wineglass. "Very good. Very very good. Next time, maybe we'll try *Le Bec-Fin* together. They have an excellent price-fixed lunch. Do you like opera, Carl?"

"Does *Tommy* count?"

"Sorry, no. Too bad that. We could have such a nice evening, just you and me. Dinner at the Striped Bass and then orchestra seats to *Rigoletto*."

"You're pushing it, McDeiss."

"Am I? Jacqueline Shaw. Hung herself in the living room of her apartment at the south end of Rittenhouse Square. Quite a place, if a bit overly baroque in decoration for my palate. Everything seemed to be in order. It was very neat, no clothes lying around, as if she was expecting guests to show up at her hanging. She had been depressed, she had tried it before."

"How?"

"Too many pills once. Slit her wrists in the bathtub when she was a teen. She was a statistic waiting to be rung up, that's all. Ahh, here's my salad." *Fresh Water Chestnut and Baby Arugula Salad with Dry Shrimp Vinaigrette ($8.00).* "Oh my goodness, Carl, this dressing is delicious. Want a taste?"

He thrust at me a forkful of greens thick with the vinaigrette.

I shook my head. "Do you think the mother arugula gets upset when the farmer takes her babies?"

McDeiss didn't answer, he simply turned the fork on himself. As he chewed, the lines in his forehead rose again.

"Who found her?" I asked.

"The boyfriend," said McDeiss. "They were living together, apparently engaged. Came home from work and found her hanging from the chandelier. He left her up there and called us. A lot of times they cut them down before they call. He just let her hang."

"Was there a doorman? A guest register?"

"We checked out all the names in and out that day. Everything routine. Her neighbor, a strange player named Peckworth, said he saw a UPS guy in her hallway that day, which got us wondering, because no one had signed in, but then he came back and said he was confused about the day. We checked it out. She had received a package two days before. Not that this Peckworth could have been any kind of a witness anyway. He's a real treat. Once that was cleared up there was nothing out of the ordinary, nothing suspicious."

"Did she leave a note?"

He shook his head. "Often they don't."

"Find anything suspicious in the apartment?"

"Not a thing."

"Candy wrappers or trash that didn't belong?"

"Not a thing. Why? You got something?"

"No."

"Didn't think so. The lady had a history of depression, history of drug abuse and alcohol abuse, years of failed therapies, and she was getting involved in some hippie dippy New Age chanting thing out in Mount Airy."

"That's the place for it," I said.

"It all fits."

"What about the motive?" I softened my voice. "She's a Reddman, right?"

"Absolutely," said McDeiss. "A direct heir as a matter of fact. Her great-grandfather was the pickle king, what was his name, Claudius Reddman? The guy on all the jars. Well, the daughter of this Reddman, she married a Shaw, from the Shaw Brothers department stores, and their son is the sole heir for the entire fortune. This Jacqueline was his daughter. There are three other siblings. The whole thing is going to be divided among them."

I leaned forward. I tried to sound insouciant, but I couldn't pull it off. "How much is the estate worth?"

"I couldn't get an exact figure, only estimates," said McDeiss. "Not much after all these years. Only about half a billion dollars."

Three heirs left, half a billion dollars. That put Caroline Shaw's expected worth at something like one hundred and sixty-six million dollars. I reached for my water glass and tried to take a drink, but my hand shook so badly water started slopping over the glass's edge and I was forced to put it back down.

"So if it wasn't a suicide," I suggested, "money could have been a motive."

"With that much money it's the first thing we think about."

"Who benefited from her death?"

"I can't talk about it."

"Oh come on, McDeiss."

"It's privileged. I can't talk about it, that's been made very clear to me. There was a hefty insurance policy and her inheritance was all tied up in a trust. Both were controlled by some bank out in the burbs."

"First Mercantile of the Main Line, I'll bet."

"You got it."

"By some snot name of Harrington, right?"

"You got it. But the information he gave me about the insurance and the trust was privileged, so you'll have to go to him." He leaned forward and lowered his voice. "Look, let me warn you, there was political heat on this investigation. Heat to clean it up quickly. I've always been one to clean up my cases, check them off and go onto the next. It's not like there's not enough work. But still I was getting the push from the guys downtown. So when the coroner came back calling it a suicide that was enough for me. Case closed."

"But even with all the heat, you're talking to me."

"A good meal, Carl, is worth any indignity," but after he made his little joke he kept looking at me and something sharp emerged from the fleshy bulbs of his face.

"And you think something stinks, don't you?" I said. "That's why you're here, isn't it? Not for the baby arugula. Where'd the heat come from? Who called you off?"

He shrugged and finished his salad, poured another glass of wine, drank from it, holding the stem of the glass daintily in his sausage fingers. "The word on the Reddmans," he said rather mysteriously, "is that it is a family dark with secrets."

"Society types?"

"Not at all. Best I could tell they've been shunned completely, like lepers. All that money and not even in the *Social Register*. From what I could figure, you and I, we'd be more welcome in certain social circles than the Reddmans."

"A Jew and an African-American?"

"Well maybe not you." He laughed broadly at that and then leaned forward and twisted his voice down to a whisper. "The Reddman house is one strange place, Carl, more a huge stone tomb than anything else, with tilting spires

and wild, overrun gardens. Veritas, it's called. Don't you
love it when they name their houses?"

"Veritas? A bit presumptuous, wouldn't you say?"

"And they pronounce it wrong."

"You speak Latin?"

His broad shoulders shrugged. "My mother had this
thing about a classical education."

"My mother thinks classical means an olive in her
gin."

"Well, this Veritas was cold as an Eskimo's hell," said
McDeiss. "As soon as I got there and started asking questions I could feel the freeze descend. The dead girl's father,
the grandson of the pickle king, the word on him is he's
demented. They lock him up in some upstairs room in that
mansion. I had some questions for him but they wouldn't
let me up to see him, they physically barred me from going
up the stairs, can you believe that? Then, just when I was
about to force my way through to get to his room, a call
came in from the Roundhouse. The family, through our
friend Harrington, had let it be known that they wanted the
case closed and suddenly the heat came down from City
Hall. See, Carl, money like that, it is its own power, you
understand? Money like that, it wants something, it gets it.
I never got a chance to see the old man. My lieutenant told
me to check off the case and move on."

"And so you checked."

"It was a classic suicide. We'd seen it all before a hundred times. There wasn't much I could do."

"No matter how much it stunk. I need you to get me
the file."

"No. Absolutely not."

"I'll subpoena it."

"I can't control what you do."

"How about the building register for the day of the
death?"

He looked down at his salad and speared a lone water

chestnut. "There's nothing there, but okay. And be sure to talk to the boyfriend, Grimes."

"You think maybe he . . ."

"All I think is you'll find him interesting. He lives in that luxury high-rise on Walnut, west of Rittenhouse. You know it?"

I nodded. "By the way, you find any Darvon in her medicine cabinet?"

He looked up from his salad. "Enough to keep a football team mellow."

"Ever wonder why she didn't just take the pills?"

Before McDeiss could answer the waiter came and whisked away his plate, with only the remnants of the dry shrimp vinaigrette staining the porcelain. In front of me the waiter placed the restaurant's cheapest entree, *Kung Pao Chicken–Very Spicy ($10.00)*, thick with roasted peanuts. In front of McDeiss he placed one of the specialties of the house, *Sweeter Than Honey Venison with Caramelized Pear, Sun-Dried Tomato and Hot Pepper ($20.00)*. McDeiss picked off a chunk of venison with his chopsticks, swilled it in the garnish, and popped it into his mouth. He chewed slowly, carefully, mashing the meat with Pritikin determination, his shoulders shaking with joy.

While McDeiss chewed and shook, I considered. Through his patina of certainty as to the suicide I had detected something totally unexpected: doubt. For the first time I wondered seriously whether Caroline Shaw might have been right about her sister's death and it wasn't just that McDeiss had doubts that got me to wondering. There was money at stake here, huge pots of money, enough to twist the soul of anyone who got too close. Money has its own gravitational pull, stronger than anything Newton imagined, and what it drew, along with fast cars and slim-hipped women, was the worst of anyone who fell within its orbit. Just the amount of money involved was enough to get me thinking, and what I was thinking, suddenly, was of

Caroline Shaw and that manipulative little smile of hers. And there was something else too, something that cut its way through the heat of the Kung Pao and slid into the lower depths of my consciousness. Just at that moment I couldn't shake the strange suspicion that somehow a part of all that Reddman money could rightfully belong to me.

McDeiss had told me I should talk to the boyfriend, this Grimes fellow, and so I would. I could picture him now, handsome, suave, a fortune-hunting rogue in the grandest tradition, who had plucked Jacqueline out of a crowd and was ready to grab his piece of her inheritance. He must be a bitter boy, this Grimes, bitter at the chance for wealth that had been snatched right out of his pocket. I liked the bitter boys, I knew what made them tick, admired their drive, their passions. I had been a bitter boy once myself, before my own calamitous failures transformed my bitterness into something weaker and more pathetic, into deep-seated cynicism and a desperate desire to flee. But though I was no longer bitter, I still knew its language and could still play the part. I figured I'd have no trouble getting Grimes to spill his guts to me, bitter boy to bitter boy.

8

I SAT DOWN AT THE BAR of the Irish Pub with a weary sigh and ordered a beer. As the bartender drew a pint from the keg I reached into my wallet and dropped two twenties onto the bar. I drank the beer while the bartender was still at the register making my change, drank it like I was suffering a profound thirst. I slapped the glass onto the bar and waved to the bartender for another. Generally I didn't drink much anymore because of my drinking problem. The problem was that when I drank too much I threw up. But that night I had already spent hours searching and asking questions and looking here and there, and now that I had found what I was looking for I was determined to do some drinking.

"You ever feel like the whole world is fixed against you?" I said to the bartender when he brought my second beer.

It was a busy night at the Irish Pub and the bartender didn't have time to listen. He gave a little laugh and moved on.

"You don't need to tell me," said the fellow sitting next to me, the remnants of a scotch in his hand.

"Every time I get close," I said, "the bastards yank it away like it was one of those joke dollar bills tied to a string."

"You don't need to tell me," said the man. With a quick tilt of his wrist he drank the last of his scotch.

The Irish Pub was a young bar, women dressed in jeans

and high heels, men in Polo shirts, boys and girls together, meeting one another, shouting lies in each other's ears. On weekends there was a line outside, but this wasn't a weekend and I wasn't there to find a date and neither, I could tell, was the man next to me. He was tall and dark, in a gaudily bright short-sleeve shirt and tan pants. His features were all of movie-star strength and quality, his nose was straight and thin, his chin jutting, his eyes deep and black, but the package went together with a peculiar weakness. He should have been the handsomest man in the world, but he wasn't. And the bartender refilled his glass without even asking.

"What's your line?" I asked, while still looking straight ahead, the way strangers at a bar talk to one another.

"I'm a dentist," he said.

I turned my head, looked him up and down, and turned it back again. "I thought you had to have more hair on your forearms to be a dentist."

He didn't laugh, he just took a sip from his scotch and swirled it around his mouth.

"I was that close today, dammit," I said. "And then it happened like it always happens. It was a car accident, right? A pretty ugly one, too, some old lady in her Beemer just runs the red and bam, slams into my guy's van. Lacerations from the flying glass, multiple contusions, a neck thing, you know, the works. I send him to my doctor and it's all set, he can't work, can't walk or exercise, he's stuck in a chair on his porch, wracked with pain, his life tragically ruined. Beautiful, no?"

"You're a lawyer," said the man as flatly as if he were telling me my fly was unzipped.

"And it set up so sweet," I said. "Workman's comp from the employer and then, wham, big bucks compensatory from the old lady and her insurance company. The insurance was maxed out at three hundred thou but we were going for more, much more, punitives because the old lady was half blind and should never have been out on the road, was a collision waiting to happen. She's a widow, some Wayne witch, rich as sin, so collection's a breeze. And I got a thirty-three-and-a-third percent contingency fee agreement in my bank vault, if you know what I mean. I had picked out my Mercedes already, maroon with tan leather seats. SL class."

"The convertible," said the man, nodding.

"Absolutely. Oh, so beautiful that car, just thinking about it gives me a hard-on."

I finished my beer and pushed the mug to the edge of the bar and let my head drop. When the bartender came I asked for a shot to go with my refill. I waited till the drinks came and then sucked the top off my beer and waited some more.

"So what happened?" said the man, finally.

I sat there quietly for a moment and then with a quick snatch downed the shot and chased it. "We show up at mandatory arbitration and I give our case, right? Fault's not even at issue. And my guy's sitting there, shaking with palsy in a wheelchair, his neck chafed to bleeding from the brace, most pathetic thing you ever saw. I figured they'd offer at least a mil before we even got to telling our story. Then the old lady's fancy lawyer brings out the videotape."

I took another swallow of beer and shook my head.

"My guy playing golf over at Valley Forge, neck brace and all. Schmuck couldn't keep off the links. He gave up work, sex with the wife, playing with the kids, everything, but he couldn't keep off the links. They brought in his scorecard too. Broke ninety, neck brace and all. I took forty thou and ran. So close to the big score and then, as quick as a two-foot putt, it's gone."

"You don't need to tell me," said the man next to me.

"Don't even try. What do you know about it, a dentist. You got it made. Everyone's got teeth."

He took a long swallow from his scotch and then

another, draining it. "You're such a loser, you don't even know."

"Tell me about it."

"You want to hear something? You want to hear the saddest story in the world?"

"Not really," I said. "I got my own problems."

"Shut up and buy me a drink and I'll tell you something that will make your skin crawl."

I turned to look at him and he was staring at me with a ferocity that was frightening. I shrugged and waved for the bartender and ordered two scotch on the rocks for him and two beers for me. Then I let Grimes tell me his story.

9

HE FIRST SAW HER AT A PLACE on Sixteenth Street, a dark, aggressively hip bar with a depressed jukebox and serious drinkers. She was sitting alone, dressed in black, not like an artiste, more like a mourner. She was sort of pretty, but not really thin enough, not really young enough, and he wouldn't have given her a second look except that there was about this woman in black an aura of sadness that bespoke need. Need was about right, he figured, since he was looking for an effortless piece and need often translated into willing cession. He sat down beside her and bought her a drink. Her name, she said, was Jacqueline Shaw.

"She was drinking Martinis," said Grimes, "which I thought was sexy in a dissolute sort of way."

"Is this going to be just another lost girl story?" I asked. "Because if that's all . . ."

"Shut up and listen," said Grimes. "You might just learn something."

After the second drink she started talking about her spiritual quest, how she was seeking a wider understanding of life than that allowed by the five basic senses. He smiled at her revelations, not out of any true interest, but only because he knew that spiritual yearning and sexual freedom were often deliciously entwined. She talked about the voices of the soul and the spirits that speak within each of us and how we need to learn to hear like a child once again to discern what the voices are whispering to us about the ineffable. She spoke of the connectedness of all things and how each of us, in our myriad of guises, was merely a manifestation of the whole. She said she had found her spiritual guide, a woman named Oleanna. Two more drinks and she and Grimes were walking side by side west, toward Rittenhouse Square. She had a place in one of those old apartment buildings on the south side of the park and was taking him there to show him her collection of spiritual artifacts, in which he had feigned interest.

"Ba-da-boom, ba-da-bing," I said.

"And it was something, too," said Grimes, "but that's not what really grabbed my interest."

"No?"

"It was that place, man, that place."

Her apartment was unbelievably spacious, baronial in size and furnishings, with everything outsized and thick, huge couches, huge wing chairs, a grand piano. There were tapestries everywhere, on the walls, draped over tables, and chandeliers dripping glass, and carpets thick as fairway rough piled one atop the other. Plants in sculpted pots were everywhere, plants with wide veined leaves and plants with bright tiny flowers and hairy phallic plants thick with thorns. It was otherworldly, that place. She put on this music which drifted out from behind the furnishings, a magical white mix of wind harps and fish flutes, drone tubes and moon lutes and water bells. And then in the center of the main room, atop hand-woven Persian rugs in deep blue, beside a fire, she showed him her crystals and sacred beads and fetishes imported from Africa, a man with a lion's head, a pregnant woman with hooves and beard, a child with a hyena's grin. She lit a stick of incense and a candle and then another candle and then twenty candles more and with the fire and totems surrounding them they made love and it was as though the power of those tiny statues and the beads and the crystals were funneled by the music, the incense, the flame, right through her body and she collapsed again and again beneath him on the carpet. And he felt the power too, but the power he felt was not of the fire or of the stones or of the fetishes, it was the power of all the wealth in that magical room, the utter power of money.

"Suddenly," said Grimes, "I developed a deep belief in the healing power of crystals."

He went with her the next week to a meeting of her spiritual group. They met in what they called the Haven, which was really the basement of some rat trap in Mount Airy. Everybody was dressed in robes, orange or green, and sat on the floor. There was enough potpourri scattered to make Martha Stewart choke and they chanted and meditated and told each other of painful moments in their lives and their efforts to transcend their physical selves. He noticed that the church members bustled about Jackie like she was a source of some sort. Extra time was devoted to her, extra efforts taken to make her comfortable. "Do you need a pad, Jackie?" "Can we get you something to drink, Jackie?" "Would you like an extra dose of aroma therapy, Jackie?" A woman came out at the end of the meeting and sat on a high-backed regal chair, a beautiful woman in flowing white robes. Jacqueline was taken to sit directly at her feet. This woman was Oleanna, and as she sat on that chair she fell into a trance and strange noises emerged from her throat, noises which bent Jackie double with rapture. Grimes didn't understand it, thought it part con, part insane, but he couldn't help noticing how the members all buzzed about Jacqueline like bees about the queen. The next morning he hired an investigator to check her out discreetly.

Three months later, in a private ceremony in her apartment, with the music and the fetishes and the candles, with a pile of crystals between their kneeling, naked bodies, he asked her to marry him and she said yes. By that time the

investigator had told him who her great-grandfather was
and the approximate amount of the fortune she was scheduled to inherit.

"I'm not going to tell you what corporation they started
or anything," said Grimes.

"Would I know it?" I asked.

"Of course you would, everyone does. You've been
eating its stuff forever. And her share of the fortune alone
was over a hundred million. Do you know how many zeros
that is? Eight zeros. That's enough to buy a baseball team,
that's enough to buy the Eagles. And she said yes."

"Jesus, you hit the big time."

"Bigger than you'll ever see, Mack, that's for sure."

With their future settled, Jackie took him one afternoon to meet her family in the ancestral mansion deep in
the Main Line, a place they called Veritas. The house
was a strange gothic castle, high on a grassy hill, surrounded by acres of woods and strange, desolate gardens. Inside it was a dank mausoleum, cold and humid,
decorated much like Jacqueline's apartment only on a
larger, more decrepit scale. One brother never rose from
his chair, wearing a creepy smoking jacket, almost too
drunk to talk. His wife flitted about him like a hyperactive moth, refreshing his drink, fluffing his pillow.
Another brother, thin and nervous, was in a den glued to
his computer screen, watching the prices of the family's
vast holdings rise and fall and rise again on the nation's
stock exchanges. The sister was a sarcastic little bitch in
black leather who laughed in his face when he told her
he was a dentist and who cut Grimes with a series of
scathing comments. The mother was overseas somewhere, vacationing alone, and the father stayed in his
private upstairs chamber, never stepping down to meet
his daughter's fiancé.

"It felt like I was visiting the Munsters," said Grimes.
"And that was before Jacqueline took me to meet her

Grammy, the daughter of the man who had founded the family fortune."

Grandmother Shaw was hunched over in a chair, her wrinkled face tilted as if one half were made of wax and had been pressed too close to a flame. Her hands were bony and long, the rasp of her breathing sliced the silence in the room. The eye on the melted half of her face was closed; from the other a pale, cataractal blue peered out. She stared at him like he was a disease as Jacqueline made the introductions. Then, with a withering smile, the grandmother insisted on taking Grimes for a little walk around the gardens.

They were alone, the two of them, except for the old gardener who held onto her arm as she walked. It was the height of the summer now and the gardens were a riot of colors and scents. She showed him her rhododendron, her hyacinths, with spikes of red flowers, her blood-red chrysanthemums. Thick yellow bees burrowed for pollen, rubbing their setaceous bodies over the open blooms in a silent ecstasy. She led him through an arch cut into a high wall of spinous hedges. Here the hedgerows were trimmed into some sort of a maze, flowers fronting tall walls of barberry bristling with thorns, barberry hiding paths of primrose and blue lobelia that spun around in circles, leading to still more barberry. She asked him about himself as they walked, listening without comment. Her cane was gnarled. The old gardener, holding her arm as he walked beside her, was silent beneath his wide straw hat. They wove slowly past bunches of phlox and violet sage, past peals of bellshaped digitalis, alongside spiny rows of purple globe thistle.

"You some sort of gardener?" I asked Grimes.

"Everyone needs a hobby, what of it?"

"Just asking is all."

They walked in a seemingly directionless path in that maze until they found themselves in the center of a very

formal space scribed by tall circular hedges, edged with
astilbe and gay-feather and gaudy red hollyhock on tall,
reedy spires. In the center of the space was an oval of rich,
dark earth, out of which bloomed bunches of gorgeous violet irises above a sea of pale yellow jewelweed. At one end
of the oval was a statue of a naked woman reaching up to
the heavens, her delicate bare feet resting on a huge marble
base, studded with pillars, encrusted with brass medallions,
the word "SHAW" engraved deep into the stone. Across
the oval garden from the statue was a marble bench, situated under a white wooden arch infested with giant orange
trumpet flowers, their stamens red as tongues. The gardener deposited the old woman on the bench and she bade
Grimes to sit beside her with two pats of the marble. As
they sat together the gardener took out a pair of shears and
began to trim the foliage behind them with shivery little
clips of the blades.

"This is our favorite place in all the world," rasped
Grandmother Shaw.

"It is beautiful," said Grimes.

"We come here every day, no matter the weather. We
feel all the power of the land in this place. We used to come
here as children, too, but it has developed more meaning for
us as we've grown older and more doddering. Mr. Shaw's
ashes are in an urn beneath the statue of Aphrodite. More
treasures are buried in this earth, keepsakes, mementos of a
better time. Everything of value we place here. We come
every day and think of him and them and replenish ourselves with all the power in this dark, rich earth."

"Your husband must have been quite a man," he said.

"He was, yes," she said. "In the last days of his life he
had become intensely spiritual in a way open only to the
scathed. You intend to marry our Jacqueline."

"Yes, ma'am."

"We take our marriage vows very seriously in this family. When we promise to marry it is for forever."

"I love Jacqueline very much. Forever is too short a time to be with her."

"We are sure you felt that for your present wife too," she said.

She was referring, of course, to Grimes's wife of seven years, mother of his two children, keeper of his house, rememberer of his family's birthdays and anniversaries, planner of the family vacations, his wife, about whom he hadn't yet gotten around to telling Jacqueline. They had been childhood sweethearts, he and his wife, had dated all through high school, her parents had put him through dental school by mortgaging their house. It had been the shock of his life when he moved out to live with Jacqueline Shaw.

"That marriage was a mistake. I didn't know what love was until I met your granddaughter."

"Yes, great wealth has that effect on people. Your private investigator did tell you the value of our family's holdings, didn't he?"

"I love Jacqueline," he said, rising from the bench with evident indignation. "And if you're implying that my intentions are . . ."

"Sit down, Mr. Grimes," she said, staring up at him with that opaque blue eye. "We need no histrionics between us. We were very impressed with the hiring of your investigator. It shows an initiative all too rare in this family. Sit down and don't presume to understand our intentions here."

He stared at her for a moment, but half her face smiled at him as she patted the bench once again, and so he sat. The gardener grunted and kneeled behind them, searching on his hands and knees for the tiniest weeds poking through the rich black mulch.

"Those purple spikes over there are from our favorite plant in this garden. *Dictamnus albus*. The gas plant. On windless summer evenings, if you put a match to its blossoms, the vapor of the flowers will burn ever so faintly, as if the spirits buried in this earth are igniting through its fragrant blooms. Jacqueline has always been a morose little girl, she had the melancholia from the start. Whether you marry her for her sadness or her money is no concern of ours."

He began to object but she raised her hand and silenced him.

"We are simply grateful she has found someone to care for her no matter what tragedies will inevitably befall her. But we want you to understand what it means to be a member of our family before it is too late for you."

"I can imagine," he said.

"No, I don't think so. It is beyond your imagining."

The gardener grunted as he stood once more and began again with the shears.

"Our blood is bad, Mr. Grimes, weak, it has been defiled. Where there was strength in my father there is only decay now. My sister died of bad blood, my son has been ruined by it. The result is the weakness evident in my grandchildren. If you marry Jacqueline you must never have children. To do so would be to court disaster. You must join us in refusing to allow the weaknesses in our family's gene pool to survive. Let it die, let it fade away. We are different from those pathetic others who try so futilely to keep alive a malignant genetic line at all costs. All that's left of our physical bodies is rot. Everything of value has already been transferred to the wealth."

The old lady sighed and turned her head away.

"Our wealth has been hard earned, Mr. Grimes, earned with blood and bone, more pain than you could ever know. But whatever remains of my father and his progeny, and of my husband too, still lives in the corpus of our family's holdings, their hearts still beat, their souls still flourish through the tentacles of our wealth. Everything we have done in what was left to us of our lives was to honor their sacrifice and to maintain the body of their existence towards three divine purposes. Conciliation, expiation, redemption."

Each of the last three words was spoken with the strength and clarity of a great iron bell. Grimes was too frightened to respond. The chiming of the gardener's shears grew louder, the pace of his cuts increased.

"Our three divine purposes have almost completely been achieved and we will never allow an outsider to undo what it has taken generations of our family to accomplish. You won't be squandering our money, Mr. Grimes. You won't gamble it away like Edward or invest it foolishly like Robert. Your sole duty will be to preserve the family fortune, to tend it and make it grow, to treat it with all the care required by the frailest orchid to satisfy its purpose. And we want to be absolutely clear on one thing. You will never leave poor Jacqueline and take a piece of her money with you. That will not be allowed. Our wealth was hard won by blood and has been defended by blood. Don't doubt it for a moment. Our father was a great and powerful man and he taught us well."

The silvery clips of the gardener's shears came closer and closer until the hairs on the tips of Grimes's ears pricked up. With each scissoring of the clippers a cold slid down the back of his neck. The old lady looked at him with her one good eye almost as if she were casting a spell.

"Well, enough family business," she said, and instantly the gardener's shears fell silent. "Tell us about your ideas for the wedding, Mr. Grimes. We are all so excited, so certain that you will make our Jacqueline terribly happy."

As he stammered a few words about their plans, how they wanted to be married as soon as possible, the old lady started to rise and the gardener was quickly at her side, helping her to stand. She left her cane resting on the bench and with her free hand grabbed tightly onto Grimes's arm.

Her grip was cold and fierce as she walked with him and the gardener back to the house.

"There is no need to blindly dash into something as deadly serious as marriage, is there?" she asked as they walked. "Take your time, Mr. Grimes, wait, be certain. That is our advice," she said and then she chatted almost gaily about the flowers, and the grass, and of how the high level of humidity in the air exacerbated her asthma.

Shortly after that visit, Grandmother Shaw died in her ninety-ninth year. She had given explicit instructions that she was to be cremated and her ashes intermingled with the ashes of her husband and placed again beneath the feet of the statue of Aphrodite. The funeral was a bleak and sparsely attended affair. It was shortly after the funeral that Jacqueline first started fearing for her life.

She claimed there were men following her, she claimed to see dark visions in her meditations. When they walked along the city streets she was forever turning around, searching for something. Grimes never spotted anything behind them but he humored her fears. When he asked her what it was that frightened her so, she admitted that she feared one of her brothers was trying to kill her. She said that murder ran in her family, something about her grandfather and her father. She wouldn't have been surprised if her grandmother died not from an asthma attack but was smothered with a pillow by one of her brothers. The only family members she ever talked about with kindness were her sister and her dear sweet Grammy. Grimes never told her of his brutal conversation with Grandmother Shaw. They would have married immediately but for a delay in Grimes's divorce proceedings. He offered his wife everything, he didn't care, because everything he had was nothing compared to all he would have, but still the case dragged on. And still Jacqueline's fears increased.

Then, one winter evening, he returned to the apartment from his dental office. She had been at the Haven all morning, meditating, but was supposed to be home when he arrived. He called out to her and heard nothing. He looked in the bedroom, the bathroom, he called her name again. He was looking so intently he almost passed right by her as she hung from the gaudy crystal chandelier in her orange robe, a heavy tasseled rope twisted round her neck. The windows were darkened by thick velvet drapes and the only light in the room came from the chandelier, dappling her with the spectrum of colors sheared free by the crystal. Beneath her thick legs a Chippendale chair lay upon its side. Her feet were bare, her eyes open and seemingly filled with relief. Looking at her hanging there Grimes would almost have imagined her happy, at peace, except for the gray tongue that rested thick and swollen over the pale skin of her chin like a stain. He took one look and knew just how much was gone. He turned right around and took the elevator down and used the doorman's phone to call the police.

Along with the police came a man, tall and blond. He obtained a hotel room for Grimes that night at the Four Seasons, an apartment in a modern high-rise on Walnut Street for him the very next day. Without having to do anything, Grimes's possessions were in the new apartment, along with a brand new set of contemporary furniture. The lease was prepaid for two years. On his new big screen television set was a envelope with twenty thousand dollars in cash. That was the last he saw of Jackie or her family. The last he saw of his hundred million.

"You're right," I told him as we sat side by side at the Irish Pub, across from his new and fully paid luxury apartment at 2020 Walnut. "That's an absolute tragedy."

"So when you talk about almost getting a piddling little share of some crappy little lawsuit," said Grimes, "I don't want to hear it."

"Why'd she kill herself?"

"Who knows? There was no note. She was always so

sad, maybe it just got to be too much. Or maybe her paranoia was justified and someone in that gruesome family of
hers killed her. I wouldn't be surprised if it wasn't that
punkette of a sister, either. But it doesn't make a difference
to me, does it?"

"Guess not. Who was that blond guy who paid you off
in the end?"

"Family banker."

I nodded. "You ever been to a place called Tosca's?"

"No. Why?"

"Just asking."

"What's that, a restaurant?"

"It's an Italian place up on Wolf Street. Great food is
all. I was thinking you can take your wife sometime, make
it all up to her.

"Fat chance, that. I tried to go back but she divorced
me anyway. I don't blame her, really. She's remarried,
some urologist, raking it in even with the HMO's. He's got
this racket where he sticks his finger up some geezer's
butt, feels around, and pulls out a five-hundred-dollar bill.
She says she's happier than she's ever been. Tells me the
sex is ten times better with the urologist, can you believe
that?"

"It's the educated finger."

"And, you know, I'm glad. She deserves a little happiness. You want to know something else?"

"Sure."

"I sort of liked her. Jackie, I mean. She was a kook,
really, and too sad for words, but I liked her. Even with all
her money she was an innocent. We would have been all
right together. With her, and a hundred million dollars, I
think I finally might have been a little happy."

He turned back to his drink and swilled the scotch and
I watched him, thinking that with a hundred million I
might be a little happy too. I took another sip of my beer
and started to feel a thin line of nausea unspool in my

stomach. And along with the nausea it came upon me again, the same suspicion I had felt before, that somewhere in this unfolding story was my own way into the Reddman fortune. I couldn't quite figure the route yet, but the sensation this time was clear and thrilling; it was there for me, my road to someone else's riches, waiting patiently, and all I had to do was discover where the path began and take that first step.

"What now?" I asked myself and I wasn't even aware I had said it out loud until Grimes answered my question for me.

"Now?" he said. "Now I spend the rest of my life sticking fingers in other people's mouths."

10

I SLIPPED MY MAZDA into a spot on the side street that fronted the brick-faced complex. I snapped on the Club, which was ludicrous, actually, since my car was over ten years old and as desirable to a chop shop as an East German Trabant, but still it was that type of neighborhood. At thirty minutes per quarter I figured three in the meter would be more than enough. I pulled my briefcase out and locked the car and headed up the steps to the Albert Einstein Medical Center.

In the lobby I walked guiltily past the rows of portraits, dead physicians and rich guys staring sternly down from the walls, and without stopping at the front desk, took my briefcase into the elevator and up to the fifth floor, cardiac care. The hospital smelled of overcooked lima beans and spilled apple juice and I could tell from just one whiff that Jimmy Vigs Dubinsky in Room 5036 was not a happy man.

"I'm nauseous all the time," said Jimmy Vigs in a weak, kindly voice as I stepped into the room. He wasn't talking to me. "I retched this morning already. Should that be happening?"

"I'll tell the doctor," said a nurse in a Hawaiian shirt, stooping down as she emptied his urine sack. "You're on Atenolol, which sometimes causes nausea."

"How am I peeing?"

"Like a horse."

"At least something's working right." Jim was a huge round man, wildly heavy, with thick legs and a belly that danced when he laughed, only he wasn't laughing. His face was shaped like a pear, with big cheeks, a large nose, a thin, fussy little mustache. He lay in bed with his sheet off and his stomach barely covered by his hospital gown. In his arm was an intravenous line and beside his bed was a post on which three plastic bags hung, filling him with fluids and medicines. The blips on the monitor were strangely uneven; his pulse was eighty-six, then eighty-three, then eighty-seven, then ninety. I wondered if Jimmy would book a bet on which pulse rate would show up next and then I figured he already had.

"Hello, Victor," he said when he noticed me in the room. His voice had a light New York accent, but none of the New York edge, as if he had moved from Queens to Des Moines a long time ago. "It's kind of you to visit."

"How are you feeling, Jim?"

"Not so well. Nauseous." He closed his eyes as if the strain of staying awake was too much for him. "Helen, this is Victor Carl, my lawyer. When a lawyer visits you in the hospital it's bad news for someone. I guess we're going to need some privacy."

She smiled at me as she fiddled with his urine. "I'll just be a minute."

"With what he's charging, this is going to be the most expensive pee in history."

"Okay, okay," she said as she finished emptying the catheter bag, but still smiling. "Just another moment."

"She's been terrific. They've all been terrific. They're treating me like a prince."

"When are they cleaning out your arteries?" I asked. For the past few years Jim had worn a nitro patch and kept the medicine by his side all the time, often popping pills like Tic-Tacs when things got tense. He had had a bypass about ten years back, before I met him, but I had never known him to be without pain and finally, when the angina had grown unbearable, he had consented to going under the knife, or under the wire at least, to clear his arteries by drilling through the calcium deposits that were starving his heart.

"Tomorrow morning," he said. "By tomorrow evening I'll be a new man."

The nurse fiddled with the drips and took some notations and then left the room, closing the door behind her. As soon as it was closed, Jim said in a voice with the New York edge suddenly returned, "You bring it?"

"I don't feel right about this," I said. "I feel downright queasy."

"Let me have it," he said.

"Are you sure?"

"Let me have it," he said.

I was reaching into my briefcase when an orderly came in with a tray. I snapped the case closed before he could see inside.

"Here's your lunch, Mr. Dubinsky," said the orderly, a big man in a blue jumpsuit. "Just what the dietitian prescribed."

"I'm too nauseous to eat, Kelvin," said Jimmy, weak and kindly again. "But thank you."

"You'll want to eat your lunch, Mr. Dubinsky. Your DCA's tomorrow morning, so you won't be getting dinner."

"I'll try. Maybe a carrot stick. Thank you, Kelvin."

"That's right, you try, Mr. Dubinsky. You try real hard."

When the orderly left, Jimmy ordered me to close the door and then said, "Let me have it."

I stepped over to the tray the orderly had just brought and lifted the cover. Carrot sticks and celery and sliced radishes. Two pieces of romaine lettuce. An apple. A plastic glass of grape juice. An orange slice for garnish. "Looks tasty."

"Let me have it," he said.

"I don't feel right about this," I said as I again opened my briefcase and pulled out the bag. White Castle. A grease mark shaped like a rabbit on the bottom and inside four cheese sliders and two boxes of fries.

He looked inside. "Only four? I usually buy a sack of ten."

"You need a note from your cardiologist to get ten."

He took one of the hamburgers and, while still lying flat on his back, popped it into his mouth as easy as a mint. He breathed deeply through his nose as he chewed and smiled the smile of the righteous.

"What about your nausea?"

"Too many damn carrots," he said in between sliders. "Carotene poisoning. That's why rabbits puke all the time."

"I've never seen a rabbit puke."

"You've never looked."

While he was shoving the third hamburger into his mouth, keeping all the while a careful eye on the door, the phone rang. He nodded with his head to the phone and I answered it. "What's Atlanta?" asked the whispery voice on the phone.

I relayed the question to Jimmy and he stopped swallowing long enough to say, "Six and eight over Houston."

"Six and eight over Houston," I said into the phone.

"This is Rocketman," said the voice. "Thirty units on Houston."

I told Jim and he nodded. "Tell him it's down," said Jimmy Vigs and I did.

"That's the problem with this business," said Jim. "It never stops. I'm scheduled for surgery tomorrow and they're still calling. I need a vacation. Want a fry?"

"No thank you."

"Good," he said as he stuck a fistful in his mouth. "They're not crisp enough anyway, you need to get them right out of the fryer." He stuck in another fistful.

"You know, Victor," he said when he was finished with everything and the bag and empty boxes were safely back in my briefcase and the only remnant of his surreptitious meal was the stink of grease that hung over the room like a sallow cloud of ill health, "that was the first decent bite I've had since I was admitted. Starting tomorrow I'm going to change everything, I swear. I'm going to Slim-Fast my way to skinny, I swear. But I just needed a final taste before the drought. You're a pal."

"I felt like I was giving you poison."

"Aw hell, they're scraping everything out tomorrow anyway, what's the harm? But you're a real pal. I owe you."

"So then do me a favor," I said, "and tell me about one of your clients, a fellow named Edward Shaw."

Jimmy sat still for a while, as if he hadn't heard me, but then his wide cheeks widened and underneath his tiny mustache a smile grew. "What do you want to know from Eddie Shaw for?"

"I just want to know."

"Lawyer-client?"

"Lawyer-client."

"Well, buddy, you know what Eddie Shaw is? The worst gambler in God's good earth."

"Not very astute, I guess."

"That's not what I tell him. He's the smartest, most informed, most knowledgeable I ever booked is what I tell him. And he's such an uppity little son-of-a-bitch he believes every word of it. But between you and me, and only between you and me, he is the absolute biggest mark I've ever seen. It's uncanny. He's such a degenerate he couldn't lose more money if he was trying. He's the only guy in the world who when he bets a game, the line changes in his favor, he's that bad. He bets a horse, it's sure to come in so late the jockey's wearing pajamas. I could retire on that guy, go to Brazil, lie on the beach all day and eat fried plantains, suck down coladas, never worry about a thing, just bake in the sun and book his losers."

"Why don't you?"

"Well, you know how it is sometimes. Collection can be a problem."

"Isn't he good for it?" I asked, wondering how much Jimmy knew about the family.

Jimmy let out an explosion of breath. "You know Reddman Pickles? Well this loser's a Reddman, and there aren't too many, either. The guy's worth as much as some small countries, let me tell you, but it's all tied up in some sort of a trust. He lays the bets based on his net worth but he can only pay up based on his income, which is less than you would figure with a guy like that. When his old man dies, then he can buy the moon, but until then he only gets a share of a percentage of what the trust throws out in income."

"Ever have any real trouble getting him to pay?"

Jimmy shifted in bed a bit and the line on his monitor flat-lined for a moment, his pulse number dropping to zilch, before the line snapped back into rhythm and the pulse registered ninety-three, ninety-six, ninety, eighty-eight. "What's up, Victor? Why so much interest in Shaw?"

"I'm just asking."

"Lawyers don't just ask."

"I heard that he got pretty far behind and you started getting tough, a little too tough."

He turned his head away from me. "Yeah, well it's a tough business."

"How much did he owe?"

"Aw, you know me, Victor, I wouldn't hurt a pussy cat."

"How much?"

"Lawyer-client, right?"

"Sure."

"Over half a mil. Normally I cut it off before it gets that high, just cut them off and work out a payment plan, but he has so much money coming and he loses so regularly, I just couldn't bear some other book taking my money. I let it get too high, and I was willing to be patient, with the interest I was charging it was going to be my retirement when his old man died. But January a year back I took more action than I should have on the game and laid off too much to the wrong guys. The refs don't call the interference on Sanders, and it was clear, so clear, but they don't call it and I'm way short. Next thing I know those bastards started squeezing. I was in hock to them, Shaw was in hock to me, so I had to apply some pressure. It was just business is all, Victor, nothing . . ."

The phone interrupted him. I picked it up. "What's the spread on the Knicks tomorrow night?" said a voice.

"Hello, Al?" I said into the phone, rapping the handset as if the connection was bad. "Al? Are you there, Al? I think the tap shorted out the wires. Al? Al? Can you get on that, Al?"

"Aw cut it out," said Jimmy, reaching for the phone.

"I don't understand it," I said. "He hung up."

"You're killing me here."

"You said you needed a vacation. Tell me what you did about Shaw."

"I went to Calvi."

"Calvi, huh?" I said. "I heard he's gone to Florida. Any idea why the sudden visit South?"

"I don't know, maybe the boss got sick of the smell of those damned cigars."

"I wouldn't blame him for that."

"I also heard some rumors about him getting impatient with his share, stuff I never believed. But I got sources say that Earl Dante was behind the rumors and his ouster."

"Dante's rising fast."

"Dante is a scary man, Victor, and that is all I want to say about that."

Just then the door opened and a thin young man in a black leather coat and a black fedora stepped into the room. On some guys the leather coat and the hat would have made them look hard, like Rocky, but not this guy, with his long face and beak nose and wide child-taunted ears. He wore thick round glasses and between his pursed lips I could see a set of crumbling teeth. When he saw me he stopped and stared.

"Hey, Victor," said Jimmy, "you know Anton Schmidt here?"

I shook my head.

"Next to you, Victor, he's the smartest guy I know."

"That's not saying much for you," I said.

"No, really. Anton's the real deal, got a mind for numbers like a computer. And don't ever bet him in chess, he's a prodigy or something. He's got a ranking. I didn't know they gave rankings, but he's got one."

"How high?" I asked.

"Nineteen fifty as of my last tournament," he said through his twisted set of teeth.

"Impressive," I said, and from the way he said it I guess it was, though I had no idea what it meant.

"He's almost a master," said Jimmy. "Imagine that, and he works for me."

"Anything going?" asked Anton.

"Rocketman bet thirty units on Houston."

"He would," said Anton.

"Other than that, Victor put on the kibosh so I think it's going to be quiet. You got that match to study for, go on home. I'll see you tomorrow after the procedure."

Anton looked at Jimmy like he wanted to say something, his eyes behind the glasses widened, then he looked away.

"It's nothing," said Jimmy. "Just a procedure is all. Get

the hell out of here and study. In two days I'll let you start me on that exercise program you been ramming me about."

Anton smiled. "They're waiting for you at Gold's."

"I'll bet they are, those bastards. I'll show them something. I can bench a horse."

"You can eat a horse maybe," I said, "but that's about it."

"Get out of here," said Jim. "I'll see you tomorrow."

Anton nodded for a moment, looked at me and nodded, stared some more at Jim, and then left.

"He worries about me too much, but he's a good kid," said Jimmy. "Keeps everything in his head now so there won't be no more ledgers should the cops come looking again."

"You trust him with that much information?"

"Like a son."

"Good," I said, "Because I'd hate to have to cross-examine a chess master at your next criminal trial. All right then, so you went to Calvi to collect what Eddie Shaw owed you."

"Met him at Tosca's," said Jimmy. "He was smoking a cigar and I almost gagged as I sat across from him. I have craps smell better than his cigars. I told him my problem and he said he'd apply some pressure. Strong-arm stuff, but nothing too radical. Raffaello doesn't go for that. He sent some boys up, sent the message, talked to the family, talked to the staff, made sure everyone knew the situation. I heard they got a little rough. Next thing I know Shaw paid off. Half of what he owed, which is all I needed to get myself clear. Had to increase my payout to Raffaello, you know, a collection charge, but it was worth it, got me off the hook. And you want to know something, that crazy loser is betting again. Just last night he took the Lakers and seven for a thousand."

"What happened?"

"Bulls blew them out by twenty-five."

"And what about the sister?" I asked.

"What about who?"

"Shaw's sister."

Jimmy shrugged, a wholly unconcerned shrug, as loose as a 275-pound man lying on his back in a hospital before surgery can shrug. "What about her?"

"She died just before her brother started paying you back. Some in her family think she was murdered."

"Who? By me? That's a laugh."

"Not so funny if it's true."

"Why would I care about the sister?"

"You don't think Calvi might have hurt the sister as a warning for Eddie?"

"What, are you crazy? His boys broke Shaw's arm in two places with the blunt end of an ax, threatening to use the blade side if he didn't pay up. Now that's a warning. Hey, we got to get tough sometimes, but we're not animals. What do you think?"

What I thought was that he was telling me the truth, which was a relief because I liked Jimmy Dubinsky and I'd hate to think that someone I liked was a murderer. So Jimmy had gone to Calvi and Calvi had broken Eddie Shaw's arm in two places and suddenly Eddie had found the money to pay back Jimmy. Where? That seemed to be the crucial question.

"All right, Jimmy," I said. "Thanks for your help. This thing tomorrow, it's not dangerous, is it?"

"A piece of cake," he said. "Roto-Rooter, that's the name and away go troubles down the drain. I'll be here for three more days. You'll visit again?"

"Sure."

"You'll bring me another little gift?"

"I thought you were Slim-Fasting."

"You're allowed one reasonable meal a day. It says it right there on the can."

"Sure, I'll bring a gift if you want," I said.

"And next time, Victor, be a sport and buy them by the sack."

My car was still at the meter, when I stepped outside the hospital, still with its tires, still with its radio, still with its battery firmly in place, all of which was a pleasant surprise. It was back in my office where the unpleasant surprise awaited.

11

"THEY JUST WENT IN," said Ellie, her hands fluttering about her neck. "I tried to stop them."

"That's all right, Ellie. Where's Beth?"

"At a settlement conference. I was the only one here."

"You did fine," I said. "I'll take care of it now." Ever since I began representing criminals I had made a practice of locking up my most sensitive files, but still I didn't like visitors free to roam about my office alone, didn't fancy utter strangers rifling the papers on my desk, the files in my drawers, eyeing which case opinions I was studying in preparation for my court appearances.

"I didn't know if I should call the police," said Ellie. "They said it was about business."

"No, you did the right thing. I don't want the police in my office either."

"The little one's creepy looking, like a troll."

"It's fine, Ellie," I said, staring at the closed door, screwing up my courage to enter my own office. "Don't worry about a thing."

"An evil troll."

I put a hand on her shoulder and gave her a falsely confident smile. "In that case, you better hold my calls."

I took three steps forward and opened the door.

Two guys. One was tall, dark, and squinty, dressed all in black, with one of those faux-cool ponytails that tries to say, "Hey, I'm hip," but which really only says, "Hey, I'm a geek trying oh so hard to be hip." He was concentrating on my tall file cabinet with the vase of dead flowers still perched on top. The cabinet was brown with fake wood grain, fireproof, batterproof, burglarproof, made of heavy-gauge steel for the most security-minded file keepers, and the ponytailed guy was fiddling noisily with the lock. The other guy, short and bearded, with the nasty eyes of a psychiatrist, was sitting at my desk, reading a document he had found there. The sheer brazenness of their actions was comforting, in a way. The most serious dangers, I have learned painfully through my ransacked life, come disguised as gifts.

I cleared my throat like a schoolteacher in an unruly class. The two men stopped what they were doing, looked up at me, and then immediately went back to work.

"Finding anything of interest?" I asked.

"Not really, no," said the little man. His voice was a natural falsetto. I guess if I was five foot three with a voice like that I'd grow a beard too. "Your desk is a mess. Is all your life this disorganized?"

"Cluttered desk, uncluttered mind."

"Somehow I don't think so."

"We have a problem, Mr. Carl," said the man in black, in a pretentious husky whisper that went all too well with that ponytail. He was still standing by the file cabinet but apparently had given up his attempt to pick the Chicago Lock Company lock and peek inside. His face was deeply lined and though I had first thought him to be somewhere in his twenties, on closer inspection I believed him to be somewhere in his forties, which made his cry-for-hip outfit all the more pathetic. "We think you can help."

"Well, I'm a lawyer. Helping is my business."

That brought a yelp of mirth from the little man.

"Why don't you gentlemen sit down where the clients are supposed to sit and I'll sit behind the desk, where the lawyer is supposed to sit, and maybe then we can discuss your situation."

The tall man looked at the short man. The short man stared at me for a moment before giving the tall man the nod. Then we all do-si-doed one around the other like a set at a square dance. When we were in our proper positions, I appraised the two men sitting across from me and found myself very unafraid, which I didn't think was their intention.

I guess it was the dealing with all those murderous mob hoodlums in the last few years that did it. It wasn't that I had turned brave from my association with them. I had been born a coward, raised a coward, and faithfully remained a coward. It was part and parcel of being my father's son and I would have taken great pride in my cowardice if I didn't realize it only meant that in my thirty sorry years I hadn't yet found a cause or a love worth dying for. No, I wasn't frightened by these two men who had barged into my office in what they had hoped was an intimidating style because my experience with the more vicious elements of the city's underworld had given me the capacity to judge the truly sadistically vicious from the bad-boy wannabees. The geezer in black, he was a wannabee. The truly sadistically vicious don't have to go around dressing like Steven Seagal to stoke fear. One look in their eyes and you know to step aside. And as for the little guy, well, would he have frightened you?

"So, gentlemen," I said. "What is this problem you were telling me about?"

"Harassment," said the man in black.

"Well, actually, that's a specialty of our firm. My partner, Elizabeth Derringer, is one of the top sexual harassment lawyers in the city. The surreptitious pat on the butt, the sexual double entendre, the sly brush of protruding body parts as your boss passes you in the hall, the inappropriate suggestion of an after-hours liaison. It's a terrible problem, yes, but there are laws now under which we can bring suits. Even the stolen kiss in the supply closet, once the province of harmless office fun, has now become actionable. And quite profitable too for the plaintiff and the lawyer. So," I said with a wide smile. "Which one of you was sexually harassed?"

"That's not what we're talking about," said the man in black.

"No? So what is it? An old girlfriend calling every night? Being stalked by a secret admirer? I want to help." I roughed my voice a bit. "I just need to know what your problem is."

"You're pretty clever, Mr. Carl, aren't you?" said the man in black.

"With enough rewrites, sure," I said.

"Well quit the cleverness and shut up."

"A child has died," skirled the short man with the beard. "She was a sweet and much-loved child. I find tragedies bring out the best and the worst in us, don't you, Victor? My name is Gaylord. This is Nicholas. The tragedy of this child's death has raised a problem for us that you are going to resolve."

"Well, as you must know, I take a keen professional interest in other people's tragedy."

"That's exactly the problem," said Gaylord.

"We don't want you interested in the tragedy of this child's death," said Nicholas in his husky whisper.

"All right, gentlemen, let's stop the playacting," I said, more curious than anything else. "Who are we talking about and what do you want?"

"You've been asking questions about Jacqueline Shaw's death," said Gaylord, shaking his head and closing his psychiatrist eyes as if with sadness. "Her death has caused us all much pain and we are trying to put the grief of her loss behind us. Your running around the city like a fool, badgering the police, bothering her friends, is only making it more difficult for our wounds to heal. You are to stop immediately."

I waited a moment and looked at them, the little squeak of a man and the fraud hard guy in a ponytail, and my only emotion was a sort of indignation that the likes of these two thought they could intimidate me. Didn't they check me out in *Martindale-Hubbell*, didn't they ask around, didn't they know that with one call to certain of my clients I could have their knees pounded into mash? I leaned forward and clasped my hands together like a choirboy and said what I had to say slowly.

"Listen, you little weenies, don't you ever again frighten my secretary by ignoring her requests and marching into my office uninvited. Don't you ever again try to play the hard guy with me when neither of you have the stones to pull it off. And don't either of you ever again, for an instant, think that I will listen to any orders that come out of pathetic losers such as yourselves. Whatever work I'm doing for my clients I will do no matter what you or anyone else says to me and whether I am or am not looking into the death of this friend of yours, whatever her name is, I will continue to do whatever I was doing before your pathetic attempt to scare me off. Now that we are finished here, get the hell out of my office."

They both remained seated, staring at me with not quite the shocked and wary eyes I had hoped for. Gaylord started shaking his head and as he did so Nicholas rose. He pushed back his chair, swooped his arms before him and lifted his left knee. He stayed motionless for a moment, his left leg raised, his left arm before him like a shield, his right arm at his side, his stance as ludicrous and as far from threatening as if he froze smack in the middle of a power walk. I think I snickered.

"I believe you underestimate our sincerity," said Gaylord. "It happens."

In that instant Nicholas hopped into his left leg as he swung his right around, cracking the heavy vase atop the filing cabinet in two with his kick before it shattered against the wall. The shards of glass hadn't hit the floor before, with a grunt and another spin, Nicholas pivoted off his right foot and buried his left heel into the side of my fireproof, batterproof, burglarproof, heavy-gauge steel filing cabinet. The concaving of the cabinet was punctuated with the slam bang of his heel against the side and the groan of bending metal, not unlike, I expect, the sound of the cracking of bones. From the force of his blow the lock popped and one of the drawers slid open.

By the time Ellie had rushed in to see what had happened, Nicholas was back in his seat, hands folded before him, and I was suddenly suitably frightened.

"It's all right, Ellie," I said, without looking at her so she wouldn't notice my watering eyes. "Just a small accident with the cabinet. Everything's fine." I smiled thinly and she left, leaving the door open.

"Sometimes you walk down the street," said Gaylord, "without realizing, until it is too late, that the fellow approaching you has the ability to reach into your chest and rip out your lungs."

"I trained in Chiang Mai," whispered Nicholas.

"You know, Victor, I think I killed you in a prior life," said Gaylord. "Were you by any chance in Jerusalem at the end of the eleventh century when Godfrey of Bouillon stormed the city? Because your aura is very familiar."

I still hadn't recovered enough from the shot into the solar plexus of my filing cabinet, wondering at what a shot like that would do to my rib cage and the oh so delicate organs encased within, to start exploring my past lives with Gaylord. The image of my heart compressing to the flatness of a plate, my lungs exhaling first air, then blood, then bronchioles, alveoli snapping, my colon popping like a pea, such images tended to wipe out all thoughts of the hereafter with obsessions of the dangers in the here and now. I was breathing hard when I said, "What is it exactly that you want?"

Nicholas, for the first time, smiled. I couldn't help but notice that his smile was excellent and he still had all his teeth. "No more questions about Jacqueline Shaw. That's what we want."

"I seem to remember that I sliced off your head with my broadsword," said Gaylord. "Does that ring a bell?"

"Being beheaded by a midget in Jerusalem? Not really."

"You scoff. Did you ever think there may be more to life than you imagine, more than eating and screwing and dying?" asked Gaylord. "Did that ever cross your mind?"

"Well, I do watch a lot of TV."

"I'm talking existence, Victor. Have you ever wondered if your existence embodies more than you could ever imagine? Or maybe even, more profoundly, less?"

"Metaphysics in the afternoon?"

"I hate that word, metaphysics," said Gaylord, "as if the truths in our souls are less real than the forces at work on pool balls clacking against one another. Let's say we're talking about a higher level of cognition. Any ideas?"

"Meaning. You're asking me about meaning." I was vamping for time, trying to figure out where this high-pitched little man was going. "Let's say I'm still searching for an answer to that one."

"Did you hear that, Nicholas? Victor here is searching. He is at least a one. There is hope for him yet."

"If he ever wants to become a two then he'll cooperate," said Nicholas. "This was just a warning but . . ."

"This supposed meaning of life you are searching for, Vic," said Gaylord, his high voice piercing Nicholas's husky whisper like a dart, "any idea of where you're going to find it?"

"I read some, talk to people, watch Woody Allen movies. In the past few years my private investigator has sort of been a spiritual adviser."

"Your private investigator, how clever. You've hired him to investigate the meaning of life, I presume."

"Something like that."

"You ever wonder, Victor, if the answer is right out there for you to see? Ever have a coincidence happen that seemed too perfect for coincidence? Ever have a déjà vu and be certain that it wasn't just a trick of the mind? Ever feel almost connected to the secret of the universe, feel that the answer to everything is just out of reach, or just out of sight? Ever think everything is so close except you are deaf to it for some strange reason?"

"Yes, actually," I said, because I had actually experienced all that.

"Wonder of wonders," said Gaylord. "You're a two."

"Gaylord is a nine," said Nicholas. "I'm a five."

"Nicholas is a five and I'm only a two?"

"Well, keep out of trouble," said Gaylord, "and maybe you'll rise. We can teach you how to see it, if that's what you really want. There are novice meetings in our temporary headquarters every Wednesday night at eight." He reached into his pocket and pulled out a card, tossing it into the clutter of my desk. "That's all, I guess," he said, slapping his chair armrests and standing. Nicholas stood too. "Be a good boy, Victor, and maybe I won't have to use the sword once again. It is so wasteful when we are forced to relive the calamities of our past lives over and over again. We'll be in touch."

With a nod from Gaylord they turned and walked out of my office. I sat and watched them go. Then I picked up the card. "THE CHURCH OF THE NEW LIFE," it read and underneath it "OLEANNA, GUIDING LIGHT." There was a Mount Airy address and a phone number and fax number and an e-mail address. The Church of the New Life.

I had always been a little leery of churches, being Jewish and all, but what really gave me the creeps was Church Lite. I could fathom the power in the somber Romanesque visions of the Catholic Church, the stained glass and incense, the passionate story of sacrifice and redemption. But there was something creepy about those pseudomodern, calorie-reduced, image-cleansed, white-washed churches that were springing up left and right. Glass cathedrals selling salvation and tee shirts. Betty Crocker as Madonna, Opie as child. And then there were those super-cleansed New Age halls, so scrubbed and shined that God had been washed right out of them, leaving crystals and pyramids and channeled entities from the fourteenth century to take His place. That was where I figured the Church of the New Life belonged. My new pals Gaylord and Nicholas were even creepier than I had thought. And none too bright either.

I mean, why would anyone bother to threaten someone off a case? Why not just put up a neon sign that flashed, "LOOK HERE FOR GOLD?" If I had still had doubts that there was something of interest to be found in Jacqueline Shaw's death before my run-in with the apostles of the Church of the New Life, I had none anymore. And as I thought about the meeting and about my two new friends, the suspicion that had been hounding me, the suspicion that there was my very own way into the Reddman fortune, suddenly burst into the open and snatched my attention out of the air in its teeth and wrestled it to the ground. The route had been so obvious, so clear, that I hadn't seen it. And now that I did I felt something ethereal flow through me. I grew light, almost light enough to float. I could barely remain seated in the chair as I felt myself suffused until bursting with the giddy sensation of pure pure possibility.

12

WHEN I HAD TOLD GAYLORD I took a keen professional interest in other people's tragedy, it hadn't been just banter. I am a lawyer and so tragedy is my business. Riches lurk for me in the least likely of places, in that dropped package of explosives at the railway depot, in that cup of drive-through coffee that scalds the thighs, in the airplane engine that bursts into a ball of flame mid-flight. Think of your worst nightmare, your most dreaded calamity, think of injury and anguish and death and know that for me it represents only so much profit, for I am your lawyer, the alchemist of your tragedy.

I had seemingly forgotten this, forgotten that one case can make a lawyer wealthy, one client, one fact pattern, one complaint. In delving into the death of Jacqueline Shaw I had belted myself too tightly inside the trench coat of Philip Marlowe and had forgotten that I was a lawyer first and foremost and that a lawyer, first and foremost, looks after the bottom line. You can make money charging $185 an hour, as long as you work like a dog and keep your expenses low, good money, but that's not how lawyers get stinkingly rich. Lawyers get stinkingly rich by taking a percentage of a huge lawsuit based on somebody else's tragedy, and that's exactly what I meant to do.

Caroline Shaw thought someone had murdered her sister, Jacqueline, and had hired me to find out who. After looking it over it seemed to me that she might just be right, and if Jacqueline was murdered I could figure out the motive right off—money, and lots of it. Why ever would you kill an heiress if it wasn't for the money? Caroline Shaw had only hired me to find the murderer, but I had other ideas. A wrongful death action against the killer would take back whatever had been gained by the killing and whatever else the killer owned, with a third going to the lawyers. All I needed was for Jacqueline Shaw to have been murdered for her money and for me to find the killer and for me to get Caroline to sign a fee agreement and for me to dig up enough evidence to win my case and take my third of the killer's fortune, which in itself would be a fortune. Long shots all, to be sure, but that never stopped me from returning my Publishers Clearinghouse Sweepstakes entry twice a year.

I was on my knees picking up tiny shards of glass and placing them on a piece of cardboard, thinking it all through, when Beth showed up.

"Redecorating?" she asked.

"Just some friendly visitors from the Twilight Zone trying to scare me off the Jacqueline Shaw case."

"Are you scared off?"

"Hardly."

I stood up and dumped the glass fragments into the trash can where they tinkled against the sides like fairy dust.

"Think on this, Beth. Eddie Shaw's money situation seems to have eased right after his sister's death. And Jacqueline herself told her fiancé that she was afraid one of her brothers was trying to kill her. And somewhere there was a load of insurance money, so said Detective McDeiss. And when I had suggested to Caroline that maybe a family member had killed her sister she had snapped that her family had nothing to do with the death, protesting far too much. I'm not sure how the two losers who threatened me are involved, but what if Eddie killed his sister to increase his income and his ultimate inheritance? And what if we could bring a wrongful death action against the bastard and prove it all?"

"A lot of ifs."

"Well, what if all those ifs?"

"You'd wipe him out with compensatory and punitive damages," she said.

"With a third for us. McDeiss estimated the total Reddman fortune at about half a billion dollars. The brother's share would be well over a hundred million. Let's say we prove it and win our case and get everything in damages. We'd earn ourselves a third of over a hundred million. That would be about twenty for you and twenty for me."

"You're dreaming."

"Yes I am. I'm dreaming the American dream."

"It probably was a suicide."

"Of course it was."

"And if it was a murder, it probably wasn't the brother who did it."

"Of course not."

"It was probably some judgment-proof derelict."

"You're absolutely right."

"There's nothing there. You're just chasing a fool's dream."

"And yet when the pot was sixty-six million you bought ten lottery tickets."

"So I did," she said, nodding her head. "Twenty million. It's too gaudy a number to even consider."

"I've dreamed bigger," I said, and I had. That was one of the curses of wanting so much, whatever you get can never top your dreams. "How are you on the meaning of life?"

"Pretty weak."

"Are you willing to learn?"

"Like you have the answers," she snorted. "Don't you think karmic questions about life and meaning are a little beyond your depth?"

"You're calling me shallow?"

"Aren't you?"

"Well, sure, yes, but there's no need to rub it in."

"Oh, Victor, one thing I always admired about you was your cheerful shallowness. Nothing's more boring than Mr. Sincere droning on about his life's search for spiritual meaning in that ashram in Connecticut. Just shut up and get me a beer."

"Well, maybe I don't have any answers, but the Church of the New Life says it does. Novice meetings are held every Wednesday night in the basement of some house in Mount Airy. From what her fiancé told me, this was the same place where Jacqueline Shaw meditated the day she died. Somehow, it seems, their connection to her didn't end with her death. They wanted me to come, but I think I'll stay away for obvious health reasons. Maybe you can learn something."

"Why don't you just have Morris give them a look?"

"I don't think this is quite right for Morris, do you?" I said, handing her the card.

She studied it. "Maybe not. Who's Oleanna?"

I shrugged my ignorance.

"Sounds like a margarine. Maybe that's the secret, low cholesterol as the way to spiritual salvation."

"You never know, Beth. That something you've been looking for your whole life, maybe it's been hiding out all this time in a rat-infested basement in Mount Airy."

"I don't think so," she said, and then she looked at the card some more. She flicked it twice on her chin before saying, "Sure. Anything for a few laughs."

Good, that was taken care of, and now I had something even more important to do. What I had was a hope and plan and the sweet lift of pure possibility. What I still needed was Caroline Shaw's signature on a contingency fee agreement before I could begin the delicate process of spinning the tragedy of Jacqueline Shaw's death into gold.

13

I CLEARED OFF MY DESK before she came, threw out the trash, filed the loose papers whose files I could find, shoved the rest into an already too full desk drawer. Only one manila folder sat neatly upon the desktop. I straightened the photographs on my office wall, arranged the client chairs at perfect obtuse angles one to another, took a plant from Beth's office and placed it atop my crippled filing cabinet. I had on my finest suit, a little blue worsted wool number from Today's Man, and a non-Woolworth real silk tie. I had spent a few moments that morning in my apartment, globbing polish onto my shoes and then buffing them to a sharp pasty black. I buttoned my jacket and stood formally at the door and then unbuttoned it and sat on the edge of my desk and then buttoned it again and stood behind my desk, leaning over with one hand outstretched, saying out loud, in rounded oval tones, "Pleased to see you again, Ms. Shaw."

It was so important to get this right, to make the exactly correct impression. There is a moment in every grand venture when the enterprise teeters on the brink, and I was at that moment. I needed Caroline's signature, and I needed it today, I believed. With it I had a chance, without it I held as much hope as a lottery ticket flushed down the toilet. That was why I was practicing my greeting like a high school freshman gearing himself to ask the pretty new girl from California to the hop.

"Thank you for coming, Ms. Shaw."

"I hope this wasn't too inconvenient, Ms. Shaw."

"Have a seat, Ms. Shaw."

"I'm glad you could make it this morning, Ms. Shaw."

"God, I need a cigarette," she said, giving me a wry look as she sat, no doubt commenting on my tone of voice, which sounded artificial even to me. She drew a pack from her bag and tapped out a cigarette and lit up without asking if I minded, but I didn't mind. Anything she wanted. From out of my drawer I pulled an ashtray I had picked up from a bric-a-brac shop on Pine Street specifically for the occasion. Welcome to Kentucky, it read. She flicked a line of ashes atop the red of the state bird.

She was wearing her leather jacket and tight black pants and combat boots. On the side of her neck was the tattoo of a butterfly I hadn't noticed before. She looked more formidable than I remembered from that morning outside the Roundhouse when she pulled her gun on me and then collapsed to the ground. Even the stud piercing her nose seemed no longer a mark of desperation but instead an insignia of power and brutal self-possession. I felt, despite my finest suit and newly polished shoes, at a distinct disadvantage. It was interesting how things between us had changed. When she first came to me she was the one begging for help, but I guess a hundred million dollars or so can shift the power in any conversation.

"Couldn't we have done this over the phone?" she asked, exhaling her words in stream of white smoke. "It's a little early for me."

"Well then, I appreciate your punctuality. I thought it best we meet in person." I didn't explain that it was impossible to get a signature over the phone. "You've disposed of your gun, I hope."

She gave me her sly smile. "I flushed it down the toilet. Some alligator's probably shooting rats in the sewers as we speak." She took a long drag and looked around nervously.

"That butterfly on your neck," I said. "Is that new? I didn't notice it before."

"Yes, it is," she said, suddenly brightening. "It's from a designer collection, available only at the finest parlors. DK Tattoo. Do you like it?"

I nodded and looked at her more carefully. She said in our prior meeting that she was in fear of her life and so the first thing she did after hiring me was to go out and get herself tattooed. If not exactly an appropriate response it was certainly telling, though I couldn't quite figure telling of what. As I was looking at her she took out another cigarette.

"Do you always smoke like this?" I asked.

"Like what?"

"Like a New Jersey refinery."

"Just in the morning. By the afternoon I'm hacking too much. So what have you learned about my sister's death, Mr. Carl?"

"I learned that you haven't been entirely candid with me."

"Oh, haven't I?"

I stared at her for a moment, waiting for her to squirm a bit under the power of my gaze, but it didn't seem to affect her. She stared back calmly. So what I did then was reach into my desk drawer and pull out a thick wad of hundred-dollar bills and slap them onto the desktop with a most satisfying thwack. Caroline flinched at the sound. Ben Franklin stared up at me with surprise on his face.

"Ten thousand dollars," I said. "The full amount of your retainer check. Take it."

"What are you talking about?" she said, flustered and suddenly devoid of her slyness.

"I'm returning your money."

She stood up. "But you can't do that. I bought you. I wrote the check and you cashed it."

"And now I'm giving it all back," I said calmly.

"You're going to have to find someone else to play your games. I don't represent clients who lie to me." This itself was a lie, actually. All my clients lie to me, it is part of the natural order of the legal profession: clients lie, lawyers overcharge, judges get it wrong.

"But I didn't lie," she said, her voice rich with whine. "I didn't. What I told you about my sister was true. Every word of it. She didn't kill herself, I know it." There were tears of shock in her eyes as she pleaded with me. It was going rather well, I thought.

"I believe you're right, Caroline. I believe your sister was murdered."

"You do?" she said. "Really?" She fell back into her chair, crossing her legs and hugging herself tightly. "Then what's the problem?"

"Didn't you think it significant that I know your sister was a Reddman? Didn't you think that would have impacted my investigation?"

"My family had nothing to do with her death."

"That's what you hired me to determine."

She looked at me, her eyes still wet. "I hired you to find out which mob bastard killed my sister and to convince him not to kill me too. That's all. I don't need anyone digging up my family graveyard."

"If I'm going to find a murderer I have to know everything. I have to know about your family, about the family fortune, about this Church of the New Life that sent its goons into my office threatening me off the case."

Her head lifted at that and she smiled. "So that's it. The chant-heads frightened you."

"Why would they threaten me?"

"You want to have a blast? Throw a brown paper bag in the middle of one of their meditation sessions and yell, 'Meat!'"

"Why would they threaten me, Caroline?"

Pause, and then in the most matter-of-fact voice:

"Maybe because their church was the beneficiary of Jackie's insurance policy."

I looked at her and waited. The room was already dense with smoke, but she took out another Camel Light.

"We all have insurance policies, to help pay our estate taxes should we die. The trust covers the premiums and the family members are named beneficiaries, unless we decide otherwise. Jacqueline decided to name the church."

"How much?"

"God, not much, I don't think, not enough to cover even half the tax. Five."

"Thousand?"

She laughed, a short burst of laughter.

"Million," I said flatly.

She stared at me for a bit and then her mouth wiggled at the corners. "Are you married, Mr. Carl?"

"No."

"Engaged or engaged to be engaged or gay?"

"I was once."

"Gay?"

"Engaged."

"So what happened?"

"It didn't work out."

"They never do, Vic. Can I call you Vic?"

"Call me Victor," I said. "Vic makes me sound like a lounge singer."

"All right, Victor." She leaned forward and gave me a smile saucy and innocent all at once. The effect of this smile was so disarming that I had to shake my head to get my mind back to the vital business at hand.

"Didn't you think, Caroline, that a five-million-dollar life insurance policy was important enough to tell me about? I can't work in the dark."

"Well, now you know everything, so take your money back."

"No."

"Take it."

"I won't."

It was almost ludicrous, arguing like that over a stack of hundred-dollar bills. Any other situation I would have knocked her to the floor while grabbing for it, but this wasn't any other situation. She stared at me and I stared at her and we were locked in a contest of wills I would win because I wanted something ever so much more than she. It was time to lay it out for her. I fought to keep my nerves from snapping.

"I'm not willing to continue under the old arrangement," I said, "not with the way you withheld crucial information from me. If we're to go forward together it will have to be different."

"What are you talking about?"

"There is a type of legal action that is perfectly designed to cover this situation. It is a civil proceeding and it is called wrongful death. If I'm going to continue to work on your behalf I will only do it as your partner in the prosecution of such a suit on a contingency fee basis."

"Ahh," she said, crossing her arms, leaning back, taking a long inhale from her cigarette. "Now I understand," she said and I could tell that she did. I suppose the very rich see the look I had just then more often than is seemly, the baleful gleam of want in the eyes of those they do business with. I wonder if it wearies them with its inevitability or thrills them with reassurance of their power and privilege.

"One third for our firm if it settles before trial," I explained. "Forty percent if I have to try it, which goes into effect once we impanel a jury. But money's not the issue," I lied. "Finding the truth is the issue. If you level with me, I'll do my best to get to the bottom of your sister's death."

"I'm sure you will," she said with an edge in her voice, as if she were talking to a somewhat unpleasant servant. "You already have."

It was an awkward moment, but that is inevitable, really, when one's business is tragedy. She was looking for help, I was looking for a gross profit, how could it be otherwise?

"I have the appropriate documents right here," I said, indicating the manila folder on my desktop. "If you'll just read them carefully and sign, we can continue our relationship as I've outlined."

I pushed the file toward her and watched as she opened it and read the fee agreements. I had already signed where I was required to sign; all that was wanting was her signature. As she read, nodding here and there, I barely stifled a desire to get down on my knees and polish her boots. I was certain it was all taken care of when she suddenly closed the folder and dropped it back onto my desk.

"No," she said.

My stomach fell like a gold bar sinking in the sea.

"Sorry, Victor," she said. "No."

"But why not? It's a standard agreement. Why not? Why not?"

She stood and slipped me that sly smile of hers. "Because you want it too much."

Out of watering eyes I stared at her with horror as she picked the wad of hundred-dollar bills off my desk and shoved it into a pocket of her leather jacket. The lottery ticket swirled round the toilet bowl to the drain.

"All I wanted you to do," she said, "was to prove that Jimmy Vigs killed my sister. Was that too hard?"

"But Jimmy didn't do it."

"How do you know?"

"I asked him."

"Nice work, Victor," she said as she turned to leave.

Panic. Say something, Victor, anything.

"But what if I'm right and it wasn't the mob? What if it was something much closer? I've been asking around, Caroline. The Reddmans, I've been told, are a family dark with secrets."

She stopped, her back still to me, and said, "My family had nothing to do with it."

"So you've said. Every time I mention the possibility that your family is involved in your sister's death you simply deny it and try to change the topic of conversation. Why is that, Caroline?"

She turned and looked at me. "I get enough of that question from my therapist. I don't need it from my lawyer, too."

Her lawyer. There was still hope. "But what if one of those dark family secrets is behind your sister's death?"

As she stared at me something at once both ugly and wistful slipped onto her face, a mix of emotions far beyond her range as an actress. Then she walked right up to my desk and started unbuttoning her shirt.

I was taken aback until she reached inside her shirt and pulled out some sort of a medallion hanging on a chain from her neck. She slipped the chain over her head and threw the medallion on my blotter. It was a cross, ancient-looking, green and encrusted, disfigured by time and the elements. In the upper corners of the cross, sharp-pointed wings jutted out, as if a bird had been crucified there.

"That is the Distinguished Service Cross," she said. "It was awarded to my grandfather, Christian Shaw, for gallantry in World War I. He led an attack over the trenches in the first American battle of the war and routed the Germans almost single-handedly. My grandmother dredged it from the pond on our family estate after his death. She gave this medal to me one afternoon as we sat together in her garden and said she wanted me to have it."

"I'm not sure I follow," I said.

"My grandmother told me that this medal symbolized more than mere heroism. Whatever crimes in our family's past, she said, whatever hurts inflicted or sins committed, whatever, this medal was evidence, she said, that the past was dead and the future full of promise. Conciliation, she said, expiation, redemption, they were all in that medal."

Those were the same three words the old lady had used with Grimes. I couldn't help but wonder: conciliation to whom, expiation for what, redemption how?

"So all those rumors and dark secrets and gossip, I don't care," she continued. "They have nothing to do with Jacqueline and nothing to do with me. The past is dead."

"If you believe that, then why do you still wear this medal around your neck?"

"A memento?" she said, her voice suddenly filled with uncertainty.

I shook my head.

She sat down and took her grandfather's Distinguished Service Cross back from me. She stared at it for a while, examining it as if for the first time. "My therapist says my ailurophobia comes from deep-seated fears about my family. She says my family is cold and manipulative and uncaring and until I am able to face the truth I will continue to sublimate my true feelings into irrational fears."

"What do you think?"

"I think I just hate cats."

"Your therapist might be on to something."

"Why is it that everyone wants to dig up my family's past in order to save me? My therapist, you."

"The police also tried to look into any familial connection with your sister's death but were cut off by Mr. Harrington at the bank."

She looked up at me when I mentioned Harrington's name.

"And, deep down, Caroline, you want to look into it too."

"You're being ludicrous."

"Why else would you pay my retainer with a check drawn on the family bank? It was as clear as an advertisement."

Her voice slowed and softened. "Do you really think Jacqueline was murdered?"

"It's possible. I can't be certain yet, but I am certain I'm the only one still willing to look into it."

"And you think with the answer you can save me?"

"Do you need saving?"

She closed her eyes and then opened them again a few seconds later. "What do you want me to do, Victor?"

"Sign the contract."

"I won't. I can't. Not until I know everything."

"Why not?"

"Because then I'll have given up all control and I can't ever do that."

She said it flatly, as if it were as obvious as the sun, and there was something so transparent in the way she said it that I knew it to be true and that pushing her any further would be useless.

"How about this, Caroline?" I said. "I'll agree to continue investigating any connection between the mob and your sister's death so long as you agree to start telling me the truth, all the truth, and help me look at any possible family involvement too. I'll pursue the case without a contract and without a retainer, providing you promise me that if I find a murderer, and you decide to sue, then you'll let me handle the case on my terms."

She stared some more at the medal and thought about what I had proposed. I didn't like this arrangement, I liked things signed, and sealed, but it was my only hope, I figured, to keep on the trail of my fortune, so I watched oh so carefully as her hand played with the medal and her face worked over the possibilities.

When I saw a doubt slip its way into her features I said, "Did you ever wonder, Caroline, how the medal got into the pond in the first place?"

She looked up at me and then back at the medal, hefting it in her hand before she grasped the chain and hung her grandfather's Distinguished Service Cross back around her neck. "You find that out, Victor, and I'll sign your damn contract."

"Is that a promise?"

"There's a dinner at the family estate, Veritas, on Thursday night," she said. "The whole family will be there. You can be my date."

"They shouldn't know we're looking into your sister's death."

"No," she said. "You're right, they shouldn't."

"Anything I should know before I meet them all?"

"Not really," she said, with an uncomfortably knowing smile. "Just don't come hungry."

14

"ABOUT HOW MANY CONVERSATIONS did you have with the defendant in the course of your dealings, Detective Scarpatti?"

"I don't know, lots. I taped five and we had others. It took awhile for him to get it all straight. Your boy, he's not the swiftest deal maker out there, no Monty Hall."

"So you were forced to lead him through the deal, is that right?"

"Just in the details, but there was no entrapment here, Counselor, if that's what you're getting at. Cressi came to me looking to buy the weapons. He wanted to buy as many as I could sell. I told him one-seventy-nine was all I could come up with and he was disappointed with that number. But he brightened when I added the grenade launchers and the flamethrower. To be truthful, I was more surprised than anyone when he showed up. We were targeting a Jamaican drug outfit with the operation. But your guy could never make up his mind on the spot. He always said he had to think about it."

"Like there was someone he had to run the details by, is that it?"

Scarpatti creased his brow and looked at me like he was straining to actually dredge up a thought and then said, "Yeah, just like that."

Detective Scarpatti was a round, red-faced man who smiled all the while he testified. Jolly was the word he brought to mind as he sat and smiled on the stand, his hands calmly clasped over his round hard belly. His was a look that inspired trust, which is why he was such an effective undercover cop, I figured, and an effective witness. All cops have an immediate advantage as they step into the witness box in front of a jury; they are, after all, men and women who devote their lives to law enforcement and competent, truthful testimony is only what is to be expected. Of course they usually get into trouble as soon as they open their mouths, but Scarpatti wasn't getting in trouble at this preliminary hearing and I sensed he wouldn't get into any trouble at the trial either. I had never met the guy before but one look at him on the stand and I knew he would bury Peter Cressi. What jury wouldn't convict on the cogent testimony of Santa Claus?

"Now in any of those myriad discussions, did Mr. Cressi ever specifically mention he had to run the details of the deal by someone else?"

"No."

"Did he ever mention that he had a partner?"

"No, he didn't. In fact I even asked once and he said he was flying strictly solo."

"In any of your phone conversations did you ever sense there was someone else on the line?"

"No, not really. But come to think of it, now that you asked, there was one conversation where he stopped in the middle of a comment, as if he was listening to someone."

"Did you hear a voice in the background?"

"Not that I remember."

"All right, Detective. Now in the course of your conversations, did you ask Mr. Cressi what he planned to do with the guns?"

"Sure. Part of my job is to draw out as much information as possible, especially in a deal of this magnitude."

"And how did he respond?"

"Can I refer to my notes?"

"Of course."

Preliminary hearings are dry affairs, generally, where the defense tries to find out as much as possible about the case without tipping any stratagems that might be used at trial. I was putting on no testimony, presenting no evidence, Cressi was remaining blissfully silent. What I was doing was sitting at the counsel desk, sitting because that's the way we do it in Philadelphia, the lazy man's bar, asking my simple little questions, learning exactly how high was the mountain of evidence the state had against my client and whatever else I could glean about his attempted purchase of the guns. I was in a tricky position, stuck between a bad place and two hard guys, defending my client while also trying to find out for my patron, Mr. Raffaello, what Cressi was planning to do with his arsenal. Tricky, hell, it was flat-out unethical, as defined by the Bar Association, but when your client is a gleeful felon buying up an armory and a mob war is brewing and lives are at stake, especially your own, I think the ethical rules of the Bar Association become somewhat quaint. I think when you are that far over the edge it is up to you to figure out your way in the world and if they decide you stepped over a line and pull your ticket then maybe in the end they're doing you a favor.

While Scarpatti was flipping through his little spiral-bound notebook, I turned to scan the courtroom. It was full, of course, but not to witness my scintillating cross-examination. Once I was finished there was another case set to go and then another and then another, as many hearings as defendants who needed to be held over for trial, and the defendants and lawyers and witnesses and families in the courtroom for those hearings that were to follow Cressi's were waiting and watching, their faces slack with boredom. Except one face was not slack with boredom, one face was watching our proceedings with a keen, almost frightening interest. Thin sharp face, oily gray hair, dapper black suit, with a crimson handkerchief peeking from his suit pocket. What the hell was he doing here?

"All right, yeah. I got it right here," said Scarpatti.

I turned around and faced the witness, whom I had forgotten about in the instant I noticed the mortician's face of Earl Dante staring at me from the gallery of the courtroom. "All right, Detective, what did the defendant say to you when you asked him what he planned to do with the guns?"

"He said, and I'm quoting now, he said, 'None of your fucking business.'"

Scarpatti laughed and the slack crowd, suddenly brought to life by the obscenity, laughed with him. Even Cressi laughed. You know you're in trouble when your own client laughs at you.

"Thank you for that, Detective," I said.

"Anytime, Counselor."

When I was finished handling Scarpatti, denting his story not a whit, the prosecution rested and I stood and made my motion to dismiss all charges against my client. The judge smiled solicitously as she denied my motion and scheduled Cressi's trial. I made a motion to reduce my client's bail. The judge smiled solicitously as she denied my motion and, instead, raised his bail by a hundred thousand dollars, ordering Cressi to be taken into custody immediately by the sheriff until the additional funds could be posted. I objected strenuously to the increase, requesting she reconsider her addition, and she smiled solicitously, reconsidered, and added another fifty thousand to the amount. I made an oral motion for discovery, the judge smiled once again as she denied my motion and told me to seek informal discovery from the prosecution before coming to her with my requests.

"Anything else, Mr. Carl?" she said sweetly.

"Please, in heaven's name, do me a favor here, Vic, and just say no," said Cressi, loud enough for the whole courtroom to laugh again at my expense. Maybe I should have given up the law right there and hit the comedy circuit.

"I don't think so, Your Honor," I said.

"That's probably a wise move." The slam of her gavel. "Next case."

Dante was waiting for me outside the courtroom, in one of the columnar white hallways of the new Criminal Justice Building. He leaned against a wall and held tight to his briefcase. Behind him, his head turning back and forth with an overstudied guardedness, was the weightlifter I had seen with Dante at the Roundhouse's Municipal Court. Dante had one of those officious faces that was never out of place, a face full of condolence and efficiency. A dark face, close-shaven, with small very white teeth. His back stayed straight as he leaned and his cologne was strong. He could have been a maître d' at the finest French restaurant in hell. *Table for two? But of course. Would that be smoking or would you prefer to burn outright with your dinner?* The only comforting thing about being face to face with Earl Dante was that he couldn't then be behind my back.

"Find out anything yet, Victor?" Dante said to me in a calm resonant voice that held a slight lisp, as if his tongue was too long for his mouth and forked.

I felt a chill even though it was hot in that corridor. "I don't know what you're talking about," I said.

"Those questions about possible partners and anything Cressi might have said about his intentions for those guns, very clever."

"I don't know what you're talking about."

"Of course you do. You keep searching, you'll find something." He stared at me for a long moment, the significance of which I couldn't gauge, and then turned his head away. "You might not have heard, Victor, but Calvi's out."

"I heard."

"You liked Calvi, didn't you? You were friends."

"We shared a few meals."

He turned his head to stare at me again. "You were friends."

"Calvi doesn't have friends. He despises everybody equally. But there were those who could stand his cigars, and those who couldn't. I could, that was all, so we had lunch now and then and chatted about the Eagles."

"He took a shine to you, all right. But he's out. The organizational chart has been changed. You should be reporting to me from now on."

"I don't report," I said. "That's not what I do. I represent my clients to the best of my ability, that is all."

"That's never all."

"With me, that is all."

"You find out anything you'll be smart and report to me, see?"

"I don't know what you're talking about."

Dante started sucking his teeth. His mouth opened with a slick leeching sound. "Want to hear a story?"

"Not particularly."

"Out of high school I enlisted," said Dante, ignoring my protest. "Want to know why? My father was an animal, that's why. I was willing to shave my head and take orders like a dog for two years because my father was an animal. But I was also patriotic, see? Still am. I hear the anthem at a ball game and tears spring. I still love my country, even after they sent me to that shithole. See, there was nothing out there that was tougher than my father. I love my goddamn country, but over there I learned there is something beyond patriotism. Do you know what that is?"

"No."

"It's called survival. I didn't survive by volunteering for every crappy mission some promotion-happy lieutenant dreamed up before we could frag him. And I didn't survive by taking one step beyond the step I had to take. I survived by remembering that I couldn't love my country if I was dead, see? Loyalty, it only goes so far. After that it doesn't go no more. Things are changing fast, Victor. Calvi's not the only one that's going, there are others. You make the right choice and you come to me first, understand?"

"I don't know what you're talking about."

"I heard you visited our friend Jimmy Dubinsky yesterday, so I thought you might like to know. He died this morning. Right there on the operating table."

"Oh my God."

"They had that wire up his heart and he had himself a massive. That's the funny thing about Jimmy, everything about him was massive, even his death. Just thought you might like to know. Funeral's Friday. Your people, Victor, they don't mess around when it comes to burying their dead. A guy doesn't even have time to cool before he's in the ground."

"But I just saw him yesterday. He can't . . ."

"Some kids they showed up in our unit, we didn't even want to know their names. You could see it in their eyes they wouldn't last. I'm seeing that look right now, Victor." He sucked his teeth again and chucked me on the shoulder. "See you at the funeral." Then he turned and started walking away, holding his briefcase, walking off to bail out Cressi once again.

The weightlifter gave me a nasty wink and followed him down the corridor.

I watched them go and then fell to the wall, my back against the porous white stone, and covered my eyes with a hand while I shook. Jimmy dead. I had a hard time fathoming it. I actually liked the guy. But the news was worse than that. That tooth-sucking Earl Dante wanted me to pick a side without a scorecard, without a rule book, without even knowing what game we were playing. The way I looked at it, if I picked wrong I would be as dead as Jimmy and if I picked right I would be as dead as Jimmy. All I knew for sure was that I was on the wrong playing field and needed desperately to get out. When I had told Beth I had to flee the law or it would kill me, she didn't know I was being literal as hell.

And I couldn't help but think, as I shook against the corridor wall, that my fate in the coming mob apocalypse and my investigation of the dark secrets of the Reddmans would somehow become entwined. I was right, of course, but in a way I could never then have even vaguely imagined.

Part 2

≡

FROGS

In a rich man's house there is no place to spit but in his face.

—DIOGENES THE CYNIC

15

LAST NIGHT I DREAMT I went to Veritas again. I woke up sweating and shouting from the dream in my room at the guest house in Belize City. No matter how hard I tried, I couldn't force myself back to sleep. It is morning now and I have sat up all night in my underwear examining the contents of my briefcase, reviewing my mission. There are documents relating to bank accounts and bank records and the flow of great sums of money. There are documents from the State Department in Washington to present to the embassy here. There are pages from the diaries of a dead woman and a letter from a dead man and last night, when I read them together, I felt the same shiver roll through me as rolls through me whenever I read them together, which is often. They are the plainest clues I have as to what curse it was that actually afflicted the Reddmans, those and a carton of ancient ledgers that are still in my office in Philadelphia. The full truth will never be learned, but the man I seek in Belize has much of it, along with my share of the Reddman fortune.

Belize City is a pit, and that is being kind. Antiquated clapboard buildings, unpainted, weathered, streaked with age, line the warrens of narrow streets that stumble off both banks of the rank Belize River. Laundry hangs from lines on listing porches, huge rotting barrels collect rain-water for drinking, the tin roofs citywide are rusted brown. The city is crowded with the poor, it smells of fish and sewage and grease, the drivers are maniacs, the heat is oppressive, the beggars are as relentless as the mosquitoes. It is absolutely Third World and the food is bad. My guest house is right on the Caribbean but there is no beach, only a grubby strip of unpaved road called Marine Parade and then a cement barrier and then the ragged rocks that break the water's final rush. It is dangerous, I am told, to walk in certain sections at night and those sections seem to change with whomever I talk until the map of danger has encom-passed the whole of Belize City. Still, last night I put on my suit and took hold of a map of the town and a photo-graph from my briefcase and walked west, away from the Caribbean, into the dark heart of the city to see if anyone had seen anything of the man I am stalking.

The night was hot, the air thick, the streets as unen-lightened as poverty. Cars cruised past, slowly, like preda-tors. Pickup trucks veered by, teenagers jammed into the beds, shouting at one another in Creole. Guards stared somberly from behind chained gates. A rat scurried toward me from an open sewer, halted and sniffed, scur-ried back. I stopped at two nightspots, three hotel bars, a wooden shack of a club that overlooked the Caribbean, black as fear in the night except for the relentless lines of iridescent froth dying on the rocks. I had been told the shack club was habituated by lobstermen and sailors and I had wanted especially to visit it, wondering if my prey was sailing on a luxury yacht somewhere off the Belizean cayes. In each joint I bought for myself and whoever was nearby a bottled beer with a Mayan temple on the label, a Belikin, and made what conversation I could. When I showed the picture I tried to see if I could detect anything beneath the denials and the shaking heads, but there was nothing, a whole night of nothing, though I had known from the start that I was trawling bait more than anything else.

Back in my room, I took off my clothes and turned the fan to high and lay on my back, staring up at the ceiling, waiting for the moving air to cool my sweat. I closed my eyes and fell into a deep sleep only to awake with a shout a few hours later when I dreamt of Veritas.

Now the dawn is just starting to ignite. I lie down again and try to sleep but it is impossible. I watch the sun rise yellow and hot out of the ocean and feel its burgeoning heat. I shower in cold water and think of cool Alaskan glaciers but am already in a sweat by the time I tighten my tie.

When I reach the Belize Bank on Regent Street I am exhausted from the heat and my lack of sleep. I have already visited the quaint white clapboard American Embassy, like a Southern manse dropped in the middle of the Third World, and had a long talk with a junior official named Jeremy Bartlett about my problem. He was freshly scrubbed and amiable enough as he listened to my story and examined my documents but there is something about State Department personnel that leaves my teeth hurting. There must be hundreds of English majors hidden in the basements of embassies all over the world, toiling away at ingenious, long-winded ways of saying, "There's nothing I can do." I took his card and asked for one tiny favor and he looked at me awhile and I left before he could find a new way to say no.

After the embassy, I crossed the swing bridge to the southern part of the city and visited a Belizean lawyer with whom I had been in contact. His office was across the street from the Supreme Court building and above a tee shirt shop. He gave me a long explanation of Belize's robust asset protection laws, which left me feeling doubtful, but then he told me of his uncle, who was a clerk of the

Supreme Court and who could manage anything with proper incentive. I wrote out a check and signed certain documents and paid certain fees and picked up certain other documents. Then it was on to the bank.

The Belize Bank building on Regent and Orange streets is almost modern, with a bright jade-green sign. It presides at the head of a rather ragged business district, its white cement and dark marble facade standing out like a shiny penny against the general disrepair of the rest of the city. In the bank I ask to speak to the assistant manager and am taken to a desk on the second floor. The man I talk to is older and distinguished, with gray hair and a proper British accent. His suit is pale beige and perfectly pressed. His face is powder dry; mine glistens, I am sure, with my sweat.

"I need information about a bank account," I say.

He smiles officiously as I explain my situation and show him the judgment and the documents I have evidencing the flow of money. He reminds me of a State Department employee as he spends five minutes explaining to me that there is nothing he can do. "We must respect the privacy of our customers," he explains rather patiently. "Our country's asset protection laws give us no other choice."

"So I have heard," I say, "but the man I'm seeking is a murderer."

"Well, I suppose murderers have their rights, too," he says.

"There is a warrant for his arrest in America."

"But this isn't America, sir. I am truly sorry but our hands are tied."

I look at him and his bland smile and I sigh. "My government is very interested in finding this man," I say. "We know you are cooperating on a number of money-laundering issues with our people and we would be very grateful, and it would go a long way to easing the pressure you must now be feeling, if you'll cooperate on this matter too."

He nods, his polite smile intact. "We are always willing to cooperate with legitimate requests from your government's law enforcement agencies." His emphasis on the word legitimate is very precise.

"Not every request can go through official channels," I say. "Not all officials can be trusted. Discretion here is of the utmost importance."

"If I could review your credentials."

"Credentials can be dangerous," I say.

"But you can understand, sir, how certain we must be that all requests are legitimate."

"Yes," I say. "I understand completely." I reach into my jacket and pull out Jeremy Bartlett's card. "Why don't you phone Mr. Bartlett at the American Embassy and ask him discreetly about whether or not cooperation with my request might be advantageous to your situation?"

He takes the card and looks at it for a moment and then excuses himself and leaves for a private office, closing the door behind him. That morning I had asked Bartlett that if anyone called hinting about my status not to dissuade him of his misconceptions. Bartlett in all likelihood will tell the assistant manager he has no idea who the hell I am and I will be sent packing, as I would have been sent packing anyway, but there is always the chance.

The assistant manager returns and gives me a tight smile. He leans over the desk and says softly, "I have talked to Mr. Bartlett at the embassy."

I stare up at him impassively.

"You understand that disclosure to us of the beneficial owner of any account is not required under Belizean law, so the information is most probably of no use."

I purse my lips and nod, while continuing to stare.

He turns his head to the side for a moment and then back to me. His voice now is even softer. "The account in which you are interested is in the name of a Mr. Wergeld. The listed address is a post office box in Switzerland. The money was withdrawn last month from our branch in San Ignacio, on Burns Avenue. That's all I can tell from our records."

I nod and pull the photograph from my jacket pocket. He looks at it for a moment and then shakes his head.

I stand and thank him for his service.

"We hope this will take care of the Carlos Santera matter your people have been giving us so much difficulty about."

"I'm sure it will," I say, before turning and walking out of the bank. I shouldn't really have doubted Bartlett. I had merely asked a State Department employee to obfuscate with innuendo, which is sort of like dropping a bloody leg of mutton in front of a shark and asking it to chew.

On my way back to the guest house I walk past Battlefield Park, where a mess of locals sit on benches and spit. A droopy-eyed man leaves the park and jogs to catch up with me. He hectors me about how I should get to know the Belizean people. I stop and look at him. He gives me a yellow-eyed smile and offers me drugs. I shake my head and ignore his shouts and curses as I continue up Regent Street to the swing bridge that will take me over the Belize River and into the north side. I loosen my tie, I take off my jacket and trail it over my shoulder. Men on bikes too small for them circle around me. I feel slow and tired in the heat. On the bridge, the sun reflects off the water in an oppressive strip of light. The heat has a presence, it feels dangerous. Sweat drips into my eye and burns. I wipe it away but it keeps flowing. I turn right at the ramshackle yellow post office, pass a Texaco, and take a turn to where I think lies the sea. I am not sure exactly where I am but once I reach the sea I can follow the water's edge back to my guest house. I find myself in a narrow alleyway behind a row of warehouses fronting the river. I walk alongside a low wall of red-washed rusted tin, with a sign that reads "QUEENS BONDED WAREHOUSE NO. 1." I think I am alone in the alley when a man suddenly steps in front of me. He is wearing filthy loose pants and a flowered shirt.

"You want some coke, *amigo*?" he says, his voice thick with accent.

I shake my head. "Thank you but I'm not thirsty." I move to my left to step around him. He steps to his right and blocks my way.

"You make joke."

"Oh. I didn't mean to, I'm sorry. No thank you."

"Maybe you want some ganj?" He puts two fingers to his lips and pretends to inhale deeply. "Finest ganj in Belize. Or girls even, we got girls. I have sweeter than you'll find at Raoul's."

"No, no thank you." I step to my right and he steps to his left, blocking me again.

"Then maybe you just give me some money, *amigo*? Just that? For an American that is nothing."

I step back and swing my jacket under my arm holding the briefcase. I reach into my rear pocket for my wallet when I feel another hand grabbing for it. I spin around and find a second man there, in cutoff shorts and a Michael Jackson tee shirt, grinning at me. "Drugs?" he says, his accent thicker than the first. "You American, no? You must want drugs."

"I don't want anything," I say loudly as I back away from both men. I feel confused in the heat. My mind has slowed beneath the press of the sun. The second man grasps my arm and yanks me back. My jacket spills to the ground. The man holding onto me starts grabbing again for my wallet.

"How much you want to give us, *amigo*?" asks the first man. "How generous are you today?"

I try to shrug my arm loose but it stays in the second man's grip. He reaches for my wallet and I spin, avoiding his grasp. My briefcase slams into him. I spin the other way and my briefcase hits him solidly on the opposite side. I had not intended to hit him with my briefcase but I'm glad that I did. I begin to spin once again, to hit him with my briefcase once again, when I see something flash shiny in the first man's hand and I stop. The second man reaches into my rear pocket and slips out my wallet and I let him, stilled into paralysis by the heat and the sight of that shining in the first man's hand. The second man lets go of me and begins to go through my wallet and I wish for him to take what he wants, to take it and leave and leave me alone, that's what I am wishing for when I hear a voice from behind.

It is loud and in Spanish and I don't understand it but the two men attacking me do and they immediately halt. The three of us turn to see who is speaking.

It is a young man with dark blue pants and a red Chicago Bulls cap. His tee shirt is printed with the words "LAS VEGAS." He has short black hair and a silver earring and a round dark face, a peasant's face, his cheekbones broad and sharp. He says something again in Spanish and the first man replies harshly.

The young man in the Las Vegas shirt says something else, says it calmly, this time in Creole, and there is a wild silence for a moment. The young man cocks his head to the left and suddenly the two men run, past the young man, back up the alley, the way I had come, and are gone. The young man walks right up to me, reaches down, picks my jacket and wallet off the street, and hands them to me.

"I am sorry for how they behaved," says the young man in slightly accented English. "Some in this city are too lazy to find honest work."

"Thank you," I say. I'm still shaking from the sight of that blade in the first man's hand, shivering and sweating at the same time. With trembling fingers I rifle through my wallet and pull out a twenty and hand it to the man.

He looks up at me and for an instant there is something hard and disappointed in his face. "Don't do that. I am not a beggar."

"I am just grateful," I stammer. "I didn't mean . . ."

"I work for my money." He is stern and noble for a moment more and then he smiles. The smile is wide and seems to come from somewhere deep in his chest. When he quickly turns serious again I want to see the smile once more. "Where are you staying?" he asks.

"At a guest house by the sea."

"I'll walk you back."

"You don't have to," I say, but I'm glad that he does.

He walks through the alleyway slowly, his back straight, his gait even, and I struggle to slow down enough to stay by his side. As I quiet my step, I find myself calming. "I'm Victor Carl. From the United States."

"Pleased to meet you, Victor," he says. "I'm Canek Panti." He says his name so that the accents are on the second syllable of each word.

"I'm very pleased to meet you, Canek. I didn't mean to insult you. I am extremely grateful. What kind of work is it that you do?"

He shrugs as he walks. "I run errands, paint houses, whatever there is. I have access to a car so I also do some taxi work and guide travelers around Belize."

"Interesting," I say. "Do you know a place call San Ignacio?"

"Of course," says Canek. "It is in the west, near the border."

"The Guatemalan border?"

"Yes."

I think on that a moment. I have read enough news reports of the CIA's activities in Guatemala, and the missing Americans, and the never-ending civil war, to be nervous about that country. "It just so happens, Canek, that I need to go to San Ignacio on business. Can you take me there?"

"Of course."

"How much would that cost me?" I ask.

He thinks for a moment. "One hundred and twenty dollars American for the day."

"That will be fine," I say.

He doesn't smile at that, he just looks seriously down at the ground as we walk, as if he is somehow disappointed. I figure he figures he should have asked for more and he is right. He could charge whatever he wants and I would pay it gladly in gratitude for what he did for me. At the end of the alleyway the pavement turns and opens up to the sea. Sailing boats are moored by ragged docks, others are moored bow to stern in the middle of the river; boats speed out of the river's mouth toward the Belizean cayes. We walk together along the water's edge and stop at a small park next to a red and white lighthouse. A pelican, brown and fat and haughty, floats by, its wings extended against a gentle current of sea air. From the lighthouse there is a view across the sea to the southern part of the city. The white buildings lining the far shore gleam in the sun and suddenly the city doesn't seem such a pit. I spin around slowly and look. There is something about Belize City I hadn't noticed before. It is old and rickety and full of poverty, yes, but it is beautiful too, in a non-Disney way, a gateway to true adventure, as if a last haven for swaggering buccaneers remained alive in the Caribbean. Canek, already acting as the guide, waits patiently as I take it all in and then we continue on together, around the ocean's edge and up Marine Parade.

"You must bargain," says Canek, finally, as we walk along the unpaved road that fronts the sea. "I say a hundred and twenty, you say seventy, and from there we find a fair price."

"I thought your price was pretty fair as it was."

"It is high," says Canek. "Most taxis will charge eighty-five to San Ignacio. The bus is only two dollars. Let's agree on a hundred dollars American."

I walk without saying anything for a bit, pondering everything carefully, and then say, "Ninety."

He gives me his brilliant smile again. "Ninety-five," says Canek Panti, "and I will allow that to include a guided visit to Xunantunich, the ancient ruins beyond San Ignacio."

"Done," I say. "We have a deal." By now we are at the end of Marine Parade, standing in front of the tidy white porch of my guest house. "Tomorrow morning?"

"I'll be here at nine," he says.

"That will be perfect. I'm suddenly very thirsty," I say, wiping sweat again from my brow. "Can I buy you a drink, Canek?"

He glances up at the guest house for an instant and then shakes his head. "No, I'm sorry, Victor, I have now to get the car ready for our trip. It needs first some work, but I will be here tomorrow at nine, on the spot."

We shake hands, solemnly, as if we had just agreed on the next day's headline in *The Wall Street Journal*, and Canek walks off, hurrying more now. I wonder in just what shape his car is in that it needs so much work but, surprisingly, I am not worried. The Caribbean shines like an emerald in the late sun. The guest house, on its stilts, seems more quaint than I remember it to be, prettier and whiter. I have met an honest and honorable man. Inside, I know, I can get a bottle of cold water and a bottle of cold Belikin and sit at a table on the veranda and rehydrate beneath a spinning fan. All of it is almost enough to make me forget what it was that led me to Belize City, almost but not quite. I think on the man I am hunting and I think on all he has committed and on the secrets he is hiding and think again on last night's dream of Veritas and even in the midst of the heat I shudder.

16

LAST NIGHT I DREAMT I went to Veritas again. I was at the base of the long grassy hill just inside the great wrought-iron gates with the forged design of vines and cucumbers that barred the entrance to the drive. The moon was bright and cold, the grass devoid of all color in the darkness. Behind, a stream swept past, its black water swirling around heavy, sharp-faced rocks. Two massive sycamores stood side by side, sentries at the base of that hill, and I stood between them, looking up the long sweep of grass to the stone portico that guarded the formal front of the great Reddman house. The wind was fragrant with the soft scent of spring flowers, with lilacs, with the thick grassy smell of a perfectly manicured lawn. Rolling down from the top of the hill, stumbling uneasily down like a drunken messenger, came the sound of music, of violins and trumpets and snappy snare drums. There were lights shining high over my head, there was the sound of gaiety, of laughter, of a world drinking deep drafts of promise. Veritas, on the crest of that hill, was alive once again.

I began to walk up the hill toward the party. The music, the laughter, the light in that dark night, I wanted to see it, to be a part of it all. I was in jeans and a tee shirt and as I got closer and began to hug my bare arms from the cold I wondered where was my tuxedo. I owned one, I knew that, and mother-of-pearl studs and a cummerbund, but why wasn't I wearing it? I patted my pants. No wallet, no keys, no invitation. Where was my invitation? Where were my pearls? I felt the sense I feel often of being left out of the best in this world. I thought of turning back but then the music swept down for me. I heard a car engine start, coughing and sputtering like something ancient, I heard the neighing of a horse, I heard voices that sounded like guards. I dropped to my knees and began crawling, hand over hand, up the steep hill.

My knees slid over grotesque fingers of roots that jutted from the soil. Pebbles embedded themselves into the flesh of my palms. I heard the faint buzz of beetle swarms infesting the lawn. I thought about stopping, about letting myself go and rolling down the hill, but the music grew louder and swept down once more for me. The violins drowned out the buzzing of the insects and the laughter turned manic. My jeans ripped on a stone, my palms bled black in the moonlight, but I kept moving toward the joy, reaching, finally, the encircling arms of the front portico's stairwell that would take me to it. On the wide swooping steps that led up to the house I crouched and slowly climbed, steadying myself with a hand on the step above my feet, my blood smearing black on the stone. I could hear distinctions in the voices now, hearty men, laughing women. Snatches of conversation flew over my head as I rose to the top of the stairs. A group, standing outside on the drive that circled the surface of the portico, seemed not to notice me as I slipped across. I was certain the guests would see me but they didn't; even as they turned to me they looked right through me. They were handsome, pretty, they laughed carelessly, they were sure of their places in the world and I realized that for them, of course, I would not exist. I stood, slapped the dirt off my ripped pants, walked past the group to one of the large bay windows to the right that studded the grand ballroom wing of the house.

It was a party like every party I had never been invited

to. Fabulously dressed women, men in white tie and tails, champagne and butlers with tiny foods and dancing. The women wore gloves, they had dance cards, the men waltzed as though they actually knew how to waltz. The celebrants stood straight and showed white teeth when they laughed. I pressed my nose to the glass. I watched their revelries and felt again what I had felt in high school and college and through my career as a lawyer, the sheer desperate pain of wanting to be inside. But where was my tuxedo, where was my invitation? I was no longer in tee shirt and jeans. I was now wearing a navy blue suit, black wing tips, a tie from Woolworth's, but still it was not enough. A pretty girl in a white dress walked by without noticing me stare at her with great longing through the window. And then I recognized him, standing tall and grand in the middle of his ballroom, recognized him from the pictures and the histories, from the portrait on the billions and billions of pickle jars. Claudius Reddman.

He was an imposing figure, with a deep chest and arrogant stance and perfectly trimmed white beard. His eyes bulged with power, his pinprick nostrils flared, his mouth stretched lipless and wide, and he was alive and in his certain glory in that room. His three young daughters, on the threshold of their womanhood, stood with him for a moment before breaking away as if on cue to their separate fates. The eldest was small and frail, her pale hair tight to her skull. She coughed delicately into a handkerchief and sat on a chair by her father's side and watched the party with a wrenching sadness. The youngest, tall and buxom, slipped from the room with a man far older than she and stood with him on the portico, talking intimately, smoking. She was the only woman in the whole of that party who was free enough to smoke. The middle child, with flowers twined in her hair, was now dancing with a strong young man, dancing beautifully, gracefully, her head lying back, pointing her raised toe. There was a drama to her movements as she swooped around the dance floor, greedily carving space for herself and her partner among the other dancers until the floor was cleared of all revelers but the two. As she spun in his arms she turned her head and stared at me and for the first time in the whole of that night I was noticed. Her mouth twisted into an arrogant smile. Her pale blue eyes glinted. Her head whipped back from the force of her ever more ferocious spins; her mouth opened with abandon; the lights of that great room bounced off the whites of her teeth with a maniac's glee.

"My grandmother was one of three children, all girls," said Caroline as we drove slowly through a crashing rain toward Veritas. "The fabulous Reddman girls." Caroline laughed out loud at the thought of it. "The *Saturday Evening Post* did a spread about them when my great-grandfather's pickles were becoming all the rage. Three debutantes and their fabulously wealthy father. Men came from all over the East Coast to court them. My great-grandfather threw lavish balls, sent invitations to every young man in Ivy at Princeton, in Fly at Harvard, in Scroll and Key at Yale. They should have had the most wonderful of lives. Hope, Faith, and Charity. I suppose my grandfather named them after the virtues to guard them from tragedy but, if so, he failed miserably."

A bolt of lightning ripped open the black of the sky; the lashing rain raised welts on its own puddles. My Mazda hit a pool of black water, slowing as the undercarriage was assaulted by a malicious spray. I had picked up Caroline outside her Market Street building with the rain just as thick. She had been a dark smudge waving at me before she opened the door and ducked inside the car. She dripped as she sat next to me, but there was something ruddy and scrubbed about her. Even her lipstick was red.

She seemed almost as nervous at seeing her family as I was.

"The first daughter, Hope, died just before my father was born," continued Caroline. "Consumption we think, it was the glamorous way to expire then. Grammy always told us how wonderfully talented she was on the piano. She would play for hours, beautiful torrents of music, for as long as she had the strength. But as she grew older she grew more sickly and then, before she turned thirty, she faded completely away. Grammy cared for her until the end. Apparently, my great-grandfather was devastated."

"The death of Hope."

"Faith, the middle girl, was my grandmother. She married, of course, to a Shaw, with much charm and fading fortunes. He was of the Shaw Brothers Department Store, the old cast-iron building at Eighth and Market, but the store was doing badly and he married my grandmother for her money, so they say, in an attempt to save the business. From everything I've heard he was a scoundrel until the war, when his heroism came as a shock to everyone. Through it all, my grandmother loved him dearly. She was widowed young and spent the rest of her life caring for her son and grandchildren, mourning her husband."

"How did your grandfather die?"

"It was an accident."

"A car accident?"

"No," said Caroline. "My grandmother never remarried, never even dated. She stayed at the house and tended the gardens with Nat and took care of the house and the estate."

"Nat?"

"Old Nat, the gardener. He's been with the house forever. He's really the family caretaker, he supervises everything. My mother's interests lay outside the house and my father cares even less, so it is all left to Nat. He's probably busy tonight."

"Why?"

"Sometimes, when it rains, the lower portion of the property floods. There's a stream that flows all around the house, leading to the pond."

"Like a moat?"

"Just a stream, but during heavy rains it overflows the road into the gate."

"What happened to Charity?"

"Aunt Charity. She ran away."

"It's hard to imagine running away from all that money."

"No it isn't," she said. "That's the only thing that makes any sense."

She pressed my car's lighter and reached into her purse for a cigarette. As she lit it, I glanced sideways at her, her face glowing in the dim red light of the lighter. What was it like to grow up weighed down by such wealth? How did the sheer pressure of it all misshape the soul? I would have loved to have found out firsthand, yes I would have, but looking at Caroline, as she inhaled deeply and mused wistfully about the grandaunt who escaped it all, for the first time I wondered if all I had wished to have been born to might not have been such a blessing after all.

"Charity was sort of a fast girl," said Caroline.

"I haven't heard that expression in a while."

"These are all my Grammy's stories. Grammy said that after her sister disappeared she had guessed that Charity had gotten pregnant and would return in half a year or so, saying she had been abroad, or something like that. That's the way it was done. But there was apparently a bitter fight between Charity and my great-grandfather, that's what Grammy remembered, and then Charity was gone. Grammy used to sit on our beds at night and tell us strange and fascinating tales of a traveler in foreign lands, overcoming hardships and obstacles in search of adventure. Grammy was a natural raconteur. She would weave these beautiful, brilliantly exciting stories, and the heroic traveler was always named Charity. It was her way, I think, of praying that her sister was well and living the life she had hoped for when she left. Of all of us, really, only Charity has been able to rid herself of the burden of being a Reddman."

"And, unfortunately for her, the Reddman money. Any word ever about the child?"

"None. I've wondered about that myself."

"Anyone ever make a claim to her share of the estate?"

"No, the only known heir is my father. Turn here."

I braked and turned off the road into a paved lane so narrow two cars could pass each other only with scratches. Foliage grew wild on the sides of the road and the trees, boughs heavy with rain, bent low into my headlights as if in reverence to Caroline as we passed. The rain thickened on the windshield so that I could barely see, even with the wipers, and there was a steady splash of water on the undercarriage of the car. I slowed to a crawl. I hoped there were no hills to go down because I figured the brakes were too soaked to stop much of anything.

"Tell me about your childhood," I said.

"What's to tell? I was a kid. I ran around and fell a lot and skinned my knees."

"Was it happy?"

"Sure. Why not? I mean, adolescence was hell, but that's true even in the best-adjusted families, though no one ever accused us of being one of those. We're all in tonight, which is a rare and oh-so-delicious treat, so you can judge for yourself. My brother Bobby, my brother Eddie and his wife, Kendall, and my mother. There may be others, too. My mother has a need to entertain and though most refuse her invitations now, there are always a few parasites who can be counted on to grab a free meal."

"We should figure out what to tell everyone about me."

"We should. I'll say you were a friend of Jacqueline's and that she introduced me to you. But you shouldn't be a lawyer—too obvious."

"I've always wanted to be a painter," I said.

I was waiting for Caroline to dub me a painter when instead she screamed.

A huge figure, shiny and black, lumbered out of the woods and stood in the rain before my oncoming car.

I slammed on the brakes. The car shuddered and slid sideways to the left as it kept humming toward the figure. It looked like a tall thin demon waving its arms slowly as my car slipped and skidded right for it.

"Stop!" said Caroline.

"I'm trying," I shouted back. I had the thought that I never really knew what it meant to turn into the skid, as I had been forever advised in driver's ed, and that if a clearer instruction had been implanted in my brain I wouldn't be at a loss at that very instant. As a row of thick trees swelled in the headlights, I twisted the wheel in what I hoped was the proper direction. The car popped back to straight on the road and then veered too far to the left. I fought the wheel again and locked my knee as I stood on the pedal. With a lurch the brakes finally took hold. The car jerked to a sudden stop and stalled.

"Jesus, Jesus, Jesus," said Caroline.

I said nothing, just sat and felt my sweat bloom. With the wipers now dead, the rain totally obscured the view through the windshield.

When I started the car again and the wipers revived I could see that my front bumper was less than a foot from the shiny black figure. It was a man, clothed in a black rubber rain slicker and cowl.

"Oh my God, it's Nat," said Caroline. "You almost hit Nat."

The man in black stepped around the car to the driver's side. I unrolled the window and he bent his body so that his dripping cowl and face loomed shadowy through the frame until Caroline reached up and turned on the roof light. Nat's face was long and gaunt, creased with deep weather lines. His eyelids sagged to cover half his bright blue eyes. Circling his left eye was a crimson stigma, swollen and irregularly shaped. There was no fear on his face and I realized there was no fear in the way he had held his body as my car headed right for him, just a curious interest, as if he had been waving his arms not to ward me off but to increase the visibility of my target.

"You need to pump those brakes, young man," said Nat in a dry friendly cackle.

"I wanted to turn into the skid but I couldn't figure what that meant," I admitted.

"Can't say as I'm sure myself, but that's what they say, all right. How are you, Miss Caroline?"

"Fine, thank you, Nat. This is a friend of mine, Victor Carl."

"Welcome to Veritas, Mr. Carl."

"Isn't this a marvelous rain, Nat?" she said.

"From where you're sitting, maybe. Stream's rising."

"Can we make it up?"

"For a little while, still. But you won't make it down again, not tonight. Not without a boat."

"Maybe we should turn around," I said.

"Your mother's been expecting your visit, Miss Caroline," said Nat.

"What about her cats?" asked Caroline.

"They're in the cage in the garden room for the evening."

"Vicious little things, her cats. And they pee everywhere. She knows I hate them, why can't they just stay in Europe?"

"Your mother's quite attached to them," said Nat. "It's good to see her attached to something. I left the front gate open for you."

"Well, I suppose it will be all right once the rain lightens," said Caroline. "And we could always stay over."

"Plenty of room," he said. "But if you're going up you should be going before the stream rises any further. Already there's a puddle where the bridge should be. Master Franklin was going to be late so I told him not to bother."

"I need to go to a funeral tomorrow," I said.

"Rain's supposed to stop tonight," said Nat. "There won't be any trouble leaving in the morning."

"Let's go, Victor," she said.

I smiled at Nat and did as I was told. In my rearview mirror I could see him watching us leave, glowing red, dimming as he fell farther away from my rear lights into the misty depths of the rain.

I followed the road onward, leaning forward so I could see more clearly through the wet darkness. After a turn left and a bend right we came in sight of two towering black gates, opened enough to let a single car through. Studding both gates were gnarled, spidery vines sprouting great iron cucumbers. On the left gate, wrought massively in iron, were the words MAGNA EST, and on the right the word VERITAS. Before the gate was a black puddle that spread ten yards across the road, its surface pocked by rain, its depth impossible to determine. I stopped the car.

"It's just the stream," she said. "It's not too deep yet."

"Are you sure? This isn't four-wheel drive. My drive's only about a wheel and a half."

"Go ahead, Victor."

Slowly I drove forward, the road sloping down, sending my car deeper and deeper into the water. I kept looking down at the floor, wondering when the water would start seeping through, kept listening to the engine, waiting for the sputter and choke as the motor drowned. The water looked impossibly deep outside my window, the car so low I felt I was in a rowboat, but then the front tilted up and the car pulled higher and soon we were out of the overflowed stream, through the gates, past two huge sycamores, driving up the long driveway to the house.

The trees and overgrowth had given way to a wide flat hillside that seemed to spread forever in the darkness. The drive pulled higher and the hillside lengthened and I realized I was driving through what must have been a vast piece of property, stunning, I was sure, in its size and depth even though I could see only the narrow strip illuminated by my headlights. And then a crack of lightning confirmed my suspicions and my eyes couldn't take in its entire breadth before darkness once again clasped shut its jaws and the sky growled and my vision was reduced to the thin strip lighted by my car. Atop the hillside was a glow, yellow and dim, a glow that strangely grew no brighter as we approached. The driveway curved away from the light and then back again and suddenly Veritas came into view. I drove around the drive as it circled tightly across the top of a wide stone portico, whose steps led down the hill which our car had just climbed, and parked in front of the house

"Charming," I said.

"We call it home."

What they called home was a massive Gothic revival stone structure with dark eaves and predatory buttresses and strangely shaped bay windows with intricate stained glass. Wings and dark additions had been slapped on with abandon. Dull yellow lamps lit the great front door, giving the carved wood a sickly look, and thin strips of light leaked weakly out some of the windows on the first floor, though a whole huge wing of windows to the right was dark as if in blackout. The second floor appeared deserted except for a window under one of the eaves at the far left end, where I saw a light stream for a moment before heavy curtains were dropped to block its exit. I gaped with amazement at the monstrosity before me, and that's what it

was, truly. Misshapen and cold, I could imagine it as one
of those demented boarding schools for the blood spawn of
the insanely rich. I had always wanted my fine home on a
hill in the Main Line, sure, but not that home.

"Come on in," she said, as she opened the car door.

"Is it haunted?" I asked.

"Of course it is." She jumped out of the car, dashing
through the rain, until she was protected by an archway
over the front door. I joined her. Before she could reach the
knob that worked the buzzer the heavy wooden door
opened with a long creak. A tiny maid with a tightly wrinkled face stared at us both for a moment, as if we were
intruders, before guiding us into the center hall.

It was a poorly lit space, cavernous, two stories high,
leading to a dark hanging stairwell at the rear. There were
huge arched beams overhead, like ribs, and dark maroon
wallpaper on the walls, the seams peeling back. A piece of
furniture sat squat in front of the stairs, round like a tumor,
its four seats facing hostilely away from one another. A
chandelier lit the space with an uneven, dingy light; three
of the bulbs were out. I felt, with those arched ribs above
and the tumor of a circular couch, that I was in the belly of
a some huge malignant beast.

"Hola, Consuelo. Como estas?" asked Caroline.

The maid, without smiling, said in a lightly accented
voice, "Fine, thank you, Miss Shaw."

Caroline gave Consuelo her raincoat and I did the
same. I hadn't noticed before, but underneath Caroline's
raincoat had been a tight black cocktail dress that was
obviously not thrift-shop quality. She was wearing stockings with black lines down the back and her black heels
were high and glossy and sharp and the stud in her nose
held a diamond. Caroline had dressed for the family; her
spirit of rebellion only went so far.

"Donde está ma familia?" she asked.

"They're all in the great room," said Consuelo. "With

the guests. They held dinner for you." She let her impassive gaze take me in and added, "I'll set another place."

"Road's out, so expect some overnights this evening."

"I've already taken care of it. I'll set up another room for your friend."

"Gracias, Consuelo," said Caroline as she grabbed my arm and led me deeper into the beast's belly.

"Pretty good Spanish," I said.

"That's all I know. *Hola* and *Como estás* and *Gracias*. The fruits of four years of high school Spanish. Pathetic." She gripped my arm ever more tightly as we approached a double doorway at the end of the hall. "Are you ready?" she asked gravely, as if I were about to enter a wax museum of horror.

"I guess so," and before I had even finished saying it she had swept me through the doors.

It was a huge formal room, ornate plaster ceiling, walls covered with wood and studded with portraits of the wealthy dead, furniture with thin legs, a huge pale blue oriental rug. I could tell right off it was a fancy room because the fabrics on the differing pieces of furniture didn't match one another and there wasn't a plastic slipcover in the place. From the ornamental facing of the fireplace a gloomy plaster head stared out with blank eyes and above the mantelshelf was a portrait of an angry man in a bright red coat, a hunting coat. He had a brisk white beard and great goggling eyes and a familiar face and it didn't take me long to recognize him. Claudius Reddman. A clot of people held drinks in the center of the room, leaning back and chatting. Others were standing by a huge blue vase from some ancient Chinese dynasty that had prospered for thousands of years for the sole purpose of providing the great houses on the Main Line with huge blue vases. Before I could take it all in Caroline, still clutching my arm, said in a voice loud enough to silence their conversations:

"Sorry we're late everybody. This is Victor Carl. He was a dear friend of Jacqueline's. He's a painter."

All eyes turned to gaze at me in my very painterly black wing tips and blue suit and green tie. And just as they were all giving me the up and down Caroline pulled me close and leaned her head against my shoulder and added:

"And in case you're interested, yes, we're lovers."

17

Serenata Notturna in D minor

1. Adagio

I WAS LYING IN BED in a dark cell of a room on the third floor of Veritas, lying in my tee shirt and boxers, staring up. The ceiling, illuminated by a dim lamp beside my bed, was made of thick beams, painted with fragile flowers, arrayed in a complicated warren of water-stained squares, all imported, I'd been told, from a famous Italian villa outside of Florence. It had once been a pretty fancy room, that room, with that ceiling. Once. As I lay staring at the ceiling and thinking of the strange evening I had just spent in the Reddman house, an uneven patter of water dropped from that wondrous imported ceiling into a porcelain chamber pot by the foot of my bed. Splat. Splat splat. Splat. And then, behind the patter of those drops, I heard a faint knock at my door.

I bolted to a sitting position and wondered if I had imagined the sound, but then it came again, just a light tap tapping, soft, hesitant. I rose from the bed and grappled on my pants and slowly, carefully, walked barefooted across the mildewed threadbare oriental rug to the door.

"Yes?" I said through the wood, hoping for some reason it was Caroline. Well that's not really true, I was hop-

ing for very specific reasons that it was Caroline, hoping
because of that dress, the shape of her legs in those sharp
glossy heels, because of the way she looked feral and
dangerous in her cocktail wear. I was hoping it was she
because I could still feel the warmth of her and smell the
scent of her from when she leaned into me and surprised
the assembled throng with her announcement of our sexual engagement. The whole horrid evening I had been
watching her out of the corner of my eye, watching her
move, watching her laugh, watching the butterfly on her
pale neck flutter as she drank her Manhattans, one after
the other after the other, a veritable stream of vermouth
and whiskey and bitters, and as I watched her I found
myself wishing that what she had announced with great
ceremony and mirth was actually true. So I said, "Yes,"
through the door, and I hoped it was she, but when I
opened it whom I saw instead was her brother Bobby.

"Mr. C-C-C-Carl?" said Bobby. "D-d-d-do you have a
moment?"

"Sure," I said, "so long as you don't mind my informal
dress."

"I don't mind," he said, and his gaze dropped from my
face, down past my tee shirt, to my pants and lingered
there long enough for me to assume I was unzipped.

"Come on in, then," I said, "and call me Victor." When
he was past me in the room I quickly checked my zipper. It
was closed.

He sat on the edge of my bed. There was an overstuffed reading chair in the corner and I switched on the
lamp beside it before sitting. I could feel each spring dis-
tinctly beneath me and the cloth underneath my forearms
was damp. The light coming through the faded lampshade
cast a jaundiced yellow upon the walls and Bobby's face.
He was a tall thin man, shy and stuttering, who slouched
his chin into the shoulder of his gray suit as if he were a
boxer hiding a glass jaw. His hair was red and unruly and

his lips were pursed in an astonished aristocratic sort of way. He kept mashing his hands together as if he were kneading dough. We had talked some at the cocktail gathering before dinner, each of us with a bitter glass of champagne in one hand and a stick of some sort of roasted gristly meat in the other. He had asked me about my art and I had described for him my imaginary oeuvre.

"I wanted to t-t-t-talk to you about Jackie," Bobby said as he sat on the edge of my bed. He avoided looking at me as he spoke, his gaze resting over my shoulder, then to the side, then again quickly on my crotch before moving up to the ceiling. "Caroline said you knew her."

"That's right," I lied. "I met her at the Haven, where we used to meditate together."

"Poor Jackie was always searching for some m-m-m-measure of meaning. I expect that place wasn't any better than the others. She tried to get me to go with her once."

"Did you?"

"No, of c-c-c-course not. Jackie was always looking outward, away, certain wherever she would find the answers was someplace she had never been. I think it's really sad that she was looking so d-d-d-desperately for something, when all along the answer was right under her nose."

"Where?"

"Here. In this house, in our history. I think m-m-m-meaning is in devoting yourself to something larger than yourself, don't you? That's what our Grammy taught us."

"And what do you devote yourself to, Bobby?"

"To our investments, our money. I go downt-t-t-town and watch the family positions on the monitors at the stock exchange building every day. And I have a hookup here, also. While most of the family money, of course, is in the company stock, we have other investments that I watch and trade."

"That must be exciting."

"Oh, it is, really," he said as he looked me straight in the eye. As he spoke of money and finance an assurance rose in his voice and his gestures grew animated. "But it's more than just exciting. See the thing, Mr. Carl, is that we're all going to die, we're all so small. But the money, it just goes on and on and on. It's immortal, as long as we care for it and tend to it. It's the only thing in the world that's immortal. Governments will fall, buildings will crumble, but the money will always be there. My role in life is caring for it, keeping it alive. Every moment as I watch it percolate on the screen, watch the net value go up and down by millions at a stroke, I feel a flush of fulfillment. That's what was so sad about Jackie, she was looking for something else when she should have been looking right here." He paused, his eyes dropped to my chest and then my crotch, and then he began to clutch his hands once more. "But w-w-w-what I wondered, Mr. Carl . . ."

"Victor."

"All right, V-V-V-V-V . . ." His face closed in on itself as he tried to get the word out and I struggled with him. I was about to spurt out my name again, to get him through it, when he stopped, breathed deep, and smiled unselfconsciously. "Some letters are harder than others."

"That's fine, Bobby," I said. "Don't worry about it."

"W-w-w-what I wondered was why do you think she k-k-k-killed herself, if you have any idea. She almost seemed happy for the first time. She was engaged to be married, she said the meditation was helping her. Why do you think she k-k-k-killed herself?"

"I don't know," I said. "I thought she was doing well too. So well, in fact, that I'm not certain that she did kill herself."

"N-n-n-no?"

I looked at him carefully as I spoke, looking for anything that would clue me that he knew something he shouldn't have known. "No," I said. "There are some things that seem suspicious about her death, little things, like even the way she died. In a group meeting at the Haven she once admitted to having a cache of pills in her apartment. They were there, in her bathroom, at the end. I don't see why she hung herself if she had the drugs."

"That is strange. But Jackie was always m-m-m-most dramatic in her despondency, m-m-m-m-maybe she wanted to m-m-m-make a statement."

I shrugged, noticing that he had seemed more nervous as he talked about her death. "I don't know. It's sort of comforting to think that maybe she was happy and was murdered rather than her being so depressed at the end as to hang herself."

"That w-w-w-would be nice, yes, but who w-w-w-w-w-w . . ."

"Would want to kill her? You tell me."

He shook his head. "No, Jackie was always unhappy. Even as a b-b-b-baby she was c-c-c-colicky. If she was going to die she would do it herself. Grammy used to say the c-c-c-curse got hold of her from the start."

"Excuse me," I said.

"The c-c-c-curse. Didn't Jackie tell you about it?"

"About a curse? No."

"We have a family c-c-c-curse. Doesn't every family have one?"

"Probably. Ours was my mother. Tell me about your family curse, Bobby."

He stood up and started pacing as he spoke, his hands working on each other as if out of control. "It's from the c-c-c-company. The c-c-c-company wasn't always named Reddman Foods. That name came in only when our great-grandfather gained control. Before that it was called the E. J. P-P-P-Poole Preserve Company. That was before Great-grandfather's special method of pressure pickling took the country by storm, when they mainly canned tomatoes and carrots and other produce. Apparently Elisha P-P-P-Poole was a drunk and the company wasn't profitable before he sold out to Great-grandfather, but as soon as the company started selling the new pickles and turning a profit P-P-P-Poole turned bitter and accused Great-grandfather of stealing the company from him. He made a couple of drunken scenes, wrote letters to the police and the newspapers, threatened the family, and made a general n-n-n-nuisance of himself. But it never got him any stock back or affected the company's profits. Eventually he killed himself. Great-grandfather did the charitable thing and took care of his family, giving the widow an annuity and her and her daughter a place to live, but he always denied stealing the company. Said P-P-P-Poole was drunk and deluded, that the lost opportunity drove him mad." Bobby shrugged. "Supposedly, before he died, he c-c-c-cursed Great-grandfather and all his generations."

"How did Poole kill himself?" I asked.

"He hanged himself from the rafters of his tenement," he said. He looked at me with his eyes widening. "M-m-m-maybe it really was the curse that got her." And then he laughed, a scary sniveling little laugh, and as he laughed his eyes dropped down from my face to my crotch again before he turned his head away. I looked down at my fly. Still zipped.

"Is there a problem with my trousers?" I said. "Because you keep on looking down there as if there was a problem."

With his head turned away and his hands still kneading one another he said, "I j-j-j-just thought you might be l-l-l-lonely up here on the th-th-th-third floor. I th-th-th-think Caroline's asleep already d-d-d-downstairs. One too many M-M-M-Manhattans. So if you want I c-c-c-could keep you c-c-c-company."

"Ahh," I said, suddenly getting the whole idea of his visit. I wondered how he had gotten the wrong idea about me. Was it my suit, my haircut? It must have been my haircut; the barber this time was a little too enthusiastic with the electric clippers. "I'm just fine, actually, and a little tired, so if you'll excuse me." I slapped my legs and stood up.

"I didn't m-m-m-mean, I'm s-s-s-sorry, I-I-I-I . . ."

"It's all right, Bobby," I said, as I held the door open for him. "Don't worry about it. I'm glad we had this chance to talk."

He stepped through the door and then turned around. "I like g-g-g-girls too."

"All right."

"I d-d-d-do. Really."

"It's all right, Bobby."

"It's j-j-j-just they don't come over much."

"I understand, Bobby. Really. And you don't have to worry, I won't tell a soul."

2. Molto Vivace

I shut off the floor lamp and stripped off my pants and crawled back into the slightly sodden bed, staring once again at the decrepit ceiling. I thought of the drunken Elisha Poole, railing at his missed opportunity for a fortune, blaming Claudius Reddman, blaming the alcohol that deadened his predatory instincts, blaming capitalism itself. I wondered where his heirs were, how they were faring. They had probably grown to be pathetic money-maddened lawyers, searching the byways of America for a case, just one case, to make them as rich as they were meant to be. Even so, they were probably in better shape than Claudius's heirs. Jacqueline, hanging dead just as Elisha Poole himself had ended by hanging dead. Or Bobby, his tongue twisted by the pressures of his family history, sexually confused, finding his meaning in the blinking numbers of a computer monitor. Or Caroline, irrationally terrified of cats, seeking solace in a perpetual state of arrested rebellion. Or Eddie, gambling away his fortune with a fat, mob-invested, now sadly dead and soon to be buried bookie.

Edward Shaw had turned out to be a short man, heavy not of the bone but of the flesh, with a cigarette constantly in his sneering lips. His eyes were round and sort of foolish, filled with the false bravado of a loser who thinks he's ready for a comeback even though the final bell has rung. His left arm was bent stiffly at his side and I smiled when I saw it, thinking it unexpectedly wise of Calvi's men to have left Eddie's check-signing arm whole. Through the entirety of that evening, through the insipid cocktail conversation, through the nauseating dinner, through the smell of those moldy cigars the men smoked in the mite-ridden library, a rancid smell of old towels burning we endured as we talked of investments and Walker Cup golf and how the Wister yacht ran aground in the sandbars off Mount Desert Island in 1938, through it all I kept my eye on Eddie, and he seemed to keep his eye on me. I tried to talk with him more than once, but I never got the chance. He successfully avoided me, as if he knew my mission there was to smoke him out. Whenever I approached to say hello he smiled tightly and slipped away. I had that effect on people, yes, but Eddie's reticence was more sinister than mere distaste at being bored by a man in a suit. It seemed to denote a wild sense of guilt, or at least so I hoped.

I was thinking of it all when I heard another knock at my door, this one less hesitant, quicker, full of some unnatural energy at that late hour. Again I grappled on my pants. In my doorway, clutching a painted canvas, I found Kendall Shaw, Eddie Shaw's wife.

Kendall was a thin pretty woman with straight honey hair cut in an outdoorsy style you often see on women who think the great outdoors is the space between their front doors and their Volvos. She wore a red wool dress that hugged her tight around aerobically trimmed hips. As soon as I opened the door she started speaking. She spoke breathlessly and fast.

"I hope I'm not bothering you, and I know it's late, but I had something I just had to show you. It's so exciting that you're an artist and a friend of Jackie's. I guess Jackie introduced you to Caroline. Caroline is just wild, but so much fun too, don't you think? We were all so disappointed about her movie. First she was raving with excitement and then, poof, she pulled the plug. That is so like her. She collapsed tonight in her old room. Too much to drink, poor dear. It always seems to happen when she comes home. Do you meditate? Jackie always used to talk about meditation. I tried to meditate but I kept on thinking of all the things I needed to buy. Maybe it was because my mantra was MasterCard. So have you met Frank yet? Frank Harrington, he's also a friend of Caroline's, an old friend. What a handsome man, clever too. You two should meet. So tell me about your painting. Where have you shown? I paint some too. Mostly landscapes. I'm not very good, heavens, but I find it so soothing. I brought one to show you. Tell me what you think, and be honest, but please not too honest."

It didn't take me long to figure out how it was that Kendall stayed so thin. The painting she had handed me was a landscape all right, an imaginary view painted right from the instructions on the PBS painting shows, with spindly trees and moss-covered rocks and majestic peaks in the background. It was actually pretty good for what it was and it could have proudly held its own on any Holiday Inn wall. "I like it," I lied.

"Do you, really?" she shrieked. "That is marvelous, simply marvelous. It's a gift, from me. I insist. I have others if you want to see them. You must. Believe it or not this isn't even a real place. I dredged the landscape out of my imagination. It's so much more psychologically authentic that way, don't you think?"

Something she had said in that first torrent of words interested me. "You mentioned a Franklin Harrington. Who is he?"

"Oh, Franklin. An old family friend, the family banker now. He was supposed to come tonight but had to cancel. I thought you knew. I was sure you did. He's Caroline's fiancé. Oh my, I hope I haven't spilled anything I shouldn't have."

"No," I said. "I'm sure you didn't." I turned my attention back to the painting, holding it before me as if I were studying it with great seriousness. "You know what this work reminds me of? That special place that Jackie used to talk about, where she would go in her most peaceful meditations."

"How extraordinary." Her eyes opened wide. "Maybe Jackie and I were linked in some mystical way."

"Maybe you were," I said. "That would be so cool. You know, sometimes people who are connected in mystical ways can feel each other's emotions. On the night she died, did you feel anything?"

"To tell you the absolute truth, Victor, I did have a premonition. I was in North Carolina, vacationing, when I felt a sense of dread come over me. Actually I thought it was Edward's plane. He flew back that morning, for business, and on the beach I had this horrible sense that his plane had gone down. I was so relieved to hear from him, you couldn't imagine. But that was the day that Jackie died. You think I was getting those horrible images of death from her?"

"I don't doubt it," I said.

"How marvelously strange."

"Tell me, Kendall. What was the business your husband flew north for that day?"

"Oh, some real estate thing. Edward dabbles more than anything else. He's waiting for the inheritance so that he can buy a football team. He's just a boy like that. And do you want to know something else very interesting about my husband, Victor? But I have to whisper it."

"Okay, sure," I said, anxious to hear whatever other incriminating facts she wanted to tell me about Eddie Shaw.

Kendall looked left down the hallway, then right, then she leaned forward until I could smell the Chanel. "My husband," she whispered, "is fast asleep."

And then she bit my ear.

3. Marcia Funebre

When I was alone in my room again, I laid the painting on a tottering old dresser, having successfully avoided laying Kendall Shaw, and once more took my pants off and fell into bed. She had been particularly ardent, Kendall had, which would have been flattering had she not been so obviously hopped up with her diet pills and suffering from some sort of amphetamine psychosis. Upon biting my ear, she performed a talented lunge, kicking the door closed with a practiced side swipe at the same time she threw her arms round my neck, but I fought her off. It wasn't that I wasn't attracted—I was actually, I have a thing for women just like Kendall, hyperactive and thin with sharp Waspish features and outdoorsy hair—it was just that it was all so sudden and wrong that I didn't have time to let my baser instincts kick in before I pulled her off and sent her on her way. I sort of regretted it too, afterward, as I lay in bed alone and waited for my erection to subside. It had been a profitable visit in any event. I had learned Eddie's whereabouts the night of Jackie's death, I had gotten a motel-quality painting, and I finally knew exactly who that Harrington was whom I had run into at the First Mercantile Bank of the Main Line. He was Caroline's fiancé and knowing that made Caroline even more attractive to me in the deep envious reaches of my petty mind, which meant it took longer for me to relax enough to even try once more to sleep. So I lay in the bed, staring at the ceiling, letting the blood flow back to my brain and trying to sort it all out in my mind, when I heard still another knock on the door.

"Oh, Mr. Carl," said Selma Shaw, Caroline's mother, through the wooden door. "I have something for you."

I bet you do, I thought, as I slipped out of bed and grappled again with my pants. I opened the door a crack and saw her standing there with a covered plate in her hand.

"I noticed you didn't eat much of the dinner," she said, her voice slipping raw and thick out of a throat scarred by too much of something. "I thought you might still be hungry."

I looked at her smile and then at the plate and then back at her smile and realized that I actually was hungry so I let her in. Selma Shaw was a tall, falsely blonde woman, so thin her joints bulged. Her face was as smooth and as stretched as if she were perpetually in one of those G-force centrifuges they use to train astronauts, and her smile was a strange and wondrous thing, a tight, surgically sharp rictus. She stepped to the bureau to put down the plate and noticed the painting there.

"So Kendall's been here already," said Selma, her smile gone.

"She wanted to show me one of her paintings."

"I assume that was not all. I wish Kendall would be more concerned with taking care of her husband than rushing to the third floor to show visiting artists her trashy little pictures. But," she said, her voice suddenly brightening, "enough of that dervish." She spun around almost gaily and smiled once more. "I assumed you were being too polite to eat, worried about the strange surroundings, so I had Consuelo make you up a sandwich."

"Thank you," I said, truly grateful. I hadn't eaten much at dinner, Selma was right about that, but it wasn't out of politeness. We had eaten in the dark, cavernous dining room of Veritas, stared at by stern brown portraits on the walls, the only bit of color the blue-and-white marble of the fireplace that looked to be carved from blue cheese aged too long. The food that Consuelo had served in the dark room had fallen to the far side of vile. A spiky artichoke, a bitter greasy salad, overcooked asparagus, undercooked potatoes, fatty knuckles of mutton with thick stringy veins snapping through the meat like rubber bands. There had been pickles of course, a platter of pickles fresh from the factory, and Dr. Graves, on my right, had advised me that pickles were always served at Veritas. The only light in the dining room had come from candelabras on the table, which, blessedly, were dim enough to make it difficult to see what the muck it was we were eating, but I saw enough to turn my appetite. I tried to look at least interested in the food, pushing it around on my plate, actually swallowing a small spoonful here and there, but when something in the bread pudding crunched between my teeth like a sharp piece of bone I figured I had had enough, spitting my mouthful into my napkin and dropping the napkin over my silver dessert plate in resignation.

"I hope you don't mind me putting you all the way up here on the third floor," said Selma Shaw, "but we weren't expecting so many people to be forced to stay over because of the flood. There are not so many rooms available to visitors anymore. We've closed down the east wing to guests because my husband is a troubled sleeper and he finds it difficult to rest with anybody in close proximity to him during the night. Me included."

"I'm sorry I didn't get to meet him."

"Don't be. I love him dearly, of course, he's my husband, but he can be a very difficult man. Childhood trauma will do that."

"What kind of trauma?" I asked.

"Oh, it's a terribly sad story," said Selma. "Too depressing for a rainy night like this. Do you really want to hear it?"

"Yes, actually."

"Well, make yourself comfortable at least," she said, almost pushing me onto the bed and sitting right beside me. The bed creaked beneath us.

She crossed her legs and put her left arm behind her so that her upper body was turned toward me. She was wearing a clinging black dress that sparkled in the dim light and the sharp points of her breasts gently wiggled at me from beneath the fabric.

"I won't bore you with the details, but in a horrible mistake Kingsley, my husband, shot his father to death on the back patio of this very house on a dark, rainy night much like this one."

Her brown eyes were looking straight into mine, as if in warning. I blinked twice, thinking that what Caroline had successfully avoided talking of during the ride to Veritas her mother had blurted to me with nary an excuse, and then I shifted away from her as politely as I could.

"Needless to say," she continued, "it has scarred my husband terribly. This house used to be so grand a place, I am told, a marvelous place for parties. But that was when Mr. Reddman was still alive. He knew how to run a house. My husband has let the house go. I've done what I could to maintain it but it is so difficult, almost as if it has become what it was always meant to be, as if its essential character is becoming exposed with all the leaks and warped floors and the browning wallpaper. Is it any wonder, then, that I spend much of my time away? Would you spend all your life here if you had a choice, Mr. Carl?"

"No," I said, shifting away from her a little more.

"Of course not, and still they carp. But enough talk of Kendall and my husband's sad past, both subjects are entirely too morbid. Tell me about you and Caroline. She said you are lovers."

"So she did."

"You know of course that she is engaged," said Selma and on the final syllable her right hand, which had been floating in the air as if held high by a marionette's string, dropped lightly onto my knee.

"Yes, I do, Mrs. Shaw," I said, looking at her hand. While her face was stretched taut and young, her hand had the look of a turkey foot about it, bone-thin, covered with hard red wrinkles, tipped by claws. I tried to deftly brush her hand off as if it had fallen there by mistake, but as I performed my gentle brush her fingers tightened on my knee and stayed put.

"Caroline has known Franklin Harrington for years and years," said Selma Shaw, not in any way acknowledging the ongoing battle over my bended knee, "ever since Mother Shaw brought him to this house as a boy. They took to each other so quickly we had always assumed their marriage. Caroline, of course, has dallied and so, I am told, has Franklin in his way, but they will be married despite what any of us would prefer. You should be aware of that as an unalterable fact. Destiny, in this family at least, must always have its way with us. Even love must yield. No one knows better than I."

"Could you move your hand off my knee, Mrs. Shaw?"

"Of course," she said, loosening her grip and sliding her hand up my thigh.

"That's not what I meant," I said, standing up.

Before I could get cleanly away, Caroline's mother goosed me.

"What is going on here?" I said, perhaps too loudly, but I believe my pique was understandable. "Are you all crazy?"

"It's just Caroline," she said, laughing. "She is so prone to exaggeration. Come sit down, Mr. Carl," she said, patting the bed beside her. "I'll be good."

"I'll stand, thank you."

"You must think me a pathetic old witch." She lifted her face to me and paused, waiting for me to inject my protestations. When I didn't say a word she laughed once more. "You do, don't you. Such an honest young man. Caroline always knows how to find them. But before you judge me too harshly, Mr. Carl, consider how noxious I must appear to myself. I wasn't always like this, no, not at all, but the same forces that have rotted out this house have turned me into the wondrous creature you see before you. You're better off without any of us, Mr. Carl."

"I just came for dinner," I said.

"Oh, I know the attraction, heavens yes. Just as Mother Shaw, may she rot in peace, brought Franklin here for Caroline, she brought me here for Kingsley. She had that way about her, of taking destiny by the hand and turning it to do her will. I had no intention of staying. It was a part-time job, to read to her son in the evenings, that was all. He was forty already and had difficulty reading for himself. I was only twenty and still in school, but already I believed I knew what I wanted. You want to know how pathetic I really am, Mr. Carl, know that this was what I wanted, this house, this name, this life, from which now I run to France to escape whenever I am able. The French say that a man who is born to be hanged will never be drowned. I was born to be rich, I always thought, in the deepest of my secret hearts. And see, I was right, but I suppose I was born to drown too." She stood, and without looking at me, walked to the door. "Do yourself a favor, Mr. Carl, leave tomorrow morning as soon as the road clears and don't look back. Leave tomorrow morning and forget all about what you think you want from Caroline."

She closed the door behind her. I stared at it for a moment and then my stomach growled. I stepped to the bureau and whisked off the cover of the plate. It was a sandwich all right, but beneath the stale bun the slices of tongue were so thick I could still see the whole of the muscle lolling between the slabs of teeth in the mouth of its cow, brawny, hairy, working the cud from one side of the mouth to the other. I went to sleep hungry.

4. Allegro con Fuoco

I had thought about keeping the bedside lamp on the whole of the night to discourage any other unwelcome visitors, but I found it hard enough to sleep in the must and damp of that room, with the splat, splat splat, splat of leaking water dropping into the chamberpot and the groans of that ancient house collapsing ever so slowly into itself, so I turned out the light and, while lying in the darkness, I thought about Claudius Reddman, grand progenitor of Reddman Foods. His legacy seemed a dark and bitter one just then, except for the wealth. One daughter dead, another run off, the third widowed by her own son's hand, and all the while Elisha Poole railing drunkenly at his ill fortune before silencing his wails at the end of a rope. Then there was the grandson, Kingsley Shaw, shooting his father on the portico of the house on a rain-swept night. Then there was the ruin that was Selma Shaw, brought to the house by Grandmother Faith to be Kingsley's wife and doomed to become the living embodiment of all her false expectations. And, of course, there was the house itself, reverting to a wild and untamed place filled with decay, like some misanthrope's heart. It was almost enough to have me swear off my desperate search for untold amounts of money. Almost. For I was sure if I was ever to be given the gift of glorious wealth I would do a better job of handling it than the Reddmans. A bright airy house, filled with light, maybe a converted barn with a tennis court, clay because I was never the swiftest, and a pool, and a gardener to mow the acres of lawn and care for the flowers. And there would be parties, and women in white dresses, and a green light beckoning from across the sound.

I lay in the bed and shivered from the damp and thought about it all, not even realizing I was slipping into somebody else's reverie, until I fell, eventually, into a dark, empty sleep. That it was dreamless was merciful, what with all I had been through and learned that night. I slept curled in a ball and stayed like that until I felt the scrape of teeth at the back of my neck.

I sprung awake and spun in the darkness, first this way, then that way, searching desperately for the rat. But it wasn't a rat. I could only make out the outlines of a figure in my bed and I pulled myself away before I heard a throaty laugh and the soft silvery rustle of metal on metal and smelled the sweet smell of vermouth.

"Jesus dammit," I said. "I thought you were passed out."

"I revived," said Caroline, in a glazed voice. "I didn't know you'd be so jumpy."

"What are you doing here?"

"I thought we should maintain our cover with a late-night rendezvous. There are always eyes open in this house."

"We could have let our cover slide, I think. They'll know soon enough, as soon as they talk to your fiancé. You didn't tell me about you and Harrington. Another lie?"

"The love of my life," she said. "And you're right, they will tell him, of course, and he will tell them exactly who you are. I guess the jig is up."

"Are you still drunk?" I asked.

"Maybe."

"You were pounding them down like an Australian frat boy."

"I have a small problem sometimes. My therapist says

I'm a situational alcoholic. It's one of the many things we're working on."

"What situations specifically?"

"Family situations, like tonight."

"I really can't blame you, Caroline. This family of yours is the screwiest I've ever seen. It makes mine look like the Cleavers, and believe me, no one ever confused my mother and father with June and Ward. And besides their general weirdness, it seems each and every one of them has the damnedest desire to have sex with me."

She gave a hearty laugh. "You said you wanted to meet them all, so I arranged it."

"You arranged it?"

"I told them you were a polymorphously perverse sexual addict and hung like a horse."

I let out a burst of embarrassed angst just as I heard the rustle of covers. I felt her palm land on my stomach and rub and then slip south, reaching under my boxers.

"Well maybe I overstated it a bit," she said, "but it is mighty perky for this late at night."

"Cut it out," I said. I reached down to grab her wrist and brushed her breast accidentally, feeling something hard and cold against the back of my hand, something round, metallic. "You're drunk and you're a client. The ethical rules say I can't get involved with a client."

I tried to pull Caroline's hand away but it stayed right where it was. She kissed my nose and cheek and then bit my upper lip. She didn't bite it hard, not at all like Kendall turtle-snapping my ear, she bit it softly, tenderly, teasing it out from between her teeth as she pulled away.

"Am I?" she whispered in my ear.

"Are you what?"

"A client?"

I thought on it, how she took back her retainer and hadn't yet signed the contingency fee contract and how our strange business relationship was not so easily described and as I thought on it she bit my lip, my lower lip this time, bit it the same way and teased it from between her teeth the same way and suddenly I didn't want her hand to leave, just to move, which it did.

"I really don't think this is such a good idea," I said.

"Then don't think."

"Caroline, stop. Don't I have any say in this?"

"Not until I sign your contract," she breathed into my ear. "Until then I'm in control."

She kissed me lightly and then scooted toward me on the bed, slipped close until our bellies rubbed and her grandfather's Distinguished Service Cross dug into my chest. The springs beneath us creaked loudly.

"They'll hear."

"Then be sure to be loud," she said. "I don't want them to miss a single groan."

She kissed me again and dragged her tongue across my gums. I tasted her breath and whatever control had stubbornly remained suddenly shifted out from beneath me and I fell.

"You are going to save me, aren't you?" she said.

It was phrased rhetorically, which was good, because I couldn't have answered just then, still falling as I was, falling. I tasted her breath and it tasted sweet from the vermouth of her Manhattans and fresh, like a warm wind off a meadow, and full of mint.

No, not peppermint. Government.

18

BREAKFAST WAS WAITING in tarnished silver chafing dishes arrayed on a black marble sideboard in the Garden Room. Consuelo had met me at the base of the stairs and asked, without inflection, how my night had been before directing me to the morning's regalement. I had been the last to rise that night and I was evidently the first to rise that morning and I had awakened alone.

The Garden Room was an exotic monstrosity, warm, humid, circular, with a grand Victorian glass dome, the panes of which were sallow and sooty and edged dark with fungus. Huge jungle plants, sporting leaves as big as torsos, stood among weedy stalks topped by tiny face-shaped blooms. Behind the jungle plants stooped pale-barked trees, gnarled and stunted. Meat-red flowers drooped from clumps of green sprouting from the crooks of tree trunks, the flowers' dark mouths yawning in hunger. The place smelled as if fertilizer had been freshly laid in the huge granite pots. I wouldn't have been surprised if General Sternwood had been there to greet me in his wheelchair, but he wasn't, nobody was, except for two black cats locked in a large wrought-iron cage. When I approached, one cooed invitingly while another snarled before hurling itself right at me, slamming its face into the iron bars. I guessed they were playing good cat bad cat.

Sunlight glared through the dirty windows. The storm had passed that night just as Nat had predicted. In my suit

and day-old shirt and socks and underwear I stepped to the
food-laden sideboard. I was ravenous and all too ready to
set to, despite the Garden Room's offal smell. I took a
plate and lifted the silver cover off the first of the warming
trays.

Eggs, runny and wet like snot, with chips of black
mixed in, either chunks of pepper or something else I
didn't want to guess at. In the next were potatoes, wet and
hard, swimming in some sort of green-colored oil. In the
next, French toast slices with the consistency of cardboard
and a reservoir of syrup, slick with the prismatic surface of
motor oil. In the last, white slabs of uncooked fat surrounding shivery pink slivers of trichinosis. I put my plate back
and looked around for something to drink.

I examined six china cups before I found one crack-
free and clean, released a splash of coffee from the urn,
and found my way outside to the rear patio and a perfect
spring morning. The sun was risen, the damp of the night
before was lifting in sheets of fog, the air was filled with
the fresh scent of newly soaked loam. A bird heckled. To
my right, a large stone wing stretched perpendicular to the
rest of the house, its windows covered with white sheets to
keep out the sun. An old ballroom, I figured. A few of the
windowpanes were cracked and it looked as if it hadn't
been balled in decades. As I examined it I took a sip of the
coffee; it spilled into my empty stomach with an acidic
hiss. I looked around and found a rusting white cast-iron
chair and placed my cup and saucer onto its seat. Then I
walked off into the rising fog to explore the grounds.

Behind the house, halfway down the backside of the
hill, was a long rectangular pool, surrounded by what
looked like a swamp. The water in the pool was a dark
algae green and it appeared to be spring-fed because the
water had risen in the storm to flow over the top of the
pool, flooding the ground beside it. There was no cement
or wooden platform around the pool for sunbathing or

relaxing with a tall drink of lemonade, just the swamped grass.

I walked around the pool and headed still farther down, to a small pond almost at the base of the hill. This was the pond, I assumed, where Caroline's grandfather had thrown his Distinguished Service Cross. Why had he ditched it? I wondered. Caroline had offhandedly promised that if I found out she'd sign my fee agreement and I intended to hold her to the promise. The pond was murky, overgrown with weeds and lily pads. As I approached, the ground grew quaggy beneath my shoes and a swarm of gnats flew into my face and hovered. I heard a sucking sound as I lifted my foot and I stopped walking and searched the water for any sign of life beneath its surface. Other than some water boatmen skimming over the top on their long legs, I saw nothing.

I moved around the pond until I reached a tree that had died and fallen into the edge of the water directly opposite the house, and it was by the tree that I noticed, with a small shock, a thousand eyes.

Frogs. The water around the branches of that tree teemed with them, hundreds and hundreds of them. They climbed one atop the other, forming layers of frogs, feet resting on heads, heads beneath bellies, all breathing their dangerous quiet breaths, their eyes open and staring, hundreds and hundreds of them, layers of them, piles of them, a plague of frogs. Slick green, the color lightening about their lower jaws, they were not large frogs, some still had tails and each of their bodies was no bigger than a thumb, but the eyes that stared at me were a malevolent yellow and they climbed one atop the other to get a better look at me, hundreds and hundreds of them, piles of them, slick green silent thumbs with eyes.

Above them, atop the hill, stood Veritas, broad-shouldered and arrogant even in its decrepitude, the mist still rising about it. I had the fanciful notion that each of the frogs was spawned by a sin transgressed by those who had once occupied that house. A thumb on the scale to cheat a customer, a thumb licked as money is counted falsely, a thumb in a competitor's eye, a thumb atop a secretary's breast, a thumb to cap a handshake to seal an agreement to cheat a partner of his fair share, a thumb jerked to the door to fire the sole support of a family of seven, a thumb rubbed gently across the subject's lip at the end game of a seduction, a thumb that cocks the hammer of a shotgun or grasps the last nail to be driven through the lid of a coffin. Which of those frogs, I wondered, was sired by Claudius Reddman's buyout of Elisha Poole before he introduced the pressure-flavored pickle that was to make him a rich and much-honored man? Which of those frogs was fathered by whichever sin it was that caused Caroline's grandfather to toss away his decoration for exceptional gallantry? Which of those frogs was begot by Kingsley Shaw's patricide? Which of those frogs was engendered by the murder of Jacqueline Shaw?

And which of those frogs, I also wondered, sprang to life as a result of my midnight fornication with a situationally drunken Caroline Shaw, youngest heir to the Reddman fortune? I had been fantasizing about screwing her all that night, admittedly, but sexual fantasies are the natural segues between my more practical thoughts, delirium over that secretary or that lawyer or that middle-aged judge wearing whatever she is wearing beneath that hot black robe, no more meaningful than the sluice of chemicals and flash of electricity in the brain that generated the imaginary idyll in the first place. There is no harm in fantasizing, no awkward moments after, no fluids to deal with, no vicious little microbes to wonder incessantly about, no ethical rules to consider. But what had started as a run-of-the-mill fantasy had twisted its way into reality and though I had not actively sought it, I had participated with a canine eagerness that seemed free and vibrant in the darkness of that bed but seemed now like nothing more than a crass exploitation of a young drunken women in a fragile emotional state for purposes of my own pleasure and enrichment. And it hadn't even been any good.

I swung my leg at the pile of frogs and a handful jumped off to the right. I followed them with my gaze as they dived into the water and then lifted my eyes to see, in a secluded grove of trees, the ruin of a house. It was Victorian and gray, not the clean gray of a rehabbed bed and breakfast but the tired gray of weathered wood long neglected. The foundation had shifted and the building sagged with the sad weariness of a tragedy whose story no one remains alive to tell. Some of the windowpanes were shattered, others were boarded with plywood, itself weathered to gray, and the lower part of half the house was charred on the outside by some sort of brushfire. It must have been an old caretaker's cottage, I figured, situated as it was so far down the hill from the main house.

While climbing back up to the main house my attention was drawn to a large bosky grove to the right of the pool. It looked to be untended and its setup completely haphazard but as I approached, I noticed a definite shapeliness about it. While each of the individual plants had a disordered look, the general shape had corners and lines, as if those bushes were once part of a wall of hedges that had long gone untrimmed. The plants were wild vicious things, the leaves spiked, the branches studded with a profusion of pale thorns, some more than an inch long. I walked around the grove until I saw a spot in the wall of green that was less dense than the rest and appeared to have been closed off only by the most recent growth. I looked left and right, spotted no one watching, glanced up at the porch, saw that still it was empty, and reached my hand into the opening. I pulled my hand back again, inspected it, and then stepped right on through.

I found myself on a pathway bright with sunlight and

wildflowers. The grass was high and the pathway was narrow, with thorny branches thrusting like spears across the
gap, but still there was plenty of room for me to walk after
brushing away the errant stalks. I followed the pathway
around a corner until I found an archway of green that led
to another pathway. The flowers were random, full of
lovely yellows and violets and a few lurid reds. Two birds
serenaded one another in the morning light. A cardinal
hopped from one bush to another. It smelled like a different world, all fresh and ecstatically fragrant, full of life, the
very opposite of the must-ridden house or the mucky pond
below.

I knew where I had sneaked myself into, of course.
This was the maze of hedges and flowers that had been
described to me by Grimes, the dentist, in his mournful
soliloquy at the Irish Pub. He had described it as immacu-
lately tended, but it had apparently not been touched in
many many months, not since, I would guess, the death of
Caroline's sweet widowed grandmother, Faith Reddman
Shaw, Grammy, who seemed to have a hand in many of
the goings-on in that house. I followed the maze like a rat
looking for cheese, ducking into almost completely covered entrances, under archways of branches, moving ever
toward the middle, until I stepped, as cautiously as a hea-
then in a church, into the clearing Grimes had described so
vividly.

The sun was brightest here and the plants had seemed
to mutate into wild stalks of color. Flies fell upon my neck.
The statue of Aphrodite was there, on her tiptoes, reaching
up to the heavens, but now it appeared she was being held
down by a thick hairy vine that cloaked the base of the
statue and wrapped itself like an arm around her rear leg.
The bench across from the statue was also covered with a
vine, but this one sported bright orange flowers. Between
the two was an oval covered with high grasses and stalks
of weedy green not yet brought to flower. I stepped around

the oval toward the statue, feeling some dark presence beneath my feet as I walked, and pushed away the hand-sized vine leaves covering the base until I could see the stone in which was deeply engraved the word "SHAW."

I felt something on my foot and jerked it away suddenly, seeing a frog hop into the surrounding bushes. Another frog leaped by. I turned and saw two more come bounding like little flashes of light from the entrance arch and then a boot.

I backed away, almost ducking behind the statue, but before I could hide the boot's owner came into view and smiled at me in an unsettling way from beneath a wide straw hat. "A little sightseeing, Mr. Carl?" cackled Nat.

"I didn't mean to," I stammered, backing away. "I wasn't . . ."

"You're allowed," he said, and his smile warmed to genuine. The spot around his left eye glowed a lurid red. "It's just a garden."

"It's beautiful," I said, trying to recover my breath.

"You should have seen it when it was tended. I spent half of each of my days maintaining it to Mrs. Shaw's specifications. She was a demon for pruning. The elder Mrs. Shaw, I'm talking of now. Not a bloom out of place, not a weed. 'Take off every shoot whose value is doubtful,' she taught me, 'and all you have left is beauty.' It was a masterpiece. Yep. Some magazine wanted to do a spread, but she wouldn't have strangers stomping through it with tripods and cameras."

I looked around at the weeds and the vines pulling at the statue. "Why'd you let it go?"

"This is the way the elder Mrs. Shaw, she wanted it. 'Just let it go when I die, Nat,' she told me." His voice took on a strange power as he imitated hers. "'Let the earth take it back,' she told me. So that's what I've done."

"It seems a shame."

"That it does, yep. Every once in a while I come with

my shears and get the urge to straighten it up, some. To prune. But the elder Mrs. Shaw, she was one who liked her orders carried out to the letter. It was the least I could do for her to honor her wishes. It was her place, you know. She'd been coming here ever since she was a girl. Built it up herself."

"What was she like, Nat?"

"The elder Mrs. Shaw? Quite a woman, she was. Like a mother to me. Brought me here when I was still a boy and made sure I was taken care of ever since, almost like I was one of her own. She's done more for me and mine then you'd ever imagine, Mr. Carl. Can't say as she was the gentlest soul I've ever met." He squatted down and pulled at a long piece of grass, wrapping it about his hand. "Nope, I could never say that. But deep in her heart she wanted to do good. N'aren't too many like that."

He stood and strolled over to the statue and kicked roughly at the base.

"She's laying right there," he said. "In some special urn of hers. Her ashes mixed up with her husband's. I'll tell you one thing, Mr. Carl. She loved him more than she loved anything else on this good earth. That kind of love coming from a woman for a man, she's got to have more than a little good in her."

"How did he die, her husband?" I asked.

Nat's blue eyes looked into mine and he smiled as if he knew that I knew the answer, though how he could I couldn't know. "It was before my time. But I'll say this, the elder Mrs. Shaw, she was probably right to let this place go. Sometimes what's buried should remain buried. No good can come from digging up the dead. Come along, Mr. Carl, I'll show you out. The way it is now, it sometimes gets tricky and you might end up here longer than you'd expect."

He winked at me before turning and starting back. I followed him, through the arched entranceway of the clearing, along passageways, through the narrow opening, thorns grabbing at my suit jacket, until we had returned to the wide lawn. The sun was bright now and there was no mist left. Nat took off his hat and wiped his head with his forearm. "Getting hot. You had best go on up and get your eggs."

I heard something from the patio. Some of the others were there now, Kendall, waving at me energetically, Caroline, in sunglasses, with a drink in her hand. I turned away and looked down the hill, beyond the pond to the wooded area in which sat that old weathered and burned Victorian house. From here I couldn't see any of it, blocked as it was by the foliage, but I could feel it there, listing in its sad way.

"There is a house down there beyond the pond, in those trees," I said. "Who lived there?"

"You did get around, didn't you, Mr. Carl?" said Nat. "Feeling a bit frisky this morning, I suppose." He turned toward the relic. "That was the caretaker's house. Mrs. Shaw's father, he deeded it for the whole of her life to the widow Poole. She lived there with her daughter until the widow Poole, she died. Then it reverted back to the estate."

"What happened to the daughter?"

Nat, still looking down the hill, his back to me, shrugged. "She up and left. Rumor was she died in an asylum New England way. She was supposed to be demented. Caught the pox, or some such fever, and gave up the ghost. The whole family Poole sort of just withered away. I guess that's the way of it. The good Lord's always pruning, trying to get it right at last."

Before I could respond he started walking away from me, down the hill, toward the pond with all those frogs.

"You remember what I said about leaving the buried be, Mr. Carl," he said without turning. "Some patches of this earth are better left unturned."

19

IT WAS A TOUCHING LITTLE SERVICE for Jimmy Vigs at the funeral parlor on North Broad Street. The rabbi spoke of the joy that Jimmy Dubinsky had given to his family and his friends, of the sage advice and prompt service he had given his clients, of his generous spirit in running the charity bingo events at the synagogue. A tall straw of a man with flighty hands stood up and spoke of how Jimmy was always there for him in his times of deepest need, when the fates conspired against him and OTB was closed. He was a giver, said the man, and he gave without complaint, so long as the call was laid in time. Anton Schmidt, a tie beneath his leather jacket, looking almost like a yeshiva student in his wide fedora and evident sadness, talked in soft halting sentences of Jimmy's fairness and kindness and his facility with numbers. And then the son spoke, a young heavy man, just in from the Coast, the spitting image of poor dead Jimmy, talking of how his dad was the greatest dad in the whole wide world, always taking him to the ball game, watching sports with him on television. The son spoke of the joy they had in traveling together, father and son, to Vegas, to watch a Mike Tyson fight, and here the son choked up a bit and grabbed tightly onto the lectern before continuing. His father had taught him how to play craps, he said through a blubber of sobs, how to handicap the horses. He would remember his father, he said, for the rest of his life.

Jimmy would have liked it. And with the over and under at seventy-five and the higher than expected turnout in the chapel, Jimmy would also have liked that the over pulled through. But even with the turnout, when I arrived a little late and went to sign the guest book I wasn't surprised to see it totally devoid of names. I was the only mourner willing to be identified.

The rabbi started reading the Twenty-third Psalm and, right at the part about walking through the valley of the shadow of death, Earl Dante slid into my pew, jamming his hip into mine. With the yarmulke neatly on his head and the white rose pinned to his lapel he could have been mistaken for the owner of the joint. Like I said before, he had that kind of face.

"Glad you could make it, Victor," he said in his slurry voice. "We were counting on you to show."

"Just paying my respects."

"There was a rumor that the feds were tapping Jimmy's phones at the end. Any truth to it?"

"How would I know? I'm just the lawyer."

"Always the last to know, right, Victor?"

"That's right."

He reached into his jacket pocket and pulled out a piece of paper. "I have you down as a pallbearer. When they turn the bier around we need you to go on up and grab a handle."

"I can't believe there aren't six men who were closer to Jimmy than me."

"There are," said Dante, leaning forward in preparation to stand. "But it will take more than six to carry Jimmy off to his final reward. There's a limo for the pallbearers that will ferry you to the cemetery. They'll need you there too."

"I wasn't planning to go to the cemetery," I said.

He looked at me and sucked his teeth. "Take the limo."

When it was time to wheel the coffin out, there were

ten of us jockeying for position at the handles. From the other side of the coffin I caught Cressi grinning at me. "Yo, Vic," he mouthed, bobbing his head up and down. Anton Schmidt was also there, red-eyed beneath his thick glasses. Then, with the rabbi silent and the mourners standing, we walked beside the coffin on its journey out of the chapel. At the side door, with the hearse waiting, its back door swung wide, we all tightened our grip on the handles and heaved. The coffin didn't budge.

"Put your backs into it," said the guy from the funeral home. "Ready, one, two, and three."

We were able, with much grimacing, to lift the coffin and, each of us taking tiny steps, carry it, amid groans and curses, to the hearse, where it slid through on rollers to the rear of the cold black car.

Our limo was long and gray and just as cold as the hearse, though we didn't have as much room to stretch out as did Jimmy. I sat shotgun, with the window to the back open so I could hear the conversations of the other men jammed shoulder to shoulder inside the rear benches.

"That was a very moving service," said one of the men in the back.

"I thought the son was touching, just touching," said a second. "When he talked about Tyson it almost brought tears."

"If you see a McDonald's or something," said a third man to the driver, "why don't you pull over. I could use a little lunch."

"What kind of slob are you, Nicky, we're burying a man here."

"He'd a understood."

"We can do drive-through," said a different man.

"I have to follow the hearse," said the driver.

"So tell the hearse to go too. Get an extra value meal for Jimmy. Like a gesture of respect, you know. One last stop at them golden arches."

"Too many stops at the golden arches," said Anton Schmidt softly, "that's why he's dead."

"What, he got wacked at a McDonald's?"

We drove up Broad Street to the Roosevelt Extension of Route 1 and then hit the Schuylkill Expressway, west, to get us to the cemetery. Buzzing past us were a horde of speeding cars and vans, swiping by each other as they changed lanes with a frenzy. I turned around and over the heads of the pallbearers I saw the long procession of cars, their headlights lit, following us slowly, and I imagined them all lined up at the McDonald's drive-through, each putting in its order for fries and Big Macs.

"Maybe there's a party or something after," said Cressi. "Hey, Victor, your people, they throw wakes after they bury their dead?"

"We sit *shivah*," I said. "That's where we visit the families and say *Kaddish* each evening."

"*Kaddish*, all right," said Cressi. "I used to date a Jewish broad. You're talking booze, right?"

"That's *Kiddush*, which is different," I explained. "*Kaddish* is the prayer for the dead."

"I thought I'd see Calvi at the ceremony," said someone else.

"Probably has gotten too fat to leave the pool down there."

"Last I heard, the fuck had prickly heat."

"You dated a Jewish girl, Cressi? Who?"

"That Sylvia, what lived in the neighborhood, remember her?"

"Stuck up, with the hats and the tits?"

"That's the one."

"You dated her?"

"Sure."

"How far you get?"

"You think I dated her for the conversation? I want conversation I'll turn on the television."

"Why'd she go out with a bum like you?"

"What do you think, hey? I got charm."

"You got crabs is all you got."

"You ever tell your mother you were dating some Jewish girl?"

"What are you, a douchebag?" said Cressi. "My mother would have fried my balls for supper I'd had told her that."

"With a little garlic, some gravy and mozzarella, they'd probably taste all right."

"Yeah but such small portions."

General laughter.

"Hey, Victor, about this shiver?" said Cressi.

"*Shivah.*"

"They have food?"

"Usually."

"Well then, after the burial, I say we do some shivering."

"But if you pass a McDonald's before that . . ."

At the cemetery, we strained our backs lugging the heavy metal coffin from a hearse to the cart and then pushing it over the uneven turf to the hole in the ground. As we shoved our way into places around the hole, like a crowd at a street show, a man from the funeral parlor handed out yarmulkes and little cards with prayers and then the rabbi began. The rabbi spoke a little about one-way journeys and the son sobbed and the rabbi spoke some more about ashes and dust and they lowered the casket into the hole with thick gray straps and the son sobbed and then a few of us who pretended to know what we were doing said *Kaddish* for James Dubinsky. I read the transliteration of the Hebrew on the little cards they handed out so I don't know if my words counted, but as I read *yis-gad-dal v'yis-kad-dash sh'meh rab-bo*, as I struggled through the faintly familiar pronunciation, I thought of my grandfathers, whom I had helped bury, and my grandmothers, whom I had helped bury, and my father, who was coughing out the blood in his lungs as he got ever closer to that hole in the ground, and I hoped with a strange fervor that my words were doing some good after all.

The rabbi tossed a shovelful of dirt onto the wide wooden lid of the coffin, some pebbles bouncing, and then the son, and then the rest of us, one by one, tossing shovelfuls of dirt, one by one, and afterward we walked slowly, one by one, back to the road where our cars waited for us.

"It's a sad day, Victor." A thick, nasal voice coming from right next to me. "Jimmy, he was a hell of a guy. Hell of a guy."

"Hello, Lenny," I said. "Yes, Jimmy was something."

The nasal voice belonged to Lenny Abromowitz, a tall barrel-chested man of about sixty, with plaid pants and the nose of a boxer who led with his face. He had been a prizefighter in his past, and a professional bruiser, so I'm told, who did whatever was required with that brawn of his, but now he was only a driver. He wore a lime-green jacket and white patent leather shoes and, in deference to the somber occasion, his porkpie hat was black. And as he walked beside me he draped one of his thick arms over my shoulder.

"Haven't seen much of yas, Victor. You don't come to the restaurant no more?"

"I've been really busy."

"Ever since the *Daily News* put those pictures on the front page, people they don't come around so much as before."

"Oh, were there pictures?" Of course there were pictures. The *Daily News* had rented a room across the street from Tosca's and stationed a photographer there to capture exactly who was going in and going out of the notorious mob hangout, plastering the pictures on a series of front pages. Politicians and movie stars and sports heroes and famous disc jockeys were captured in crisp blacks and whites paying court to the boss. Each morning everyone in

the city wondered who would be the next cover boy and
each evening the television news broadcasts started with
pointed denials of any wrongdoing by that day's featured
face. The only ones who weren't impressed were the feds,
who had rented the room next to the *Daily News*'s room
and were busy taking pictures of their own. As would be
expected, since the front-page series, Tosca's business had
been cut precipitously.

"Yeah, sure there was pictures. Front page. Surprised
you missed it."

"I read the *Inquirer*."

"Hey, Victor, let me give you a ride back to the city."

"That's okay," I said. "I'll go back with the limo."

"Take a ride with me, Victor."

"No really, it's taken care of."

His hand slid across my shoulder onto my neck and
squeezed, lightly sure, but still hard enough for me to
know how hard he could squeeze if ever he wanted, and
with his other hand he reached over and gave my head a
few light knocks with his knuckle.

"Hello, anybody home? Are you listening? I think
maybe you should come and take a ride with me, Victor.
I'm parked over there."

We crossed the road with the hearse and the limousine
and the other cars and kept going, across a field of tomb-
stones with Jewish stars and menorahs and torah scrolls
carved into the stone, with names like Cantor and Shure
and Goodrich and Kimmelman, until we reached another
road, where, down a ways, was parked a long white
Cadillac.

We approached the passenger side and Lenny opened
the rear door for me. "Hop on in, Victor."

I gave him a tight smile and then ducked into the car. It
must have slipped my mind for a moment, what with all
the wiseguys at the funeral and the sadness of the pebbles
scudding across the top of the coffin and the words of the

Kaddish still echoing, but Lenny was not just any driver, and his invitation of a ride was less an invitation than a summons. When I entered the cool darkness of the car's interior my eyes took a second to dilate open and I smelled him before I saw him. The atmosphere of the car was rich with his scent: the spice of cologne, the creamy sweetness of Brylcreem, the acrid saltpeter tang of brutal power waiting to be exercised.

Slowly, the car drove off along the cemetery road.

20

"I THOUGHT IT BEST IF I PAID my respects from a distance," said Enrico Raffaello, sitting next to me on the black bench seat in the rear of his Cadillac. He was a short, neat man in a black suit and flowered tie. His hair was gray and greased back, his face cratered like a demented moon. His voice was softly accented with a Sicilian rhythm and a genuine sadness that seemed to arise not from the surface mourning of a funeral but from a deep understanding of the merciless progression of life. Between his knees was a cane tipped with a silver cast of a leopard, and his thick hands rested easily atop the crouching cat. "Jimmy was a loyal friend and I didn't want to ruin his day."

"I think that was wise," I said.

"Did you like the service?"

"It was touching. The son especially."

"Yes, so I've heard. I arranged for it to happen like that."

"Flying him in from L.A. was very generous."

"That is not quite how I arranged it. You see, Jimmy was not a diligent family man. He hadn't seen his son in years and the son refused to come after what Jimmy had done to his mother. Jimmy was wrong in how he handled his wife, granted, but that was no reason for a son to show such disrespect for his father."

"So how did you get him here?"

"I didn't. Such rifts can be wide and deep and I am not a psychologist. I hired an actor instead."

"That was an actor?"

"I told him I wanted some emotion. This actor, he said that crying was extra. I could have wrung his fat neck, but I am a sentimentalist, so I paid."

"I never knew you were such a soft touch."

"I'm getting too old, I think. It is one thing when my colleagues die, that is the natural order of things. But when the new generation start dying from natural causes and I'm still around, there's nothing but a weary sadness. Maybe they are right. Maybe it is time to loosen my grip on the trophy."

He sighed, a great sad sigh, and turned away from me to look out the window. We were just heading out the gates of the cemetery, turning into traffic. Lenny was breathing through his mouth as he drove. Though it had become a warm sunny day outside, with the darkened windows and the cool of the air conditioning it felt like fall.

"Have you found out anything from Pietro?" he asked still looking away.

"I wish you would let someone else do this."

"Tell me what you know," he snapped.

"Cressi wasn't working alone," I said. "He had to check the details of the arrangement with someone else before agreeing to the purchase of the guns. I've made some inquiries to area Mercedes dealers, no one reported stolen cars. I also talked with the ATF about the group to whom Peter says he was going to sell the guns. White supremacists, skinheads. Those brothers who butchered their parents up in Allentown were members. ATF has been watching them for years and says they do buy guns, but not in quantity. They're too strapped for cash to even mail their newsletters out. I don't believe he was going to resell them."

"Then what were they for?"

"I don't know yet."

He sighed again and lifted a hand so he could examine

his fingernails. "I believe I can trust you, Victor, and that is good. You are my scout. Like in the old cavalry movies, every general needs a scout to find the savages."

"I hope I'm not the only one."

"I'm being betrayed from within. I'm ready to step down, to retire to New Jersey and paint flowers, like Churchill, but I won't be pushed out by a Judas."

"Who do you think it is?"

Raffaello shrugged, his shoulder rising and falling as gently as a breath.

"Dante wanted me to report directly to him," I said. "That is not our arrangement."

"He is overeager perhaps, but a good man."

"How did he rise so fast?"

"He is the eye in back of my head."

"Maybe he needs glasses."

"Do you have any reason to doubt him?"

"No, but I don't trust him. What happened to Calvi? I thought I could trust Calvi."

"We had a disagreement."

"Over what?"

"What do you think this is about, Victor, the cars, the secrets, the deals, the threats? It's all about money, rivers of money. We drive around in our Cadillacs and people give us money. When they don't, we get a little rough and then they do. I keep the peace because that way we make more money. I distribute what we get fairly so everyone will stay in line and we'll make even more money. It's fun, sure, and we eat well, but we're not in it for the pasta or the fun, we're in it for the money. Now the animals who are against us, they want more than their share and to get it they'll do whatever they need to, commit whatever crime they have to. It would be no different if we were selling cars, or canned goods, or cannoli, we'd still have the same fight. Just the tactics would be different and there would be more survivors. They want me gone so they can control the city and decide who gets what and once they control the city they're going to milk it dry. And then it will grow too ugly to even imagine."

We were on the Schuylkill Expressway again, going east, toward the city. We were in the center lane and all about us cars were surging and changing lanes and halting abruptly as another car got too close. Lenny was driving remarkably steady, never rising above fifty-five, acting as if we were being followed by a cop car at all times, which we very well might have been. A red convertible pulled even with us to the right, the driver's blond hair flying behind her like a dashing scarf, before she rammed her way ahead.

"What about Calvi?" I asked.

"Calvi became unreliable. He hated everybody, trusted no one, and everyone hated him back. He had risen beyond his abilities and he knew it, but he wouldn't step down. And then we discovered he was taking more than his share, so I was forced to step him down."

"How did you find out?"

"Like I said, I have an eye in the back of my head."

"Have you ever wondered why if you got rid of Calvi you still have trouble? Have you thought maybe that Calvi wasn't the problem? That maybe it's that damn eye in the back of your head that is the problem?"

"Be my scout, Victor. Find out who is behind Pietro and I'll call in the cavalry to take care of the betrayer."

"And then I'm out. Completely. No one so much as even walks in my door or calls my number."

An old white van, its side rusted out with holes, slid up on the left of us, passing the Cadillac, before slowing down again. The van fell back behind us as a station wagon slowed in the left lane before cutting sharply in front of our car and then in front of a bus before exiting.

"That's the deal, yes," said Raffaello. "But before that can happen you must find out what I need to know. I try to govern with reason, Victor. I'm a peaceable man at heart. But I know for certain when reason battles strength it is strength that will win. You tell me who the traitor is and I will show you strength. Tell me who the traitor is and I will cut out his tongue and mail it to his wife."

Outside, on our left, the white van again pulled up to our side and this time from one of the rusted holes stuck a black metal tube. There was a puff of smoke and a fierce whine and the window next to Enrico Raffaello's face suddenly sprouted crystal blooms of glass.

21

THE CRY OF METAL being torn apart. A shriek of brakes. A shout. The white van shooting ahead of us and then coming back as if on a string. A twist of the wheel. A force slamming me into the door and then down off the seat. The scream of twisting steel. A shout. A shattering of glass. A splash of cool crystals on my neck. A shout. A hand in my face and a voice telling me to shut up. An explosion beneath us and a wild series of bumps. A jerk forward. The shriek of breaks. The grind of the engine and a force pushing me further into the floor. A shout. A shout.

"Shut up already, Victor," said Raffaello. "Just please shut up."

"What? What?"

"Just shut up and calm down. We're getting off the highway."

A loud acceleration. A flash of a green hillside and then a jerk upward and to the right.

"Superb, Lenny. Absolutely superb. Did you see anything?"

"The window was blacked," said Lenny with an utter calm. "Couldn't see a thing, Mr. Raffaello."

"That's fine. We'll find out soon enough. You were superb."

"I slammed the hell out of them," said Lenny, "but I couldn't see who they was."

"What? What happened?"

"What do you think happened?" said Raffaello. "The bastards they tried to whack me. You can sit up if you want. They've gone past."

I sat up cautiously. The rear windows were all cracked and pitted with holes. Through the cracks I could see we were speeding off the highway, not bothering to stop at the stop sign before swerving violently to the left and onto a city street. The ride was terribly rough, even for a Philadelphia street, so I figured a tire must have blown. Lenny was searching the rearview mirror as he sped along. The car door on Raffaello's side was fluffed with spurts of coffee-colored foam.

"We need to let Victor off now, Lenny."

"Yes sir, Mr. Raffaello. I'll slow us down under the bridge."

"I don't want to get out."

"It has started, Victor. It doesn't do either of us any good for you to be with me right now, you understand? When Lenny slows you will jump out of the car."

"But no. No. I can't."

The Cadillac eased slower just a bit and edged to the side as it slipped under a cement bridge.

Raffaello leaned over to open my door. As he leaned I saw him wince. The left side of his suit was wet with blood.

"You've been hit. You're bleeding."

"Get ready to fall," he said as he clicked down the lever.

"I can't do this. They're probably following us. They'll run right over me."

"Then be sure to roll," he said as the door yawned and I saw a primitive mural of cars in traffic pass and beneath that the rush of black asphalt.

"Wait!"

"We'll be in touch," said Enrico Raffaello before he shoved me out of the car.

A sledgehammer bashed into my shoulder, a pile of rocks fell all at once along my side, claws scraped at my face as my head was pummeled. A line of pain edged into my back and then I was up, over the curb, lying splayed on a narrow cement walkway just beyond the cover of the cement bridge. I picked my head up as a set of tires sped inches from my left hand, which lay in the street, pale and still like a dead fish.

I pulled it back and scooted to my knees and tried to figure out where I was. It all looked vaguely familiar. The stone tunnel to my left, the traffic lights, the banners on the poles. A ludicrous bouquet of balloons. Wait a second, balloons and banners? Over there, by that parking lot, gingerbread kiosks and barred entranceways and a great green statue of a lion pride at rest. Suddenly I knew. Lenny had pulled off the expressway at the Girard Street exit and left me just outside the front entrance to the Philadelphia Zoo.

When I figured out where I was I also realized that the murderous white van must also have known the Cadillac's escape route. It would give chase, along with any other vehicles that were tagging along to finish the job. No doubt they'd come right up this road, looking for whatever they could to kill off and what they'd find, if I stayed there, on my knees, like a scared penitent, would be me.

I stood and did a quick inspection. My jacket was ripped at the shoulder and blood was leaking through the white of my shirt. I wiped thin lines of blood from the scratches on the left side of my face. The right knee of my pants was slashed and through the opening I could see jagged gashes from which bright red oozed. Move, I told myself. Where? Anywhere, you fool, just move.

I cantered past the balloon guy and across a narrow road that encircled the zoo and then, with a stiff side step, I passed the lion statue and headed for the open gate between the kiosks.

"That will be eight-fifty," said the young woman in the

ticket window after she eyed my tattered jacket and the blood that had seeped through the shoulder of my shirt. She had a wide mole on her cheek that creased when she smiled. "But if you want to buy a membership now, you can apply today's admission charge to the forty-dollar total."

"I don't think so."

"It's a tremendous deal. You get free parking anytime you come and free admission all year long. If you just want to fill out this form."

"Really, no thank you," I said, handing her a twenty. As she counted out my change I looked behind me. Nothing suspicious, nothing at all, until I spotted the nose of a long black Lincoln sniff its way slowly down the same road Lenny had taken the Cadillac. I rushed through the gate and into the zoological gardens before the woman could give me back my change.

I galloped across the wide stone plaza with the fountain in the grand iron gazebo, past the statue of the elephants, into the rare animal house, a long semicircular corridor flanked by cages. Fruit bats, to my right, scurried across their caged ceiling like a puppy motorcycle gang in black leather. Naked mole rats, pale pink and toothsome, huddled together in a warren of tunnels to my left. I glanced quickly behind me as I walked through the interior. Owl-faced guenons, marmosets, colobus monkeys with fancy black-and-white furs. It was mostly empty of viewers, the rare animal house at that time of the day, a few kids in strollers with their mothers. I stopped for a second to listen. The screech of a monkey, the rustle of the bats. The place smelled of dung and the musk of simian sweat. Two tobacco-colored tree kangaroos humped on a branch high in their cage. I was about to start moving again when I heard a door swing open and the tap of running feet.

I couldn't see who was coming because of the curve of the wide corridor, but I knew enough not to want them to see me. There was an exit to the left marked EMPLOYEES ONLY and I darted to it, but the handle wouldn't turn, as if the door knew exactly who I wasn't. I looked back down the corridor, still saw nothing, and started running, past the mongoose lemurs from Madagascar, running to the far door, the sound of the footsteps gaining. Just as I hit the first of the double doors a herd of schoolchildren stampeded in, followed by their teachers. They pushed me back, drowning out the sound of the following steps with their excited baying. I found myself unable to wade through the waist-high gaggle and as the kids streamed by, I stopped and turned to face whatever fate it was that was chasing me.

The woman from the ticket window.

"Sir," she said, her mole creasing with a smile, holding up two bills in her fist. "You forgot your change."

I forced myself to take a deep breath. Even as I trembled, I stretched my lips into a smile. "Thank you," I said softly, "that was very kind."

"Here you go."

In her outstretched hand was a ten, a one, and two quarters. I took the one and the quarters and said, "Thank you, you can keep the rest."

"I can't do that sir. Really, I can't."

"Think of it as a tip," I said, "for restoring my faith in human nature."

She blushed and her mole creased considerably and she tried to protest but I raised a hand.

"Thanks a lot," she said. "Really, that's great," and finally she spun around to leave. Then I, with my faith in human nature restored, stepped slowly from the building, searching about me all the while for the men who were trying to kill me.

There was nothing suspicious on the wide brick walkways. Huge Galápagos turtles, safe in their shells, stared passively as I hurried by. Emus strutted and hippos wallowed and a black-and-white tapir lumbered about, looking suspiciously like a girl I used to date. At the rhino pen I leaned on the fence and watched a mother rhino and her calf. I was jealous of their great slabs of body armor. A girl in a purple dress stood on the tips of her Mary Janes and slipped her golden elephant key into the story box. A voice poured out.

Throughout Africa and Asia the rhinoceros is being hunted almost to extinction. For centuries certain cultures have believed the rhinoceros horn, blood, and urine possess magical and medicinal power.

While leaning on the bars and listening to the lecture, I slyly looked back along the path. As I did I spotted a figure at the top of a rise and my breath stopped. A beefy man in a maroon suit, looking around with a fierce concentration.

Scientists estimate there are only fourteen hundred greater one-horned Asian rhinos remaining in India and Nepal.

I didn't know him, and I wouldn't have recognized him except for the suit. Maroon suits are rare enough, but that shade was simply radiant in its repulsiveness, and not easily forgotten. I had seen it just that morning, at Jimmy Vig's funeral. Its owner was one of the downtown boys for sure and not, I was sure, here to commune with nature. I froze and let my breath return in tiny spurts.

To help preserve this endangered species the Philadelphia Zoo cooperates with other zoos in a program called a species survival plan.

I waited, watching the man in maroon from the corner of my eye, and when he turned around to wave at something behind him I ran for the nearest building and rushed inside the doors.

I was in a wide, modern corridor, with huge plate glass windows fronting scenes of natural glory. Massive tortoises stared; a gray anaconda slept. A monitor, half submerged in a jungle pool, observed me with carnivorous eyes. At the end of the wide hallway were two huge windows with the superstars of the Reptile House, the alligator, squat and fierce, and the crocodile, pale and patient and hungry. Where the corridor made a sharp turn to the left I stepped away from the great predators so that while I was hidden, a view of the doors I had come in was reflected for me in the alligator's window. Just be calm, I tried to tell myself, wait patiently and let him pass the building by as he searches the rest of the zoo. Better waiting and hiding then darting around the zoo's maze of walkways like a zebra on the loose. Slow and patient, like my friend the crocodile, I told myself, while the bruiser lumbered past and disappeared. I evened out my breathing and the lump in my throat had almost dissolved when off the windowed front of the alligator's cage I saw the door open and a flash of maroon.

I backed away until I hit a large wooden cube in the middle of the corridor. I slipped around it into the desert alcove. The windows here were smaller, like terrariums studded into the wall. Rattlesnakes, coachwhips, skinks, lots of skinks. I passed the Gila monster and then, using the wooden cube as a shield, I made my way into the older section of the building, toward a second set of doors. The atmosphere turned slippery and green. I backed my way to the far exit, past ropy snakes and tiny poisonous dart frogs and a North American bullfrog, staring at me with passive eyes that seemed to discount my fear. Your legs look mighty tasty, you bastard, I thought as the bullfrog sat comfortably on a synthetic log and watched me sweat. With the wooden cube still acting as a screen, I turned and made fast for the far doors, trotting then running then sprinting, sprinting too fast to stop when the doors opened and a figure, blackened by the light streaming in from behind, stepped through.

I ran right into it, bounced off as if hitting a wall, sprawled backwards onto the floor. The figure took one step toward me. When I recognized Peter Cressi looking down at me I quailed.

"Yo, Vic," he said. "How's it hanging?"

Behind me I heard steps.

"Geez, what happened wit' you?" said Cressi as he eyed my tattered condition. "You crawl into one of the cages? Did some gorilla take a shine to you?"

I staggered up and immediately felt a hand fall onto my shoulder. I spun around. The beefy boy in maroon was grinning at me. He was missing a tooth. "Dante said we'd find someone here and he was right."

I spun around again and stared at Cressi.

"Quite a thing what happened with that van," said Cressi. "Quite a thing. To think such a thing like that could happen in this day and age."

I tilted my head in thought while still staring at Cressi. "How'd you find out about the attack, Peter?"

"Dante, he told us and sent us on over."

"And how'd he find out about it?" I asked.

"How do you think?"

"You tell me, Peter, dammit."

My anger and fear all balled together and went directly to the muscles in my arms and in a tremendous shot of energy I slammed my hands into his chest, pushing him back against the doors.

"How'd he know, Peter?" I said. "Tell me that, you bastard."

Again I pushed him back, this time so hard he hit his head on the glass.

"How'd he know unless he set it up? And you set it up with him. You bastard. Why the hell are you trying to kill me?"

I meant to slam him again but before I could two arms slithered fast as cobras around my shoulders and behind my neck and suddenly I was lifted off the ground.

"You bastard!" I shouted.

"Whoa, Vic," said Cressi, giving me a strange look. "You're going ballistic on us. Quiet yourself down or Andy Bandy here is going to have to quiet you for me. We don't want no scenes in such a public place."

Still struggling while held aloft, I said, "How'd you find out?"

Cressi gave me a look and then reached into his jacket and I stopped kicking as I waited for what I knew was coming. But what he pulled out of his jacket was a cellular phone.

"Lenny called Dante from the cell phone in the car once they dumped you. Dante sent me over to check out you was okay. We was only trying to take care of you is all."

With that, Andy Bandy loosed the iron snakes around my shoulders and neck. Once again I dropped in a sprawl onto the ground.

"Pull yourself together, Vic," said Cressi. "I'm not used to seeing you squirm like a slug such as you're doing here. It's enough to get me thinking, you know. It's not a good thing to get me thinking, pal. It ruins my whole day."

He reached into his pants pocket and jiggled what was in there for a moment before pulling out a small peppermint swirl wrapped in cellophane. He lifted his hand and with a quick squeeze he squirted the candy into his mouth before tossing the wrapper to the side.

"I can understand you being all shook up and all, but I hate to see you down there afraid of me." The peppermint candy clicked in his teeth as he spoke. "What do you think I am, an idiot? You're my lawyer. What kind of idiot would hurt his own lawyer?"

He leaned over me, but I found myself unable to look him in the face. Instead I was staring at something else, something I couldn't yet understand the significance of, cringing and sniveling on the floor as I was, numb with fear of the two men standing over me. I couldn't yet understand the significance but still I couldn't stop staring, as if somewhere within me I knew the truth, that what I was staring at from the floor of the Philadelphia Zoo's reptile house was the first loose thread in the eventual unraveling of the darkest secrets of the Reddman demise.

22

CRESSI AND ANDY BANDY drove me home and waited for me to enter the vestibule before they drove away, waited as if I were a schoolboy dropped off in the middle of the dark. "You want I should stay around some and keep an eye out for you, Vic?" had asked Peter from the front seat of the Lincoln. "No," I had answered. The problem with Peter guarding my back was that I would have had to turn it to him and I didn't trust him far enough for that. So I went into my apartment alone and stripped off my ragged suit and took a shower and put on a new white shirt and a relatively fresh suit and tightened my tie and looked at myself in the mirror. Then I loosened the tie and took off the suit and took off the shirt and the shoes and the socks and went to bed. It was now early afternoon and there was much work to be done at the office but still I went to bed.

I get this way, I guess, after I stare death in the face and she laughs at me. The fierce whine that had slid by my head in that car was death's chortle, there was no doubt about that, and I had all but accepted her embrace when Andy Bandy held me aloft and Cressi reached into his jacket for what I was certain was a gun. But then death had slipped away for the moment, satiated, so it would seem, by the acrid scent of fear secreted by my endocrine system, satisfied with having reminded me once again of exactly what I truly was. I know people who look at the stars and say the night sky makes them feel insignificant, but I don't believe them when they say it. When I look at the stars I don't shrink but grow, filled with the perverse certainty that the whole of the universe has been put here solely for my amusement and enlightenment. But face to face with the grinning mask of death I know the truth. I am a randomly formed strand of DNA no more significant than random strands of DNA that define the leaf of grass upon which I tread or the cow whose charred muscle I gnaw. I eat Chinese food and crap corn and sweat through my socks and stink and the same DNA that gave me this nose and this chin and my ten fingers and ten toes has also sentenced me to oblivion. It directs my arteries to clog themselves with calcified fat, it directs my liver to wither, my kidneys to weaken, my lungs to spew bits of itself with every cough. And in the face of this utter randomness and planned obsolescence I can't even imagine mustering enough energy to get out of bed and to walk the streets, to dry clean my suits, to return my library books, to vote for judges whose names I can't pronounce, to act my part as if any of it really matters.

So for the whole of that afternoon I lay with my head beneath the covers, shivering, though I wasn't cold, smelling the dried sweat of the fifty nights it had been since I last had laundered my sheets, trying and failing to come up with a reason to get out of bed. As if the smell of fifty nights of my dried sweat was not reason enough. Trying and failing until the phone rang.

Should I answer it? Why? Who could it possibly be that would matter at all? The answer was that it could be no one. I let it ring almost long enough for my machine to answer it, but maybe four hours of smelling old sweat was enough, because I peeked my head out of the covers, picked up the phone, and, with a little high-pitched squeak of a voice, said into the receiver, "Yes?"

"Did you hear what happened on the Schuylkill Expressway today?" said Beth in a gush. "A van with a hole bored into its side slid up to Raffaello's Cadillac and shot it all to hell. It's all over the news. Somehow the Cadillac got away. Raffaello is recuperating in some unnamed hospital, they won't say, but can you imagine? Everyone's talking about it. On the Schuylkill Expressway. Everyone wants to know who was driving the Cadillac. Apparently it got away even with one of its tires blown to pieces. The driver's an absolute hero. I want him driving for me. Amazing. I think, Victor, it's time to find ourselves another class of clientele, don't you? Where have you been anyway?"

"I'm feeling a little under the cosmic weather, so to speak," I said. Beth didn't need to know I was part of it all. No one needed to know, no one ever needed to know, which was exactly why Raffaello had pushed me from the careening Cadillac.

"Are you all right?" said Beth. "Is there anything I can do?"

"No. Did they say on the news who did the shooting?"

"They have no idea. Just that there is apparently an internal dispute of some sort. The authorities are all mystified. You sound terrible. Do you need some soup or anything? Have you eaten?"

I had to think about that for a moment. It had been a day and a half, really. I had a quick lunch yesterday afternoon, but then there had been the repulsive offerings at Veritas and I hadn't had time for an edible breakfast before Jimmy Dubinsky's funeral. I wondered if my deep existential soul searching was less a result of my brush with the grinning mask of death than mere sugar depletion. Maybe there did exist a surefire solution to all our deep metaphysical dilemmas—a Snickers bar. "No," I said. "Not for a while."

"Let's do dinner."

"You sound obscenely cheery."

"I've been going to that place in Mount Airy you

wanted me to look into. The Church of the New Life. We should talk about it."

"Anything interesting?"

"Interesting as hell," she said.

We met at a restaurant on a deserted corner in Olde City. Beth had suggested a retro diner off Rittenhouse Square but all I could think of was its wide plate glass windows. I didn't want to be behind wide plate glass windows just then, so I suggested this place well off the beaten track, and on the other side of the city from my apartment, and she had agreed. Café Fermi was a pretentious little restaurant with a pickup bar and bad art and an ingenious menu one step above the chef's ability to deliver. I took a cab to the funeral parlor and picked up my car and still got there ahead of her. I ordered a Sea Breeze and drank it quickly to give myself a brave front. I went through a basket of bread while waiting. Beth arrived with a strangely serene smile on her face. A guy on his way out bumped her slightly and she just turned that smile on him.

She sat down and looked at me closely and put a hand on my cheek. "What happened to your face?"

"I cut myself shaving."

She squinted. "That must have been some blade. How was James's funeral?"

"Touching."

"They said Raffaello was coming back from the cemetery when they shot up his car."

"Oh yeah? I didn't see him there. You hungry? Let's order something. How does the veal look?"

She rubbed her thumb along the cuts on my cheek. "They didn't say exactly who was in the car with him."

I just shrugged and was surprised to feel tears well behind my eyes. I was about to lose it, but I didn't. I held it in and looked away. I blinked twice and twice more. I raised my hand for the waitress and by the time she came it was all back inside where it belonged and I was once again as dry-eyed as a corpse.

Our waitress was a tall leggy woman, wearing all black, with heavy earrings and some demented metal *objet d'art* on her blouse to make it clear how *au courant* she was and we weren't. "Yeah?" she said, and I didn't like the way she said it, like we were disturbing her evening.

"We're ready to order."

"Sure," she said, "I'll be right back," and then she shuffled off to serve someone more important.

"Is it just me," I said, "or was she rude?"

"She has a tough job," said Beth, which was very unlike her. Beth had the marvelous ability to take umbrage at even the mildest slights in our slighting culture. It derived directly, I think, from her natural optimism. She was a generous tipper, generally, but when a waiter was rude or a bartender nasty it was fun to sit back and watch the sparks fly. She was not the type to say, "She has a tough job," not the type at all.

"What are you," I asked, "in love?"

"No," she laughed.

"All right. Tell me about the kooks in Mount Airy."

"They're not kooks," she said quickly and quietly.

"Aaah," I said slowly. "I begin to see."

"Begin to see what?"

"Tell me about Mount Airy."

Her head tilted as she stared at me and I could see something working its way in her eyes and I flinched from the expected tongue lashing but then that strange smile arose and all was once again serene.

"Well they're not a cult, or anything like that," she said, fiddling with her silverware. "They're just a lot of nice people trying to find some answers. They believe that the voices of the spirit and of the soul are always there to tell us the secret truths of our existence, but we need to learn how to hear them. We need to somehow cut through the murk of our omnipresent reality and learn to listen and see in a spiritual way. The purpose of the Haven is to teach us how."

"Okay," said the waitress with a roll of her eyes. She had slinked upon us as silently as a predatory cat. "You said you were ready."

"We've been ready," I said. "I'll have the Caesar salad and the veal in the apple cream sauce. Is the veal any good?"

"I haven't gotten any complaints," said the waitress.

"A ringing endorsement. And another Sea Breeze."

"I'll just have the bean chili," said Beth.

"They have that Texas ribeye I thought you'd like," I suggested.

Beth made a face, an I-don't-eat-red-meat kind of face. I had seen that face on many women before but never before on Beth.

"Aaah," I said slowly once again. "I do see."

"You see what?"

"Go on about your new friends."

"What they're trying to gain is a way to see into the spirit world, what they call initiation into the temple of higher cognition, where they drink from the twin potions of oblivion and memory."

"The twin potions of oblivion and memory," I said, nodding. "And this is not a cult."

"Not really. They teach a series of practical exercises that will help you climb up the twelve-step path to initiation. You can do it with them or on your own, with proper knowledge. There's some chanting and incense, sure, but no magic. And no Kool-Aid. Just a natural way to a higher wisdom. Twelve steps with explicit instructions for each step. There's actually nothing so unique about it. They've been doing it for centuries in the East. This is just a way for the Western mind to train itself."

"And I assume you're in training."

"As part of my cover, of course." She fiddled with a packet of Sweet'n Low. "But I will admit it seems to speak to a certain void I have been feeling. Maybe even what we talked about before, the something I had been missing."

"Wouldn't a few dates be more practical?"

"Shut up, Victor, you're being an asshole."

I was, actually. I didn't know if it was the vodka talking or an outgrowth of my false brave front or the feeling I had that the last bastion had fallen, but I didn't like to hear about Beth's voids or her search for spiritual meaning. I could always count on Beth to stay rooted in the real world. Her idealism had nothing to do with any mystical esoterica, just the realization that we had a job to do and let's get to it. And if her job was helping the disadvantaged it was no big thing. I never thought I'd see her groping for meaning in the spirit world. That was for mixed-up losers who couldn't make it on their own and wanted an excuse. That was for hipsters too cool to accept the Western way in which their minds moved. That was for phony shamans in orange robes, not for Beth.

When my drink came, plopped in front of me without ceremony, I took a deep gulp and felt the bitter sweetness of the juice and the cut of the vodka. "All right," I said. "I'm sorry," and I was. Beth was the last person who took me seriously, I think, and for me not to take her seriously was a crime. "Tell me about the twelve steps."

"I don't know them all yet, but I'm trying to learn. The first step is just wanting to find meaning. It's walking in the door. The second is understanding that the answers are all around us, both internal and external, but in the spiritual, not physical world. To access that world we are required to develop new ways of seeing, to develop our spiritual eyes."

"The creep who came into our office and threatened me said I was a two."

"Gaylord. He's one of the teachers. A sweet man, really."

"Sweet enough to remember cutting my head off with a broadsword."

She raised her eyebrows. "You must have deserved it in your past life," she said, "and as far as I can tell not much has changed." It was good to see her laugh.

"Well, at least I've been consistent through the ages."

"That's nothing to be so proud of. Your level refers to the steps you have mastered on your way up the ladder. Practically anyone who enters the Haven has satisfied the first two steps or they wouldn't be there, so it's no great honor to be a two. It is on the third step that the exercises begin. You have to prepare your mind for the journey and you do that by learning devotion. You take the critical out of your thinking, you clear your mind of the negative, you fight to see the good in everyone and everything you come in contact with."

"That rules me out. My one true talent is seeing the negative in everyone and everything."

"You should try it, Victor. It's rather refreshing. One result of being completely uncritical, I've found, is that I stop surrendering myself to the outside world, stop chasing one sense impression after another. Instead I try to take each sense impression as a unique gift and orient myself by my response to its singular beauty. I don't rush to see a hundred flowers, hoping to find the prettiest, but examine one completely, uncritically, and feel my inner self responding to it. It is that response which is most enlightening. Respecting our own responses to sense impressions is the first step to developing an inner life."

"I can't manage my outer life, what am I going to do with an inner life?"

"Why so defensive, Victor?" she said with a condescending

smile. "No one's saying you shouldn't keep eating animal flesh and watching *Matlock* reruns and chasing all the money you want to chase. You should do as you like and be happy. I, on the other hand, am practicing devotion."

"And that's why you're so sweet to our rude waitress."

"I can't let my inner life be disoriented by minor annoyances in the physical realm. Only benevolence will lead to spiritual seeing."

"I'd rather chase the money."

"And do you think being rich will make you a complete and satisfied person?"

"Maybe not, but at least I'd be able to dress better."

"You're no different than the rest of us, Victor. We all see ourselves as this dissatisfied thing, this ego, looking outside ourselves for just that one other thing that will make us complete. That job, that lover, that pot of money. Even enlightenment, as if that too is a thing we can grab hold of to complete what needs completing. There is always something, we believe, that will make us whole. But if you take a finite thing, like body and mind, and look for something outside it to make it complete, something like money or love or faith, what you are seeking is also just a finite thing. So you have a finite thing reaching for the infinite by grabbing for some other finite thing and you end up with nothing more than a deeper sense of dissatisfaction."

"So what's the answer?"

"I don't know. I haven't trained myself to see it yet, but it's out there, it has to be. I think it starts with changing our conception of ourselves."

It all made more than a little sense and I had to admit that some of what Beth was saying resonated with what I had been feeling that very afternoon while hiding beneath my sheets. I thought for a moment about pursuing it further with her, to see if maybe there might be some answers there for me, thought about it and discarded it. Maybe I was succumbing to the same impulse that made it so hard for me to ask directions when I was temporarily misplaced on the road, or to ask for help from my father, but I figured I'd rather suffer in existential limbo than give myself over to a bunch of chant-heads, as Caroline had so finely described them.

"In the course of your spiritual search, Beth," I said, "did you happen to find out why, maybe, your sweet teacher Gaylord and his muscle threatened me?"

"The group is building a spiritual center in the suburbs," she said softly. "In Gladwyne."

"Funny, isn't it, how even in the spiritual realm it all comes down to real estate. Henry George would be much gratified."

"They collect dues and hold fund-raising events, but there is also talk about a benevolent soul who left a great deal of money to Oleanna."

"Jacqueline Shaw, and the five-million-dollar death benefit on her life insurance policy."

"I think we can assume that. It appears when that money from the policy arrives it will finance the new building. Until then the group seems nervous to discuss it."

"What's the story on this Oleanna?"

"A very powerful woman, apparently. I haven't had the honor of meeting her yet, but she is the only true seer in the group."

"A twelve, I suppose."

"She's beyond twelve, so they say, which means her powers are beyond the noninitiate's capacities to understand."

"So this Oleanna exercised her powers to kill Jacqueline in order to finance her spiritual palace in Gladwyne."

"It's possible, of course, and it's what I figured you'd figure," she said. "But it doesn't really jibe. These people truly seem to be after something nonphysical. They

seriously believe in karma being passed along through
recurrent lives. I can't imagine them killing for money."

"That's the difference between us," I said. "You can't
imagine them killing for money and I have a hard time
imagining anyone not being able to kill for money, so long
as there's enough of it at stake."

"Your cynicism will be a definite handicap as you
climb the ladder of spiritual seeking."

"Well at least it has some use. So you're rising?"

"Step by step. I'm now a three."

"A three already? Once again you outpace me. What's
the next rung?"

"Level four," she said. "Finding an inner peace through
meditation."

23

THE SHRIEK OF SKIDDING TIRES sliced through the dark stillness of my room and I jerked to a sitting position, a cold sweat beading on my neck. It was the middle of the night but I wasn't sleeping. Maybe it was being in a Cadillac riddled with bullets just that afternoon, maybe it was the vision of Beth climbing her mystical ladder step by step and leaving me behind, maybe it was the coffee I had taken with my dessert. "Decaf is for wimps," I had said, and not being a wimp I had taken a second cup, but whatever it was I was lying awake, under the covers, shivering, letting a raw fear slide cold through my body, when the sound of the skidding car skived the night quiet.

I leaped out of bed and searched Spruce Street from my window.

Nothing.

I spun around and paced and bit and threw myself on the couch, remote control in hand. I spent twenty minutes watching an Asian man explain how I could become as lavishly rich as he by sending him money for a pack of cassettes that would teach me to purchase real estate cheap and put cash in my pocket at the settlement table. I knew how he was getting rich, by suckering desperate insomniacs like me into sending him money, but I severely doubted that I would profit too. Except there were testimonials, all of them convincing as hell, from people I imagined to be stupider than me, and I was seriously debating whether to pick up the phone and make the call that would change my life when I decided instead to masturbate. I tried that for a while but it wasn't quite working, so I looked in the refrigerator for something to eat. There was nothing to eat but there was a beer, so I drank that, but it was old and not any good and left a bad taste in my mouth. I opened a *Newsweek* and then tossed it aside. I picked up an old Thomas Hardy paperback I had bought for a dime off the street and had been meaning to read, but who was I kidding? Thomas Hardy. I flicked on the television again and watched babes in tights hump the HealthRider and tried to masturbate again but again it didn't work. I turned off the television and paced around some more. Then I decided I would follow Beth up her ladder and try to find some inner peace through meditation.

I had of course tried meditation in college, in an undergraduate sort of way, with an exotic redhead, a senior yet, braless, in tight jeans and a low-cut orange crepe peasant shirt. She had explained to me the whole transcendental thing while I had stared transfixed at her breasts. We were kneeling on the floor. We were probably high. David Bowie was probably playing in the background. I remember the soft warmth of her breath on my ear when she leaned close, one breast brushing my arm, and whispered to me my mantra. It was "Ooma" or "Looma" or something like that. When I crossed my legs and made O's with my fingers and repeated "Ooma" or "Looma" over and over again, I tried, as she had instructed, to force all thoughts from my mind. I generally succeeded, except for thoughts of her breasts, which I thought about obsessively the whole of the time my eyes were closed. "Ooma, Ooma, Ooma," or "Looma, Looma, Looma." I imagined her breasts from beneath my closed eyes, all thick and ripe and mysteriously scented. I ran my tongue across my lips as if I could taste them. Sweet, like vanilla wafers in milk.

I don't think I had quite the right attitude for proper

meditation in college and it hadn't worked for me: I neither fell into a meditative trance that night nor got closer to those marvelous breasts than my feverish imaginings. But I was not closed to the idea of meditation and could see no other nonpharmacological solution to my restlessness. So I sat on the floor in front of my couch and crossed my legs and checked the digital clock and closed my eyes and did as Beth had instructed me over dinner that evening. It was two twenty-three in the morning.

I concentrated on my breathing, in, out, in, out, and tried to keep my mind blank of any thoughts other than of my breathing, in, out, in, out. A vision of the white van slid into my consciousness and I slid it out again. I thought about the decrepit remains of Veritas and the venous piece of mutton I had been served and how disgusting all the food had been and I wondered how anybody could have eaten anything in that place and then I realized I was thinking about that when I should have been thinking about nothing and I pushed the thoughts away and went back to my breathing, in, out, in, out. The darkness beneath my lids looked very dark, out, in, out, in, and I remembered how Caroline had felt in bed, how her muscles had slackened and her eyes had glazed even as she was telling me to go on and how kissing her was like kissing a mealy, flavorless peach. I opened my eyes and looked at the clock. It was two twenty-five. I closed my eyes, in, out, in, out. A thought about a woman hanging from a tapestry rope started to form and shape itself until I banished it and kept concentrating on my breathing, in, out, in, out, and the darkness darkened and a calm flitted down over my brain. I opened my eyes and saw that the clock now read two forty-six. I closed my eyes again, in, out, in, out, in, out, and slowly I directed my consciousness to pull free from my body, stretching the connection between the two, stretching it, stretching it, until the spiritual tendon snapped back and my consciousness was loose, free to float about the room on its own power.

"The point of the early stages of meditation," Beth had said, "is to view yourself with the dispassion of a stranger in order to gain perspective on your life. Only with the perspective you gain by placing yourself in a position to observe your life from afar can you dissolve the niggling concerns of the here and now that keep you from hearing the true voices of your spirit." That was why I had directed my consciousness to escape from my corporeal self, so I could dispassionately see what I was up to. Of course it was all self-directed, and most certainly delusional, but with my eyes closed I imagined my consciousness moving about the room and examining the contents with its own vision.

The seedy orange couch. The framed Springsteen poster. The empty Rolling Rock bottle on the coffee table beside the television remote control. The little washer-dryer unit, the dryer door open and half filled with pinkish-hued tee shirts and socks and boxer shorts. Three-day-old takeout Chinese food cartons on the red Formica dining table. I tried to send my consciousness out of the room, to take a Peter-Pannish tour of the city, but I couldn't lift it through the ceiling. It could gaze out the window at the desolately lit scene on Spruce Street, but it couldn't go through the glass. I tried again and again to hurl my consciousness through the ceiling, trying to gain the faraway perspective Beth had told me I needed, but my consciousness simply would not go. And then, almost of its own volition, it turned around and looped low until it was face to face with my body.

Crow's feet, deeper than I ever thought possible, gouged out from the corners of the eyes. The scabs on the cheek were like the scrapes of hungry fingernails. The brown hair short and spiky, the neck too long, the shoulders too narrow. A white tee shirt hung from the shoulders as loose as if from a hanger. Where was the chest? The boxers were striped and only a shade paler than the bony knees. I was trying to view my body with the tranquility of an observer, as Beth had advised, but it was hard to keep down the dismay. Didn't that stack of bones ever exercise? I went back to the face and tried to find some thought or emotion playing out on its features, but it was as inanimate as wax. I couldn't even tell if the body was breathing, it looked more like a corpse than corpses I had seen.

I wondered what would happen if I opened my eyes just then. Would I see my consciousness staring back at me or would I have a clearer vision of the body I was now inspecting? Or would my consciousness, caught outside my awakened body, simply flee, leaving the body there as still and as lifeless as a salami? I started to back up again, to gain more perspective. The body seemed to shrink in both size and significance. I flew back until I was hovering over the dining table, as far from the body as I could get in that room. The whole scene, the sad, nondescript apartment, the mess, the stiff waxy body with its pale legs crossed on the floor, the detritus of loneliness scattered all about, the whole scene was pathetic. And then I noticed something in the body's right hand.

I flew around the room, just zipped around for the sheer pleasure of it, before drawing close to get a better look. The hand was open, as if presenting an offering. Lying on the palm was a cellophane candy wrapper, one end twisted, one end open, and printed on the wrapper's side in red and green were the words: MAGNA EST VERITAS.

I opened my eyes.

The light in the room forced me to blink away the hurt as I stared down at my right hand. It was open, just as I had seen it with my eyes closed, but now it was empty. My ankles hurt, I realized, from sitting cross-legged for too long. The cool blue numbers of the digital clock now read three thirty-one. I pushed myself to standing and walked around a bit, let the stiffness of my legs dissipate. I thought of that wrapper I had imagined my consciousness seeing in my opened hand and I started shaking. When I had calmed myself enough to sit and dial I called up Caroline Shaw.

With a voice drowsy with the remnants of a deep and most likely disturbing sleep, she said, "Victor, what?"

"I need to see you."

"What time is it? What? Victor? Okay. Okay. Wait." I heard her grope for a cigarette, the click of a lighter, the steady soft breath of an inhale. "All right, yes. You can come on over, I guess. I've been thinking about you too. It was nice, wasn't it?"

"No, not now," I said. "Tonight. Let's have dinner tonight."

"I wanted to talk to you this morning but you just ran away. I saw you on the lawn with Nat but then you were gone."

"I had to be somewhere."

"But it was nice, wasn't it? Tell me it was nice."

"Sure, it was nice."

Another inhale. "Your talent for romance is over-whelming."

"We'll have dinner tonight, all right?"

"I'll make a reservation someplace wildly expensive."

"That's fine. But make it for three."

She laughed a dreamy laugh. "Victor. I wouldn't have imagined."

"I want your Franklin Harrington to join us," I said, and her laughter stopped.

"I don't think so."

"I need to talk to him."

"I think that's a terrible idea, Victor."

"Listen to me, Caroline. I believe I know who killed your sister. Now I need your fiancé to help me figure out why."

24

I SPENT MUCH OF THE NEXT MORNING inside my office, door closed, reading the news reports in the *Inquirer* and the *Daily News* about the shootout on the Schuylkill Expressway. The information was sketchy. The white van had been found deserted in Fairmount Park. Police were still searching for clues as to the identity of the hit men but there were still no suspects. Authorities had confirmed that Raffaello was inside the Cadillac when it was attacked and was now in a hospital in serious condition, but no one, for obvious reasons, would say where. The police would state only that Raffaello and the unidentified driver of the car were both cooperating. There were reports, though, of another occupant, a white male, tall, thin, in a blue suit, who may have fallen from the car near the zoo. My skin crawled as I read about the mysterious figure stumbling his way across the street. The sighting was made by a balloon vendor outside the zoo entrance but the police apparently were discounting the story. Still, it worried me, and I pored over the reports nervously looking for any other information.

After I had read the papers, twice, I began playing catch-up at the office, returning phone messages, responding to letters, filing motions to continue those matters that I didn't have time to deal with just then, freeing up my afternoon and the many days to follow. I was, in effect, putting off the whole of my practice while I pursued my ill-starred quest for a chunk of the Reddman fortune. When I cleared my calendar for the next week, I took a deep breath, grabbed a file, stuffed it in my briefcase, and sneaked out of the office, heading for Rittenhouse Square. Before my dinner meeting with Caroline Shaw and Franklin Harrington I had some things I needed to check on.

Rittenhouse Square is a swell place to live, which is why so many swells live there. It is the elegant city park. There are trees and wide walkways and a sculpture fountain in the middle. Society ladies, plastic poop bags in hand, walk their poodles there; art students, clad all in black to declare their individuality, huddle; college dropouts looking like Maynard G. Krebs walk by spouting Kierkegaard and Mr. Ed in the same breath; hungry homeless men sit on benches with handfuls of crumbs, luring pigeons closer, ever closer. It is a small urban pasture, designed by William Penn himself, now imprisoned by a wall of stately high-rises jammed with high-priced condominiums: The Rittenhouse, the Dorchester, the Barclay. It was the Cambium I was headed for now, a less imposing building on the south side of the park, hand-wrought iron gates, carved granite facings, million-dollar duplexes two to a floor. A very fashionable place to die, as Jacqueline Shaw had discovered.

"Mr. Peckworth, please," I said to the doorman, who gave me a not so subtle look that I didn't like. I was dressed in a suit, reasonably well groomed, my shoes may have been scuffed, sure, but not enough to earn a look like that.

"Who then can I say is visiting this time?" he asked me.

"Victor Carl," I said. "I don't have an appointment but I expect he'll see me."

"Oh yes, I'm sure he will," said the doorman.

"Do we have a problem here?"

"No problem at all."

"I don't think I said anything funny. Do you think what I said was funny or is it just the way I said it?"

"I did not mean in any way to . . ."

"Then maybe you should stop smirking and get on the phone and let Mr. Peckworth know I'm here."

"Yes sir," he said without a smile and without a look.

He called up and made sure the visit was all right. While he called I looked over the top of his desk. The stub of a cigar smoldered in an ashtray, a cloth-bound ledger lay open, the page half filled with signatures. When the doorman received approval for my visit over the phone he made me sign the ledger. A few signatures above mine was a man from UPS. "All UPS guys sign in?"

"All guests and visitors must sign in," he said.

"I would have thought they'd just leave their packages here."

"Not if the tenant is at home. If the tenant is at home we have them sign in and deliver it themselves."

"That way stuff doesn't get lost at the front desk, I suppose."

The doorman's face tightened but he didn't respond.

While I waited beside the elevator, I noticed the door to the stairs, just to the left of the elevator doors. I turned back to the doorman. "Can you go floor to floor by these stairs?"

"No sir," he said, eyeing me with a deep suspicion. "Once inside the stairwell you can only get out down here or on the roof."

I nodded and thanked him and then waited at the elevator.

Peckworth was the fellow who had seen a UPS guy outside Jacqueline Shaw's apartment when no UPS guy should have been there. He had later recanted, saying he had confused the dates, but it seemed strange to me that anyone would not remember the day his neighbor hanged herself. That day, I figured, should stick in the mind. On the elevator I told the operator I was headed for the eighth floor. It was an elegant, wooden elevator with a push-button panel that any idiot could work, but still the operator sat on his stool and pushed the buttons for me. That's one of the advantages of being rich, I guess, having someone to push the buttons.

"Going up to visit them Hirsches, I suppose," said the operator.

"Are the Hirsches new here?"

"Yes sir. Moved in but just a few months ago. Nicest folk you'd want to meet."

"I thought there was a young woman living in that apartment."

"Not no more, sir," said the operator, and then he looked up at the ceiling. "She done moved out."

"Where to, do you know?"

"Just out," he said. "So you going up to visit them Hirsches?"

"No, actually."

"Aaah," he said, as if by not going to visit the Hirsches I had defined myself completely.

"Is there something happening here that I'm not aware of? Both you and the doorman are acting mightily peculiar."

"Have you ever met Mr. Peckworth before, sir?" asked the operator.

"I don't think so."

"Well then that there explains it," said the operator.

"I guess I'm in for a treat."

"Depends on your tastes is all," said the operator as the elevator door slid open onto a short hallway. "Step to your right."

I nodded, heading out and to the right, past the emergency exit, to where there was one door, mahogany, with a gargoyle knocker. A round buzzer button, framed with ornate brass, glowed, but I liked the looks of that knocker,

smiling grotesquely at me, and so I let it drop loudly.
After a short wait the door opened a crack, revealing a
thin stooped man, his face shiny and smooth but his
orange shirt opened at the collar, showing off an absurdly
wrinkled throat. "Yes?" said the man in a high scratchy
voice.

"Mr. Peckworth?"

"No, no, no, my goodness, no," said the man, eyeing
me up and down. "Not in the least. You're a surprise, I
must say. We don't get many suits up here. But that's fine,
there's a look of desperation about you I like. My name is
Burford and I will be handling today's transaction. In these
situations I often act as Mr. Peckworth's banker."

"I don't understand."

"Well come in, please," said the man as he swung the
door open and stepped aside, "and we'll begin the bargaining process. I do so enjoy the bargaining process."

I entered a center hallway lined with gold-flocked
paper and then followed Burford into another, larger room
that had traveled intact from the nineteenth century. The
room was papered in a dark maroon covered with large
green flowers, ferocious blooms snaking their way across
the walls. There was a dark old grandfather clock and a
desk with spindly animal legs and an overstuffed couch
and thick carpets and dark Gothic paintings of judges in
wigs with a lust for the hangman in their eyes. Thick velvet
drapes framed two closed windows, the drapes held to the
wall with iron arrows painted gold. The place smelled of
not enough ventilation and too much expensive perfume.
On one wall was a huge mirror, oval, sitting like a giant
cat's eye in a magnificent gold-leaf frame.

Burford led me to the center of the room and then, as I
stood there, he circled me, like a gallery patron inspecting
a sculpture he was interested in purchasing.

"My name is Victor Carl," I said as Burford continued
his inspection. "I'm here to see Mr. Peckworth."

"Let's start with the tie," said Burford. "How much for the tie? Is it silk, Mr. Carl?"

"Polyester, one hundred percent," I said. It was a stiff black-and-red-striped number, from which stains seemed to slide right off, which is why I liked it. Wipe and wear. "But it's not for sale."

"Come now, Mr. Carl," said Burford. "We are both men of the world. Everything is for sale, is it not?"

"Yes, actually, that's been my experience."

"Well then, fine, we are speaking the same language. Give me a price for your one hundred percent polyester tie, such a rarity in a world lousy with silk."

"You want to buy this tie?"

"Isn't that why we're here?"

"One hundred dollars," I said.

"A tie like that? You can buy it in Woolworth's for seven dollars, new. I'll give you a profit on it, though, seeing that you've aged it for us. Let's say fifteen dollars? Who could refuse that?"

"Is Mr. Peckworth in?"

"Twenty dollars then."

"I didn't come here to haggle."

"Thirty dollars," said Burford.

"Let me just talk to Mr. Peckworth."

"Well, forget the tie for the moment. Let's discuss your socks. Tasty little things, socks, don't you think? So sheer, so aromatic."

"One hundred dollars," I said.

"The thing about socks," said Burford, "is you take them off, sell them, and all of a sudden you look more stylish than you did before. See?" He hitched up one of his pants legs. A bare foot was stuffed into a tan loafer. "Stylishness at a profit."

"One hundred dollars."

"That's quite high."

"Each."

"Did you shower today, Mr. Carl?"

"Every day."

"Then they wouldn't quite be ripe enough for the price you are asking. But that tie, that is special. We don't see enough man-made fibers these days. You don't happen to have a leisure suit somewhere in the recesses of your closet, do you?"

"I'm afraid not."

"Fifty dollars for the tie, but no more. That is the absolute limit."

"Seventy-five dollars."

Burford turned his face slightly and stared at me sideways. Then he took a thick roll of bills out of his pants pocket, licked his thumb with pleasure, and flicked out three twenties. He fanned the bills in his hand. "Sixty dollars. Take it or leave it," he said, smiling smartly.

I took the bills and stuffed them in my pocket.

"Come now, come now," said Burford. "Let's have it. Don't balk now, the deal's been done, money's been passed. Time to pay the piper, Mr. Carl."

At the same time he was demanding my tie he stepped aside, a smooth glide slide to the left which I found peculiar. What that smooth step did, I realized, was clear my view of the large oval mirror so that I would be able to watch myself take off my tie. There was something so neat about that glide slide, something so practiced.

I turned toward the mirror and gripped the knot of my tie with my forefinger and started slipping it down, slowly, inch by inch. "Now that you've bought my tie, Mr. Peckworth," I said to the mirror, "I have a few questions I'd like to ask."

For a moment I felt like an idiot for having spoken to a mirror but then, over an intercom, I heard a sharp voice say, "Take the tie and bring him here, Burford," and I knew I had been right.

Burford stepped up to me and held open a clear plastic

bag. "You're such a clever young boy, aren't you," he said with a sneer.

I dropped the tie in the bag. "I try."

Burford moved to the desk, where a little black machine was sitting. I heard a slight slishing sound and a thin waft of melting plastic reached me. "Yes, well, I would have paid you the seventy-five. I'll take you to Mr. Peckworth."

Peckworth was in a large garish room, red wallpaper, gold trimmings, the ceiling made of mirrored blocks. He was ensconced on a pile of pillows, leaning against steps that ringed the floor of what we would have called a passion pit twenty years ago. There were mounds of pillows and a huge television and a stereo and the scent of perfume and the faint scent of something beneath the perfume that I didn't want to identify. On one wall was a giant oval window looking into the room in which I had taken off my tie, a two-way mirror.

"Sit down, Mr. Carl. Make yourself comfortable." Peckworth was a slack-jawed bald man with the unsmiling face of a tax auditor, looking incongruous as hell in his pink metallic warmup suit.

I looked around for a chair, but this was a passion pit, no chairs, no tables, just pillows. I sat stiffly on one of the steps and leaned back, pretending to be at ease.

"I hope you'll excuse the entertainment with the tie," said Peckworth in a sharp, efficient voice. "Burford sometimes can't help himself."

"I hated to part with it for sentimental reasons," I said, "but he made me an offer I couldn't refuse."

Peckworth didn't so much as fake a smile. "It is nice to be able to mix business and pleasure. Unfortunately, we'll lose money on the tie, but you'd be surprised how much profit we can earn from our little auctions. The market is underground but shockingly large."

"Socks and things, is that it?"

"And things, yes."

I imagined some room in that spacious luxury duplex dedicated to the storage of varied pieces of clothing in their plastic bags, organized impeccably by the ever-vigilant Burford, their scent and soil preserved by the heat-sealed plastic. The reheating directions would be ever so simple: (1) place bag in microwave; (2) heat on medium setting for one minute; (3) remove bag from microwave with care; (4) slit open bag with long knife; (5) place garment over head; (6) breathe deep. Follow the directions precisely and the treasured artifact would be as fresh and as fragrant as the day it was purchased. That's one of the things I loved about Philadelphia, you could learn about some foul new pleasure every day of the week.

"What can I do for you, Mr. Carl?"

"I'm a lawyer," I said.

"Oh, a lawyer. Had Burford only known he would have negotiated a better deal. I think he mistook you for a man of principle."

"I'm representing the sister of your former neighbor, Jacqueline Shaw." That was technically a lie, but it wouldn't matter to Peckworth. "I wanted to ask you some questions about what you saw the day of her death."

"Nothing," he said, turning his slack face away from me. "I already told the police that."

"What you originally told the police was that you saw a UPS man in the hallway the day of her death. Which was interesting since no UPS guy had signed in that day. But later you changed your story and said you saw the guy two or three days before. The change conveniently matched the guest register at the front desk, so the police bought it. But the change of memory sounded peculiar to me and I wanted to ask you about it."

"It happens," he said. "I'm older than I was, my memory has slipped."

"This man you saw, can you describe him?"

"I already told that to the police."

"So you shouldn't mind telling it to me."

"Tall and handsome, broad shoulders, dark curly hair. His brown shirt and slacks, I remember, were impeccably pressed."

"As if they had just come out of the box."

"Yes, that's right."

I opened my briefcase and took out a file. Inside was a folder with eight small black-and-white photos arranged in two rows and glued to the cardboard. The photos were head shots, all of men between twenty-five and thirty-five, all with dark hair, all facing forward, all aiming blank stares at the camera. It was a photo spread, often used in lieu of a lineup in police investigations. I stepped down onto the base of the passion pit with the photo spread. The ground tumbled when I stepped on it and then pushed back. It was a giant water mattress. I fought to remain upright while I stumbled over to where Peckworth reclined. Standing before him, maintaining my balance steady as she goes, I handed the spread to him.

"Do you recognize the UPS man you saw in these photos?"

While he examined the photos I examined his eyes. I could see their gaze pass over the photos one after another and then stop at the picture in the bottom left-hand corner. He stared at it for a while and then moved his eyes around, as if to cover the tracks of his stare, but he had recognized the face in the bottom left-hand corner, just as I suspected he would. I had received the spread in discovery in one of my prior cases and that figure on the bottom left had a face you wouldn't forget, dark, sculpted, Elvesine. A guy like Peckworth would never forget the likes of Peter Cressi or his freshly pressed brown uniform. I wondered if he had made him an offer for the uniform instantly upon seeing it on him.

Peckworth handed me back the spread. "I don't recognize anyone."

"You're sure?"

"Perfectly. I'm sorry that you wasted so much of your time." He reached for the phone console beside him and pressed a button. "Burford, Mr. Carl is ready to leave."

"Who told you to change your story, Mr. Peckworth? That's what I'm really interested in."

"Burford will show you out."

"Someone with power, I bet. You don't seem the type to scare easy."

"Have a good day, Mr. Carl."

Just then the door behind me opened and Burford came in, smiling his smile, and behind Burford was some gnomelike creature in a blue, double-breasted suit. He was short and flat-faced and impossibly young, but with the shoulders of a bull. I must have been a foot and a half taller than he but he outweighed me by fifty pounds. Look in the dictionary under gunsel.

"Come, come, Mr. Carl," said Burford. "It's time to leave. I'm sure you have such important things to do today."

I nodded and turned and made my careful unbalanced way across the great water mattress. When I reached the wraparound steps leading to the door I turned around again. "An operation like this, as strange as it would appear to authorities, must pay a hefty street tax. Probably cuts deeply into your profits."

"Let's go, Mr. Carl," said Burford. "No time for nonsense. Time to leave. Everett, give Mr. Carl a hand."

The gunsel skipped by Burford with an amazing grace and grabbed hold of my arm before I could grab it away. His grip was crushing.

"I might be able to do something about the tax," I said. "I have certain contacts in the taxing authority that might be very grateful for your information."

Everett gave a tug that nearly separated my arm from its socket and I was letting him pull me up and out of that room when Peckworth said, "Give us a minute."

After Burford and Everett closed the door behind them, Peckworth asked me, "What could you do about it?"

"How much are you paying?"

"Too much."

"If the information proves as valuable as I expect, I might be able to convince my contacts to reduce your tax substantially."

"Is that so? And do we even know who is in charge after yesterday's dance macabre on the expressway?"

"I'm betting the old bull holds his ground."

"And if he does, and you get me the break you say you can get me, what do you get out of it?"

I was about to say nothing, but then realized that nothing wouldn't satisfy the suspicions of a man like Peckworth. There had to be an angle to it for him to buy in. "I get twenty percent of the reduction."

"That seems steep."

"My normal contingency fee is a third, but I'm giving you a break out of the goodness of my heart."

Peckworth nodded and said, "I understand." They always know you have an angle when you say you're doing something out of the goodness of your heart. "You must understand something, Mr. Carl. We don't choose the things that give us pleasure in this life, we only choose whether or not to pursue them. I have chosen to pursue my pleasures and with the money I earn in my side enterprise I am able to do just that. But the life is more precarious than you can imagine and those thugs are killing my cash flow."

"Well, that's the deal," I said. "Take it or leave it."

He thought about it for a moment, I could tell, because his brow knitted.

"I had some visitors," he said, finally. "Two men, one very well dressed, short and dapper. The other a stooge in an impossible maroon suit. They suggested that I was mistaken as to the date I saw the UPS man outside Miss

Shaw's door. After they explained it all to me I realized
that I must have been."

"Did they give you their names?"

"No, but they did give me the names of a few of my
suppliers."

"You mean from the auctions."

"Yes."

"And that troubled you."

"Yes."

"Let me guess," I said. "Were these suppliers maybe
under a certain legal age?"

"Never underestimate the delicate piquancy of the
young, Mr. Carl."

"So suddenly the entirety of your pleasure quotient was
at risk."

"Exactly, Mr. Carl. You're very quick for a lawyer."

"Any idea who these men were, or who they represented?"

"None, but I knew enough to step away. There is an
aroma that follows particularly dangerous men."

"And the stooge smelled bad, huh?"

"Not the stooge, Mr. Carl. They are a dime a dozen.
Beside being monstrously strong, Everett is very loyal
and can handle those that come my way with relative
ease. It was the well-dressed man, extremely handsome,
with even white teeth and groomed gray hair. There was
something frightfully languorous about him, but even
that languor couldn't hide the scent of danger he carried."

"What did he look like, an accountant?"

"Oh no, Mr. Carl. If he was anything he was a funeral
director, but one who never had to worry about supply."
He leaned forward and said, "If your friends can lower my
tax and take care of these men for me, Mr. Carl, you can
take your full one third."

"That's very generous of you," I said. I reached for the

door and then stopped reaching and turned around. "Bottom left picture was your UPS guy, wasn't it?"

"There was a brutality to his native good looks that I found unforgettable."

"Mr. Peckworth, I hope you don't mind my saying so, but for someone who has chosen to pursue his pleasures with such devotion, you don't seem so very happy."

"Mr. Carl," he said, with a straight, stolid face, "I'm so happy I could burst."

25

EVERETT LUGGED ME THROUGH the apartment and spun me into the hallway. Burford blew me a kiss before he closed the door. A fond farewell, I'm sure, but I was glad to be left alone in the hallway. I didn't take the elevator down, instead I went into the emergency exit. The stairwell was ill lit and smelled furry. The door hissed slowly shut on me. When I tried to open it again I discovered, as I had expected, that it was locked.

I started climbing up the stairwell, twisting around the landings as I rose. I tried each door on my ascent and discovered each to be locked, until the last. This one I opened, slowly, and found myself on the roof. It was flat and tarred, with assorted risers here and there, and a three-foot ledge all the way around. Scattered about were plastic lounge chairs, which I imagined were used by bare-chested sunbathers on hot summer afternoons. The knob on the outside of the door wouldn't turn, but all those melanoma seekers would need a way to get back inside once the sun dimmed. I searched the floor and found a wooden wedge, well worn, which I jammed into the crack. With the door stuck open I stepped onto the roof.

I wasn't really concerned with the roof of the Cambium. What I wanted to see were the surrounding roofs. The building fronted on the park and one side bordered on Nineteenth Street, as the road continued its way south after being interrupted by Rittenhouse Square.

Behind the Cambium was a building three flights shorter, so that was probably out. But to the side opposite Nineteenth Street was another fancy-pantsed doorman building, whose roof was roughly the same level, separated only by a six-foot gap. The drop between the two was deadly enough, but six feet was not too long a jump for an athlete with a brave heart. Too long for me, of course, as I was no athlete, which I learned painfully enough in junior high gym class, and my heart was more timorous than brave, but not too long for a committed gunman out to kill an heiress, for my client Peter Cressi.

It was the cellophane candy wrapper Cressi had tossed out in the Reptile House of the zoo that clued me, of course, one end open, one end still twisted, just like the wrapper Caroline had found behind her sister's toilet. It took a dose of meditation for my unconscious to show it to me because to my conscious mind it didn't make any sense, Cressi killing Jacqueline Shaw. He had nothing to gain. But others did, others who may have been hunting for a fortune. Maybe Eddie, maybe Oleanna, maybe some other legatee in line for a great deal of money with one or more of the heirs to the Reddman fortune dead. There was someone, I figured, who had enough to gain from Jacqueline's death to pay for it. And that someone paid enough to allow the killer to purchase a hundred and seventy-nine fully automatic assault rifles, three grenade launchers, and a flamethrower from an undercover cop. This was where Cressi's money had come from, I now was sure. He had probably run into whoever wanted to do the killing while shaking down Eddie Shaw for the half-million Eddie owed Jimmy Vigs. He had been nosing around, harassing Eddie, harassing his relatives, making his presence known, when an offer was made. And then, after the offer and an acceptance and a meeting of the minds, Peter Cressi had dressed in a UPS outfit and gone to the roof of that building over there and jumped the six-foot gap and rushed down the stairs of the Cambium to knock casually on Jacqueline's door with the words, "UPS, ma'am." And after the door was opened and Peter had entered and done his lucrative wet work, he had gone into the bathroom to straighten up, to smooth back his hair, to tuck in his shirt, all the while with Jacqueline hanging there, twisting from the chandelier, probably still moaning out loud. And to freshen his breath, of course, Cressi would pop into his mouth one of the mints he had boosted from Tosca's and, from force of habit, toss aside the wrapper, just as he had tossed aside the wrapper at the zoo. Sweet Peter.

Dante was in it with him, that was clear too. It was Earl Dante who went to cover Cressi's tracks after Peckworth had spotted Cressi outside Jacqueline's door. It was Earl Dante who had convinced Peckworth to change his story and so it must have been Earl fucking Dante who was directing Cressi as Cressi hired himself out as a hit man to get the bucks to purchase the guns that would allow Dante to win his war against the boss. What a little scab, that Dante. He had picked me as a pallbearer and probably advised Raffaello to have a chat with me, all the while knowing there was a white van with a hole in the side waiting to slide up to the Cadillac and blast away. What a murderous pus-encrusted little scab.

I only had one question left now, as I backed away from the edge of the roof and stepped toward the open door. Who, I wondered, had left the little wedge of wood in the door crack for Peter Cressi before Cressi made his leap?

I went back down the stairs, checking each door all the way down. On the third floor the door opened, even though the knob wouldn't turn. The latch was taped down, as at the Watergate the evening Nixon's hoods were discovered by the night watchman. Someone moving surreptitiously between floors, I guessed, a little hanky-panky that the elevator operator had no business knowing. It wasn't much of a tape job, but it was all that was needed and I was sure that whoever had left the wooden wedge had done the same type of tape job to let Peter into the eighth floor. I ripped the tape off the lock with a quick jerk, just as Cressi must have done on his way back up from Jackie's apartment.

When I came out of the emergency exit in the lobby, the doorman gave me a look. I guess he was wondering what I was doing in the stairwell. I guess he was wondering where I had left my tie.

"Nice building," I said.

He nodded and said nothing.

"I hope you're not still sore about how I spoke to you earlier. I had never met Mr. Peckworth before so I didn't understand."

"Everything, it is fine, sir," he said with a formality that let me know everything, it was not fine. I would need to build some bridges with the doorman.

"What's your name?" I asked.

His eyes slitted. "Roberto," he said.

"You like cigars, Roberto?"

He tilted his head at me. "A good cigar, sure, yes."

"You like them thick or thin?"

"You can tell much about a man, I've found, by the cigar he smokes."

"Thick then, I take it. I'll be back in a minute."

I walked across Rittenhouse Square and then east to Sixteenth Street and down to Sansom. A few steps east on Sansom Street I walked into the Black Cat Cigar Company. It was like walking into a humidor, warm and dry and redolent of fall leaves. "I need to buy an impressive box of thick cigars," I told the stooped gray man with an unlit stogie in his teeth.

"How impressive?" he barked.

"Oh, about a hundred dollars impressive," I said. "And I'll need a receipt."

*   *   *

Roberto took a bowie knife out of his pocket and slit open the seal on the box. He held up one of the thick and absurdly long cigars and rolled it in his fingers, feeling the texture of the tobacco. He smelled it carefully, from one end to the other and back again. With the knife he cut off a piece of cellophane and licked the end of the cigar as if it were a nipple and then licked it again. He finally smiled and put the cigar back into the box.

"I have a few questions I'd like you to answer," I said.

"Surprise, surprise," said Roberto.

"Jacqueline Shaw, your former tenant. I represent her sister."

"And you think you can buy me with a box of cigars. You think my honor can be bought so cheaply?"

"Of course not. They're yours, whether you help or not. And I wouldn't call them cheap. I just felt bad about how I snapped at you before and wanted to make amends."

He pursed his lips at me.

"Now, in addition to that, I do just happen to have some questions about Jacqueline Shaw."

"I've already told the police everything."

"I'm sure you did, Roberto. And Detective McDeiss has even provided me with a copy of your guest register for the day of her death. What I'd like to know is whether anybody ever went up to her place without signing in?"

"All guests and visitors must to sign in."

"Yes, so you've already told me, Roberto. But I noticed Mr. Grimes didn't sign in that day."

He stared at me stiffly. "He was living there."

"Yes, but I figure he wasn't a listed owner of the co-op so, technically, he was a guest. What I want to know, Roberto, is who else could pop up to her apartment without signing in."

He hesitated a moment, stroking the smooth top of the

box with his fingers. "These are Prince of Wales, fancy cigars just to make up for a harsh word."

"I have an overactive conscience. And like I said, they're yours whether you help or not. All I'm trying to do is figure out exactly what happened the day of her death."

I smiled. He examined my smile carefully, searching not for the insincerity that was surely there but for the glint of disrespect that was not. "Well, Mr. Grimes could just walk in," he said finally, his right hand on the box of Macanudos as if it were a Bible. "And since it was a family place, her brothers, Mr. Edward, Mr. Robert, and her sister, were allowed up whenever they wanted. Mrs. Shaw of course went up often."

"The mother, you mean."

"Yes, and the grandmother, too, before she died. She used to come visit the old lady who lived there before, years and years ago. Mr. Harrington, too, came frequently. He paid the maintenance fees each month to me personally, gave out the Christmas tips. And the gardener would come up to take care of her plants. She had many plants but she wasn't very good with them."

"Nat, you're talking about."

"That's right. With the red eye. A quiet man, but he always smiled at me and said hello."

"You told all this to the cops?"

"They did not ask."

"All right, the day of Jacqueline's death, who came up and didn't sign in?"

"I didn't start work until twelve that day. The only one I remember coming in was Mr. Edward. He seemed to be in a hurry, but he left before Miss Jacqueline arrived."

"You sure of that?"

"Oh yes, I remember. He rushed in very harried, like he was being chased. I told him Miss Shaw was not home but he insisted on checking for himself. I opened the door for him on the way out and he didn't even nod at me."

"Did you tell that to the cops?"

"They did not ask."

"You said it was an old family place?"

"Yes, the Shaws had it for as long as I've worked here. The old cripple lady was in it and then it was empty for a while before Miss Jacqueline moved in. The family only recently sold it, after the unfortunate accident."

"It's funny how many hangings are accidental. Is it a nice place?"

"Very."

"Well lucky for the Hirsches, then. One last thing. Any of your tenants besides Jacqueline belong to some New Age religious group out in Mount Airy?"

"How the tenants pray is none of my business. I'm just the doorman."

"Fair enough." I winked. "Enjoy the smokes, Roberto."

"Yes, I will. You come some afternoon, we can savor one together," he said, as he stepped from behind his desk and opened the door for me.

"I'd like that," I said.

I walked again through Rittenhouse Square and down to Walnut. I headed east for a bit and then quickly turned on my heels and headed west. I saw no one behind me similarly turn. I darted into a bookstore on Walnut, just east of Eighteenth. As I browsed through the magazines I checked the plate window and saw nothing suspicious. Then I took the escalator to the second floor and went to an area in the rear, by the mysteries, and found the phone. With the receiver in my hand I swung around and saw no one paying the least bit of attention to me, which is just the way I liked it. I dialed.

"Tosca's," said a voice.

"Let me talk to table nine," I said, roughing up my throat like I was Tom Waits to confuse the guys at the other end of the tap.

"I'm'a sorry. There's no one at'a table nine right now."

"Well when you see the man at table nine again tell him the scout needs to talk to him."

"I don't'a know when it will be *occupato* again."

"Tell him the scout knows where the money came from and who's behind it all," I said. "Tell him I need to talk to him and that it's urgent," and before he could ask for anything more I hung up the phone.

It was as I was walking out of the bookstore that I spotted the late edition of the *Daily News*, whose front-page photograph instantly set my teeth to clattering.

26

I PAID THE FOUR BITS, folded the tabloid in half to hide the front, and took the paper straight to my apartment. I locked the door behind me. I pulled the shades down low. I flicked on a lamp by the couch and unfolded the paper beneath the artificial arc of light. Staring up at me was the picture that had shaken me so when I first glimpsed it in the bookstore. It was a picture of a man, stretched out on his back like an exhausted runner, a dark shadow slipping from beneath his head. The man's mouth appeared to be laughing and at a glance it might have seemed a cheery picture except I knew the man and he was not much drawn to laughter. What seemed to be laughter was really a twisted grimace and the shadow was not a shadow and the man was no longer a man but now a corpse.

Dominic Volare, an old-time mob enforcer with strong ties to the boss. They had clipped him when he left his favorite diner in South Philly, waited as he leaned down to stick his key in the door of his Cadillac, rushed at him from behind, blasted him in the back and the neck, leaving only his face nicely unmarred for the picture. I had played poker with Dominic Volare, lost to him, been frightened by him, but he had never hurt me and had actually done a few favors for me along the way. I had thought him retired and now, I guess, he was.

There was a story inside linking the Schuylkill Expressway attack on Raffaello to Dominic's murder and to another hit, just as deadly, if less photogenic. Jimmy Bones Turcotte, massacred in his car, a Caprice, the windows blown to hell by the fusillade that took with it his face. I didn't know Jimmy Bones, had never had the privilege of standing in court beside him and saying "Not Guilty," but I knew of him, for sure. He was another longtime associate of the boss. It was getting dangerous just then, I figured, to be a longtime associate of the boss, especially in or around your car.

The headline above Dominic's death mask on the front page said it all: WAR!

It was on, yes it was. Dante's battle for the underworld had begun in earnest and no one was safe, especially not a nickel-and-dime defense lawyer who had been roped into scouting for one side or the other. I turned off the light and thought about fleeing, maybe to Fresno, where mobsters in the movies always seemed to flee, Fresno. Or I could just cower in my apartment until it passed. I'd be all right, I had a television and a freezer for my frozen dinners and there was that Thomas Hardy book I had been meaning to read. I could hide out until it all blew over, lose myself on the bleak heaths of Hardy's Wessex, I could, yes. But I wouldn't. I had things to do, a fortune to hunt, and no slick-haired tooth-sucking loan shark like Earl Dante was going to push me off my path. What I needed was advice, serious advice, and there was only one man I trusted who knew enough of the ins and outs of the family business to give it to me.

With trembling fingers I dialed the 407 area code and then information. It was a shock to actually find his number there, as if all he was was another retiree, waiting by the phone for calls from his grandchildren. "Be there," I whispered to myself as his phone rang. "Please to hell be there."

"Yes?" said a woman's voice, squeezed dry by massive quantities of cigarettes.

"Hello," I said. "I'm looking for Walter Calvi."

"He no here now."

"I need to speak to him, it's very important."

"He's gone two, three days, fishing."

"Fishing? I didn't know Calvi fished."

"Big fish," she said. "From a boat."

"When will he be back?"

"Two, three days."

"Can you give him a message for me?"

"He's fishing," she said.

"Can you give him a message for me? Can you tell him Victor Carl called and that things are going on up here and that he should get in touch with me?"

"Okay," she said. "Victor Carl."

I gave her my number and she repeated it to me.

"Could you tell him it's important?"

"Nothing more important down here than big fish," she said. "Except maybe cleaning the air conditioner and feeding the cat. But I tell him, okay?"

I hung up the phone and waited in the dark of my apartment for a while, waited for the light outside to grow dim, waited for Calvi to get his butt off his boat and tell me what to do. At least it had turned out all right for him, I guess. He was sitting on some boat off the Florida Keys, snapping marlins from the cool Atlantic waters, while the rest of us were stuck up here ducking Dante's bullets. Of all the deals that were handed out Calvi got the best, for sure. I just hoped he would get his butt off that boat in time to tell me how to get one for myself.

When it was time I quietly left the quiet of my apartment, stepped down the stairs, looked both ways along the now dark street. Cautiously I slipped out onto the sidewalk. I passed my car and left it there. After what had happened in Raffaello's Cadillac, and seeing what I had seen in the paper, I wanted nothing to do with cars for a while. I walked along Spruce, then down through the park at Nineteenth, and over to Walnut, to restaurant row. It was time, I figured, for me to do some fishing of my own.

27

"HOW'S THAT GROUPER, CAROLINE?" asked Franklin Harrington, with a surfeit of politeness.

Caroline was leaning back in her chair, arms crossed, moodily separating the pale flakes of fish with her fork. She wore her leather jacket and black jeans and combat boots and would have looked terribly out of place among the well heeled and well coifed except that Harrington, in his perfectly pressed Ralph Lauren, covered for her. "Succulent," she said, her voice dry and devoid of enthusiasm.

"Terrific," said Harrington, who had instinctively taken on the role of the host, either through the dictates of good breeding or his unbridled arrogance, I couldn't yet figure. "And your crab cakes, Victor?"

"*Trayf,*" I said.

"I don't understand."

"It's the Jewish word for succulent."

"And I thought that was *shiksa,*" said Caroline, with a sly smile, as she reached for her wineglass.

"*Trayf* is broader than that." I explained. "Not all *trayf* are *shiksas,* though *shiksas* are surely the most succulent *trayf.*"

"Well then why don't you just go right ahead and order the *shiksa,*" said Harrington.

Caroline spit out her mouthful of Chardonnay.

Welcome to the lifestyles of the rich and the Yiddish.

We were in the Striped Bass, a gaudy new restaurant on Walnut Street, more stage set than anything else, with palm tress and rattan chairs, with marble pillars three stories tall, with the kitchen open so the diners can see their fish's firm flesh being pan-seared. It's not enough to just eat anymore, restaurants are now theme parks. Ride the gingered seafood fritto misto. Thrill to the bite of clam fritters with Asian slaw. Test your courage with the raw Malpeque oysters and your manhood with the hunk of burning blackened sea bass. The Striped Bass served only seafood, that was the hook, but it was more show biz than anything else, no different than the Hard Rock Café and Planet Hollywood, though many steps up in class and price. Instead of hamburgers, mahimahi with arugula pesto. Instead of fajitas, sautéed Maine lobster with somen noodles. Instead of gawking teenagers, gawking adults, wondering who was rich enough or famous enough to be at the chef's table that night. And despite this burden of atmosphere the food was actually brilliant. Reservations at the Striped Bass were taken months in advance, but guys like Harrington had their ways, I figured, and so there we were, Caroline sulking, Harrington as gratingly pleasant as a cruise director, and me, who had convened this awkward congregation, waiting for the appropriate moment to unload my questions.

I hadn't liked Harrington when we first met at the bank and I still didn't like him. There was an air of false importance about him, a sense that what he said actually mattered. He had been somebody's blue-eyed boy for too long. He needed to be stepped down a peg and I was just the guy, I figured, to do the stepping. I wanted to be sure, by the end of the night, after all was said and done, that he knew I had screwed his fiancée, and even though I hadn't liked it much, he didn't need to know that. Class divisions as clear as those between Harrington and myself always bring out my best, or at least my most petty.

I took a forkful of crab, swirled it in the mustard sauce, and swallowed. It was too good. Harrington was working on his swordfish. Caroline was still flaking her grouper with the tines of her fork, showing no inclination to eat despite the thirty bucks her fish cost. It was almost getting beyond awkward, so I thought I'd lob in the first of my little bombs and liven things up.

"Who," I asked nonchalantly as I picked at my crab, "was Elisha Poole?"

Harrington looked up from his plate with a sharp surprise on his face. He glanced at Caroline, who rolled her eyes with boredom, and then back at me. "What do you know about Poole?"

"Bobby told me a little when I was at the house the other night."

"Yes," said Harrington, his pale cheeks darkening, "I heard you were there."

I smiled a competitive little smile. One of the evening's goals, at least, had been scored. "Bobby told me that his great-grandfather had bought the company from Poole just before he started pushing his pressure-packed pickles and that, later, Poole claimed he was swindled. Bobby said that Poole had cursed the whole family for it."

"So that explains everything," said Caroline. "I rather like the idea that we are cursed. It's more comforting than knowing we screwed it up ourselves."

"Everything Bobby told you is correct," said Harrington. "It was Poole's company before Claudius Reddman bought it, one of a score on the docks canning produce. Poole was a tinsmith and started the company by tinning tomatoes and corn brought over from New Jersey. Claudius was first hired as an apprentice tinsmith but soon took on other responsibilities."

"When did you learn all this, Franklin?" asked Caroline.

"I find it prudent to study the history of any family whose wealth I administer."

"How did Reddman end up buying the company if he was just an apprentice tinsmith?" I asked.

"We're not sure," said Harrington, "but it appears that Poole liked his drink and as Claudius was able to handle more and more of the business side of things, Poole spent more time with a bottle. Poole's father was a notorious drunk, apparently, and so it was only a matter of time before it caught up with the son."

"Can you get us more wine, Frankie," said Caroline. "I'm suddenly thirsty."

I gave Caroline a glance as Harrington snapped for a waiter and ordered another bottle.

"As Poole's drinking grew worse," said Harrington, "Reddman started taking control of the company. Bit by bit he purchased Poole's stock, paying cash for the shares. The company wasn't earning much in those days and Poole was finding himself falling into debt and so he took the money eagerly."

"Where did the cash come from?" I asked.

Harrington shrugged. "There's the mystery. But just before the company expanded production of its soon to be famous pickles, Reddman took out a loan to buy the rest of Poole's shares. By that time the company was in the red and Poole was apparently only too ready to sell out. It was quite the gamble for Claudius Reddman, taking a loan to buy a profitless company."

"But it paid off, didn't it?" I said. "Reddman became a wealthy man, an American industrial giant, and Poole was left to hang himself."

"That's right," said Harrington, turning his attention back to his fish. "Poole ended as an embittered old drunk who had pissed away his chance for a fortune, that's one way to view him. Or, if you take his side, he was an honest, trusting man, swindled by an avaricious swine who built his own fortune off the carcass of Poole's life work."

"Who is left to take his side now?" I asked.

"Pardon?"

"Who is around who still thinks Poole was swindled?"

"I don't know," said Harrington. "The Pooles, I suppose."

"Are there any?"

The sommelier came with another bottle of wine, red this time, and poured a sip's worth into Harrington's glass. Harrington tasted it and nodded at the waiter and then said offhandedly, "I would think there are."

"Where?" I asked.

"How should I know?"

"What about the daughter," I said, "who lived in that house by the pond at Veritas with her widowed mother? You know the place, right?"

Caroline and Harrington glanced at each other and then away.

"Can you imagine her," I continued, "living in that sagging little hovel, all the time looking up at the great manor house that her father had told her should have been hers? Do you ever wonder what she was feeling?"

"Probably gratitude that great-grandfather had given her a place to live," said Caroline, who proceeded to empty her wineglass in three quick gulps before reaching for the bottle.

"Did you know Caroline was a Republican?" asked Harrington with an ironic smile I wouldn't have expected from a banker.

"Somehow I don't think Poole's daughter was gratified at all," I said. "Have you ever seen that Andrew Wyeth painting *Christina's World*? That's what it must have been like for her, staring up with longing at the large house on the hill. Can you imagine it? She lived there until her mother died, in the shadow of that huge stone house. How twisted must her tender little psyche have become? That she ended up in an asylum is no wonder."

"Who told you she ended up in an asylum?" asked Harrington with a curious puzzlement.

"The gardener, Nat. I asked about the old cottage on the other side of the pond and he told me."

"How the hell would Nat know anything about her?" asked Caroline. "This is all ancient history. Jesus, has it gotten cold or something?" She swallowed a gulp of wine. "Can't we talk about a cheerier subject than the Pooles, for God's sake. Victor, you're the mob lawyer, tell us about the mob war that's in all the papers. It even made the *Times*. What about that attack on the expressway?"

"Amazing," said Harrington.

"What happened to your face anyway, Victor?" said Caroline. "It looks like you were in a fight with a cat and lost."

"I wonder if she had any children?" I said.

"Who?" asked Harrington.

"The Poole daughter."

"Jesus, Victor," said Caroline. "Why are you so interested in the goddamned Pooles? It's enough to drive a girl to drink. Pass the wine." I couldn't help but notice that she was now completely ignoring her grouper and had begun to drink like, well, like a fish. I guess our conversation about her family had turned this into what her therapist would have called a situation.

"I'm intrigued by the whole of your family history, Caroline. You asked me to find out if Jacqueline was murdered. Well, after looking into it, now I'm sure that she was."

"Is Victor acting as your lawyer?" asked Harrington, bemusement creasing his face. I found it interesting that he was more surprised that I might be lawyering for Caroline than that I believed Jacqueline was murdered.

She gave a half smile rather then attempt to describe our peculiar legal relationship.

"So that explains the check and the visit to Veritas."

"You thought what?" said Caroline. "That he was a gigolo, maybe? Victor?"

"You also wanted me to find out who killed her," I continued, ignoring Harrington's laughter. "I think I now know who."

"What?" said Harrington, his laughter dying quick as a scruple in a bank. "Who, then?"

"That's not important right now," I said.

"Of course it is," said Harrington. "Have you told the police?"

"The evidence I have is either inadmissible or would disappear before a trial at this point. I'll need more before I go to the police, and I'll get it, too. But the guy who killed her was hired to do it, I believe, paid. Just like you would pay a servant or a bricklayer or a gardener. And so the question I still have is who paid him."

"And you suspect the answer is in our family's history?" asked Caroline.

"I'm curious about everything."

Harrington was staring at me for a moment, trying, I suppose, to guess at exactly what I was doing there. "You know, Caroline," said Harrington, still looking at me, "I knew Victor was a lawyer, but law was not the game I thought we were playing here. Silly me, I thought you brought me here just to show off another of your lads."

"I announced him as my lover at the house just to get mother's goat," said Caroline.

"And you succeeded. She was apoplectic."

"Thank God something worked out right."

"Well, then, let's have it out," said Harrington. "Are you, Victor?"

"Am I what?"

"Caroline's lover."

I glanced at Caroline and she reached for her wine and there was an awkward silence.

Harrington laughed, a loud gay laugh. "That was clear enough an answer. Now, I suppose, I must defend my honor." He patted his jacket. "Damn, you can never find a glove when you need one to toss into a rival's face."

"Shut up, Franklin."

"I'm sorry. You're right, Caroline. I'm being rude. Don't worry, Victor, what you and Caroline do after school is fine by me. All I want is for Caroline to be happy. Truly. Are you happy with Victor, Caroline?"

"Ecstatic."

"Terrific then. Keep up the good work, Victor." He turned back to his swordfish and lopped off a thick gray square. "Any help you need keeping her happy, you let me know."

Caroline emptied her glass and let it drop to the table. "You're a bastard, you know that."

"Maybe I'll order some champagne to celebrate."

"A goddamn bastard. And you want to know something, Franklin. Victor's amazing in bed. An absolute acrobat."

I couldn't stop my jaw from dropping at that.

"Well then, instead of the champagne I'll call for the check, get you both back to your trapeze."

"You're too heartless," said Caroline, her arms now crossed tightly against her chest, her chin tilted low.

"I wasn't the one who invited us all out to dinner together." Harrington picked up the bottle and said nonchalantly, "More wine, Victor?"

"Am I missing something?" I asked. "It sounds like I'm in the middle of an Albee play."

"Yes, well, the curtain has dropped," said Harrington, putting down the bottle. He looked at Caroline and the arrogance in his face was replaced by something tender and vulnerable. It was as if a tribal mask had suddenly been discarded. The way he looked at her made me feel small. "You have to understand, Victor, that I don't care for anyone in this world as much as I care for Caroline. I couldn't love a sister any more than I do her. She caught a bad break, getting born a Reddman. Any normal family and she'd have been a homecoming queen, happy and blithe, and she deserves just such blind happiness, more than anyone else I know. I'd die to give it to her if I could. I'd rip out my heart, bleeding and raw, and present it to her on a white satin cushion if it would turn her sadness even for a moment."

Caroline's sobs broke over the last few words of Harrington's speech like waves over rock. I hadn't even known she was crying until I heard them, so entranced I was by this new Harrington and his proffer of love. Caroline was hunched in her chair, thick mascara tears streaking her cheeks, and there was about this jag nothing of the rehearsed dramatist I had seen when she collapsed in the street with her gun that first day I met her. Whatever strange thing was between Caroline and Harrington, it cut deep. She was about to say something more, but she caught her lip with her teeth, tossed her napkin onto her plate, stood, and walked quickly away, toward the ladies' room.

"She's an amazing woman," said Harrington after she had gone.

"Yes."

"You're very lucky."

"I suppose."

"Don't hurt her," he said, picking up his knife and slicing into a dinner roll.

"I may be wrong," I said, "but I don't think she's in the bathroom crying over me."

He sighed. "No."

"What are you, gay?"

Harrington's face startled, and then he laughed, a warm guttural laugh, charismatic and comforting. I watched him laugh and I couldn't help but start laughing too. "No," he said when he finally calmed and had wiped the tears from his eyes. "But that would have been so much easier."

While we were waiting for Caroline's return,

Harrington, now under the assumption that I was Caroline's lawyer as well as her lover, explained to me the intricacies of the Reddman demise. The family's entire share of Reddman stock was in one trust, controlled by Kingsley, Caroline's father. While the bulk of the dividends remained with the trust, a portion was designated for division to Kingsley' heirs, the four children. When an heir died, each survivor's share of the designated division increased proportionally. Upon Kingsley's death, the shares in the trust were to be divided equally among the surviving heirs.

"How much?" I asked. I knew the general numbers, but I still liked hearing them.

"Right now, with three heirs, each share is worth about one hundred and forty-five million dollars, before taxes, but the share price has been rising so it may be more."

"Uncle Sam will be happy with his cut."

"Both Eddie and Bobby are considering moving to Ireland permanently to defray taxes."

"And they say patriotism is dead. It's funny though, talking about so much money, but I thought it would be more."

"Yes, well, over the years many of the shares have been sold, to pay the expenses in maintaining the house and other properties, and a large stake has been put into a different trust, pursuant to the direction of a former trustee."

"Which trustee?"

"Caroline's grandmother."

"And who are the beneficiaries of that trust?"

"I don't know. It is not being run by our bank and the documents are sealed."

"Any ideas?"

"Not a one."

"I heard a rumor that Charity Reddman, Caroline's grandaunt, ran away after she became pregnant. Any possibility that the trust could be for the benefit of the child or the child's heirs?"

"Possible, I guess. But you can't honestly suspect some mysterious heir of Charity Reddman of being responsible for Jacqueline's death."

I shrugged. "Tell me about the life insurance policies."

He raised his eyebrows. "Five million, term, on each heir, premiums paid by the trust. The beneficiary of the policies was designated by the trust as the surviving heirs."

"So if one killed off another," I said, "that one would get a third of five million?"

"That's right."

"Nice motive," I said, thinking of Edward Shaw and his gambling debts. "Except I was under the impression the money from Jacqueline's insurance went to her church."

"Yes. Jacqueline changed the beneficiary just before her death."

"Did her brothers and sister know?"

"She wanted me to keep it quiet, so I did."

"And so when she died her brothers and sister were in for a nasty surprise."

"Some were none too pleased," admitted Harrington. "And neither, of course, was the insurance company. It was ready to pay the death benefit but now it's holding off payment until all questions of Jacqueline's death are answered."

I was surprised at that, wondering who had raised the questions with the insurance company, but before I could follow up, Caroline returned. Her eyes were clean of mascara and red, her face was scrubbed. She looked almost wholesome, about as wholesome as you can look with a diamond in your nose. She didn't sit, instead she placed a hand on my shoulder.

"Take me home, Victor."

Harrington stood immediately. "Don't worry about the check," he said.

Out on Walnut Street, as I raised my hand for a cab, I couldn't help but ask, "What is going on between you two?"

"Have you ever been in love, Victor?"

I thought about this for a little bit. "Yes."

"It wasn't any fun, was it?"

"No, not really."

"Just take me home and fuck me, Victor, and please please please please please don't say another word until you do."

28

HER PLACE WAS ABOVE an abandoned hardware store on Market Street, just a few blocks west of the Delaware River. It was a huge cavernous space supported by rows of fluted cast-iron pillars, easily more than three thousand square feet. It had been a sweatshop of some sort in its more productive days and must have been a brutal one at that. Plaster scaled from the walls leaving them mottled and psoriatic. The ceiling, warped and darkened by leaks, was a confused configuration of wires and old fluorescent light fixtures and air conduits. Here and there patches of the ceiling's metal lath showed through where huge chunks of the plaster had fallen to the floor of roughened wood, unfinished, dark, splattered with paint. The windows were yellowed and bare of adornment, staring forlornly out onto the street or the deserted lot next door. The bathroom was doorless, the shower a cast-iron tub with clawed feet, the kitchen one of those stainless steel kitchenettes that looked to have been swiped from a motor home. Piled in one of the corners on the Market Street end were scraps of metal, old bed frames, chairs, evidence of a failed rehab. The loft smelled of wet plaster and dust and sorrow.

There was a couch in the middle, lit by a ceramic lamp on an end table, and there was a love seat that matched the couch and a coffee table to prop up feet and place drinks when entertaining. It looked to have been bought at a place like Seaman's, the whole setup, and it would have been at

home in any suburban split level, but here, in the midst of
this desolation, it seemed so out of place it was almost like
a work of art, commenting wryly on the easy comfort
bought at places like Seaman's. And then, beneath an
industrial light fixture that hovered over it like a spy, there
was the bed, a king-sized sleigh bed, massive as a battle-
ship, carved of dark mahogany. Red silk sheets covered the
mattress. The comforter, a masculine gold and green pais-
ley, was twisted and mussed atop the silk. Four long pillows, covered in a golden print, were tossed here and there
across the bed. And tossed among the pillows and the
twists of the comforter were Caroline and I, on our backs,
staring up at that spy of a light fixture and the ragged ceiling beyond, following with our gazes the rise of her
cigarette smoke, naked, our bodies at right angles one to
the other, not touching except for our legs, which were still
intertwined.

"Tell me about her," said Caroline.

I immediately knew which woman she was asking
about. "There isn't much to tell, least not anymore."

"Was she pretty?"

I knew which woman she was talking about and I knew
why she was asking and the reasons were so sad I couldn't
help but answer her. "She was very pretty and very deca-
dent and very vulnerable. When I met her she was with
someone else, someone very powerful, which made her
wildly attractive to me and so far out of reach she wasn't
even worth fantasizing about."

"What was her name?"

"Veronica."

"How did you two get together?"

It was a funny-sounding question, like you would ask
about high school sweethearts or an innocent pair of newly-
weds, not two depraved lovers like Veronica and me. "I
don't know, exactly. It was a time of my life when I was
full of desires. I wanted money and success, I wanted to be

accepted and admired by my betters. I wanted to be the guy
I saw in the *GQ* ads, the smiling man-about-town in those
society photos. I wanted to be everything I could never be.
And for a while, most of all, I wanted Veronica. Then, like
a dream, I had a chance for everything, the success, the
wealth, the entree into a world that had kept me out just for
the sheer joy of it. And I had a chance at her too. In the
blink of an eye we were sleeping together and she had
become more than a desire, she had become an obsession."

"Was it as marvelous as you had imagined?"

It was, actually, the sex was beyond glorious, over-
whelming all my better intentions, and soon nothing had
seemed to matter but the sex, except I didn't want to tell
Caroline that, so I answered her question with another
question. "Is anything ever as marvelous as we imagined?"

"Never," she said, "never, never, never."

I couldn't help but wince a bit at that.

"And then it all turned bad," I said. "Everything I
thought I was being offered was a lie, everything I thought
I wanted was a fraud. Everything I knew for certain was
absolutely wrong. And finally, when I put myself on the
line, she betrayed me. That was the end. I thought I was in
love, and part of it was that, I think, but it was also that for
the times I was with her I felt I was on the verge of becoming something else, and that was what I had been most desperately seeking all along. I still am, I guess. I've thought
about it a lot since she disappeared from my life and it
doesn't make a whole bunch of sense, but then I guess
obsessions never do."

"You want her back?"

"Nope. Well, maybe, yes. I don't know. Yes. Even
still. But all that other stuff I wanted, they can blow it out
their asses. I don't want their success, I don't want their
admiration or their acceptance. Last thing I ever want is to
slip on my tux and make nice with high society."

She reached out her arm and slid a finger up my side,

from my hip to my armpit. "So what is it that you want now, Victor?"

"Just the money," I said, rather cruelly, and then it was her turn to wince.

But I was troubled enough about my whole burgeoning extracurricular relationship with Caroline Shaw that I wanted to keep certain things clear, and they were. Absolutely. The reason she was asking about the time I was in love, I was sure, was because while there we were, naked in bed, our legs intertwined, my condom, pendulous with fluid, already tied off and disposed of, the sweat still drying on our overheated bodies, fresh from making whatever it was we had been making, the one thing missing had been love. Its absence was as chillingly palpable as a winter's fog.

I had brought her home as she had requested, and escorted her upstairs, as propriety required, but I had decided not to take her up on her belligerent invitation to screw. It wasn't just that I wanted her as a client more than anything else and as a client any coital relationship would be highly suspect in the eyes of the bar, not the corner bar, where my reticence would have been laughed at, but the legal bar. And it wasn't that it had not gone so well that night at Veritas, because I knew that the first time is often disappointing and no indication of the wonderful fruits to be reaped from regular and intense practice. And it wasn't that I didn't want to get caught in the middle of whatever tortured mess lay between her and Harrington because, well, I have to admit that only served to make her all the more attractive. No, the problem here was that there was something venal about my interest in Caroline Shaw and while I didn't mind that in the usual lawyer-client relationship, where venality properly belonged, having it manifest itself in command performances in the sack, as part of my effort to get her signature on a contingency fee agreement, gave me the unwelcome, though not wholly unfamiliar, sense of being a whore. I had enough of that in my day job, I didn't need it at night too.

So I had intended to pull away, but she had insisted on pouring me a drink, single malt whisky she had said it was and whatever it was it was pretty damn good and thank you, ma'am, I'll have another. And as she drew closer to me on the Seaman's couch I had intended to pull away, but then she took off her boots and tucked her pointed stockinged feet beneath her and curled next to me on the couch in that feline way she had. And I had intended to pull away but she leaned close to me and tilted her face to me and her eyes glistened and her mouth quivered with a sadness so damnably appealing that I couldn't help but bend close enough to her that our lips almost brushed. Oh I had intended to pull away all right, I had intended intended intended to pull away, and then in the middle of all those good intentions what I found myself pulling was my tie off and my shirt off and her jeans off and my shoes off and her stockings off and my pants off and my socks off, hopping ludicrously around as first one fell and then the other, and the next thing I knew, as if just thinking it had made it so, she was spread-eagled and naked beneath me and I was sucking on a golden ring while I rolled her right nipple between my teeth.

Beside the multiple hoops in her ears and the stud in her nose there were rings on each nipple, there was a ring in her belly button, there was the rose tattoo on her ankle and the butterfly tattoo on her neck and a tattoo of a snake crawling dangerously up her hip. On each shoulder blade were rows of tattooed gashes, as if some giant cat had pounced upon her back with its claws extended. For a moment, as I worked on her breasts, first one nipple, then the other, letting my tongue lick each and caress each and then pull at its ring with a languorous tug, first one then the other and then back again, I could feel a slight tremble rise through the softness of her skin. I pushed her grandfather's medal to the side and buried my face between her breasts before dragging my lips down, over the belly ring and down, until she arched her back and the magnificent musk of her shortened my breath with involuntary want. And then with the swiftness of a light being clicked off it happened again as it had happened before and I lost her.

"It was strange," I said to her afterward, when we were lying face up on the bed. "Your friend Harrington. First time I met him I thought he was the biggest prick in the world. But tonight, I sort of liked him."

She turned away from me, onto her stomach. Her butt was as round and as fresh as a melon. "Franklin's a charmer."

"You two have a peculiar engagement," I said, reaching instinctively out to touch that butt and then thinking better of it and pulling my hand back before I actually did. "He finds out we're sleeping together and asks, with all sincerity, if he can help. It was the strangest . . ."

"He's a real charmer, all right," she said, reaching over to the night table, smashing out her cigarette, pulling another out of the pack, fiddling with the lighter, holding up a flame.

I waited a beat before I asked, "What is it with you two?"

"Old wounds."

I stared up at the ceiling and waited as she took a couple drags on her new cigarette. She took a few drags more and I waited still. She didn't want to tell me, I could feel it, but I lay quietly on my back, certain that eventually she would. And then she did.

She had known Franklin pretty near all her life, she told me. Grandmother Shaw had found him at an orphanage, one of her special charities, and decided to take responsibility for the young foundling and give him a chance in the world.

She was very special that way, her grandmother was, said Caroline. Very giving. She couldn't give enough, especially to Franklin. She gave him clothes, toys, he had his own room in the servants' section. It was always clear that he was different from the rest of the family, of course. How could that be avoided? He was expected to help Nat in the gardens while the Shaw children and their guests played freely in the house and he always had chores, but he often ate with the family and went on vacations with the family when the family, all but Caroline's father, left Veritas for the Reddman house by the sea. In almost every way possible, Grandmother Shaw treated him like a member of the clan.

"So long as he helped Nat in the garden," I said.

"Yes, well everything has its price, doesn't it? It was a pretty good deal for Franklin, considering Grammy paid his way through Episcopal Academy and then Princeton."

"He looks like a Princeton man."

"He's grown into the part."

As a boy, she said, he was wild, hyperactive. He seemed to always be angry, charging here and there for no apparent reason, a handsome little towhead bursting with energy. He was the only real friend she had at the house. Her father was never there for her, hiding from the world and his family in his upstairs bedroom; her mother was so preoccupied with being a Reddman she had nothing left to give to her youngest daughter. Brother Edward was too busy looking for trouble to be interested in his little sister. Brother Bobby was shy and bookish and sister Jacqueline moped about melodramatically, wearing long flowing gowns, carrying her dog-eared copy of *The Bell Jar* everywhere. But Franklin was wild and full of some exciting anger that drew her to him. Whenever he wasn't working they were running off together like wolves, the best of friends.

"How did Grammy feel about that?"

"You don't understand my grandmother. She wasn't a snob at all. If anything, she encouraged Franklin and me to play together, at least when we were young."

They liked the same sports, hated the same people, read the same comic books. They watched *The Love Boat* on television every Saturday night, religiously. They both thought the Beatles were overrated, that Springsteen was the boss. They agreed that *Annie Hall* was the most important movie ever made. They were almost a perfect match, which is why it seemed so natural, so inevitable, when they first started having sex.

"Out there on the ancestral moors. How old were you the first time?"

"Fifteen."

"Fifteen? That's statutory."

"He's only two years older than me."

"When I was fifteen I hadn't even slow-danced with a girl."

"It was absolutely innocent. We were absolutely in love. We decided we were going to be married, so why not, though we swore not to tell anyone."

"Grammy wouldn't have approved you messing with a servant, I guess."

"She never knew, no one ever knew. It was Franklin who insisted it be an absolute secret, and I understood. He was never quite sure of his place among all us Reddmans."

They'd hide out together in the old Poole house down by the Pond. They brought in a mattress, sheets and blankets, a radio. They turned that ruin of a house into a love nest and whenever they could get away that's where they'd run. They read books, poetry, reciting the lines to each other. They listened to the newest songs on WMMR. They made love in cool summer evenings to a cricket serenade. They experimented with each other's bodies.

"When I was fifteen," I said in amazed envy, "I wasn't even experimenting with my own body."

"Cut it out," she said. "It's not a joke. I shouldn't be telling you."

We lay in the bed for a while, quietly. Our legs were no longer touching.

"So what happened to you two?" I asked finally.

"I don't know."

"What do you mean you don't know?"

"I still don't know," she said.

Somehow their secret was discovered. They never knew by whom or how, but they had no doubt. Someone had sneaked into the old Poole house and rummaged through their things. They could feel a chill when they were together, as if they were being watched. And then one night, when he was eighteen, Franklin disappeared. No one knew what had happened or where he had gone, he had simply vanished. A letter came for him from Princeton. Caroline opened it anxiously, recklessly; he had been accepted, but there was no one to tell. She searched for him, called all their friends, checked out all their places, found not a trace. And when he reappeared, finally, after months and months, reappeared without explanation, he was somehow different. Whatever had been wild about him was gone. The anger in him that she had loved so much had disappeared. And when she finally got him back to the Poole house and demanded he tell her where he had been, he sat her down and told her it was over. Forever. That though he loved her with everything in his soul they would spend the rest of their lives apart. She clutched hold of him and cried and begged to know what she had done but he wouldn't answer. He just stood and left and never went back into the house and never slept with her again.

"And there was no explanation?"

"None."

"Any ideas?"

"None. At first I thought he might have a disease that he didn't want to spread to me, or that he might be gay. I announced our engagement publicly, a childish attempt to force him to change his mind, and he didn't disabuse anyone of the notion, so the expectation remains in the family that we will be married, but he hasn't touched me since. He can barely stand to look at me now. Franklin has other women, I know that. What I don't know is why he'd rather be with them than with me. But desertion seems to be the pattern, doesn't it? My father hides from me in his room, my one true love flees from me."

"Do you regret anything now?"

"I regret everything now, but not that. It was the finest, purest time of my life. The last innocent period where I still believed in the myth that life was a thrilling adventure and everything was possible and there was true happiness to be found in this world."

"What do you believe in now?"

She inhaled from her cigarette and let it out slowly.

"Nothing," she said finally. And I believed her. It was in the dead look in her eyes, in the body piercing, as if to gore a great emptiness, in the tattoos, as if to scrawl onto her body some evidence of faith. It was in the way she drank in her situations, intently, the way she smoked, with the incessant dedication of a suicide, the way she held herself, like an actress searching in the wings for a line because she had none of her own. And most of all, it was in the way she screwed.

After she had clicked off into passivity I didn't give up trying to bring her back. I kissed the flesh behind her ear and rubbed her crotch with my thigh and took hold of her hair. Though at Veritas I had been expecting something more, I wasn't surprised this time when she left me alone in her bed with her body. But despite how I tried to revive her, she was gone, to someplace calm and innocent, to someplace full of youth and love, to someplace I could never follow, leaving me with only her flesh and my heightened desire. So what else was there to do? I caressed her pale flanks, indelibly marked in the green ink of her tattoos, sucked at her neck, dragged my tongue across the rough skin beneath her arms. Her mouth, newly rinsed with Scope, tasted as minty and new as a newly minted hundred-dollar bill and I grew ever more excited despite myself. To have sex with Caroline Shaw, I realized whilst astride her, was to peer into Rockefeller's soul.

She lay there quietly for me, eyes open, saying not a word as I did what I willed with her. Her very passivity spurred me, her eyes staring at me, rich and blue, challenging. I straddled her and turned her around so those rich eyes were away from me and I entered her, pumping hard, pumping furiously, filled with anger at her stark passivity. And in the moment that I came, my teeth clenched in release, it was as if Mammon itself opened up its secrets to me and I started to grasp its dark power. It is utter emptiness, a vessel formed of nothing, filled with nothing, believing in nothing, an emptiness into which we are urged to pour our most essential truths. And what spurted out of me was not love nor compassion nor charity nor even need, what spurted out was all my wanting and my coveting, all my deep yearning for anything that anyone else might ever have, all my darkest ambitions for prestige and power and glory and ultimately what? Godhood? God help me. That was the next-to-worst part of screwing Caroline Shaw, the part that brought to light the ugliest shadows of my crippled soul.

The worst part was that I liked it.

"Do you think all that crap about Elisha Poole and my great-grandfather might have something to do with Jacqueline's death?" asked Caroline.

"I don't know. Maybe. Harrington seemed interested enough."

"He did, didn't he?" She took a drag from her cigarette. "I had a strange feeling in the restaurant when you and he were discussing this thing about Poole. It was more like a déjà vu than anything else, but I felt it. It was like there weren't only three of us at the table anymore, there was someone else, sitting with us, casting a coldness over everything."

"A ghost?"

"No, a presence, maybe just a memory. But it made me shiver."

"Who? Your grandmother?"

"Someone else, someone strange to me. It was almost like my great-grandfather was there, listening to us talk about him. Is that weird?"

"I don't know. Maybe it was just a draft."

"Whatever it was, it was really cold." She took another drag and then stubbed out her cigarette right on the table's surface. "I think it's time I learned the truth about my family's history. I think I want to know everything that happened, from the very beginning to what is left of us now. I want to know if it was always rotten or if there was a moment of brightness before it turned."

"Conciliation, expiation, redemption," I said.

"Yes, I want to know about that too. Especially the redemption."

"You might not like what you find."

"I don't care. What could I ever learn that could make things worse for me?"

"Are you sure?"

"Positive, as long as you'll do it with me."

"If that's what you want."

"That's what I want. You'll see it through to the end, won't you, Victor? You won't desert me like every other man in my life, will you?"

Perhaps it was all part of the masculine ego rush that comes after hard sex, accentuated by the glimpse I had caught of the dark truths in my soul, but just then I didn't feel like every other man. Just then I felt within me a strange and unique power, not only to do financial good for myself but to do good for Caroline, too. She had said before that she wanted to be saved; maybe the truths I would unearth in her family's past could provide the first crucial steps toward her salvation. It was a maybe, only a maybe, but a maybe could warrant a hell of a lot. As a lawyer I had gotten pretty damn good at self-justification.

"I won't desert you," I said. "I'll see it through."

"So where do we start?"

"I have an idea, but you'll think it crazy."

"No I won't."

"Forget it," I said. "It's too wild."

She turned over on her stomach and drew her fingers lightly across my chest. "What is it, Victor? Whatever it is, no matter how insane, we'll do it, I promise."

"Anything?"

"I promise."

"Well, what I think we should do next," I said, sitting up and looking straight into those rich, blue eyes, "is dig up your grandmother's garden."

29

THE VAST STRETCH OF LAWN within the iron gates of Veritas was a sea of blackness, the windows of the mansion were dark. I parked the car on the upsweep of the driveway so as not to wake anyone who might have been in the house. It was a pitchy night, the moon was new, and in the expanse of sky that spread over the estate the stars peered forth like a million frog eyes. Caroline led with the flashlight as we made our way quietly around the house and to the rear gardens. In my right hand was a shovel we had just purchased from Home Depot for $9.99, a long-handled discount jobber with a sharp blade of flawed steel ready to chip at the first pebble. In my left hand was a kerosene lantern I had dug out of my closet from among my camping gear. We had stopped at a gas station to fill it with unleaded but I had misjudged the process and had drenched my pants with gasoline. Along with the fear of self-combustion was the dry sour smell that followed me wherever I moved.

As we sneaked around the ballroom side of the house, I tripped over a stone and cracked my shin. I let out a short sharp cry. Caroline turned the beam of her light into my face.

"Shut up," she whispered fiercely, a shadow behind the blob of light. "If you can't be quiet we'll just forget it."

"I'll be quiet," I said quietly. I rubbed my shin. "I just fell. Get that light out of my face." I pushed myself back to standing. "Let's go."

"This was a bad idea," she said, her inquisitor's light still blaring in my face. "We should forget it."

"You said you wanted to dig into your family history," I said. "That's just what we're doing. It's your house. I don't know why you're so jittery."

"You don't understand my grandmother. She wanted her garden left alone and she was not one to be defied."

"She's dead, Caroline."

"If there's anyone with the power to control this world from her grave, it's my grandmother."

I was surprised to see how nervous Caroline had become. When I first mentioned the idea a few nights before she seemed amused by it, as if it were a prank as harmless as toilet-papering a house or leaving a burning bag of manure on a doorstep. But as I explained my reasons she grew more and more apprehensive. She was afraid Nat would find out, or her father, or her mother, or Consuelo. It was clear that for a woman who claimed she believed in nothing, she found much in the Reddman family to fear, including her dead grandmother. She had insisted she would only go along if we were silent and did our best to replace the torn-up garden, all of which I had agreed to.

"I'll be quiet," I said. "Just stay close, I don't know the property as well as you do."

Side by side now, we followed the distorted oval of light on the ground. It led us across a side porch, around the swampy pool, to the giant square of untrimmed hedges looming large and mysterious in the night.

"Are you sure?" she said.

"I'm sure," I said, though in the presence of those living walls I was not so positive as I sounded. Maybe I was just catching some of Caroline's fear, or maybe there was something inside those thorny walls that resonated at the low pitch of horror, but whatever it was, as I approached the secret garden I felt more and more uneasy about what we were about to do.

We moved around those great walls until we arrived at where the entrance to the maze should have been. In the flattening beam of the flashlight it was hard to see any gaps. There was an irregular dark line of an opening at one spot. I put down the lantern and stepped up to the uneven line. When I reached through I felt something bite my hand. I snatched it back and found a thorn embedded between my forefinger and thumb.

"Damn it," I said as I yanked it out with my teeth. "These thorns are lethal. That's not it."

"Maybe over there," she said.

She was pointing the light now at a ragged vertical line that looked just like the last ragged vertical line in which my hand had been attacked. I reached in again and this time felt nothing impeding my hand once I got past the first layer of scraping branches. I pulled out my hand and turned around to look at her. She was almost cringing. Behind us, like a huge black bird extending its wings, crouched Veritas. Not a light was on inside. I picked up the lantern, whispered vague encouragements to Caroline, and slipped through the narrow opening, feeling the scrape of the spiny leaves on my arms and neck. Caroline squeezed through right behind me.

In the darkness, the pathways seemed narrow and malevolent. I remembered how bright and fresh they had been when I entered in the daylight, how the birds had sung and the butterflies had danced, how the smell of wild-flowers had suffused the atmosphere with a sweet fresh-ness, but we were no longer in the daylight. The air was thick with moisture and smelled of rot, as if whatever had been infecting that dinosaur of a mansion seeped out from the stones and mortar and wood, under cover of darkness, to taint everything within its reach. We followed the path-ways from one entrance to another, searching for our way through the maze. I wondered if this was how rats felt. I slashed the shovel into the ground as I walked, using it like a walking staff. Finally, after a few wrong turns and a few dead ends and a few moments of blind panic when there appeared to be no way out, we entered upon the very heart of Grandmother Shaw's private garden.

Caroline didn't go beyond the arched entranceway, halting there as if kept out by the type of invisible fence used to restrain dogs. From the entranceway she flicked the flashlight's circle of light around the area. The statue of Aphrodite, struggling against hairy arms of vine, was to our right; the bench, its orange blossoms closed in the darkness, was to our left. The oval plot at the center that had been populated with violet lilies and pale yellow jewelweed when Grimes had visited was now overgrown with thick grasses that were strangling the few perennials that had survived.

I placed the lantern on the ground and kneeled before it. "Put the light here," I said.

The circle of light jerked around the little garden and landed on the kerosene lantern. There was a tiny button on the side which, when I pulled, extended itself into a pump. I jacked the pump back and forth, priming the lantern. Then, when the pressure made the pumping difficult, I lit a match and turned a knob to the highest level and heard the sweet hiss of the pressurized fuel escaping. As I slipped the match under the glass windshield the inside of the lantern exploded into fire, which, after a few seconds, centered with a fury on the mantle. The white-hot flame blanched the scene for a moment before our eyes adjusted to the harsh light and long shadows.

I took the lantern and hung it from one of the arms of Aphrodite. Then I took the shovel, stepped through the weeds in the garden's central, oval plot, and, right in the middle of the oval, jabbed the shovel deep into the earth. As I levered the shovel's blade upward the roots of the weeds and flowers snapped and groaned until the shovel's load of dirt and weed pulled free, revealing bare black earth beneath. I tossed what I had dug to the side and jabbed the shovel into the groaning earth once more.

It was not as crazy an idea as it sounds, digging up that garden. When Grimes, Jacqueline Shaw's fiancé, had told me in the Irish Pub of his audience with Grandmother Shaw in that very same place, I had been left with the distinct impression that there was something hidden in the ground there. "Treasures are buried in this earth," Grammy Shaw had said, "keepsakes, mementos of a better time. Everything of value we place here." It had sounded figurative at best, but it had left me with an uneasy feeling, accentuated by her explanation of how, when the vapors of her gas plant burned, it was as if the spirits buried in that earth were igniting. On my first visit to that garden I had almost felt it beneath my feet, a presence of some sort, something dark and alive. And then Nat, the gardener, who seemed to know more than anyone else of the Reddman family's secrets, Nat, trailing frogs like a twisted Pied Piper, Nat had come upon me in that overrun oval and told me that Grandmother Shaw was right to order that this place should remain untended and allowed to turn wild. "Sometimes what's buried should remain buried," he had said. "No good can come from digging up the dead."

There were no shortage of suspects for Jacqueline Shaw's murder. Peter Cressi had killed her, sure, and somehow I would make sure he paid the price, but, financially speaking, pinning the death only on Peter did nothing for me. There had to be someone who paid him to do it, who arranged for the roof and stairwell doors to be open as he slipped down and performed his UPS impersonation, someone with assets on which I could collect once I filed and won my civil suit. Was it the Church of the New Life, that bogus cult of rehashed New Age excretion that was scheduled to reap a cool five mil from Jacqueline's death and tried to threaten me off the case? Or was it Eddie Shaw, pressured by the mob to pay up his debt, his arm shattered, his life threatened? He had been at the Cambium that afternoon, having flown in just for that purpose from North Carolina, looking for Jacqueline, so he had said, in perfect position to wedge the roof door open, to tape back the automatic lock on the stair shaft door, setting up Cressi's murderous visit. How he must have howled when he found out there was no insurance money coming to him. Or maybe it was Bobby Shaw, the diffident sexually confused stutterer, whose life was devoted to increasing the value of his fortune, or Harrington, who also had access to Jacqueline's building and was refusing marriage to a Reddman for some unknown reason.

There were enough suspects in the present to keep me busy, sure, but I wasn't digging up Grandma Shaw's garden just to find for Caroline the truths buried in her family's history. Something strange was at work here, something old, something hidden deep within the story of the Reddmans. Everything seemed to center around that crazed relic, Grammy Shaw, with her twisted face and one good eye, controlling the destiny of her entire dysfunctional family. Grammy had brought Nat and Selma and Harrington into the clutches of the Reddman family; Grammy had diverted great sums of money into a secret trust for some unknown purpose; Grammy had decreed that the garden was to grow wild and be left untouched. I couldn't shake the feeling that whatever secret Grammy had been trying to hide she had buried in this garden. I could have respected her wishes, sure, the rich old hag with half a face, but protecting her secrets wasn't going to get me any closer to my hard-earned share of her fortune. "No good can come from digging up the dead," had said Nat, the gardener. But it wasn't my dead.

I was three feet down when I heard the clang of my shovel against something hard and metallic. Behind me was a heap of dirt and ripped-out plants. The air was filled with the smell of old earth being turned. I had been digging out the heart of the little oval garden for almost an hour now, digging an area about eight feet long and four feet wide, trying to keep the floor of the pit level, like an archaeologist searching for pottery shards through strata of time. It was hard going, all except for one patch. I had stripped down to my tee shirt in the warm night. My hands slipped along the shiny surface of the new shovel's handle and had started to blister, forcing me to grip the wooden shaft awkwardly, so as to keep the tender portions from continuing to rub. My muscles ached and my back was only a few strains from spasm. In my few breaks, Caroline had dug a bit, but without much enthusiasm or progress, so it was mainly up to me. Without a pickax, I was forced to chop at the dirt with the shovel to loosen the packed earth before I could scoop it up, all except for the one patch I mentioned before. It was a small area roughly in the middle of the garden where the dirt was softer. I thought about just digging there, but I didn't want to miss anything, so I kept at the whole of the pit. Still, it was no surprise that, when I heard the clang of metal against metal, it came from the loosely packed center.

When I first heard the clang I wasn't sure what it was, my blade had already sparked against a few rocks, but then I clanged again and Caroline let out a small gasp, and then another, one for each time I wracked my shovel against the metal. It didn't take me long to figure out the rough rectangular dimensions of the object and to dig around it until my shovel could slip beneath and then to leverage it up out of the earth.

It was a box, a metal strongbox, dark, with rusted edges. There was a handle on the top, which I pulled, but it broke away quickly, weakened by rust and decay. I grabbed the box from beneath the sides and lifted. It was heavy and it smelled richly of old iron. When I gave it a tender shake I could feel its insides shift. The primary weight was the box itself, I could tell, for what had shifted inside had been relatively light. There was a lock integrated into the body of the metal and then another lock, an old rusted padlock, holding together two bars welded onto the top and the bottom. With the box in my arms, I stepped out of the pit and brought it to Caroline.

"You ever see this before?" I asked.

"No," she said, backing away from it as if it were a cat. "Never."

"I can't believe there was something actually here."

Staring, as if transfixed by the sight of that box, she said, "My grandmother put that there."

"Looks like it."

"Open it," she said.

"I don't think I can."

"Knock it open," she said. "Now."

As I carefully laid the box on the ground I glanced up at her. She stared down at the box as if it were something alive that needed killing. I took a breath, raised the shovel, and slammed the edge into the lock. It held. I raised the shovel again and slammed it again, and then again, and each time the padlock jumped in its frame and then sat back again, whole and tightly shut. I went at it a few times more, waiting for the padlock to explode, but they don't make things like they used to because they used to make them pretty damn well. The padlock held.

I swore as I swung futilely, the clangs of the shovel against the metal rising above the night calls of the crickets.

"You're making too much noise," she said.

I stopped, leaned over to gasp for air, turned my face to her. "You wanted me to open it. I don't think asking it nicely to unlock itself is going to work."

"You don't have to be nasty."

"We'll take it with us," I said. "You want me to fill in the hole?"

"Not yet," she said. "There might be something else down there."

"What else would be down there?"

"I don't know, but we've gone this far."

She took the shovel from me and hopped into the hole. She was trying harder now than before, as if some weakness of resolve had been strengthened by the sight of that box, by the knowledge that there were indeed secrets to be unearthed, but even so she was still making little progress. This far down the earth was hard-packed. I didn't expect she'd find anything else, but it was boring just to watch.

"Let me try," I said.

I stepped in the hole and took the shovel and ignored the pain in my hands as I went at it. A half an hour later my hair was wet with sweat, my tee shirt was soaked through, my hands were bleeding where the blisters had rubbed off. I was just about to give up when I jabbed the shovel into the earth and the ringing of the metal blade was strangely muffled. I tried it again and again heard the same soft sound.

"What's that?" I said.

I cleared as much dirt as I could and saw a piece of something rising from the packed earth, something folded and soft. I looked up at her as she stood over me and I shrugged.

"It's a piece of canvas or something," she said. "It almost looks like a sail."

"What's it doing there?"

"Who knows," she said.

I scraped some more around it and cleared the dirt away. A long ridge of a darkened fabric was rising from the floor of the pit.

"I'm going to pull it to see what it is," I said.

The fabric was thick and still strong within my fingers. Pulling at it was like pulling at time itself. Nothing moved, nothing budged. I jerked and pulled and made no progress. I moved around to get a better grip and started yanking again. Nothing, no shift, no budge, nothing. Caroline jumped down and took hold and helped me pull, but there was still no movement, still nothing—and then something.

The ridge of cloth lengthened, dirt started shifting. A dark smell, ancient and foul, slipped from the ground.

"It's coming," I said. We pulled hard and yanked again and more of the cloth started coming free.

"On the count of three," I said as we both tightened our grips. "One, two, three."

I put my weight into it and yanked back, pressing with my legs against the dirt, and Caroline did the same and suddenly the cloth gave and there was a cracking sound and we both fell flat onto our backs and that ancient ugly scent covered us like a noisome blanket.

Caroline was the first to scamper up and so I was still on my back when I heard her breath stop as if blocked by a chunk of half-chewed meat. I looked up at her. Her hands were pressed against her face and her eyes were screaming even though her throat was making not a sound.

I pulled myself to my feet and took hold of her and shook her until she started breathing once again. While she was gasping for air she pointed to the other side of the pit and I looked to where she was pointing and there I saw it, lit by the white light of the lantern, and my breath caught too.

A hand, its fingers outstretched, reaching out of the ground from among the folds of what looked now to be an old cloth coat, reaching up to the unblinking stars, a human hand but not one that had seen the softness of the sweet night sky for scores of years. It stuck out of the dirt, pointing up as if in accusation, and from the white light of the lantern came the gleam of a gold ring still riding a finger of bone, the flesh and muscle having long been devoured by the foul creeping life that prowls the loam for death.

The first thought that came to my mind upon seeing that skeleton hand with a ring on its finger was that maybe now it was time to call in my private investigator, Morris Kapustin.

Part 3

≡

FAITH

Those who set out to serve both God and Mammon soon discover there isn't a God.

—Logan Pearsall Smith

30

Belize City to San Ignacio, Belize

WHAT HAD BEEN MERELY rumors of dark doings in the Reddman past were absolutely confirmed by our finding of the corpse with the gold ring behind Veritas. I was certain when we found it that the root of the evil from which redemption had been sought by Grammy Shaw was buried beneath the dead woman's garden, but I was wrong. That death was an offshoot of some older, more primal crime, and only when that crime was discovered could we begin to unravel the mystery of what had murdered Jacqueline Shaw and threatened the destruction of all traces of the Reddman line. It was that discovery that led me, ultimately, to Belize, where a killer awaits.

I am sitting with my cases on the steps outside the guest house in Belize City, waiting for Canek Panti to take me to San Ignacio. Before me is a guard of low palms and then the unpaved road and then the Caribbean, turning from gray to a brilliant turquoise in the distance. It is five minutes after nine and already the sun is broiling. I look down both sides of Marine Parade but do not see my guide. Sweat is dripping down my shirt and I am thirsty, even though I drank an entire bottle of water at breakfast.

There is a grinding of gears and a hoot and the shaking sound of doubtful brakes. I look up and see Canek Panti

leaping out of a battered brown Isuzu Trooper, rushing to
grab hold of my bags. He is hatless today, wearing serious
black shoes, a clean shirt, his work clothes, I suppose. His
face is solemn. "I am sorry I am late, Victor," says Canek.

"You're right on time," I say as I grab my briefcase
and take it into the front seat with me. Canek hauls my
suitcase into the rear and then jumps back up into the
driver's seat.

"You have a lot to see today," he says.

"Well, let's have at it. San Ignacio or bust."

"Or bust what?"

"It's an American expression. It means it's time to go."

"San Ignacio or we bust apart, then," he says, nodding
seriously, as he grinds the gears and the engine whines and
the car shoots forward. He jerks the wheel to the left and
the car takes a sharp leaning turn and we are now heading
away from the Caribbean.

Canek honks the horn repeatedly on the narrow roads
as he edges our way out of the city. He doesn't talk, concentrating on his maneuvering, biting his lip as he works
past the crowds, children wearing maroon or blue or white
school uniforms, women with baskets of laundry on their
heads, panhandlers and artisans, Rastafarians striding purposefully, thin men, in short sleeves and ties, riding to
work on their too-small bicycles. Finally we reach a long
narrow road lined with cemeteries. The ground around us
is littered with shallow stone tombs, bleached white or
dusty black, covered with crosses, guarded by little dogs
staring at us impassively as we pass. Once past the cemeteries we begin to speed through the mangrove swamps
that grow like a barrier around Belize City and onward
along the Western Highway.

Lonely clapboard houses on stilts rise above the sodden ground. The rusted-out hulks of old American cars are
half covered by the swamp. Canek leans on his horn as he
passes a bus. The landscape is flat and wet and flat and

smells of skunk. A ratty old sign in front of nowhere announces that we have reached the Belize Country Club, another urges us to check our animals to keep Belize screwworm free. Canek keeps his foot firmly on the pedal and soon we pass out of the swamps and onto a vast, sandy heath littered with scrub palmetto.

"This used to be a great pine forest," shouts Canek over the engine's uneven whine, "and mahogany too. But they cut all the trees and floated them down the river to the ships."

We drive a long while, seeing nothing but the occasional shack rising askew out of the flat countryside, until to our left we spot the vague outlines of strange peaks, like great haystacks jutting from the flat ground. As we pass by these toothlike rises I begin to see, in the distance, the jagged outlines of the mountains to the west. At a colorful sign planted in the earth Canek slows the Trooper and turns off the highway, pulling the car into the dusty parking lot of a windowless and doorless shack-bar call JB's Watering Hole.

The place is studded with wooden placards bearing the names and emblems of British Army squadrons that were once stationed in Belize to protect it from Guatemala: "34 Field Squadron, Royal Engineers"; "1st Battalion, No. 2 Company, Irish Guards"; "The Gloucester Regiment, QMs Platoon–25 Hours a Day." A few men in ratty clothes are drinking already, a young girl is wiping a table. Canek says he needs some water for the car and so I sit under a spinning fan as he works outside.

After a few moments he comes in grinning and tells me everything is fine. "The car gets thirsty," he says. "Let's have lunch." He orders us both stewed chicken in a brown sauce. It comes with coleslaw and rice and beans and even though it is already spicy hot he covers his with an angry red habanero sauce. As we eat we both have a Belikin and he tells me stories about the place, about the wild ex-pat who owned it and how the British soldiers turned it rowdy and how Harrison Ford drank here while filming *Mosquito Coast*.

"You're a good guide, Canek. The good guides know all the best bars."

"It is my country and there are not many bars."

"This chicken is wonderful."

"Outside of Belize City it is best to stick with chicken. You don't have to store it or refrigerate it. When you are ready to eat you just go outside and twist off the head."

I stare at the thigh I am working on for a moment and then slice off another piece. "What is San Ignacio like?"

"Small and fun. It used to be wilder when the loggers were there but the loggers have moved on and now it is not as wild."

"Are there good bars there?"

"Yes, I will show you. And on Saturday nights they have dancing at the ruins above the city."

"If a man was hiding out, would he hide out in San Ignacio?"

"No, not in San Ignacio. But it is the capital of the Cayo and the Cayo is wild country. There are ranches hidden from the roads and rivers that flow through the jungle and places you can only get to by horseback or by canoe."

"Is it pretty?"

"It is very pretty. You haven't told me what is your business there, Victor."

"I'm looking for someone," I say. "Someone who owes me money."

"This is a long way for an American to come to collect on a debt."

"It's a hell of a debt."

Back on the road, the highway starts kinking and slowly the landscape around the road changes to pine-covered hills and rocky pasture lands holding small villages. We pass a two-room schoolhouse, no windows or doors, old men sitting on the railing outside, listening to the lessons. Now and then we begin to pass boys on horseback. Canek shows me the turnoff to Spanish Lookout, where a Mennonite community farms the land in their straw hats and black buggies. He asks me if I want to see and I shake my head. Lancaster is only forty minutes from Philadelphia and I have never had the urge to visit the Pennsylvania Dutch there; I don't need to see them in Belize.

The land begins to undulate more and more violently and the mountains grow closer and on the mountains we can now see the forests, a dangerous green spilling thickly down the slopes. We pass a horseback rider sitting straight in his saddle, a rifle strapped to his shoulder, the muzzle jutting forward, serving as an armrest. Finally, in the middle of a valley, on the banks of a slow river, ringed with high hills, we find San Ignacio.

We wait at the end of a long one-lane bridge for a rickety red truck to pass before Canek drives us across the Macal River. The metal surface of the bridge rattles loudly beneath us. Canek takes us through the twists and turns of the town, filled with old storefronts and narrow streets, and then we are back on the Western Highway, traveling toward the ruins of the Mayan stronghold of Xunantunich.

"The word means 'stone maiden,'" says Canek as he drives us further on the paved road, alongside a wide shallow river. "The legend is that one of its discoverers saw the ghost of a woman on the ruins. It is set on a level hilltop overlooking the Mopan River and it guarded the route from the great city of Tikal, now in Guatemala, to the sea. It was a ceremonial center, along with Caracol, to the south, when this area had a greater population than the entire country of Belize has now. There was an earthquake in the year nine hundred that caused the abandonment of the city."

"It's amazing," I say, "how the Maya just disappeared."

"But that's not right," says Canek. "We haven't disappeared at all."

I turn and stare at him. He is very serious and his broad cheekbones suddenly look sharper than before.

"I didn't know you were Mayan."

"We have our own villages here and in Guatemala where we continue the old ways, at least some of the old ways. We don't go in for human sacrifice anymore." He smiles. "Except for during festival days. This is San Jose Succotz. The first language here is Mayan."

He pulls the car off the road onto a gravel shoulder. To our left is a village built into a hillside. A pair of ragged stands flank a small drive that leads straight into the water to our right. On the far shore of the river is a wooden ferry, short and thick and heavy, big enough to hold one car only. We wait in the car for the ferry to make its way to our side of the river. Boys come to the car's window, offering slate trinkets and carvings with Mayan designs. "You buy here when you come back," says one of the boys to me. "Don't believe what they say on the other side, they are escaped from the hospital, you know, the crazy house." On the other side I see more boys waiting to sell their slate. Further down the river, women are scrubbing laundry against the rocks and children are splashing in the water.

When the ferry arrives, its leading edge of wood coming to rest on the gravel drive, Canek slowly pulls the car down the small drive and onto the ferry. An old ferryman patiently waits for Canek to situate the car in the middle before he begins to twist the crank that winches the wire that drags the ferry back across the river. The water is calm and the ferry barely ripples as the old man draws us forward with each turn of the crank. Canek and the ferryman talk in a language which is decidedly not Spanish. "We were speaking Mopan," he says. "This village is Mopan Maya. I am Yucatec Maya but I know this dialect as well as my own."

When the ferry reaches the far bank, Canek drives the Trooper off onto another drive, takes a sharp right, and begins the climb up the rough, rock-strewn road that will take us to the ancient fortress. Canek tells me we are only a mile and a half from the Guatemalan border. After a long uphill drive we reach a parking grove. When Canek steps down from the car he pulls from it a canteen of water and a huge machete, which he slips into a loop off his pants.

"That's a fancy knife," I say.

"The jungle overgrows everything in time," he says.

As we climb the rest of the way, mosquitoes hover about my face and from all around us comes the manic squall of wildlife. The jungle rises along the edges of our path, green and dark and impenetrable. Canek, ever the perfect guide, offers me the canteen he carries and I stop to drink. Finally, out of the dark canopy of jungle we come upon the ceremonial plaza of Xunantunich.

The plaza is bright with sun, verdant with grasses and cohune palms and the encroaching jungle, as flat as a putting green. At the edges of the plaza hummingbirds hover among brilliant tropical flowers, darting from one bright color to another. Rising from the verdant earth in great piles of plant-encrusted rock are the remains of huge Mayan structures. There is something frightening in the immensity and the solidity of these ancient things, once hidden by centuries of jungle growth, like painful truths that have been unearthed. And dominating it all to our left, like the grandest truth of all, is El Castillo, a huge man-made mountain of rock.

Canek gives me the tour, as authoritative as if he had lived here when the plaza was still alive. He shows me a ceremonial stone bench in one of the temples and a frieze of a king and his spiritual midget in the little museum shack. "Midgets are sacred to the Maya," says Canek. "They are the special ones, touched by God as children, which is why they have stopped growing. They are able to journey back and forth between this world and the underworld. Some still claim to see the sacred little ones walking along the roads." He takes me to the residential buildings off the plaza, hacking with his machete through the jungle to get us there, and shows me the ball yard, a narrow grassy alley between the sloping sides of two of the temples. "The games were largely ceremonial," says Canek, "and the ceremony at the end involved the sacrifice of the losers."

"And I thought hockey was tough," I say.

We make our way around the grounds until we face the immensity of El Castillo, which towers above us, cragged and steep, stained green with life, banded with a reconstructed frieze of beige.

"Can we climb it?" I ask.

"If you wish."

"Let's do it."

I take a drink of water and we begin to ascend the long wide steps along the north side of El Castillo. The thing we are climbing is a ruin in every sense of the word, churned to crumbling by the jungle, but as we turn from the wide steps and climb off to the left and around, past the huge ornate glyphs of jaguars reconstructed on that side, the structure of the artificial mountain becomes clearer. It is a tower built upon other towers, an agglomeration of buildings perched one atop the next. From the path on the east side the vista is magnificent but Canek doesn't stop here. He takes me around to the south side, where a set of steps leads to a wide plateau. We scoot around a narrow ledge to a balcony with steep walls on either side and a broad view east, into the jungles of Belize.

"You can go farther up," says Canek.

"Let's go then."

"You should go alone, Victor. It is better alone."

He gives me a drink of water. I look again down from the balcony and realize I am already over a hundred feet above the plaza. I take another drink and then head back, across the narrow ledge, to the south side. It appears there is no way up but then I spot a narrow set of stairs cut into the stone. I climb them, one hand brushing the wall, to a ledge where I find a similar set of narrow stairs, this set leading up to a high room, stinking incongruously of skunk. There is no way out of that room, but I follow the ledge to the west, to another room, with a set of steep stone stairs spiraling up through a hole cut into the room's ceiling. I grab the steps above me to keep me steady and begin my climb. Slowly I rise through the ceiling and then step onto a narrow plaza with five great blocks of stone, seated one next to the other, like five jagged teeth. I am so relieved to be again on solid ground that it takes me a moment to calm myself before I look around. When I do my breath halts from the sight.

I can see so far it is as if I can see through time. I trace the indentation of the river as it flows through the jungle. In the distance to the east is San Ignacio and the rest of Belize. But for a slight haze I'm certain I could see the ocean. To the west is the absolute green of the wilds of the Petén region of Guatemala. I am being held aloft by the ruins of a temple thousands of years old and for a moment I feel informed by the ancient wisdom of those who built and worshiped in this edifice. There is more to the universe than what I can see and feel, this ancient knowledge tells me, more than the shallow limits of my own horizons, and this limitlessness, it tells me just as surely, is as much a part of me as my hand and my heart and my soul. It comes to me in an instant, this knowledge of my own infinitude, as solid as any insight I have ever held, and disappears just as quickly, leaving the unattached emotional traces of a forgotten dream.

I wipe the sweat from my neck and wonder what the hell that was all about. I figure I am suffering from dehydration and should quickly get to the hotel in San Ignacio, suck down some water, relax, take it slow for a day or two before continuing my search. But I look around and think again on what it was I thought I understood. The story of the corpse we found beneath the garden behind the great Reddman house twists and turns through love and war and ever more death, but it also contains one man's understanding of his place in the universe that gave solace and serenity and maybe even something akin to forgiveness. For the first time since I learned of it I have an inkling of what it might have done to him to see the world and his life that way. Jacqueline Shaw, I think, was looking for the same sort of understanding during her time with the Church of the New Life, as was Beth after her. There are truths, I know with all certainty, that I will never grasp, but that doesn't make them any less true. And some of those truths might be the only antidote to the poison that passed like a plague through the Reddman line.

And as I spin around and look once more at this grand vista I know something else with an absolute certainty. I don't know how I know it, or why, but I know it, yes I do. What I know for certain is that the man for whom I am searching is somewhere down there, somewhere hiding in the wild green of that jungle.

And I'm going to find the bastard, I know that too.

31

MORRIS KAPUSTIN WAS SITTING at my dining room table with his head in his hands. He had a naturally large head, Morris did, and it seemed even larger due to his long peppered beard and mass of unruly hair, the wide-brimmed black hat he wore even inside my apartment, the way his small pudgy hands barely covered his face. His black suit was ragged, his thin tie was loose about his neck, he leaned forward with his elbows on the table and his tiny feet resting on the strut of his chair, listening with great concentration. Across from him sat Beth, who was explaining her most recent meditative exercises to him. On the table between Beth and Morris was the metal box Caroline and I had disinterred from the garden behind Veritas the night before. Deep ridges slashed through the surface of the metal where I had futilely chopped at the box with the shovel. It sat there, dirty and crusted, still unopened, large with mystery.

"We start with a small seed," said Beth. "We place it before us and meditate upon it, thinking all the while of the plant that will grow from the seed. We visualize the plant inherent in the seed, make it present to us and in us, and then meditate on that visualization, allow our soul to react to it. Eventually, we begin to see the life force in the seed as a sort of flame."

"And this flame, what does it look like?" asked Morris.

"It's close to the color purple in the middle, with something like blue at the edges."

"And you've seen this hallucination?" I said.

Beth looked up at me calmly. "Yes," she said.

"Fascinating," said Morris, the final "ng" sounding like a "k." "Simply fascinating."

"And then we concentrate on a mature plant and immerse ourselves in the thought that this plant will someday wither and decay before being reborn through its seeds. As we concentrate on the death and rebirth of this plant, banishing all thoughts other than those of the plant, we begin to see the death force inherent in the plant, and it too is like a flame, green-blue in its center and yellow-red at the periphery."

"I can't believe you're buying into this crap, Beth," I said.

"I've seen it," she said. "Either that or my lentil casserole was spiked."

"And now, after you've seen all this," said Morris, "what are you supposed to do with all that you are seeing?"

"I don't know that yet," said Beth with a sigh. "Right now I'm struggling to develop my spiritual sight so that, when the truth does appear, I'll be ready to perceive it."

"When you perceive something a little more than these flamelike colors," said Morris, "then you come back to me and we'll talk. The spirit world, it is not unknown to Jews, but these colors, they are no more than *shmei drei*. Just colors I can see every day on cable."

Morris Kapustin was my private detective. He didn't look like a private detective or talk like a private detective or act like a private detective but he thought like the best private detective you've ever dreamed of. I liked him and trusted him and, after Beth, the list of those whom I actually liked and trusted was rather short. Like all good things in this life I had first had him rammed down my

throat. A group of insurgent clients had thought a settlement offer I had jumped at was less than their case was
worth. They ordered me to hire Morris to find a missing
witness. Morris found him, which increased the value of
the case tremendously, and in the process he sort of saved
my life. Since then he had been my private dick, my spiritual adviser, and my friend. I had thought I would do my
dance around the Reddman fortune without him but, after
discovering that skeleton the night before, I realized that
the mysteries were deepening beyond my minimal capacities and that I needed Morris.

"I think," I said to Beth, "that Morris is pretty firmly
entrenched in a spiritual tradition a few thousand years
older than your Church of the New Life. I'm sure he's not
interested in your New Age rubbish."

Morris picked his head up out of his hands. "On the
contrary, Victor. It is just such rubbish that interests me so
much. Did you ever hear, Victor, of Kabbalah?"

"I've heard of it," I said, though that was about the
limit of my knowledge. Kabbalah was an obscure form of
Jewish mysticism, neither taught nor even mentioned in
the few years I attended religious school before my father
quit the synagogue. It was said to be ancient and dangerous
and better left untouched.

"Your meditation, Beth, this is not a foreign idea to
Jews. The Hassidim, they chant and sing and dance like
wild men and they say it works. I always thought it was the
way they drank, like *shikkers* in a desert, but maybe it is
something more. And this is what I find, Miss Beth. Every
morning, in *shachris*, when I strap on my *tefillin* and
daven, I find often something strange it happens. Some
precious mornings all the *mishegaas* around my life, it disappears and I find myself floating, surrounded by something bright and divine and infinite. The Kabbalists, they
have a term for it, the infinite, they call it the *Ein-Sof.*"

"But that's very different," said Beth. "We're being

trained in our meditation to focus and join with a great emptiness, not a deity of some sort."

"Yes, of course, that is a difference. But there are those who claim that any true knowledge of the infinite, it is so beyond us that we can only experience the *Ein-Sof* as a sort of nothingness. The Hebrew word for nothing, it is *Ayin*, and the similarities in the words are said to be of great significance."

"How come I never learned any of this?" I asked.

"This is all very powerful, very dangerous. There were people, very devout people, great rabbis even, who were not ready to ascend into certain of the divine rooms and never returned. The rabbis they think maybe you should get off your *tuchis* and learn more about the bolts and the nuts of our religion before you start to *potchkeh* with the Kabbalah. Maybe learn first to keep the *Shabbos* and keep kosher and learn to *daven* every day. They have a point, Victor, no? These are not games or toys. They take intense commitment. True devotion comes from following all God's *mitzvoth*. The righteous, they reach a point where every act in their daily rituals is full of meaning and devotion and life itself, it becomes like a meditation."

"If this is all so darn terrific, how come I never saw it being hawked on an infomercial?"

"Not everything in this world can be bought, Victor," said Beth.

"Maybe not," I said, "but have you seen what the stuff Cher sells can do for your hair? Tell me something, Beth. If your friends are so exclusively devoted to the spirit world, why are they so anxious to get their mitts on Jacqueline's five-million-dollar death benefit?"

Beth looked at me for a moment. "That's a good question. I've been wondering about that myself."

"Until we find an answer," I said, "I think you should be extra careful. They might just be as dangerous as they think they are."

"That's exactly why I set it up so you're the one who's going to ask Oleanna all about it."

"Oleanna?"

"Tomorrow night, at the Haven. I told her you had some important questions."

"And the great seer deigned to meet with me?"

"It's what you wanted, right?"

"Sure," I said, suddenly and strangely nervous. "What is she like?"

"I think you'll be impressed," said Beth, laughing. "She is a very evolved soul."

"Her past lives were thrilling, no doubt," I said. "She was a queen or a great soldier or Nostradamus himself. Why is it no one ever sold insurance in their past lives?"

"You should not be scoffing so quickly," said Morris. "Someday, when you are ready, I'll tell you of the *gilgul*. As Rebbe Elazar ha-Kappar once said, 'Those who are born are destined to die, those who are dead are destined to be brought to life again.' Be aware, Victor, there is much to learn in this world, and not all of it can be found in the *Encyclopedia Britannica*."

I stared at him. "Did you ever go to college, Morris?"

"Aacht. It's a *shandeh*, really. I regret so much in this life but that I regret most of all. No. I had plans, of course, when I was a boy, the Academy of Science at Minsk, they took Jews, they even taught in Yiddish, and the whole of my family we were saving each day zloty for my fee. I was to be an intellectual, to sip slivovitz in the cafés and argue about Moses Mendelssohn and Pushkin, that was my dream. Then of course the war, it came and plans like that they flew like a frying pan out the window. Just surviving was education enough. I won't go through the whole *megillah*, but no, Victor. Why do you ask such a thing?"

"Because I could just see you hanging out in the dormitories, eating pizza, drinking beer from cans, talking all night about the cosmic mysteries of life."

"And Pushkin, we could maybe discuss Pushkin?"

"Sure, Morris. Pushkin."

"I don't even like the poetry so much, I must admit, but the sound of the name. Pushkin, Pushkin. I can't resist it. Pushkin. Sign me up, *boychick*, I'm in."

"He is less the skeptic than you, Victor," said Beth. "At least he listens and takes it seriously."

"I tried it, Beth, really I did, I sat on the floor and meditated and examined myself and my life like a detached observer, just as you suggested."

"How did it make you feel?"

"Before or after I threw up?"

"You know, Victor," said Morris. "A very wise man once said that nausea, it is the first sign of serious trouble in this life. Very serious. Such nausea, it should not be ignored."

"What, now you're quoting Sartre?"

"Sartre, *Schmatre*, I'm talking about my gastroenterologist, Hermie Weisenberg. Maybe what you need is a scope. I'll set it up for you."

"Forget the scope." I gestured at the box. "You sure you can open it?"

"I can try."

"I thought Sheldon was coming." Sheldon Kapustin was Morris's son and a trained locksmith. "I asked for Sheldon."

"Sheldon, he was busy tonight. He's of that age now that I want for nothing to get in the way of his social life. A man my age, he should have granddaughters, no? So don't be disturbing my Sheldon. Besides, who do you think taught him such about locks anyway?"

"You, Morris?"

"No, don't be silly. A master locksmith named McCardle, but this McCardle he taught me too. Victor, this girl, when is she coming, *nu*?"

"Any minute now," I said, and just as I said it my buzzer rang.

Caroline, when she entered the apartment, was nervous and closed. She came right in and sat on the couch, away from the table and the box. She crossed her legs and wrapped her arms around herself. As I introduced Morris and Beth to her, she smiled tightly and lit a cigarette.

After Caroline and I had discovered the bony corpse the night before we pondered what to do with it. We discussed it in tense whispers while we stood over the skeleton hand that pointed skyward from the grave and we both agreed to cover up the pit as best as we could, shoveling back the dirt, stamping it down, replacing as many plants as might survive, leaving the body right there in the ground. It was not like the corpse was going anywhere, and any hot clues as to the perpetrator were already as cold as death. We convinced each other it was to our advantage to not let on to what we had found as we probed further into the Reddman past. So we left it there under the dirt, the bones of that poor dead soul, left it all there except for the gold ring which clung to the bone until, with force and spit, I ripped it free. We took the ring to help us identify the body and once we examined the ring there wasn't too much doubt about who was there beneath the dirt. The ring had been engraved, in a gloriously florid script, with the initials CCR.

"What's the word?" I said.

"I checked an old photograph with a magnifying glass," said Caroline. "It's her ring, all right."

"So there's no doubt," I said.

"No doubt at all," she said. "The body we found is of my grandmother's sister, Charity Chase Reddman."

32

WITH CAROLINE SITTING on my couch, smoking, her legs crossed, her arms crossed, sitting there like a shore house boarded up for a hurricane, I brought Morris up to speed on the mystery of the Reddmans. I told him about Elisha Poole, about the three fabulous Reddman sisters, about how Charity, the youngest, had apparently found herself pregnant and then disappeared, seeming to wrest the shackles of her oppressive family off her shoulders and be free, only to turn up eighty years later in a hole in the ground behind the Reddman mansion. Morris listened with rapt attention; it was the kind of puzzle he liked most, not of wood or of stone but of flesh and bone and blood.

I showed him the ring. "What's this on the inside?" he asked. "My eyes such as they are, I can't read printing so small as this."

"'You walk in beauty,'" I read from the inside of the band, "and then the initials C.S."

"Any idea who this C.S. fellow is?" asked Beth.

"Could be anyone," I tried to say, but Caroline, who had remained remarkably silent during my background report to Morris, interrupted me.

"They were my grandfather's initials," she said flatly. "Christian Shaw."

"What about the inscription?" I asked. "Anyone recognize it?"

"'She walks in beauty, like the night,'" recited Morris.

"'Of cloudless climes and starry skies; and all that's best of dark and bright meet in her aspect and her eyes.'"

I was taken aback a bit by such melodious words coming from Morris's mouth, where only a jumbled brand of immigrant English normally escaped.

"Byron," said Morris with a shrug. "You know Pushkin, he was very much influenced by this Byron, especially in his early work."

"Pushkin again?" I said.

"Yes Pushkin. Victor, you have problem maybe with Pushkin?"

"No, Morris. None at all."

"This girl," asked Morris, "this Charity, how old was she again when first she disappeared?"

"Eighteen," said Caroline."

"Then that fits then. It is a poem, this, for a young girl. It ends talking of a heart whose love is innocent."

No one said anything right off, as if there was a moment of silence for the dead girl whose heart was suffused with innocent love.

"Open the box," said Caroline.

"I'm ready if you're ready," said Morris.

"I'm ready," she said.

"Are you sure?" I asked her.

"I told you I want to find out everything I can about my family, all the bitter truths. I won't stop at a corpse. Open it."

From his seat Morris bent down and lifted onto the table a leather gym bag. He opened the bag, peered mysteriously inside, reached in, and took out a small leather packet from which he extracted two thin metal picks. I looked at Caroline on the couch, arms still crossed, her front teeth biting her lip. I smiled encouragingly at her but she ignored me, focusing entirely on Morris. Morris turned the box until the front was facing him and then began working on the padlock.

"Are you sure you can't get hold of Sheldon?" I said, after Morris had tried for ten minutes to work the lock with the picks and failed.

"It's a tricky, tricky lock. Very clever these old lock makers. I must to try something else."

He put the picks back in their leather packet and the packet back into the gym bag, reached in, and pulled out a large leather envelope from which he took a jangling ring of skeleton keys. "One of these will work, I think," he said. He began to try one after the other, one after the other after the other.

"Do you have a number for Sheldon?" I asked after all the keys had failed to fit the lock.

"Enough with the *nudging* already," said Morris, anger creeping into his voice. "These locks, they are not such a problem for me, not at all. For this I don't need Sheldon."

"I've seen Sheldon work," I said. "He is in and out in seconds."

"On second-rate locks, yes," said Morris as he put the skeleton keys back into the bag and rummaged around. "But this is no second-rate lock. I have one special tool in such situations that never fails, a very special tool."

With a flourish he pulled from the bag a hacksaw.

"This lock it is very clever but the metal is not as strong as they can make now. Is this all right, miss, if I hurt the lock?"

"My grandmother's dead," said Caroline. "I don't think she'll miss it."

It took only a few minutes until we heard the ping that signaled he had cut through the metal hoop. He opened the lock and took it off the metal guards soldered into the box. That left only the internal lock, which Morris looked at carefully. "For this again I need the picks."

"It's getting late, Morris," I said.

He took out the picks and began to work the little lock. "This second is not so tricky," he said as he twisted the picks once and twice and the lock gave way with a satisfying click. Morris beamed. "Sheldon maybe would be a *bissel* faster, but only a *bissel*."

Caroline rose from the couch and sat beside Beth at the table. Morris turned the box to her. She looked around at us. I nodded. She reached down and, slowly, she lifted the metal lid.

Beth let out a "Wow," as the lid first cracked open and Caroline shut it again.

"What?" I asked.

"I just thought I saw something."

"One of your flames?" asked Morris.

"I don't know."

"What color was it?" asked Morris.

"Yellow-red," said Beth.

Morris nodded. "The color of the death force."

"Enough already," I said. "Just open it."

Caroline swallowed and then flipped up the top of the metal strongbox. Inside were dust and dirt and a series of old manila envelopes, weathered and faded and torn. Not very encouraging.

"Let's see what they're holding," I said.

One by one Caroline lifted the envelopes out of the box.

The first envelope contained a multitude of documents on long onionskin legal paper of the type no longer used in law offices, each dated in the early fifties. The documents were all signed by Mrs. Christian Shaw, Caroline's grandmother, and witnessed by a number of illegible signatures, all probably of lawyers now surely either dead or retired. As best as I could tell, as I plowed my way through the legal jargon of the era, replete with Latin and all types of convoluted sentences, the documents created a separate trust to which a portion of the Reddman estate was to be diverted. The trust was named Wergeld and so a person or a family named Wergeld was apparently the intended beneficiary, though nothing more specific was provided in the documents. It wasn't clear exactly how much was to be transferred, but it appeared to be considerable, and over the past forty or so years the amount in the trust must have grown tremendously.

"This must be the trust Harrington was talking about the other night," I said to Caroline while I examined the documents. "Ever hear of a family named Wergeld?"

"No."

"Are you sure? Anyone at all?"

"No, no one," she said. "Never."

"That's strange," I said. "Why would she set up a trust for someone you never heard of? All right, let's go on."

The next envelope contained a series of bank documents, evidencing the opening of accounts all in the name of the Wergeld Trust. The signatory on each account was Mrs. Christian Shaw. The banks to which the money was to flow were in foreign countries, Switzerland, Luxembourg, the Cayman Islands. "All tax havens," I said. "All places where money could arrive and disappear without anyone knowing, and where the banks are all governed by secrecy laws."

"Why would my grandmother care about secrecy?" asked Caroline. "While she was alive she had control of all the money in the trust, she could have done anything she wanted and no one could have stopped her."

"Maybe so," I said, "but it appeared she wanted the trust hidden and this Wergeld person to remain anonymous."

Along with the bank documents was a three-by-five card with a list of long combinations of letters and numbers. The first was X257YRZ26–098. I handed it to Morris and he examined it carefully.

"To my untrained eye these are code numbers for certain bank accounts," he said. "Some of the banks in these places you need mention only the code numbers and a matching signature or even just a matching phrase to release the funds. This was obviously the way your Mrs. Shaw, she could access the money from that trust you were reading us about, Victor."

"But why would she bury it?" asked Caroline.

"She knew where it was if she needed it, I suppose," said Morris with a shrug. "But I would guess the beneficiary person of this trust, or whatever, would have these very same numbers."

The third envelope contained a packet of old photographs. Caroline looked at them each carefully, one by one, and then went through them again, for our sakes, telling Beth and Morris and me what she could about the people in the pictures. "These are of my family," she said, "at least most of them. I've seen many of them before in albums. Here's a picture of Grandmother when she was young, with her two sisters."

The picture was of three young women, arms linked, marching in step toward the camera, dressed as if they were young ladies on the make out of an Edith Wharton novel. The woman in the middle wore a billowing white dress and stared at the photographer with her chin up, her head cocked slightly to the side, her face full of a fresh certainty about her future. That woman, full of life and determination, Caroline said, was her grandmother, Faith Reddman Shaw. To Faith Reddman's right was a smaller, frailer woman, her stance less sure, her smile uneasy. Her hair was pulled tightly back into a bun and her dress was a severe and prim black. This was Hope Reddman, the sister who was to die of consumption only a few years later. And to the left, broad-shouldered and big-boned, but with her head tilted shyly down, was Charity Reddman, poor dead Charity Reddman. Her dress was almost sheer enough to see her long legs beneath, she wore a hat, and even with her face cast downward you could see her beauty. She was the pretty one, Caroline had been told, the adventurous one, though that thirst for adventure was not evident in her adolescent shyness. Beautiful Charity Reddman, the belle of the ball, who was destined to disappear beneath the black earth of Veritas.

"That's your great-grandfather," I said, pointing to the next photograph, a picture of a fierce, bewhiskered man, his bulging eyes still burning with a strange intensity even as he leaned precariously on a cane, his knees stiff, his back bent. He was leaner than I had remembered from other pictures, his stance more decrepit, but the fierce whiskers, the burning eyes, the wide, nearly lipless mouth were still the stuff of legend. Claudius Reddman, as familiar a figure as all the other icons of great American industrial wealth, as familiar as Rockefeller in his starched collar, as Ford with his lean angularity, as Morgan staring his stare that could maim, as Gould and Carnegie and Frick.

"That was just before he died, I think," said Caroline. "He lived to be ninety, though in his last years he suffered from palsy and emphysema."

She flipped to the next photograph and said, "This is my grandfather." It was a photograph of a handsome young man, tall and blond and mustached, with his nose snootily raised. His suit was dark, his hat nattily creased and cocked over his eye. He had the same arrogant expression I saw in Harrington the first time we met at the bank. There was something about the way he stood, the way his features held their pose, that made me pause and then I realized he held himself in the same careful way I often saw in drunks.

"Who's that?" I asked, pointing at a photograph of a thin, bald man with a long thin nose and small eyes. He wore a stiff, high collar and spectacles and through the spectacles his tiny eyes were squinted in wariness. Beside him was a handsome woman with a worried mouth. There was something fragile about this couple. There was a sense in the picture that they were under siege.

"I don't know," said Caroline.

I turned it over, but there was no description.

The next was another picture she couldn't identify, a photograph of an unattractive young woman with a dowdy print dress, unruly hair, and a long face with beady eyes. She looked like a young Eleanor Roosevelt with a long thin nose, which was rather sad for her since Eleanor Roosevelt was the ugliest inhabitant ever of the White House, uglier even than Richard Nixon, uglier even than Checkers. The woman in the photograph was just that ugly, and she seemed to know it, looking at the camera with a peculiar passion and intensity that was almost frightening.

"I don't know who she is," said Caroline. "I have no idea why my grandmother would save these pictures."

"Who might know something about them?" I asked.

"These all seem very old, from the time before my father was born, but he might recognize them. Or Nat. They are the only ones who have been around long enough to possibly know."

There were other photographs, more of the unattractive young woman, more of Christian Shaw, one of which showed him haggard and miserable in a mussed suit. It was taken, Caroline said, shortly before he died. She could tell, she said, because the sleeve of his jacket was loosely pinned to the side. "He lost his arm in the war," she said. "In France, during the battle in which he won his medal." There was also a postcard with a picture of Yankee Stadium on its grand opening, a sellout crowd, the Yankees, in pinstripes, at bat. From the distance it was impossible to tell, but maybe it was Ruth at the plate, or Jumping Joe Dugan, or Wally Pipp. There was no message written on the back.

The final picture was more modern, in faded color, a young couple with their arms around each other. The boy was tall and handsome, his hair long, his shirt tie-dyed, his

jeans cut into shorts and his shoes sandals. He was laughing at the camera, giddy with life. The girl was wildly
young, wearing jeans and a tee shirt, her brown hair as
straight and as long as a folk singer's. She was staring up
at the boy with the glow of sated passion on her face.
Caroline didn't say anything and I blinked a bit before I
realized who it was: Caroline and Harrington, just a couple
of kids crazy in love.

"Who took it?" I asked.

"I don't remember," she said softly, "but not Grammy.
I don't remember her ever taking a picture."

When we had finished with the photographs, Caroline
reached again into the box and took out a white business
envelope with the words "The Letters" written in script on
the outside. The handwriting was narrow and tight, the
same as the writing on the trust documents. Inside the
envelope was a key, an old key, tarnished, with an ornate
head and a long shank and a bit that looked like a piece
from a jigsaw puzzle.

"Any idea where the lock is?" I asked Caroline.

"None," she said.

Morris took hold of the key and examined it. "This key
is a key to a Barron tumbler lock of some sort. Such a lock
I could open in a minute. Maybe three."

A thin envelope taken from the box contained only one
piece of paper, a medical bill from a Dr. Wesley Karpas,
dated June 9, 1966, charging, for services rendered,
$638.90. The services rendered were not specified, nor was
the patient. It was addressed, though, to Mrs. Christian
Shaw. I asked Caroline whether she had any idea about the
medical services referred to in the bill and she had none.

The final envelope was a thick bundle that felt, from
the outside, not unlike a bundle of hundred-dollar bills.
Caroline opened the envelope and reached in and pulled
out a sheaf of papers separated by clips into four separate
sections, the whole bundle bound with twine. The papers

were old, each about the size of a small envelope, yellowed, covered with the tight narrow handwriting that was already familiar, the handwriting of Faith Reddman Shaw. One edge of each of the papers was slightly ragged, as if it had been cut from a book of some sort.

Caroline looked at the top page, and then the next, and then the next. "These look to be from my grandmother's diary, but that can't be possible."

"Why not?"

"She burned them all shortly before she died. She kept volumes and volumes of a diary from when she was a little girl, she would scribble constantly, but she never let anyone see them and a few years back she burned them all. We begged her not to, they were such a precious piece of our history, but she said her past was better forgotten."

"I guess there were some pages," I said, "she couldn't bear to incinerate."

Caroline, who was scanning through the excerpts, said, "This first one is about meeting my grandfather."

"Maybe there are clues in these diary pages of who these people in the photographs, they are," said Morris, "and why your grandmother, she kept this box buried like she did. We should maybe be reading these pages, no?"

"It's up to Caroline," I said.

She looked up and shrugged.

We all took seats around the table. The rusted and mangled box sat between us. We leaned forward and listened carefully as Caroline read out loud the surviving sections of her grandmother's diary, one by one, the sections torn from the bound volumes before they were burned, the sections that her grandmother could not suffer to destroy. Halfway through, Caroline's voice grew hoarse and Beth took over the reading. It grew still in the room, except for the song of the reader's voice, as strangely foreign to the two women who shared the reading as if channeled from the dead Faith Reddman herself. At one point, while Beth read, Caroline suppressed a sob, and then waved us away when we offered comfort and told Beth to keep reading. The last line was a fervent wish for peace and love and redemption and after it was over we sat in silence for a long time, still under the spell of that voice from long ago.

"I think," said Morris, "I know now who are these people in the photographs, but the crucial questions I can't yet figure out."

"Like what?" I asked.

"Like why these pictures are in her box, or who it is that killed the woman you found in the ground," said Morris.

"Don't you see?" said Caroline. "Isn't it clear?"

"No," said Beth. "Not at all."

Caroline took the Distinguished Service Cross from around her neck and tossed it into the box, where it clanged, steel on steel. "My grandmother only said the kindest things about him. She worshiped him as if he was the most wonderful, most gentle man in the world. A war hero, she said, and so how could we think otherwise. Even in her diary she could barely say ill of him, but it's all there, beneath her words of love and devotion, it's all very clear. How could we ever have known it, how could we ever have imagined that our grandfather, Christian Shaw, was an absolute monster?"

33

I

May 24, 1911

*Three new young men came for tea today,
bringing to only twelve the number that have called
this month. It would have been more, I am certain,
except for those ugly rumors that continue to
plague us. Is there no way to halt the lies? I fear if
it weren't for my mother's wondrous teas, with her
sugared almonds and her famous deep-fried
crullers, we wouldn't have any visitors at all, and I
don't understand it, I don't understand why they
insist on being so mean to us, I simply don't. Of
today's young men one was fat and one was a
dwarf, but one was interesting, I must admit. He is
a Shaw of the department store Shaws. Their fortunes have declined in the last decades, but what
matter is that to me? Why else would my father
have given so much and fought so hard to earn his
money if not to allow his daughters to be free of
such worries, and so I won't judge him by his lack
of wealth, but by his pleasing manner and the way
his suit drapes his thick shoulders. I think him even
more splendid than Mr. Wister of the other day.*

We were sitting on the lawn, having tea, the two other men and Christian Shaw, that is his name, and Mother, who was knitting, and Charity, who was sitting on the grass looking up at us as we spoke. Hope was playing the piano and despite Mother's entreaties wouldn't join us, but her music, floating from the instrument room, added the perfect note to the afternoon. The men promised to come to our ball and seemed genuinely excited at the prospect. We talked of school and Mr. Taft's bathtub and we all laughed and laughed. Someone mentioned that awful Mr. Dreiser and his harsh books and then Mother mentioned the poetry she had studied as a girl in Europe. Suddenly Christian Shaw started reciting something beautiful. He is obviously well read and can quote poetry at length to great effect. The poem was about a lover's tears at parting, the best I could grasp it, but as he spoke he spoke at me, as if the others were no more than statues, and the words ceased to have meaning beyond their music. It was only the sound his voice made as he pronounced the verse and the look in his eye that mattered. I could feel the blush rising in my cheeks. It ended with clapping and Charity said that Lord Byron was her favorite too and there was much gaiety as I fought to compose myself. For the rest of the afternoon I could barely look at his sharp features and yet I could not bear to look away.

I've already made certain his name has been added to the list for the ball. I learned today that the Scotts are having an affair that same weekend, which is spiteful of them, but Naomi Scott is such a plain old thing and, besides, Father has more money than Mr. Scott, which would be of interest, of course, to a Shaw. So I think I have good reason

*to hope to share a waltz with our Mr. Shaw some-
time soon and the thought of it makes my breath all
fluttery.*

June 16, 1911

*What a simply horrible horrible day! I was told
today that old Mrs. Poole was to be invited to the
ball and I was horrified. I had a terrible row with
Mother about it that lasted much of the afternoon.
When Father came home I stamped my foot and
insisted but he refused to talk about it so that I
knew it was his doing that added her to the list. He
has done enough for that woman and I told him so.
Must she haunt us for the rest of our lives? They sit
in that house, the two of them, mother and daughter, taunting us with their very silence. But it was
not Father's fault that the pinched old man drank
himself to ruin, it was not Father's fault that
Father had vision where the other had only a bottle. The great cat of tragedy that smote their lives
was born on their own doorstep. Father was more
than kind to that man after the dissolution of their
business partnership and what did Father get in
return? Spite and vindictiveness and a smear cam-
paign that has survived that man's suicide and
spoilt our standing. And still it continues. Father
should have simply put them in a farmhouse in New
Jersey and been done with them but, ever the
humanitarian, he wanted to keep an eye on their
affairs. Had they any pride they would have
refused his kindness, but they have no pride, no
sympathy, nothing but their cold sense of deprivation, and I won't stand for it. It is evil enough to
have them so close we can smell them from the*

lawn, but to have them at our affairs in addition is too much. How can we be joyous and gay when they stand, the two of them, side by side, staring at us, their mouths set sternly, their figures a constant reproach.

As if that weren't bad enough, we received regrets today from Mr. Shaw. My heart nearly broke when the note came. Why men seem so attracted to the wan figure of Naomi Scott and her powder-white skin I can't for the life of me figure, but I assume that is where he will be. At least Mr. Wister will be coming. Once that would have sent my heart to racing, but no longer. I can't imagine Mr. Wister reciting a note of poetry, even though his uncle wrote that novel about cowboys. Well, maybe Mr. Wister can teach me how to throw a lariat so that I can toss it over Mr. Shaw's broad shoulders.

June 29, 1911

My fingers tremble as I write this. I could never forget this night, never, never. I will carry it with me like a diamond buried deep within my chest for the rest of my life. The ball was a humiliation. I am certain they are laughing at us right this moment in the homes of the Peppers and the Biddles and the Scotts. They have done all they could to keep us out and now they will have more reason than ever. All the first-rank families stayed away, which was expected after Naomi Scott played her dirty trick on us, but most of the second rank abandoned us too, leaving for our party a rather undistinguished group. While disappointing, that would have been acceptable if all had gone as it seemed in the beginning.

The dress I had ordered of the finest white silk taffeta was as beautiful as a wedding dress. I cried when the seamstress brought it to the house for the final fitting. The ballroom was iridescent with flowers and light, as finely dressed as any on the Main Line. Mother had ensured that only the best buffet was set, Virginia ham, three roasted turkeys, platters of fresh fruits and berries and ripe Delaware peaches, and Mother's famous confections, her sugared almonds, her striped peppermints, her cookies and crullers and chocolate truffles, all laid out in such lovely proportions on the dining room lace that it was a marvel. And of course there were the pickles, for what would a Reddman party be without pickles? Father had hired the most famous orchestra in the city and as the violins played their warm notes I could feel the magic in the air. Then that Mrs. Poole and her daughter arrived.

They stood alone in the corner, staring out at the dancers, making their dark presence felt, that sour old woman and the girl, not yet eight, but already the youth squeezed out of her black eyes by the cold of her mother, the two of them turning their ugly angry gazes upon anyone who had the temerity to try to have a gay time. They refused the champagne or any of the food and I couldn't help but remember how Edmond Dantès had refused to sup in the houses of his enemies. It was uncanny how the whole party seemed to cringe from them, even the dancers kept their space from that corner as they whirled about the room. Mr. Wister came, as he had promised, and we danced, but he was clumsy and my mind could not free itself from the gloom of the Pooles in the corner, so I fear Mr. Wister was not suitably impressed with me. This was especially apparent as he started dancing with

*that tiny Sheila Harbaugh, whom we had invited
only because the Winters had given their regrets. I
caught a glimpse of the two of them slipping out
together onto the rear portico, his hand on the
small of her back. I had to fight to keep my smile
firm for the onlookers, though sweet Hope, who
sees everything, gave me a look full of sympathy. It
was all horrid enough, and my stomach had turned
with disappointment, when Father had the
deranged notion to ask Mrs. Poole to dance.*

*Everyone stopped and stared as he approached
their corner. It was as if a limelight were shining
on him, he was that apparent. When he came close
he bowed slightly and reached out his hand. She
just stared at him. He spoke to her, calmly, kindly,
for my father is the kindest man alive, his hand still
outreached, and she just stared at him before turning away her face. The daughter, her head down,
couldn't bear to meet his gaze, even when Father,
with his generous spirit, patted her on the shoulder. A hush had fallen on the party, and it stayed
there as my father turned and walked back to his
wife and daughters. My father had invited them
with mercy in his heart and they had come, the
Pooles, only to humiliate him. All semblance of
gaiety was by then lost and I intended to go over
there myself and toss off to them even just a small
piece of my anger, but Father restrained me. And
then one by one, under the hush of that woman's
rejection of Father's mercy, the guests began to
say farewell and leave. It all was too much to bear,
watching them call for their coaches and motor-
cars, the humiliation was actually painful, I could
feel it in my chest, and I would have run out in
tears had I not, just at that moment, when my
despair grew overpowering, spied the magnificent*

*figure of Christian Shaw, breathtaking in his tails,
walking toward me from the far end of the ballroom.*

*He asked me to dance and suddenly the music
turned dreamy and gay. He had strong hands and a
light step and never before had I waltzed so mag-
nificently. We swept around the room as one and I
could see the eyes of what was left of the party
upon us, even those of the wretched Pooles, and
once again the room glittered. Soon another couple
joined us on the floor and then another and then
another and before long the party was alive again
and filled with laughter. In the middle of a sweeping turn I happened to glance at the Pooles' corner
and noticed, with a surge of joy, that they were
gone, banished by the light that was Christian
Shaw.*

*When we could we slipped out together onto
the rear patio and then to the lawn, to the statue of
Aphrodite which my father had just purchased for
the rear grounds of the house, where we were
finally, for the first time, alone. We leaned on the
statue facing one another and spoke softly. "I had
been to the Scotts, but the whole time there I was
thinking of you," he said. "In the middle of a dance
I saw your sweet face before me and I knew I had
to come. You're not cross at me for imposing after
sending my regrets, are you?" No, I told him, no
no no. He spoke of the night and the fragrance of
the air but as at our prior meeting I lost the thread
of his words in the music of his voice. His breath
was rich with the smoky sweet scent of brandy. The
moon was casting its silvery glow on the statue and
the two of us standing before it and then he leaned
down and kissed me. Yes, like the sweetest angel
sent for my own redemption he kissed me and an*

emotion as I had never known burst from deep within my chest and I swore then to myself, as I swear now and will swear every day for the rest of my life, that I love this man and will love him forever and I will never ever so long as I can draw sweet breath let him go.

June 30, 1911

A grand bouquet of flowers came for me at noon today, full of irises and violets and baby's breath, a fabulous explosion of color. When it came I ran to it and ripped open the card with shaking fingers. It was from Mr. Wister, telling me how wonderful a time he had had at our ball and seeking again to call on me. My heart fell when I read his words. I wonder if Sheila Harbaugh received the same bouquet, the same note. I gave the flowers to Hope and sat sullenly inside through the afternoon, though the weather outside was perfectly lovely.

Another delivery came before evening fell, a dozen red roses and one white. It looked shy, that bouquet, next to Mr. Wister's grand arrangement, but the card was from Christian, my dear Christian. "For a lovely evening," the card said. "Devotedly, C. Shaw." Those roses are beside me as I write this. I am drunk on their scent, delirious.

August 12, 1911

Christian visited again this afternoon and his goodness shines through ever more clearly. He was looking, as always, elegant in his black suit and

*homburg when he visited and as quickly as possi-
ble we absented ourselves from the rest of the
household. On my instructions, two chairs and a
table had been set upon the lawn for a private tea
and I poured for him as he spoke. Like a naughty
boy he took a flask from his pocket and added a
rich flavor to our cups. His naughtiness served only
to increase the intimacy of our moment. Our conversation, while we were sitting on the lawn, looking down upon the blue of the pond, turned to the
ecstasies of nature, of which I admitted I was
unaware, preferring the parlor to the wild, and he
recited for me the words of a Mr. Emerson about
the proud beauty of a flower. Oh, to listen to his
voice is to listen to the finest, firmest of music. The
afternoon was perfect until that little dark girl with
her rodent eyes appeared at the pond's edge and
stared up at us.*

*Christian kept speaking, as if it mattered not,
but having her stare at us was too intolerable and I
couldn't keep my silence. "Why does she bother
you so?" he asked me. I couldn't answer truthfully.
I must assume he has heard the malicious stones of
gossip thrown against us. They are lies, all lies, I
know it, but they are lies that haunt our family as
surely as if they were holy truths. I feel the press of
those evil rumors upon me as others must feel the
press of history, and pray each day that the falsehoods will someday be finally buried among the
ruins of time, along with that girl's drunkard of a
father. But how could I explain all that to my pure
darling Christian? "She's a little spy," I said simply. "Look at the way she insists on watching us."
"But she's just a poor girl," said Christian and
then he spoke of graciousness, of generosity, of giving oneself over to the disadvantaged. He said he*

felt compassion for that girl, living fatherless in that house at the foot of Veritas. He had a small book about some pond in New England in his pocket and he insisted upon stepping down the hill and giving the book to her. I fear I must admit I was embarrassed at the sight and turned to see if his transgression was spotted from the house. Charity stood at the wall of the rear patio, a breeze catching her loose hair, watching as Christian loped with his long strides down the slope.

I felt a brutal anger rise as I watched him with that girl, talking to her softly, offering the book. That my Christian should be spending his attention on so tawdry an object was humiliating and I told myself that when he returned I would have to make it clear exactly what would and would not be tolerated with regard to those people. But as I watched his posture, erect and proud, and saw the girl's shyness dissolving before him, allowing her to reach out for the book and take it to her breast, I could see in that portrait all the sweet generosity in his soul and I realized that he indeed could be our redemption. The falsehoods that have been used against us might die, as we have so fervently prayed, precisely because his goodness will transcend the evil of those lies. His goodness, I can see now, will be the instrument of our salvation and take our family to a finer place than ever we had dared to hope before.

September 3, 1911

Today we took a long and glorious walk along the stream that surrounds our property,

Christian and I, our hands clasped tightly as we face our separation. I don't know how I will survive while Christian finishes out his final year in New Haven. We have become unbearably close, our souls are united as two trees whose trunks are trained to twist around each other. He confided in me for the first time about the acute dilemmas facing his family and his future and I couldn't help but feel joy at his sharing of the whole of his life with me.

It is not just I who have become transfixed by my love's goodness. He listens with exquisite patience to Hope's performances on the piano. She is generally shy in public but delights in playing her most difficult pieces for Christian and he applauds heartily whenever she concludes, even though the length of her recitals tries the most forbearing souls. And he has taken to tutoring Charity on his favorite poets, taking long walks as he recites for her. Even Mother seems to take a special joy at his compliments on her teas. He has added a grace to this family for which we all are painfully grateful.

In two days my love will be back in Connecticut. I can't believe he'll be away from me for such length, but his strength and our commitment will surely see me through the loneliness of winter's despoliation. Together, I know, we can deal with whatever the fates hurl our way and after he left I thought hard about how his family problems could affect our possible future together. Perhaps I see a way, tentative though it may be, to ensure the future happiness I believe we both deserve. I pray only that I can somewhere find the strength I need to take us there.

December 11, 1911

Father remains in New York, on business, as we continue to prepare for the holidays. Christian is staying north to study and so it will be lonely and gray here. I miss him, I miss him, I miss him terribly, but still I will do what I must to maintain the gay facade. While searching for the ornaments for our tree, I found myself in Father's library. I remembered then the secret hideaway in the paneling he showed us when we were girls and Father had just bought the house from the Ritters after they had lost all their money. I seemed to recall it was on one side or the other of the cast-iron fireplace. On a spur, I wondered if I could find it again. Behind which of the dark sheets of mahogany did the secret place lurk? It took almost an hour of rapping my knuckles on the wood and looking for imperfections in the lines, but I found it at last. My heart leaped when I slipped up the piece of wood trim and spun open the panel. Inside was not the ornaments I had sought, or even private treasures, only books, ledgers, old accounting journals. How very boring a discovery for such a secret place. Someday maybe I will look inside these books and see why Father has hidden them away, but for now I am still wondering about the ornaments.

January 12, 1912

My love's letters become more desperate. All our hopes seem on the verge of collapse. He talks of using his engineering training and joining Mr. Goethals's endeavor in Panama, hoping somehow

to find in the wilds of Central America the fortune
that will save his family. They are dying in droves
from malaria and other foul diseases in Panama.
The thought of my love suffering in that far-off
wilderness drives a stake of fear through my heart.
It is time, somehow, to bring to fruition the plans I
made last fall and to forestall the coming tragedy. I
don't know if I am capable of doing what must be
done, but what I have learned in the past weeks
provides a peculiar strength that I had never felt
before. I must keep reminding myself that I am my
father's daughter and whatever power it was he
could muster in pursuit of his deepest desire, I can
muster the same dark power in pursuit of my own.

January 20, 1912

My father was at his desk in the library, working on his figures, when I approached with my crucial errand. A fire was blazing in the cast-iron
fireplace off to the side, but still the room was cold.
All my life I had come into that room with the low
bookshelves and mahogany paneling and the red
flock wallpaper and asked him for things and
always he had granted my requests, a new toy, a
new dress, a party to liven up the spring. He had
spoiled us, never denied us a thing, and I had
always thought of that room as a generous place
where dreams were fulfilled, but I realized now, for
perhaps the first time, that in this room of business,
where so many of my own shallow dreams had been
made reality, others' dreams had been crushed by
the power of my father's wealth. For the first time,
this day, I knew what it was to fear my father. But
from necessity I pushed that fear far from my heart

and twisted my lips into a smile. I stopped perhaps ten feet from his desk and waited for him to raise his head and acknowledge me. Those few seconds seemed to me then to be an eternity. "Come here, daughter," he said when he noticed me there. "How can I please you this evening?"

"I've come today, Father," I said, "to talk of business."

It did not take long to explain the dire situation facing the Shaw Brothers Company and when I finished my father stared out at me with eyes I had never seen in him before. They were cold, and black, and full of ugly calculation. Looking at those eyes, the business eyes of my father, and comparing them to the sweet blue lenses of my Christian, I fell, for the moment, though I am loath to admit it, out of love with my father. But we are blood and bone, my father and I, a match for one another. I know now all he was capable of in pursuit of his fortune; I am still learning the depths of my own formidable capabilities.

He didn't reject the proposition right off. Instead he had questions, questions about the books, the assets and liabilities, the market and the market share, the equity positions of the varying parties, all questions I wouldn't and couldn't answer. Those questions, I told him, would have to be taken up with the principals. Finally, my father asked the last, most important, question.

"Three hundred and fifty thousand dollars," I responded.

My father's cold ugly eyes didn't so much as flinch.

"And without this money the banks will close the company and sell the store?" asked my father.

"That is what I have been told," I said.

"And you want me to provide this company with the capital needed to survive its most current crises?" asked my father.

"You must," I said. "You simply must."

"Three hundred and fifty thousand dollars is a substantial sum of money, daughter," he said.

"Consider it," I said, "my dowry."

My father stared at me for a moment more and then dropped his head back to the figures in the ledgers before him. I didn't know whether to stay or to flee, but this was too important to leave without an answer and so, despite my faltering heart, I waited, shivering, while he wrote in the ledgers. Finally he said, without an ounce of warmth, as if he were addressing an employee, "You may go."

"Not without an answer," I said, my voice trembling as I said it.

Without looking up from his ledgers, my father said, "I will make appropriate arrangements to provide the capital."

Oh happy happy happy day! The fondest plans of my soul have been realized. I am in awe of the Lord's grand designs, that something so base and awful, something derived by such means, can be used to purchase an unearthly paradise. Just as Jesus turned water to wine He has turned my father's black wealth into a love so pure and a happiness so deep that it acts as praise itself for His beneficence. That my father made me beg and wait I shan't hold against him; I understand him completely, we are of the same coin. But today is a day for happiness, for joy, for love. My Christian, my Christian, my Christian, forever, my love, we drink together from the cup of joy held in the very hand of grace.

II

March 29, 1912

I am puzzled by the reactions of my sisters to our glorious news. When father announced the engagement at dinner tonight I had worried that Hope would be distraught. I feared her reaction upon learning that her sister, two years younger than she, was to be married while she was still without a suitor, but Hope seemed genuinely pleased at my good fortune. I have forgiven her the earlier remarks about Christian, they were of course figments of a natural jealousy, and take her wishes for my future to be of the utmost sincerity. It is Charity whose face turned dark when she heard the announcement and unaccountably bolted from the room.

It was a rather gay dinner before that moment; I haven't spent a less than gay moment since Christian's arrival on the train from New Haven and his proposal. The last of the Shaw Brothers, after whom the store is named, Christian's Uncle Sullivan, was at the dinner, as were Christians' four cousins, with all assorted wives and children, a regular convocation of Shaws. It was a group that I don't believe would have deigned to enter our house just a few years before, but all that now has changed. The dinner had been called to celebrate the resurrection of the fortunes of the Shaw Brothers Company, of which my father is to be a majority partner, once the lawyers finish the appropriate paperwork. A fire was burning in the blue and white marble fireplace and the squab was a crisp delight. Father brought his best wine from the cellar and there were generally good feelings all

*around at the new arrangement. I must say that
Uncle Sullivan is more dour a man than I had been
led to believe, though Christian attributed his
mood to weariness at dealing with the difficulties
that preceded this proud new venture. It is beyond
my understanding how he could think my father is
anything other than a saint for agreeing to provide
the needed money and sign onto all their shaky
notes in order to save the company, but the world
of business, I have been taught, is by necessity
rather cruel and ungrateful. It was during a speech
toasting the new partnership that father announced
our engagement. There were a few exclamations of
joy and then general applause and I felt the admiration flow about me like the waters of a joyous
bath. And then it was that Charity fled the room.*

*Hope started to run after her but Christian,
being the most generous of souls, volunteered to set
things right, and himself followed her out to the portico. A few moments later he returned and sat down
and straightened his napkin on his lap as if nothing
had happened. I gave him a questioning look but he
gestured me to remain calm and soon Charity herself reappeared. I don't know what dilemma caused
her alarm but Christian was able to solve it as I
believe he will be able to solve all the problems that
can hereafter arise in our family. A new era for the
Reddmans, an era of light and fellowship, has been
embarked upon and I am not being too immodest
when I say I feel myself at its very center.*

April 12, 1912

*Our list keeps growing, as if it had a life of its
own, and Mother continues to meet with the cook to*

ensure that the wedding dinner will be of the highest quality. Christian has been so busy preparing that he is almost a stranger at the house, but a future of infinite togetherness beckons. There are barely two months till the wedding and so much remains to be decided upon, flowers and invitations and table settings. I have not yet chosen my dress. So much still to be decided upon my head spins.

I already sense the change in attitudes to our family since my engagement was publicly announced. Even Naomi Scott, that pale cat, called on me the other day to say how excited she was about my coming nuptials. The Shaws have always been one of the most highly thought of families in the city and so, it appears, my marriage to Christian will break down the final barriers to our acceptance. Father has even been asked to join the board of the Art Museum, which pleases Mother immensely. It is as if the stain of our past has been removed entirely. I would breathe a little more easily if Father's business arrangement with the Shaws was fully executed, but the lawyers continue to bicker and I am told that Christian's Uncle Sullivan is making things difficult. Closing on the deal will have to take place sometime after the wedding, but Father has already paid money to the banks and they have developed a new patience, so Christian says. I believe Father is looking forward to running the store. It is so much more elegant than his briny-smelling pickle and canning factory on the river.

It is good to see Charity so happy these days. While I can't say she has been warm to me as of late, I believe she is truly excited about the wedding. Much of her time is spent away from the house, so we have no idea what her newest interests

*are, she has always a keen interest in some subject
or the other, but whatever it be it gives her a true
joy. She won't confess anything to me, but I
believe she has a beau. She has filled out beautifully in the past few months and carries with her
everywhere a smile that can denote only a woman
who has found her place in the world through
love. Just today she was wearing a gold ring with
her initials. When I asked her where she had purchased it she blushed wildly and refused to say. I
only hope she can find for herself someone as loving, as faithful, as generous with his spirit as my
dear Christian.*

May 23, 1912

*Something is terribly wrong with Charity and
she refuses to tell us what loss has befallen her. I
pray that the wedding is not the cause of her difficulties, though it is not rare for sisters to fall into a
melancholia when another sister marries. We have
never been a competitive family but I'd be less than
honest if I wrote that the natural rivalries have not
existed among us. Hope has been marvelous, considering her age and my out-of-turn nuptials, and I
would have expected Charity to feel none of the
pressures, being still so young, but one never
knows how youth will react. Charity has been testy,
her wicked sense of humor gone. When she is home
she sits and pouts and her eyes are often red. I am
loath to admit it but I fear that whatever it is that is
troubling her has driven her to overindulge and
her waist is gaining girth by the day. I don't
believe she'll be able to fit into the dress we bought
her only last month.*

June 5, 1912

This is so like her. Father has spoiled her terribly and now she has taken to ruining everything. They had a terrible row, Father and Charity, their voices spilled out of his library with a venom that I had never heretofore heard in this house. Father's voice was deep and angry, like a furious owl, hooting with indignation, and Charity was crying out her false pain, punctuated by her crocodile tears. The thunder outside was monstrous, as was the force of the rain, and still we heard their angry voices, sharp as the bolts of light that crashed their way through our shuttered windows. I am to be married in less than a week and I have barely seen my love for all the preparations. I need not Charity's histrionics to distract me from my plans.

We are having the ceremony before the statue of Aphrodite, where Christian and I shared our first, glorious kiss. At least some arrangements are proceeding well. Just yesterday we decided to add, in front of the statue for the ceremony, an oval of the richest, brightest flowers to help celebrate the day. The gardeners have dug and prepared the oval plot before this evening's rain and we will plant the flowers shortly before the wedding so their blooms will be freshest when we take our vows and their color contrast most vividly with my white silk gown. And, gratefully, the Pooles will soon be leaving the property for a two-week sojourn to Atlantic City, financed by my father. I insisted he send them away and, finally, he agreed, so we won't have their anger to poison our reception. My wedding stands to be the most glorious affair of the season if we can keep our sister from

*falling apart or eating a swath through the buffet
with her newly revitalized appetite.*

June 6, 1912

*Charity is missing, she has fled. Her satchel is
gone and so are some of her favorite clothes. After
her argument with Father she packed her satchel
and left the house for we know not where. Mother
is distraught, Father is brooding silently but has
determined not to summon the police to find her,
though I know not why. With her missing it is as if
the family is in mourning. How could she do this to
me just five days before the most important day of
my life? Whatever joy I was to feel about that day
has been destroyed by her hateful behavior and
poisonous attitude toward my future. I will go
through the motions and smile at the guests and
take my vows with my husband to be, but it can
never be the same. Never shall I forgive her this
complete disregard for my happiness. If only
Christian were here to comfort me, but I have not
seen him since she disappeared, as if he is avoiding
to tread on our tender emotions while the wound of
her disappearance is still fresh. Even in the most
trying times his warmth and generosity cannot be
overstated.*

June 9, 1912

*The pall of Charity's disappearance remains
with our family. The wedding rehearsal was a
dispiriting affair which Christian, wisely, failed to
attend. I have not seen him since the stormy night*

*of Charity's disappearance from the household
with her satchel and her problems and I wonder
how our family's current instability is affecting
him. At the rehearsal, the minister joked about
whether the groom would make it on the grand day
itself and there was an uncomfortable silence, but I
have no doubt that Christian understands that
despite my sister's disappearance there is too much
at stake for the two of us, and for his family's fortunes, to allow her absence to affect in any way our
future. Our marriage must go forward as a necessity of our undying love. Everything would have
come apart except for Father's strength. He has
insisted that the wedding proceed as planned and
he refuses to let our sorrows get in the way. I
believe until now I never understood the truly glorious power of his will, his single-minded devotion
to whatever cause he has made his own, damn the
costs. It is a lesson I have well learned from him
and one I shall never forget. I understand him now
as I never did before and I forgive him everything.*

*The gardeners have finished planting the flow-
ers in the oval plot before the statue and they are
magnificent, whites and pinks and violets in
ordered rows like a tiny guard of honor. No matter
how morose our family may be over Charity's selfishness, the wedding itself will be a triumphant
reminder that the more responsible members of this
family will carry on.*

June 10, 1912

*My nerves have gotten the best of me. I can't
stop crying. Even as I write this my tears blot the
ink. So much joy, so much worry. Still no word*

from Christian, not for days and days. It is bad luck of course to see the bride too soon before the wedding so his absence is absolutely excusable, but still with Charity and Christian both absent from the house there is an abject loneliness that infects my joy with a strange sorrow. Hope has been a rock, staying with me at all hours, sleeping in my bed with me as I shake with worry. She is so good and pure and I think she is the best of us. Should anything happen to her I will be lost. I can only imagine what impossible difficulties will come my way tomorrow.

June 11, 1912

The most glorious day of my life has passed like a dream. Christian Shaw and I were married in the eyes of the Lord and the world at precisely 1:30 p.m. in the afternoon, under an unceasing sun, before my father's statue of Aphrodite, the goddess of love and beauty. That it was a more somber affair than could be wished for was only to be expected, as my sister Charity remains among the missing.

I'll always remember my dear Christian as he awaited my walk down the aisle. He was the most endearing sight, hesitant, uncertain as a boy, tottering from nerves. I can barely describe in words how much I adore him. He was late of course, what groom isn't, and due to the difficulties we had faced in the previous week it is no wonder that he fortified himself with brandy before the ceremony, and continued on through the reception, so much so that he was later struck with sickness, the same sickness that has him lying in bed asleep as I write this in our New York hotel.

We took our vows before the excited throng on the back lawn. The minister's service was short and full of love. Between us and the audience was that plot of flowers whose colors seemed brighter than life. I said "I do" as firmly as a banker but Christian acknowledged his love for me with a squeak that brought welcome twitters from the guests. In front of everyone he was becomingly shy when it was time to kiss but I put my hand on his neck and brought his face to mine and his lips to mine and we kissed again as sweetly and as powerfully as when we kissed that first time.

The revelry was subdued, of course, with my sister absent, but it was celebratory nonetheless and there was much to celebrate. Christian and I will surely have the finest of lives together, and the restructured Shaw Brothers Company, which my father has saved from the terrible jaws of bankruptcy, will be signed into existence within a very few days. All has come together as I planned the summer last upon first hearing of the Shaw family's distress.

So I am now Mrs. Christian Shaw, a name I will cherish into eternity. Christian is snoring loudly on the bed, the result, of course, of the brandy. Our first night of passion will have to be delayed but that could not be helped, what with the way Charity's disappearance has affected all of our nerves. But enough of her. We are embarking on a long voyage to Europe, leaving on the boat tomorrow, traveling all the way from London to Istanbul in the grandest of styles, and for the whole of that time I don't want once to discuss my ungrateful sister. The future belongs only to me and my dear dear husband.

III

March 4, 1914

My Dearest Charity,

It has come again like a flood of red death to curse me in my sorrows. Need I be reminded of all that has gone wrong in the past years of my life? Must my agony continue indefinitely? Must I never be forgiven? It is no surprise that it came, of course, as my husband prefers the leather chairs and narrow bunks of his club to our marriage bed, and when he does touch me it is only from the twin spurs of anger and drink, but still I prayed this month, as I pray every month, for the Lord to grant me some surcease from my lonely misery, and so it is with profound bitterness that I see my prayers fall uselessly upon the ground like empty seed.

The questioning has stopped, thank goodness, but that doesn't make the hole any less deep. Ever since Mother passed away Father has stopped asking about grandchildren. Instead, he stares at me sullenly over dinner, as if I were the cause of his heartbreak. His glower is little different than the brooding darkness of my husband's countenance and I wonder if they are not conspiring against me for some devilish purpose. I think it may have been a mistake, dear sister, to insist that my husband and I should reside at Veritas, but I couldn't bear to be away from it and all it carries, including my memories of you. Christian, by the time we returned from Europe, had ceased to care about anything but his brandy and so he went along with the decision, but I fear our being here has not helped our marriage. My only remaining comfort is my family.

I couldn't survive without Hope and I spend hours each day by her bedside, reading to her, feeding her the broth I've prepared. Christian too, when he is at home, spends much of his time with her, confiding, I fear. I think only Hope is able to ease the secret burden that seems to so weigh down his heart. I would be jealous of her evident close-ness to my husband except that Hope is the nearest thing I shall meet to a saint in this world. I am sure she is my champion and won't tolerate even the smallest hint against me. She is grace incarnate and always full of patience for my woes. I gain strength from her, and strength from my thoughts of you, wherever you are, making your way in this world. You are my inspiration, dear sister, and every day I await the mail for some word of you. It will come, I know it will.

I don't know if I can bear another spell like this one. I must do something to fill the yawning chasm within me, I must be strong, as strong as you, sweet sister, because you chose your path as only I can choose mine.

March 12, 1914

My Dearest Charity,
   Our sister Hope climbed out of bed today, put on a frock, and walked unassisted down the stairs. Dr. Cohn says if she watches herself and avoids drafts and too much exertion she can live a normal life, which is what we all have prayed for the many years since she became ill. Father was in tears as she made her way down the staircase, I was clap-ping, and your spirit, dear sister, was hovering over us all. She sat at the piano and let her fingers drift

*across the ivory. The smile on her face was painful
in its gratitude to the Lord for giving her this recovery. It was an unseasonably warm spring day and
the sun was bright and I insisted Hope come out to
the yard, to my garden by the statue of Aphrodite.
The barberry hedge is now almost waist-high and
the daffodils and tulips are bursting forth as if sum-
moned by the warm kiss of the spring. The intricate
design I planned is now fully evident and in the center of everything is that glorious oval of good black
earth from which the perennial stalks have begun to
rise. When she saw it, Hope's eyes glowed with a
joy that told me the hours I have lavished on the
garden have not been wasted.*

March 18, 1914

My Dearest Charity,

*I have sent word to Christian's club that our
sister is failing and he should come home at once.
In truth, a comforting color has risen to her soft
cheeks and Dr. Cohn says that as long as her spirit
remains steadfast her chances for improvement are
real and our prayers for her recovery might yet be
heard. Still, this was not a time of the month for
Christian to absent himself from his adopted family
and his loving wife. If am being reckless then the
Lord will forgive me for my purpose is noble and in
furtherance of His ends. I would be surer of my
path if my husband didn't frighten me so. Father is
in Pittsburgh for the week, meeting with the
Heinzes and the Carnegies, and so there is no protection for me here should things take a turn that I
cannot now gauge, but desperate needs breed desperate means.*

I know how he will behave when he comes home; I can imagine the scene as clearly as if it were in one of Mr. Belasco's theatrical productions. The automobile will let him off in front of the house and he will charge in, his rain cape splaying blackness in his wake, and he will leap up the steps, two at a time, to get to sister Hope's room. I will be in the center hall, hands clasped before me, but he will ignore me as he climbs to the one person in this family who still has some claim to his affection. And in that room, with all the melodrama he has sucked this night from his bottle, he will fall to his knees and clasp dear Hope's cold tiny hands in his own and place his head on her stomach and allow his tears to drip upon her blanket, only to be startled by Hope's irreverent laughter.

He will spend a few moments more with her, grateful for her condition, and he will be forced to hear the kind words from our sister's lips about me that this very afternoon I implored her to speak to my husband at her first opportunity. In her faltering voice she will tell him of her fervent hopes that Christian and I can reconcile our difference and be husband and wife in more than name and create for ourselves an heir. He will keep his smile through the speech, and try to show only love for the saintly convalescent, but his face will redden and his eyes darken and when he takes his leave there will be only anger, anger at my scheming and the deceptive note that cut his precious evening short so that he could be forced to hear a lecture. My dear husband Christian hates to be lectured to and hates most of all to be lectured to about his manly duties. I have noticed that it is after lectures of that sort by my father or Christian's Uncle Sullivan that my husband's anger is most aroused.

I only pray he had enough time to guzzle his stomach's worth at the club before the note came, that his mind is suitably enraged and his sensibilities suitably dulled.

I hear his car rattling with desperation up the rain-slick hill of our drive as he rushes to our sister's bedside. I must leave my room now, must take my place on the stage as the curtain rises and the drama is about to be unleashed.

June 24, 1914

My Dearest Charity,

I feel like a blindfold has been lifted from my eyes and finally, for the first time in my life, my path is visible. I won't dwell on the selfishness of my history except to say that suddenly I see it as a wasteland, full of regret and lost opportunities for grace, and am grateful to the heavens that I have come through it alive and with child. This life within me, still as yet unformed, contains the roots of all meaning for me now. I am as blessed as the Mary herself, and certain every mother feels this same sense of divinity. Father is delirious with joy, Hope fusses over me for once, and everyone moves about the house as if in a dance around the soon to be crowned king, including my dear husband.

The shock of the announcement has worn off and, though he tries to hide it, I can see the excitement in his eyes too. Whatever dark and heavy load it is he carries, it seems to have lightened with the news of his impending fatherhood. He can bear once again to touch me with a gentle hand, caressing my swelling stomach. Sometimes, at night, we stay up late together and talk of the future, almost as it was on those long nights of our innocence before the tragedy of our wedding. Just last night he told me, with all his earnestness, that everything must be done to secure our child's future in every respect. His devotion is an inspiration. Everything I do from here on to forever, every breath I breathe, will be devoted to nurturing that life to fullness and ensuring its blessed future.

August 29, 1914

My Dearest Charity,

Our sister has relapsed into a crushing illness. She has taken once again to her bed and lost all strength. The news from Europe has disturbed everyone but it appears that our dear sister's sensibilities are finer then the rest of us and it has affected her more, weakening her defenses against whatever beastly curse has been afflicting her all these years. We hired the finest nurse but still I insist on making her broth every morning and spooning it past her quivering jaw. I can feel the power of this life that swells within me flowing into the broth I cook each morning for our sister and in my heart of hearts I feel that power will be the key to her recovery. Her eyes are as ever alive with goodness and strength but there is about her body a feebleness that is frightening. I spend hours with her, reading her the latest novels and some poetry from the collection in your room, I hope you don't mind, and her spirits are buoyant still, but there is about this spell something deeper and darker then previous bouts. Dr. Cohn patted our shoulders but his eyes were the eyes of worry.

September 18, 1914

My Dearest Charity,

As I was making the broth this morning for our dear sister, I felt the life inside me contract. With each stir of the spoon my baby twisted and turned and then the contractions sent me to the red tile floor with a scream. It isn't time yet, it can't be yet. The nurse rushed down and seeing what had happened helped me to the parlor couch where I stayed until Dr. Cohn came. He gave me some medicine and prescribed rest and so I have been banished to the bedroom for the time being. When Christian heard he rushed home and clasped my hands and we prayed together for the health of our child. I have never seen him so devoted, never seen him so full of love.

October 9, 1914

My Dearest Charity,

Hope was well enough today to sit up in her bed. Due to my condition I cannot spend the time with her I would but Christian is by her side for hours every evening, reading and talking. She is goodness incarnate and it appears the ministrations of dear Christian have delivered to her another measure of strength. Christian is a saint, doting on dear Hope's every wish. It seems my pregnancy and Hope's illness have finally turned us into the family I've dreamed we could be.

November 15, 1914

My Dearest Charity,
  While under Christian's care Hope relapsed into her deep illness and fear has now replaced whatever good cheer had been extant at Veritas. The doctor has allowed me to rise from my bed and I do so with the gravest concern for our dear sister. This morning I was back in the kitchen, chopping the vegetables by hand, butchering the chicken, spooning off the scum from the bones and stirring the sweet, clear broth that I pray will cause the wishes I hold most dear to become realities. I work with all the will passed to me by my father. She barely takes a drop, but it is enough, I pray, to do its work. It is uncanny but with each stroke of the long wooden spoon this morning I again felt my child turn within me, to kick out, and I again felt my stomach contract around my fetus, but still I continued, in silence, wanting nothing or no one to get in the way of my sacred duty. Our father is desolate with worry, Christian wrings his hands with pain and dulls his sense with drink through the long evenings while she sleeps. That tragedy should swipe at us again is unthinkable. If only you were here, dear sister, to encourage us with your loveliness and give us the strength to bear the future's pains.

November 19, 1914

  Struck numb with heartbreak, I can barely lift the pen. What have we done to deserve such misery? What? What? Why are we so cursed? It seems that from the moment I first laid eyes on

Christian Shaw tragedy has stalked me on clawed paws and I can't yet figure out why. Why? All I know is that life has become too much to bear alone.

November 20, 1914

    The cook came into my room as I was still wracked with tears and showed to me a metal canister filled with a soft white powder. She found it, she said, among the tins stored in the great wooden cabinets in our kitchen. It was not hers, she assured me, but the scent was reminiscent of what the gardener has put out in the basement for the rats. I told her to throw it out and to tell no one, ever, of what she found. What mistake could have brought such powder to our kitchen cabinets? I can't bear to even consider the possibilities of what other tragedy might have befallen us. The gardener will be fired, immediately, I will see to it. To be forced to contend with the daily concerns of this house while my sweet sweet sister lies so peacefully in her coffin is impossible. I pray even that the life inside me stops its ceaseless battering so that I can lose myself in the strong and welcoming arms of this abject grief.

December 29, 1914

My Dearest Sisters,

    Early this morning, just past the stroke of midnight, my son was born. Whatever pain we have suffered these last few years pales beside his magnificence. He is robust and pink and when he first cried as he gulped the air outside my body it was the sound of life itself asserting its glory against the tragedies of our days gone past. The labor was exquisitely painful, I shouted for hours and bit the nurse's hand until it bled, but I welcomed the agony too, in a strange part of my soul, as expiation for everything that came before it. My son exists for all of us, dear sisters, and your spirits will be as real a presence for him through his childhood as my own. He was born of violence and tragedy and death but his cry is regal and he will inherit the whole of the Reddman empire and so I have named him Kingsley. Kingsley Reddman Shaw.

To see Father's joy as he held our baby, dear sisters, his sole heir, is to be lifted to the heavens. His life has been one of continued grace, and the fame of his philanthropy has outstripped the notoriety of his business acumen, but still he has lost so much in the past years, not the least your companionship and love, that he was starving for some new victory over loss. He sees in his grandson that victory, I believe, and a justification for all he suffered as he fought to make his mark.

Christian has been absent from the house since Hope's death, grieving deep in his soul for the purest life to ever touch this earth, and so my husband has not yet seen his son, but word has been sent to his usual places and I expect him shortly. I can imagine him leaping the stairs two at a time to reach his child and that vision fills me with sublime hope for the future. Our child is all the hope we need. He will be the redemption of the Reddmans, the savior of us all. He will honor your legacy and your sacrifices, dear sisters. You can be certain that Kingsley will carry on the greatness of our father as the Reddman family is once and forever reborn.

IV

March 28, 1923

My Dearest Sisters,

A mountain cougar has been spotted in our county. It has slipped down from the heights north of us in search of food as this long wearying winter continues or has simply lost its bearings, but the effect is either way the same. A dog was mangled on a farm not far from us and one of Naomi Scott's famed dairy cows was found dead in a far pasture, its haunch chewed to the bone. The presence of this wild beast has cast a pall upon the spring and the men are out with their guns, combing the hills in search of its tracks in the soft earth.

Christian has gone out with Kingsley hunting for the cat. He has taken his father's shotgun out of the case and given it to our son to carry, against my objections. Kingsley is too young to handle a firearm and Christian is obviously unable to handle it correctly, but as always, as regards dear Christian, my objections went for naught. It is as if he does not even hear me as I speak. There is for him only his son and the pond and the woods, where he sits for hours on end with nothing but the birds and the tiniest creatures to keep him company. His unhappiness is so evident it crushes any attempt to reach out to him. We have almost passed through his fourth year back and still he acts as if the battlefield is just behind him. Sometimes I think it would have been kinder had the jagged piece of metal that severed his arm slipped into his throat instead and saved him from the misery he has come home to.

Seeing them walk off together, the quiet boy with the oversized gun cradled in his arms and the crippled man, I marveled again at the relationship they have forged. Kingsley barely speaks two words together, so shy and withdrawn he has become, and Christian's wretchedness infects with melancholy all with whom he comes in contact, but together they seem a natural whole, like two wild animals perfectly at ease with one another. I had hoped that Christian would help me speak to the boy about his studies, for Kingsley obviously fails to heed my importuning, but Christian refuses to hear one word ill against his son. Kingsley's newest tutor has failed to connect with the boy and reports that his pupil is still unable to read even the most simple-minded passages or add his figures correctly. I suspect, though I dare not breathe this to Christian or Father, that the problem is with the boy, not the pedagogue, but even so I am searching again for a more rigorous teacher.

March 31, 1923

My Dearest Sisters,
I can't sleep, I can't read, my mind is racing with an anger that I can only release in words addressed to you, my darlings. I had another row with Father about those people. I insisted once again that he force them from the property, that they be banished to where their anger can no longer infect our lives. New Jersey, I suggested, where they can do no more harm than has already been done, but once again Father ignored me. What is past is past, I argued with him, let it go, let

*them go. He reminded me that the property is
deeded to the widow Poole and he is powerless, but
even had there been no deed his answer would
have been the same. I understand Father's reasons,
better than he can know, but the time for pity has
passed, as the events of this afternoon demonstrate
with utter clarity.*

*I was in my room when the window darkened
and a great cloud drifted overhead. In the face of
that fearful sky I thought of the cougar and then of
Kingsley and immediately went in search of my
son. He was neither in the playroom nor in his area
on the front lawn. The governess was having tea in
the kitchen with Mrs. Gogarty. When I asked about
Kingsley she sputtered something foolish and then
lapsed into guilty silence. With admirable restraint
I told her to find the boy. While she searched the
house, I stepped onto the rear portico and down
into the yard.*

*The sky was gloomy and threatening, the wind
brisk and undeservedly warm, like a tease of summer before cold again sets in. I first searched
through the garden, peering as best I could over
the shoulder-high hedges. I stepped carefully, with
an unaccustomed caution, not knowing what kind
of animal could be stalking me in the interstices of
my maze, but the garden was empty of man and
beast.*

*From out of the garden I thought of returning
to the house but for some reason felt drawn to the
pond. It was with a dread that I stepped down the
hill. That pond had scared me often, yes, and I had
worried that someday my son would lose his foot-
ing and fall within its murky depths. But the surface was clear and the ducks still floated
undisturbed upon the chop. Beyond the pond was*

the stand of woods where I dared not step and prayed that my son was wise enough to stay out while that animal was still alive and on the roam. It was at the edge of the pond that I first heard the sound, high and trilling, a voice like a bird's almost, as best as I could tell from the distance. I followed it, moving around the pond, followed it to that decrepit wreck of a house.

There on the decaying wooden steps sat Kingsley, leaning on his side, listening to the Poole daughter read to him. The sight of that hideous-faced girl, and the book she was holding, that book, filled me with the hatred that rises every time I see that family. But now it came from someplace deeper. She was sitting there with my son, reading from that book, and he was listening to her, raptly, absorbing every word of the vile hatred that was spewing from her throat. Is it not enough that they have wreaked their vengeance on our father and his children, must they now infect my son? It was too much to bear and the shout of outrage came unbidden from my throat.

Kingsley jumped to his feet. I told him to get back to the house immediately and he hesitated for a tense moment, his head hanging in indecision, before sprinting past me and up the hill. I then turned my attention to the girl.

She was still sitting on the steps, her frayed frock loose about her, her dark eyes staring at me with an indifferent hatred. As calmly as possible I said, "I don't want you speaking ever again to my son."

"I was just reading to him from Thoreau."

"I know very well what you were reading," I said. "Kingsley has a trained tutor who is helping with his reading. He doesn't need your interference

with his studies. You are not to see him again, do you understand?"

"He's a sweet boy, but lonely I think."

"His state is not your concern, ever. Any further interference in his affairs by you or your mother will have dire consequences to you both."

"My mother is too ill to even rise from her bed," she said, as she reached behind and pushed herself awkwardly to standing. "There is not much more you or your family could do to her now."

It was only then that I noticed what should have been obvious from the first, the grotesque fullness of her stomach that even the loose frock could not hide. I am not proud of the words that next came from my lips before I turned and stalked away but they were drawn from my throat by the glaring triumph in her eyes as surely as water from a hand pump.

And so I went to Father and once again pleaded that they be sent away. It is bad enough that they have stayed in that house as a reminder for all these many years, but that they should plague us with their bastard is too too much. My only solace is that the deed grants the mother only a life estate and that upon her death the land and that house revert back to our family. With the mother's evident illness we should soon be finally free of the shackles of their enmity.

April 3, 1923

My Dearest Sisters,

This night, in the strange light of a full moon, I felt compelled to again walk down the sloping hill of our rear yard and around the pond to the house *in the woods, despite the danger posed by the predator cat that stalks our county. I have not stopped thinking of my encounter the other day with the Poole daughter and of learning of her shameless pregnancy. The Pooles have been a presence in that house for most of my life, ever since the death of the father, but I had never come to know them, never had a conversation with either woman until our remarks that afternoon. Their whole lives, I had been certain, were devoted entirely to the deep wounding rage they held for our family. It was a shock to imagine that girl filled with another emotion, lost in a passion that, even if for only a moment, cut her off from her angry sense of deprivation. The image of that girl rolling on the ground with another, lost in a world that admitted not the Reddmans, has haunted my mind. I see it as I bathe, as I prune the dying stalks in my garden, as I awake alone and cold in my bed.*

I stood behind the tall thin trunk of an oak and watched the house through the windows. The mother was in a bed on the first floor, weak, white, her face drawn and tired. The room was lit by a harsh bare bulb in the ceiling. The girl sat by her mother, book in lap, and read out loud. Once, while I was there, the girl rose and walked into the kitchen, bringing back a glass of water, and she helped her mother hold it to her thin lips. There passed between them the habitual tenderness of family and I thought of you, dear sisters, as I watched and I wept for what we have lost. After a time the mother's eyes closed and the girl laid the back of her hand softly upon her mother's brow. She sat there, the pregnant girl, alone with her sleeping mother, before she rose and turned out the light.

I walked back up the hill and into our mon-strously empty house. Kingsley was asleep in his room and I stood over him and stared as he slept, transfixed by the very rhythm of his breath. In many ways my boy is as foreign to me as those people down the hill, so full of mystery. There was a time when I was his whole world.

How is it possible to survive in this life when we can never forget all we have destroyed?

April 5, 1923

My Dearest Sisters,

Her movements, as she works about the kitchen, are full of a surprising grace, despite her condition. She was making a soup tonight, and I watched as she chopped the vegetables and placed them into the pot and fed the old wood stove as the water came to a boil. With an almost dainty move-ment of her wrist she pulled from the pot one ladle full of scum after the other. There was a innocent intentness about her work, as if nothing was in her mind to disturb her preparations other than the necessities of the soup, not her evident poverty, not the failing health of her mother, not the bleak prospects for the bastard child she carries within her. For a short moment she came outside, a shawl wrapped around her shoulders, and lit for herself a cigarette. I pulled back behind the tree I was lean-ing against but still I stared. The light from the house was streaming from behind her as she smoked and so I could not see her face, but there was an ease in the way she held herself, even with her bloated belly, a comfort in the way she casually brought the cigarette to her lips. She is a woman who feels secure in the love that surrounds her. There also must be more than I could ever have imagined to the old woman awaiting death in that house, if her love can provide such comfort.

April 7, 1923

My Dearest Sisters,
It is a wonder that I had once thought her ugly. It is true that her features are not perfectly regular, and her nose is somewhat long, but there is about her movements and her face a brightness and a beauty that is unmistakable. All day I think about her in that house, hopelessly pregnant but still caring for her mother. I await anxiously for the night so I can see her. When Kingsley is to bed and Father alone and drinking in a vain effort to quell his shaking hands, I slip from the house as quietly as I am able and I glide down the hill to my spot at the oak. This evening I watched as she prepared for bed, watched her disrobe and wipe the sweat from her body with a sponge. Her round belly, her swollen breasts, the areolae thick and dark as wine, the nipples erect from the cold of the water. She must be farther along than I had imagined. Her skin is fresh and taut about the white round of her belly. She carries her burden with a dignity that is remarkable. I feel cleansed just in the watching of her. She prepares for the night as if she were preparing for a lover, which is heartbreaking, knowing that she has only her dying mother to keep her company. We are sisters in our loneliness.
I have been thinking of that child she is carrying. It may be a chance to make amends with all

*that has colored our past. When the time is right I
will raise the possibility with Father.*

April 8, 1923

My Dearest Sisters,
     *When I returned from my nightly vigil I was
startled to see Kingsley at the twin French doors to
the rear portico, waiting for me. He asked me if I
had heard it. The light mist of the evening had
turned suddenly into a rain and I wiped the wet
from my face.*
     *"What are you talking about, dear?" I said,
fighting to compose myself.*
     *"The cougar," he said. "Daddy told me their
mating calls are like a wild scream. I heard it just
down the hill."*
     "It must be something else," I said.
     *"No," he said, his face revealing a rare cer-
tainty. "It's the cougar, I know it."*
     "Then what are we to do?"
     *He didn't answer me, but with all the sureness
of his eight years he turned and led me into
Father's library, to the case mounted on the wall in
which Christian stores his guns. It was locked but
Kingsley reached beneath the case and pulled out
the key. He stood on a chair and inserted the key
into the lock. The glass door swung wide.*
     *The gun he pulled off the rack was the largest
of the four. It was Christian's father's gun.
Kingsley cracked the barrel open and checked to
be sure the cartridges were inside. Then he
smacked it shut again. I shivered at the sound of
the gun closing.*
     He led me back through the house to the doors

leading to the portico and opened them to the night. The rain had grown heavy, drowning whatever light escaped from the house before it could touch beyond the patio. The night was preternaturally dark.

"Turn out the hall lights," my son commanded and I did so.

"Shouldn't we get Grandfather?" I asked when I had returned to my place behind him.

"He shakes too much," he said simply.

"What about your father?"

"He's out," he said, and in those two short words there was not a note of judgment against the parent who had more and more absented himself from his family, who had betrayed it, abandoned it to the fearful felines of the night. "But if the cougar comes this way," he said, his voice suddenly shaky, "Father taught me what to do."

We waited there together inside the frame of those doors, just inches from the fierce rain, my son with the gun and I behind him, my hand tentatively on his shoulder. It felt wrong to me, being there with him and that gun, as if our positions were terribly reversed. It was I who should be protecting him, but I was too devastated to act on my feelings and was warmed into acquiescence by my son's evident concern for my safety. We were a team, together, just the two of us, guarding the homestead from intruders, and I couldn't break myself away from the delicious warmth I felt beside him, even as I could feel a shivering terror pass through his body to my hand. The minutes flicked away, one after another, flicked and died away and I couldn't even begin to tell how many passed before I saw something crawl upon us in the rain-blanked night.

"What's that?" I whispered.

A shadow flitted across the edge of the portico.

"There," I said.

The boy swung the gun to his shoulder.

"Now," I said.

The explosion tore the night, the light from the barrel blinding for a second before it disappeared, leaving the night darker than before. We were deafened to any sound, even the flat patter of the rain was swallowed by the burst of fire.

The boy steadied the gun and fired again and once again. The night tore apart. I screamed from the sheer beauty of the power and then a quiet descended.

The servants scuttled from their rooms and down the stairs and they saw us there, standing in the doorway, Kingsley with the gun. I explained to them what had happened and ordered them back to bed. Father was too sedated, I assume, to have even heard.

Kingsley wanted to go out and see if he had actually killed the cat but I refused to let him. "It will wait until tomorrow," I said as I closed the portico doors. "I don't want you outside in the dark until we're sure it is dead."

"I need to clean the shotgun," said Kingsley. "Father told me to always clean it before I put it away."

"Clean it tomorrow," I said. "Everything tomorrow."

I followed him as he went back into Father's study and replaced the gun. When he locked the cabinet I took the key. It is beside me now as I write this. I can't explain it, dear sisters, but I feel purged by the sudden explosions of this evening. I have regained my son, regained my power, suffered and survived the betrayals of the last twelve years.

I can make everything whole, I believe. With our father's strength and the deep desires of my soul I can heal our world.

April 19, 1923

My Love,

It is ten days now since we found you and I still bear the agony of the sight. Our dear Kingsley has not left his bed for a week. I sit with him and feed him broth but he is insensible with longing and pain. How he will survive his misery and guilt I do not know, but he must, he absolutely must, or all our dreams and hopes are for naught. He is your legacy, dear husband, and you will live forever through him.

You will be warmed to know that the Pooles have left us for good. Mrs. Poole succumbed to the illness that had been plaguing her. Father attended the funeral, I could not. It was a lonely affair, I am told, and at the internment in the gravesite beside her husband only the daughter and my father were in attendance. Father offered, he said, to help the girl in whatever way he could, but she refused his proffer and has now disappeared. Their house is empty, all their possessions crated up and taken or abandoned. Just this morning I walked among the empty rooms, the floorboards creaking beneath my feet. It feels haunted, my love, inhabited by a drove of ghosts.

I am bereft without you. Every day I visit the statue where we passed our vows. I sit before it for hours at a time and think of you. I have not yet found the courage to enter your room and touch your things, to smell your precious smell as it has lingered on your shirts. For the rest of this life that the Lord has cursed me with, know that I will love you and honor you and do all I can to glorify your name. I pray for you, my darling, as I pray for our son, and I am confident now that the paws of tragedy which have pounced upon our family far too many times will no longer threaten us and that what is left of our future will be full of peace and love and redemption. I will do all in my power to make it so.

34

I WAS SITTING AT MY DESK, staring at the message slip as it glowed pink in my hand. My secretary's handwriting, normally only barely legible, was this morning a series of mystical hieroglyphs. I had to squint to make it out. "Rev. Custer," it read, atop a phone number. I called out to her from my desk. "Who the hell is this, Ellie?"

She scurried into my office and stood behind me, peering over my shoulder at the slip of paper. "Your reverend."

"I don't have a reverend, Ellie, I'm Jewish, remember? We have mothers instead, and mine's in Arizona."

"Well he said he was a reverend, he said, Rev. Custer, just like that. You don't know him? He only left a number."

What I figured just then was that this Reverend Custer guy was one of the wackos in Beth's cult, calling about the meeting Beth had set up for me with Oleanna, guiding light, so I called. What I got was not a New Age answer line but instead a soft-voiced little girl of about six.

"Hello," she said, "you want my mommy?"

"No, sweetheart," I said, pronouncing my words with utter care in that annoying way all unmarried and childless men seem to have when they talk to strange little girls. "I'm really looking for a Reverend Custer."

"Mommy's in the shower."

"What about the reverend?"

"In the shower."

"He's in the shower too?"

"Mommy."

"No, the reverend."

"Are you a stranger?"

"I don't know, am I?"

"I'm not supposed to talk to strangers."

Click.

I had a headache and my eyes were blurry and I hadn't slept nearly enough. The night before we had opened the box disinterred from the garden behind Veritas and read together, Beth, Caroline, Morris, and I, the self-selected excerpts from the diary of Faith Reddman Shaw. That would have been exhausting enough, but afterward Caroline insisted on spending the whole of the night in my apartment. It was not sex she was after this night, which was too bad, actually. Instead she was after solace. Solacing is up there with having a toothache as the least pleasant way to stay awake through the night. I had to stroke her hair and wipe her tears and comfort her when all I really wanted was to sleep, but some things we suffer for money and some things we suffer for love and some things we suffer because we're too polite to kick her out of bed.

Ignore that last crack, it was only my testosterone speaking; besides, I am not that well mannered. It was indisputable that Caroline and I were easing into some sort of relationship, though the exact sort was hard to nail. Maybe it was just that we were both lonely and convenient, maybe it was the twin gravitational pulls of her great fortune and my great wanting, maybe it was that we found ourselves in the middle of an adventure we couldn't really share with anyone else. Or maybe it was that she saw herself in desperate need of saving and I, inexplicably, found in myself the desire to save. If all there was was love then there wasn't much to it, that was clear to us both, but life is not so soggy as the Beatles would have had us believe.

In the middle of our long late night conversation, as we

lay in my bed, still clothed, she reached around and gave me a hug. "I'm glad you're here for me, Victor," she said, out of nowhere. "There's no one else I can talk to about this. It has been a long time since anyone's been there for me."

And it had been a long time since I had been there for anyone. I smiled and kissed her lightly on the eye and I wondered if now might be a providential time to mention the fee agreement she still had not signed, but then thought better of it.

"This is harder than I ever imagined," she said. "Finding Aunt Charity down there and then that diary, my grandmother's words, reliving such tragedy. It's like the entire foundation of my life has shifted. Things that were absolutely true have turned out to be lies. I thought I had my life's history figured out, organized in a way that made sense, but it doesn't make as much sense anymore."

"Should we stop digging? Should we give it up?"

She was silent for a moment, a long worrying moment, before she shook her head and said, "No, not yet," and held me closer.

Her hair tickled my nose uncomfortably and made me sneeze. I had the urge to roll away, onto my side, to sleep, but I didn't. While the bounds of the relationship we were easing into were still narrow and unclear, they at least encompassed money and sex and now, I was learning, solace. But it wasn't as though she was faking her distress. Even as she held me she shook slightly, as if from a cold draft blowing in from the past, and it is no wonder.

Family histories are a series of myths, embellished and perpetuated through gossamer tales retold over the Thanksgiving turkey. They are blandly reassuring, these myths, they give us the illusion that we know from whence we came without forcing upon us the details that make real life so perfectly vulgar. We know how Grandmom met Grandpop at a John Philip Sousa concert at Willow Grove Park but not how they lived unhappily ever after in a loveless marriage and fought like hyenas every day of their lives. We know how Daddy proposed to Mommy but not how he first plied her with tequila and then conned her into the sack. We're told by our mother all about that magical night on which we were born but she never mentions how our head ripped apart her vagina or how her blood spurted or the way the placenta slimed out of her and plopped onto the floor like an immolated cat. Well, that night Caroline had seen the cat.

She had listened to her grandmother's voice come forth from the grave and she believed she could understand now all the misery her grandmother had suffered, and why she had suffered it. She was certain that her grandfather, the moody and ofttimes soused Christian Shaw, had only agreed to marry Faith to save his family's fortune. After proposing to Faith, he had started playing around with Charity, seducing the sister of the woman to whom he was engaged without a care in the world, and then, when Charity found herself inconveniently pregnant, had found it more convenient to murder Charity and bury her in the fertile oval beside the statue of Aphrodite than to tell the tale to her father, the man who was poised to save the Shaw Brothers Company from bankruptcy. In his marriage he had been mostly absent, often drunk, primarily abusive, and Caroline couldn't help but notice how sister Hope's health took a turn for the worse when Faith was forced to her bed with premature contractions and it was left to Christian to nurse the ill woman. She could figure why the rat poison was in the kitchen cabinet even if her grandmother couldn't. With Charity and Hope both gone, the whole of the Reddman fortune demised to Christian Shaw and his heirs, another convenience. It seemed to Caroline that the best thing that could have happened to her family was the accident that rainy April night in 1923 when her father shot her grandfather, except for the crippling guilt her father carried from that day forward. That was how

Caroline saw it that night in my bed, explaining her version to me through clenched teeth and tears.

I wasn't quite sure I bought it. Her interpretation of what we had heard sounded like the plot of a bad feminist novel from the seventies, where the women would all be just fine if it wasn't for those murderous men who engaged in the foulest of schemes to further their own ends. There was something too calculating, too controlled, in the voice of the woman who spoke to us from the dead that night for her to be so innocent a victim, something peculiar in the way she seemed so easily to absolve those around her of whatever crimes they had committed. As a lawyer I had had enough experience with unreliable narrators, had been one myself in fact, to fail to recognize the signs. But all of us had agreed on one thing, the ghosts that had been unleashed in the terrible events disclosed in the diary we had found in that box were still among us and the death of Jacqueline was quite possibly related.

"You haven't by any chance, Miss Caroline," said Morris as we decided on what to do next, "ever found that secret panel in the library your grandmother in the diary, she talks about?"

"No," she said. "I never heard of it before."

"It would be helpful, maybe, if you could spend some time, just like she did, and try to find it. Inside, I think, maybe there is something interesting, don't you think?"

"I'll do what I can," said Caroline.

"But don't tell anybody what you're doing," I said. "No one should know what we're digging into. What about the numbers on the three-by-five card we found?"

"A banker friend I know," said Morris, "very upstanding now but he got his start funding *Irgun* when such was not allowed and had to be done in secrecy. This was many years ago, just after the war, but not too far removed from the time of those papers you found. I'll take them to him. He might know."

Morris also agreed he would try to discover what had happened to the Poole daughter, who had disappeared, pregnant, just days after her mother's death. I took for myself certain of the photographs, and the strangely retained receipt from the doctor. I also took the key out of the envelope entitled "Letters" and slipped it into my wallet.

That was what we had done about the box, but I still knew the likelihood was greatest that whoever had paid off Cressi to kill Jacqueline Shaw had done it not as an avenging ghost of the past but for the most basic of all reasons, for the motive that underlies most all of our crimes, for the money. Which was why tonight I was seeing Oleanna, the guiding light of the Church of the New Life, named beneficiary in the five-million-dollar insurance policy taken out on Jacqueline Shaw's life. And it was why I had asked Caroline to set up a meeting for me that very afternoon with her brother Eddie, the worst gambler in the world, who had somehow, suddenly, upon the untimely murder of his sister, paid off his debt to Jimmy Vigs. In my short career I had discovered that to find a crook you follow the money. But first there was that message from the good Reverend Custer.

"Hello."

"Can I talk to your mommy, please?"

"She's in the bafroom."

"Yes, sweetheart, can I talk to her please? I'm looking for a Reverend Custer and I was given this number."

"She told me to say she's not in. Do we owe you money?"

"Not that I know of."

"Mommy says we owe a lot of money."

"You know, sweetheart," I said, "I think I may just have the wrong number."

I hung up and stared at Ellie's hieroglyphs for a little while and watched as they rearranged themselves before my eyes. Then a thought slipped through the fog of my mind and I felt myself start to sweat.

"I'm exhausted," I told Ellie as I stepped out of my office, the phone slip in my pocket. "I'm going to get some coffee. You want anything?"

"Diet soda," she said, and she started fiddling in her purse before I told her it was on me. Then I thought better of my generosity and took her four bits. I needed change for the phone.

I guess he assumed my line was tapped or my messages somehow not secure, and I couldn't really blame him. Whoever was coming after him had the audacity to try to make the hit in the middle of the Schuylkill Expressway. To someone that brazen it wouldn't be a thing to slap a wire on a phone or rifle through a pack of pink slips looking for a number to trace. "You are my scout," had said Enrico Raffaello. "Like in the old cavalry movies, every general needs a scout to find the savages." And what beleaguered general was ever more in need of a ferret-eyed scout than George Armstrong Custer. I just wish Raffaello had picked a less-ominous example. He wasn't at the number I had dialed because that number was absolutely wrong. I took the Rev. literally and reversed the numbers when I made the call in the phone booth. This time it wasn't a little girl who answered.

"This is a private line," came a voice over the phone, a dark voice and slow.

"I'm looking for Reverend Custer," I said.

"Boy, do you ever have the wrong number," said the voice and then the line went dead.

I puzzled that for a moment, thoroughly confused about everything. When the hell was Calvi going to get off his boat and tell me what to do? Until he did I had no choice but to fake it. I took the second of Ellie's quarters and dialed again.

"I said this was a private line," said the same voice.

"I'm calling from a pay phone and this is my last quarter and if you hang up on me it will be your ass in a sling. Tell the man it's his scout calling. Tell him I need to speak to him now."

There was a quiet on the line as if my request was being considered by a higher authority and then I heard the scrape of chairs and a rap of knuckles on wood in the distance.

"What do you have for me?" came the familiar voice.

"How are you? How seriously are you hurt?"

There was a grunt.

"Where are you?" I asked.

There was a dangerous pause where I realized I had asked exactly the wrong question. "Tell me what you've learned," he said finally.

"Our friend with the guns, I know how he got the money now. Murder for hire. One of his victims was an heiress name of Shaw."

"Who paid him?"

"I'm not sure yet, but it's nothing to do with you. For our friend it was just a way to finance the war. But he got a little sloppy and there was a witness and that is what's so damn interesting. Under pressure, the witness changed his story, taking the heat off our guy."

"Who applied the pressure?"

"Our little buddy who's moved up so fast, the pawn-broker. He's in on it, I know it."

"Is there any other connection between the two of them?"

"Other than your friend was all too happy to get me into the car with you before our incident?"

"Other than that, yes."

"No. But it's him."

"If it is him, or another, it no longer matters," he said, and then he sighed. "You're a good friend. You've been very loyal. I will remember this after it is over. I have one last favor to ask."

"I want out."

"I know that is what you want and I now want the same. I'm tired of it, and these animals have no restraint. It was bad enough going after me, but what they did to Dominic, who was already out, and then to Jimmy Bones was too much. They'll go after my daughter, I know it, and then I will have no choice but to enter a war in which no one will win and everyone will end up dead. I could send my men out hunting right now, but it won't solve the problem, and with every murder, every attempt, the case the feds are building grows stronger and more of our own will feel marked and turn. I'm a tired man, I don't want to spend the last years of my life hiding or in jail or dead. I want to paint. I want to spend a whole month reading one poem. I want to dance naked in the moonlight by the sea."

"You sound like a personal ad."

"I'm a romantic at heart."

"The bastards tried to kill us."

"I was never a man of war. It was forced upon me once, I won't let it be forced upon me again. You will be approached about a meeting."

"Why would they approach me?"

"You were in the line of fire. You were the last neutral to see me. You will be approached. That is the way these animals work."

"What do I tell them?"

"You are to tell them that I want peace. Tell them that I will meet them to accept their terms. Tell them if they can guarantee my security and the security of my family then it is over. Tell them we will meet to arrange a truce and then the trophy will be theirs."

35

THE EDWARD SHAWS LIVED in a townhouse on Delancey Place, a very fashionable address on the Schuylkill side of Rittenhouse Square. It wasn't a through street, so it was quiet, and the cars that sat before the houses seemed to have been parked there for half of eternity, parked in prime, unmetered spots undoubtedly willed from one generation to the next. Of course the Shaws wouldn't deign to park on the street, their property would include a garage in the back, which I had checked out through the garage-door window before I pressed their doorbell. A two-car garage with only one car inside, a sedate silver BMW. Not the kind of car the worst gambler in the world would tool around in, I figured. He'd want something flashier, something red, something more phallic to make up for the continual humiliation of his certain winners dropping dead of coronaries in the middle of the track. Eddie Shaw, it appeared, had skipped out on our meeting. It was enough to give a guy a complex, the way he was avoiding me.

When I saw who was at the door, I expected a torrent of words, but all I got from Kendall Shaw was a subdued, "Hello, Victor. Caroline told me you'd be coming and that I was to help you any way I could." When I was inside, she turned around and led me into her family room.

To get there we passed through a formal carpeted foyer. The walls were an eggshell blue, marked with rectangular patches of a slightly darker shade. There were formal chairs and a sofa, but in the center, off to the right, there was a strange open area. As I passed the opening I glanced down at the carpet and saw four indentations in an irregular quadrangular pattern, about the size and the spacing of the feet of a grand piano.

The family room was still intact. Comfortably furnished, it was filled with deep sofas, recliner chairs, framed posters, an exhibition of some of Kendall's latest landscapes. In the center of the room, like a shrine, was a gigantic television set. I guess that's right, take the paintings, take the piano, but Lord please don't let them take my La-Z-Boy or my big screen Panasonic TV. Kendall gestured me onto the sofa and sat herself on the facing love seat. She was dressed today rather primly, a beige skirt, a white blouse, and her drug-induced mania was somewhat depressed. She was on a different set of pills this week, I figured. Valium anyone?

"I've come to see your husband," I said.

"You're not really a painter, are you, Victor?" she said.

"No, ma'am. Actually, I'm a lawyer. But I admired your work very much."

"That was kind of you and Caroline to play such tricks on me."

"I'm just here to ask your husband a few questions."

"So Caroline said. He's out at the moment, but you can wait with me, if you'd like." She glanced at her watch. "He must be running a little late."

"When did you expect him back?"

"Two days ago," she said, and then she almost jumped to her feet. "Can I get you something? Coffee? Fish sticks?"

"Coffee would be fine," I said, and I watched her walk briskly out of the room.

Well, this had become nicely awkward.

She came back after ten minutes carrying a tray with a

teapot and two cups and an arrangement of fancy cookies. As she poured, I told her I liked my coffee black. She handed me the cup and I sipped daintily. It was scalding. I wondered how much I could take her insurance company for if I spilled it on my lap.

"What exactly did you want to ask my husband about?" she said nonchalantly while she poured a cup for herself.

"Are you sure you should be having caffeine, Mrs. Shaw?"

There was a pause. She stirred in some milk and a packet of Sweet'n Low and sat back in her love seat. "I'd like to apologize for my behavior at Veritas that night, Victor. You caught me on a bad evening. I was ovulating. I tend to grow a little overeager during ovulation."

"Yes, well right there is more than I ever wanted to know, but still, apology accepted."

"How's your ear?"

"Healing, thank you. I didn't mean to disturb your afternoon, I had just a few questions about your husband's finances."

"Don't we all."

"Maybe I should come back."

"Maybe you'd have better luck asking me what you want to know. Edward is not forthcoming with or about his money, except to his bookies."

I took a sip of my coffee and stared at her for a moment. I hadn't noticed it beneath the hysteria the night she bit my ear but there was about Kendall Shaw, as she bravely sat in her posh townhouse while it disassembled before her eyes, an aura of strength. I had seen in Eddie Shaw's eyes the weakness of a gambler who, despite all evidence to the contrary, expected to win. Kendall had the eyes of a gambler too, but a gambler who had bet it all and lost and could live with that. She had rolled the dice on Eddie Shaw, a pair of dice she was sure was fixed in her favor, and still, against all laws of probability and physics, had thrown craps.

"All right," I said. "I'll ask you what I was going to ask him. The day Jacqueline died, your husband flew to Philadelphia from his beach vacation for some business. That afternoon he stopped in to visit Jacqueline, but she wasn't home. What was the purpose of that visit?"

She took a sip of coffee and looked to the side. "Edward would tell you he just went over to say hello to his dear sister."

"But he didn't just go over to say hello?"

"That would have been a kind and loving gesture on his part, so we can assume the answer is no. Cookie, Victor?"

"No, thank you. So why the visit?"

"Edward needed money to pay off his gambling debts. They had busted up his Porsche and broken his arm. He thought they were going to kill him next. He hoped his sister would give him some of her money to get him out of immediate trouble."

"Why Jacqueline?"

"Process of elimination. Bobby lost his in wild investments and Caroline wasted most of hers on her film."

"You mentioned before that Caroline had tried to make a movie."

"Yes. In a burst of unexpected enthusiasm she lavished great sums of her dividend money on a writer and a director and some actors and a crew and shot a film, a horror film about a crazed plastic surgeon, but then she cut off her financing and closed the picture down before they could complete postproduction. She has the piles of raw stock in a vault somewhere. She said that the end result didn't satisfy her standards, but that was just her excuse. It was so like her to pull the plug like that, another way of ensuring the continued failure at which she has become so accomplished. All the Reddmans, I've learned, are brilliant at failure."

"But Jacqueline still had her money?"

"Loads. For years she was too depressed to step outside her apartment. Her dividends just piled up. Edward figured two hundred and fifty thousand dollars would get them off his back. She was his last hope."

"And she wasn't home when he visited."

"No, she wasn't, and by the time he could get free to go see her again she was dead."

"Which wasn't so inconvenient for him, actually, at least so he probably thought, since she was insured for five million and he expected he was a beneficiary."

"Edward would tell you that he knew the beneficiary of her policy had been changed, that Jacqueline had told him so."

"But that would be another lie, I guess."

"The day after she was found hanging he had borrowed money on the death benefit to pay off a chunk of his debt. He had promised the borrower that he would repay the loan as soon as the insurance money came in. The night he found out the money was going to those New Age lotus-eaters he literally howled in desperation."

"Like a werewolf."

She laughed lightly but not nicely. "My charts had showed that evening to be propitious."

"Astrology?"

"Temperature. But he was so full of blubbery fear he was useless."

"Why are you telling me all this, Kendall?"

She stood up and put her now empty cup onto the tray and then walked over to one of her paintings on the wall. It was in a fine oval frame and the oil had also been laid on in an oval, a night scene, with a stream running through spindly bare trees and a huge white mountain peak in the background, all illuminated by a bright moon. "Did you really like my painting?" she asked.

"Well, no, actually. But I'm no critic."

"And I'm no painter," she said. "Caroline told me you were looking into Jacqueline's death for her. That you and she both believe that Jacqueline was murdered."

"That's right."

"Well, Victor, don't you think that I've thought what you're thinking? Don't you think I've stayed up at night, lying beside that snoring shit, wondering with fear of what kinds of beastly things he is capable? Don't you think?"

"I guess I hadn't thought."

"Well think."

"And if it turns out to be your husband, what will you do?"

"I married him for better or for worse, and unlike the rest of this world I believe in that. I'd move out to wherever they send him and visit him in prison once a week, every week. I'd be the most loyal wife you've ever seen until his father dies and his stock shares vest and then I'd divorce the bastard and take my half and move to Santa Fe. Georgia O'Keeffe painted just outside Santa Fe. Did you know that?"

"No."

"They must have the most erotic flora in Santa Fe. Any other questions, Victor?"

"Just one. This money he found to pay off a piece of the gambling debt. Where did it come from?"

"Edward would tell you he got lucky at the track."

"I bet that's exactly what he'd tell me."

"He told me he found someone to help him," she said. "He told me he found someone willing to factor the insurance payout for a few points a week. He made me sign something but then said the man would bail him out."

"Who?"

"Some pawnshop operator from South Philly. His place is on Second Street, I think, a shop called the Seventh Circle Pawn. A cute name, actually, since this man's name is Dante."

First thing I did when I left Kendall Shaw was to find a phone and tell Caroline to get the hell out of her apartment, right away, to get the hell out and hide. I had learned enough to figure that her life was in danger and who exactly it was who would want her dead.

36

I WAITED IN MY CAR outside the large shambling house in Mount Airy, watching the acolytes enter the Haven. I could tell they were acolytes because they wore sandals or colored robes beneath their denim jackets or their hair was long or their heads were shaved or they had the self-righteous carriage of those on the trail of life's one true answer. They would have looked out of place in every part of the city but Mount Airy, which has long been a refuge for earnest granola eaters and committed activists in long batik skirts. I felt sorry for them as I watched them walk in that house, even as I knew they would feel sorry for me had they crossed my path. I thought they were deluded fools buying into some harebrained promise of enlightenment for a price when all there really was was the price. They would have thought me a materialistic loser who was totally out of touch with the sweet spiritual truths in my life. All we had in common was our mutual scorn, edged with pity, but, hey, I had suffered through long-term romantic relationships that were built on less.

There was five million due to go to the woman in that Mount Airy house. If I could connect her to the killing and get Caroline's signature on my agreement I figure I'd be able to wheedle my third of the five either from a suit against her or from the insurance company. One million six hundred, sixty-six thousand, six hundred, sixty-six dollars and sixty-six cents. It wasn't all I had hoped to get out of this case in the middle of my most fervently hopeful night sweats, but there was a comforting sibilance to the number. It would do. I slapped on my armor of incredulity, stepped out of the car, and headed to the Haven for my meeting with Oleanna, Guiding Light.

The house was stone, trimmed in dark green. There was a narrow front porch with a painted wood floor, scarred and uneven. Across the porch were some old wicker chairs arrayed in the form of a discussion group, empty now. I stepped around a red tricycle, past a pile of old brown cushions left out to rot, past a stack of lumber. Though it was late spring, the storm windows were still up and green paint was peeling from the window sashes and the door. On the edge of the door frame was an incongruous *mezuzah*, covered with thick layers of paint. I rang the bell and nothing happened. I dropped the knocker and nothing happened. I looked around and twisted the door-knob and stepped into another year: 1968 to be exact.

Incense, Jerry Garcia, the warm nutty smell of a vegetarian casserole baking in the oven, posters of India and Tibet, earnest conversations, bad haircuts, the thick clinging scent of body odor.

We just missed all this, those of my generation, born too late as we were to ever remember a time when Martin Luther King and Bobby Kennedy weren't dead. The cool kids in our classes didn't dress in tie-dye and bell bottoms, didn't sport long straight hair, didn't march in solidarity with the migrant farm workers; they wore polo shirts and applied to Harvard Business School and crushed beer cans on their heads. We didn't listen to the young Bobby Dylan warble his warning to Mr. Jones, we had Bruce Springsteen and the Pretenders and the Sex Pistols just for the hell of it. There were plenty, like Beth, who felt they missed out on something, that the best was gone before they got there, but I was just as glad it passed me by. Too much pseudoactivism, too much pressure to try too many drugs, too little antiperspirant, too much godawful earnestness, too much communion with the masses, too much free love. Well, the free love I could have gone for, sure, I was as horny as the next groovester, but the rest you could stuff inside a time capsule and rocket to Aquarius for all I cared. I felt out of place in that house with my suit and tie and I liked that.

A woman without any hair, wearing an orange robe, stepped over to greet me. She put her hands together, fingers pointing up, and bowed slightly.

Yeah, sure. "I'm here to see Oleanna," I said. "I have an appointment."

"I'm sorry," said the woman in a voice that was genuinely sweet, "but Oleanna doesn't make appointments."

"Why don't you check and see," I said.

Before she had time to apologize again I spotted what looked like a hairy boy walking down the stairs. At first I could just see his sandaled feet beneath the overhang of the ceiling, and then the hem of his yellow robe, and then, as more of his body was revealed, I recognized Gaylord. He surveyed the room as he descended and spotted me.

"Victor Carl, what a pleasure to see you," he said in his high-pitched voice and the conversations that buzzed around us quieted. A smile burrowed out of his beard as he approached. "Welcome to the Haven. We've been so looking forward to your visit."

The woman in the orange robe clasped her hands together and bowed slightly to Gaylord before she backed away from us. Gaylord grabbed me at the crook of my elbow, his smile still firmly in place.

"Come," he said. "I'll take you downstairs."

He led me to the rear of the house, toward the kitchen. The congregants quieted when we approached and backed away from us. Some were dressed in street clothes, but most were in orange or green robes. Only Gaylord was wearing yellow.

"What's with the different colors?" I asked.

"How much has your friend Beth told you?" he said.

"Beth?"

"Come now, Victor, we are not fools. We knew from the first who she was when she came and were only too happy to allow her to join our family. You did us a favor bringing her to us. She has a spiritual gift that is very rare. Oleanna thinks she is a very evolved soul."

"Beth?"

"She has taken the steps faster than any seeker we've ever had other than Oleanna. The colors of our robes correspond to the twelve steps through initiation. The first five steps are called preparation, in which the seeker wears orange. Steps six through nine are called illumination, in which the seeker wears green. The final steps are initiation, in which the seeker suffers through three trials, the fire trial, the water trial, and the air trial. Those in the process of initiation wear yellow."

"You're the only one I see in yellow."

"It's a very advanced state," said Gaylord.

The kitchen was large and bright, with yellow-and-white linoleum on the floor and avocado Formica counters. A group of acolytes in orange and green were chopping vegetables and stirring pots on an oversized commercial stove. "Only a few live in the house," said Gaylord, "but all members are invited to share in the preparation and consumption of the evening meal. You're invited to stay."

"Very hospitable from someone who had threatened me with severe bodily harm just a few weeks ago."

Gaylord stopped and turned to face me and then did something that truly shocked me. He put his hands together and fell to his knees and bowed his head low, touching his forehead to my wing tips. The scene felt horribly awkward, but no one in the kitchen seemed to think much of it. One orange-robed acolyte raised an eyebrow as he watched us for a moment before turning back to his work on the counter.

"I apologize to you with all my will, Victor Carl, for my behavior in your office. I felt my family was being threatened and besieged and I responded with anger and violence instead of benevolence and kindness. You should know that the karmic wound from my behavior has yet to heal and my spiritual progress has been halted for the time being as I continue to deal with my transgression."

"Get up, Gaylord."

His head still pressed to my shoes, he said, "I plead now for your forgiveness."

I stepped back and he raised himself to his haunches, his hands still out in front of him.

"Just get the hell up," I said. "I'd rather you threaten me again than do this penitent bit."

"Do you forgive me then?"

"Will you get off your knees if I forgive you?"

"If that's what you want."

I looked down at him uncertainly. I would have felt worse about the scene had there not been a strange formality to his words, as if he had performed this same act of contrition when he blew up in the supermarket at a shopper with fifteen items in the twelve-item line or at a taxi driver who took the long way around. But even with the formality of his apology, I realized I didn't like being bowed to like that, which was a surprise. Who among us hasn't dreamed, at least for a moment, of being a king? But one robed penitent bowing at my feet had steeled my determination that if ever the Sacred College of Cardinals in their secret conclave in Rome decided to make a Jew from Philadelphia the next Pope, I would turn them down flat. Last thing I ever wanted was the huddling masses sucking on my ring.

"Rise, Gaylord. I forgive you."

Gaylord smiled a sly victory smile as he rose.

He took hold again of my arm and led me to the rear of

the kitchen to a doorway which opened to a flight of low-ceilinged stairs. I ducked on my way down to what turned out to be a cramped warren of tiny rooms linked to one central hallway. Some of the doors to the rooms were open and small groups were inside, on the floor, in circles or in rows, chanting or bowing forward and back or sitting perfectly still. The walls were cheap drywall, the carpeting was gray and had an industrial nap.

"In the practice rooms," said Gaylord, "we teach the many different techniques of meditation."

"More than just crossing your legs and saying 'Om'?"

He stopped at a room and opened the door. There were five orange-robed followers sitting around a green-robed woman, who knelt before them with a serene, peaceful expression on her face. Three of the orange robes were breathing in and out quickly, as if they were hyperventilating. One man was leaning forward, crying, his eyes still shut. A final woman was shaking as she held herself tightly and screamed like a scared child. No one came to help her as she shook and screamed. Slowly Gaylord closed the door.

"They're practicing dynamic meditation," said Gaylord. "It's the most efficient way to reintegrate the past with the present. This is how many of our followers begin to see the integrity of the inner spirit through its ascendant journey from life to life."

"You're talking about past lives?"

"Finding a connection with our pasts is the final step of preparation before we move to illumination. We can't know where our soul is heading until we know where it has been."

"Then you weren't kidding what you said about being a crusader."

"Dynamic meditation is very powerful," said Gaylord. He smiled unselfconsciously and led me further down the hallway.

I could feel it all about me, the bustling work of the robed minions searching for that spiritual salvation they know must be there for them, or else why would they ever have been placed on a slag heap such as this. I felt like a stranger in my suit, watching them all hard at their mystical work. I wonder if this was how James Bond felt as Auric Goldfinger led him on a tour of the facilities from which he was planning to detonate an atomic bomb and destroy America's supply of gold: distant and amused and impressed and appalled all at the same time. I would have gone back to that room and opened the door and hugged the woman who was shaking and crying except that I was certain it was the last thing she would have wanted me to do. She had shaved her head, that woman, and her face was red with her tears and pain. At the end of it they would each tell her how far she had come and she would feel ever so proud, feel ever so much closer to it all. Even Bond would have been at a loss.

Finally Gaylord led me to a room at the end of the basement. He asked me to take off my shoes before entering. I had suspected there might be some shoe discarding so I made sure my socks were without holes that day. Gaylord slipped off his sandals and then opened the door.

The doorway to this room was small, low enough that I had to duck to get inside, and once inside I noticed that the room was very different from the others, more spacious, the floor covered with beige tatami mats, the walls lined entirely with fine wood. On either side and around the back were steplike risers, each also covered with tatami. Flower petals were scattered on the mats and a strong floral incense burned in a bronze pot. In each corner of the room stood columns carved with what appeared to be Sanskrit and on one of the walls was a framed architectural drawing of a futuristic sort of churchlike building looking very Mormonish with its spires and looping curves. There were windows high at the far end and beneath the windows was a niche in which a stone Buddha sat, his belly full and his smile empty, and before the Buddha, resting on a small stone pedestal, were two bronzed feet, a perfect pair, life-sized, cut off at the ankles.

Gaylord walked right up to the wall with the Buddha, dropped to his knees, bent forward until his forehead touched the bronzed feet. Then he stood and gestured to one of the risers and said, "Wait here for a few moments, please."

I walked around the room for a bit in my stockinged feet, examining the woodwork, the engraved columns, the architectural drawing of what I assumed to be the Church of the New Life building proposed for Gladwyne, the cornerstone to be laid as a result of Jacqueline's timely death. I stared for a moment at the carved Buddha, it looked to be old and precious, and then at the bronzed feet on the pedestal. I had to admit that the feet were more than passing strange. They were a woman's feet, slim and gracefully arched, the toes even and slightly curled. They were very attractive for feet, actually. They might have been the prettiest feet I had ever seen. I couldn't help but reach down and touch one of them, to rub my fingers lightly on the underside of the arch, to place my hand firmly atop of the rise of the tarsal ridge. The bronze beneath my palm was smooth, rubbed shiny over time like on the feet of a statue of a Roman Catholic saint. I let out a long breath, spun around, and then sat on one of the risers, across from the architectural drawing. The risers were wide enough to sit cross-legged, as I assume they were intended, but I just let my legs dangle as though I were sitting in the bleachers for a high school football game.

I waited for about a half an hour, growing steadily more impatient, when I heard a knock at the door. I stood.

The door opened slowly. In came Gaylord, looking unusually somber, his hands pressed one to the other before him as he entered and stepped to the right. Behind Gaylord was our Steven Seagal wannabe friend Nicholas, still wearing his black outfit. No robes for Nicholas, I guessed, while he was in his bodyguard mode. He glared at me as he bent to enter through the low wooden door and stepped to the left, forming a sort of honor guard at the doorway. Then through this guard of honor walked a small white-robed woman.

I gasped to myself when I saw her because she might have been the most beautiful woman I had ever seen, strong yet delicate features, like those on a statue of a Greek goddess, green eyes that literally sparkled. Red hair circled her face like a halo and from her slim ears dangled a shimmering pair of silver and pearl earrings. Looking at her was like looking at a soft shot in a movie. Even from a distance I could smell the scent of her musk. I found myself embarrassed by my reaction to the loveliness of her face and I tore my gaze away from it, down, to her bare feet, slim and gracefully arched, the toes even and slightly curled. They were prettier in person then in bronze and I had to stifle the desire to fall to my knees and bow until my forehead rested on her flesh.

I looked back up at her face and Oleanna smiled at me, a smile I felt viscerally, like an old song that echoes with the sadness of lost love.

"Thank you for coming, Mr. Carl," she said. "I am extremely grateful that you agreed to meet with me."

I had assumed it was I who had arranged for the meeting but I was too dazzled to care.

"We at the Haven," she continued, "are in desperate need of your help."

37

CRITICAL

WHEN I CAME HOME from the Haven, Caroline was waiting for me in my apartment. She was wearing jeans and a sweatshirt, her face was free of makeup, and my first reaction upon seeing her was wondering why I had never considered her dowdy before. It was an unfair thought, really, but it couldn't be helped, still under the thrall, as I was, of Oleanna.

Caroline was at my apartment because as soon as I learned that Eddie Shaw had borrowed a load of cash from Earl Dante I realized that she was in utter danger. The way I saw it, Eddie had borrowed cash from Dante, the loan shark, to relieve the pressure from Jimmy Vigs and had arranged for his sister's death at the same time. The Seventh Circle Pawn, your one-stop shop for shark loans and murder-for-hire and mayhem. Dante had gladly lent Shaw the money, at three points a week, with the expectation that he would be repaid by the insurance policy on Jacqueline's death along with a lucrative bonus for the murder itself. Eddie had visited his sister's building the day of her death not to ask for money, as Kendall had suggested, but to tape open the lock of the Cambium's stairwell and wedge the wood in the Cambium's roof door, opening the passageway for Cressi's murderous visit. When Dante discovered that the money from the policy was not going to Eddie but instead to some New Age guru he must have turned a pleasant shade of green. Now Eddie Shaw was missing, probably running for his life, and the only way Dante would be getting his loan repaid in the near future was by killing off another Shaw. So I had warned Caroline, told her to make herself scarce and to suggest the same to brother Bobby. Bobby, I figured, had lifted off to some exotic locale but Caroline insisted on staying in Philadelphia. Insisted, in fact, after making a quick trip back to Veritas, on hiding out at my place. I had left a key for her before I visited the Haven. I guess our vague relationship was vaguely entering a new phase.

"What did you find out from the chant-heads?" asked Caroline as soon as I entered my apartment.

I looked at her for a moment and then stepped around her, toward the bedroom. "They didn't do it."

"How do you know?"

"I just know."

"Did you meet with that Oleanna person?" she asked as she followed me through the bedroom doorway.

I squinted into a mirror as I untied my tie. "Yes."

"Well, what did she say? How did she explain the life insurance policy?"

"They didn't do it," I snapped. "All right?" I sat on the bed and started untying my shoes. "It was someone else. If you want my thinking, I'd bet it was your brother Eddie that hired the killer."

"But the cult is where the money went," she said. "Aren't they the most likely to have hired a hit man to get five million dollars?"

"They're not a cult and they didn't do it." With my shoes off I stood and undid my belt. "Do you mind, Caroline, I'm getting undressed here."

"Yes, I do mind," she said. "You suspect my brother of killing my sister, you suspect some deranged descendent of Elisha Poole, you suspect everyone except for the mob bookie, who you represented, and this wacko New Age church, which stood to gain a swift five million dollars from my sister's death. There is no logic in any of that. So tell me, Victor, how are you so damn certain? How?"

How indeed?

It was hard to remember the whole of my meeting with Oleanna, it still was more like a dream than reality. We had a fairly normal conversation on the surface but it felt the whole time I was with her as if a current of some sort was being passed through her to me. I found it difficult to concentrate, to keep my place in our discussion. Being with her was like I remember reefer to be, without the paranoia or the intense desire to stuff my cheeks with Doritos. She looked at me with a penetration I had never experienced before, as if she was looking at something not connected to my physical body. She wasn't reading my mind exactly, it was more like she was keeping visually abreast of my emotional state. There was a power to that woman, it was undeniable, and for the time we were together I felt it reaching out to me. And I guess I succumbed, because by the end of our meeting, when she took my hand in hers and I felt the pulsing warmth beneath her skin, by the time she said good-bye I was not only certain that the Church of the New Life was not involved in the murder of Jacqueline Shaw, but I was also pledged to find out exactly who had hired her killer and to prove it to the insurance company so that the death benefit would be promptly paid.

It wasn't like I didn't ask the questions I had prepared, because I did. I asked her how she had convinced Jacqueline to change her life insurance policy and she said she hadn't, that Jacqueline had volunteered to make the church her life insurance beneficiary, as do many of the church's followers. I asked her how important the five million dollars was to her church and she indicated, with a smile, the architectural drawing of the building on the wall and said the bequest from Jacqueline was the great bulk of the funds that would be used to construct their new ashram in the suburbs. When I remarked on her expensive taste in real estate she shrugged and said simply that they were outgrowing the house in Mount Airy. I asked her if she knew an Earl Dante or a Peter Cressi or a Jimmy Vigs and the answer each time was no. "Ever hear of a man named Poole?" I asked, but still the answer was no. I asked her how she had found out I was looking into Jacqueline's death in the first place and she said that Detective McDeiss had called the insurance company to ask some further questions and the insurance company had called her lawyers asking why a shady criminal defense attorney would be so interested in a suicide. And then I asked her the most puzzling question: why, if she hadn't been involved in Jacqueline's death, had she sent Gaylord and Nicholas to threaten me off the case? She apologized profusely for their behavior, though not as profusely as Gaylord, and explained that at the time the insurance company was on the verge of disbursing the death benefit and she was certain my investigation would raise alarms that might delay still further the payment. "And, of course, I was right," she said, a sweet smile on her face, "and so we have been forced to sue." Those were her answers to my questions and they were pretty good answers, not great answers maybe, but good enough, I guess, though to be truthful, it wasn't the content of the answers that convinced me of her innocence.

What had convinced me was the current I had felt flowing from her to me, a strange nonverbal communication that bypassed the logic centers of my left brain and flowed straight into the emotional centers in my right. I was convinced she was telling the truth because she was telling me so in a way I was ill-equipped to refute. Emotionally I believed every word she said and after my emotions were engaged my logic swiftly followed. Of course the Church of the New Life wouldn't hurt Jacqueline Shaw. They loved her, they cared for her, she was family, so said my emotions. And she was a sugar tit that they could suck on for the rest of her life, draining, over time, enough of her share of the Reddman fortune to make the five mil look like a pittance, so said my logic, hustling to catch up.

And then, as if she were reading my spirit like a billboard, she convinced me to do all I could to find Jacqueline's killer, not by pure emotion, not by reason, not by virtue of her rare beauty, but through the one medium most designed to catch my attention. She offered me cash.

"If you can convince the insurance company to stop holding up the payment, Mr. Carl," she said, "by proving to them that we were in no way responsible for Jacqueline's death, we will be sure you are rewarded. Generally the rewards we give to our church members are karmic in nature, designed to benefit the soul in future lives. But seeing as you're not a member of the church, how about a portion of the recovery? Say five percent?"

To give you an idea of my state of mind, I promised to do my best immediately, I didn't so much as haggle. Had I been thinking more clearly I would have seen the offer for what it obviously was, a bribe to turn the direction of my investigation away from her church. But I wasn't thinking clearly. In fact I didn't even do the calculation until I was in the car, on Kelly Drive, on my way back into Center City. Two hundred and fifty thousand dollars. She was offering me two hundred and fifty thousand dollars to prove that someone else, and not she, was the killer. It was an obvious bribe, yes, but I was certain that it was no such thing. How was I so certain? How indeed? Because I had felt something flowing from Oleanna, something pure and innocent and irrefutable, something I almost couldn't recognize because of my pathetic lack of experience. What I had felt flowing from her to me was something close to love.

* * *

"So what was going on at Veritas?" I asked Caroline as we sat at my red Formica dining table and ate a pizza I had called out for.

"Nothing," she said.

"Did you look for the hiding place your grandmother mentioned in her diary?"

"Sort of," she said.

"Well? Did you find it?"

"Sort of."

"Sort of? What does that mean?"

"Okay, I found it. By the cast-iron fireplace, like my grandmother wrote in her diary. I tapped around with my knuckle until I found a hollow part. There was a piece of wood trim that slipped up." She shrugged. "So I pushed the panel and it opened."

"Hell, Caroline, that's fantastic. What did you find? Another corpse?"

"No, thank God. Nothing important, really, just books, ledgers, different kinds of financial journals. Worthless stuff."

"I'd bet not. Did you get them for us?"

She nodded slowly.

"Where are they?"

She didn't answer.

"Where are they, Caroline?"

She waited a moment and then gestured to my hall closet.

Inside I found a cardboard box, sitting on the floor among my loose jackets and assorted balls and racquets. I pulled out the box, kneeled down, and looked through it quickly. Old ledgers with their pages crumbling and the moth-eaten cloth on their frayed bindings seeming to be a step away from complete disintegration. The numbers inside were written in a fading ink, numbers over numbers over numbers, in progressions that meant absolutely nothing to me.

"This is amazing," I said. "I'd never be able to make head nor tail of it but I'll have Morris take a look."

I put the books back and stood up and thought for a moment and then turned to look at her. She was staring at a piece of pizza where the cheese had pulled off and was now in a clump on her paper plate.

"Why didn't you tell me about what you found right off?" I said.

She shrugged without looking up, staring at the denuded slice of pizza as if it was the most fascinating sight she had ever seen.

"I thought if I lied and told you the hiding place was empty," said Caroline, finally, after not responding to my question for hours, "what was inside would go away."

"What do you think is in those books?"

"I don't know. I don't want to know."

"I don't think the truth ever goes away, Caroline. I think it just sometimes lies in wait for us."

We were now side by side in my bed. It was late. We had made it halfway through Leno before I had retired to the bedroom. I had wanted some time alone that night but I didn't know how to tell her that, so I stayed up past my bedtime, hoping she'd get the hint to go to sleep by herself, had stayed up watching the local news and Jay's monologue and an insipid conversation with some long-legged starlet, Jay fawning over her so assiduously that she had to wipe the slobber from her leather dress, and I would have happily slept right there on the couch except that Caroline was sitting right there with me. So I stretched and yawned and said I needed to get some sleep and that was her cue to follow me into the bedroom. I had never lived with a woman before and I wondered if this was what it was like to be married. I could tell right off I didn't like it.

"I have an idea," said Caroline. "Let's go to Mexico."

"It's not easy learning the truth, is it?"

"Cancun, just me and you."

"You don't really want to stop our search."

"Oh yes I do."

"Really?"

She waited a moment before she said, "I thought I could control what we did and what we found, but now I'm not so sure."

I realized just then how close she was to actually quitting and I felt a twang of fear. I wasn't ready yet to stop, neither for my sake, nor for hers. I mean, however could I save her if she wasn't willing to be saved? What I needed to do was to keep everything together for just a little longer.

"What did you think we were going to find," I asked, "when we started looking into your family's history?"

"I'm not sure, maybe some good. Is just one good thing too much to ask?"

"You once told me you had a happy childhood. Wasn't that one good thing?"

"I don't know. Maybe not. It would have been happy as hell, I guess, if it wasn't me that was living it."

I thought on that for a moment. "Perhaps the problem wasn't yours, Caroline. Perhaps there was something else going on, something dark and cold and rooted in your family's past."

"Don't start telling me about my childhood."

"We found a corpse. We found your grandaunt buried in your grandmother's garden. There are secrets at work here that were alive all through your childhood, secrets that affected your entire life, secrets you should know. You are asking the right questions, Caroline."

"But what happens if I don't like the answers?"

"Whether you like them or not they manifest themselves every day, in that crumbling house and your deteriorating family, in your father, who never leaves his bed-room, in your dead sister's sadness, in your situational drinking, in your tattoos and pierced flesh, in your wild fear of cats and your aggressive promiscuity. Maybe it's time to rethink your past, to incorporate all we're learning into how you view it and yourself."

She took a moment to take all that in before saying, "You think I'm a slut?"

"I think you are hurt and scared and don't know what to do with your life."

"I'm not a slut."

"Okay, you're not a slut."

She was quiet for another long moment. "It's just I don't really believe in love anymore."

I didn't say anything because there was nothing to say.

"I think love is a trick and when we fall for it we end up less than we were before, that's what I think. It eats your guts out because you think it's real and you count on it to save your life and then it turns out it's only a trick."

"I don't know, Caroline."

"True love is a myth, and if I sleep around it's only to keep proving it to myself."

"It's late. We've been through a lot today."

"And I do, over and over again."

"Let's get some sleep."

"Hold me."

"I'm too tired."

"Please just hold me. Please."

And that's how it started, simply as my holding her, trying to quiet her so I could get some sleep in my own bed, but that's not how it ended.

I wasn't especially interested in sex with Caroline that night. After my meeting with Oleanna, after feeling what I had felt in Oleanna's presence, the love and the compas-sion and the warm pulse beneath her skin, after all that, sex with Caroline was not what I wanted at all. I wanted to remember what it was like to be near Oleanna, to hold her hand, to rub her bronzed feet. I wanted to think of Oleanna, not of Caroline, so no, I wasn't interested. Really. But she turned to me and kissed my unparted lips and kissed my neck and rubbed her hand across my chest. She was persistent and I am admittedly weak when it comes to the carnal in this life; I have a hard time turning down either prime rib or sex.

So that night we screwed once again. She was, as she always was, once the engine started revving, distant, passive, not really there, but I didn't care, I barely noticed, because it wasn't her I was thinking of as I pressed my tongue to her body and pounded out that rhythm known only by the blood. I was on top of her and I was pinning her hands above her head and I was taking her breasts into my mouth and I was pressing her legs to the bed with my own, but it wasn't she I was thinking about. What I sensed beneath me in the darkness was not Caroline's breast or Caroline's lips or Caroline's scent, but instead a halo of red hair and soft green eyes and classical features and warm pink skin and perfect feet and the exhilarating aroma of musk. I was screwing Caroline all right, but I was making love to Oleanna.

When my heart had stopped its throbbing and my breath had subsided to normal, I rolled off her and onto my back. Caroline laid her head on my chest.

"I like it here with you," she said.

I said what I was supposed to say. "I like it too."

"We'll keep looking, all right?"

"All right."

"Thank you."

"For what?"

"For just being here with me."

I felt just then about an inch and a half.

38

"I'VE BEEN TOUCHED BY IT TOO," said Beth.

"It was fabulous," I said.

"Yeah," she said. "It's pretty interesting."

"I mean really fabulous. I can't stop thinking about it."

"That's fine, Victor. What are you getting?"

"Anything with caffeine." I looked up at the board and was assaulted by choices. "How does a double mocha latte sound?"

"Nauseating. Just get me a decaf, black. I'll grab us seats."

We were at the Starbucks on Sixteenth Street. I was waiting in a slow line for a fast cup of joe. It wasn't too long ago when it was enough to walk right up to any street vendor in the city and pick up a coffee. It came in a blue cardboard cup and cost fifty cents and right there you could add a pack of Tastykake Butterscotch Krimpets to the order and still get change back from a dollar. But that was before Starbucks came to town. Now you waited in line for steamed milk and cutely named brews from exotic lands with more all-natural flavors than nature could have imagined and after the long wait, and the deciphering of the menu, and the condescending smiles from the coffee people who were far cooler than you, what you got back was a fine cup of coffee doctored to taste like something else and maybe change back from a ten. One more reason to hate Seattle.

Beth was waiting for me at a counter which fronted a window onto Sixteenth. She sipped her coffee, a Brazilian decaf mix, while I took a gulp of my latte. Too sweet, too frothy, like a hot chocolate trying to act tough. I should have known better.

"They're very impressed with you there," I said. "Gaylord thinks you're a very evolved soul."

She didn't smile at the compliment, she just looked out the window and drank her coffee.

"She has very beautiful feet," I said. "Have you noticed?"

"Oleanna?"

"And hands too, but it's the feet that most struck me. Pink and very shapely. And it's not just me who thinks it. They bronzed them, have you seen that."

"Yes," she said, still looking outside. "I've been in that room. I think it's creepy."

"Is she, like, married or seeing someone?"

"Don't think too much about Oleanna, Victor."

"I can't stop. The rest of your New Age friends can go jump in a lake for all I care but this Oleanna, wow. What I was feeling was very potent. And this isn't just my normal quantum of lust. It was something else."

"She has a power," said Beth, "an ability to consciously project certain emotions. I don't wholly understand it, but it has something to do with her control over her spiritual sense organs and a way of communicating directly on the spiritual level. I can't quite tell if it's a wonderful and advanced gift or a parlor trick."

"It was pretty fabulous, I must say."

"Yes, I'm sure it was. But she used it to manipulate you for nonspiritual reasons and that seems all wrong."

"Was I manipulated?"

"You walked in with serious questions and you came out, after one session, convinced of her innocence and pledged to help her. Yes, Victor, I'd say you were manipulated. There is something very calculating about Oleanna. She is very determined to get her building built. I'm not sure how much I trust her."

"So you have doubts about their innocence?"

She picked up a plastic stirrer and spun it lazily inside her coffee. "Not really."

"Doubts about the church itself?"

"Yes," she said.

"Really?"

"Some things are troubling. After I heard what happened in your meeting I confronted her. I told her I thought it was wrong of her to use her gifts to twist you around like she did."

"What did she say?"

"She said it was none of my business, that I was still too low on the ladder to understand. I might not yet understand how she did what she did, but I think I understand her motives well enough."

"So you're having doubts. Doubts are good. My entire spiritual system is based on doubt. Let's go to Morton's tonight, we'll each get a steak the size of third base and discuss our doubts between mouthfuls."

"You're a snake," she said, smiling. "I'm just confused. It feels half right and half wrong and I don't quite know what to do about it."

"Kick the bastards out of your life is what I say."

"But it feels half right, Victor. They are helping me tap into something real and powerful. At the same time I think they're dressing it up with all kinds of crap. Those bronzed feet, those robes that they try to make us wear, the cult of personality surrounding Oleanna."

"Speaking of cults of personality," I said, rapping on the window.

Morris Kapustin, who had been walking down the street, stopped and turned and waved when he recognized us. He was wearing a dark suit without a tie, his white shirt open to show his silk undershirt, his broad black hat propped back on his head so that the round brim acted as a sort of halo. Four white tzitzit flowed over his belt. Through his mostly gray beard he smiled and there was about Morris's smile something so genuinely pleased at seeing me that it was almost heartbreaking. I didn't often draw out that reaction, never, in fact, except from Morris. It was how a father might react upon unexpectedly running into his successful son in the middle of the day in the middle of the city, not my father of course, being as he was not prone to smiles and I was not truly successful, but someone else's father, a kind, loving father, a father like Morris.

"Your secretary," said Morris after he made his way inside, "Ellie," as if I didn't know my secretary's name, "she said I would find you here. Such a fancy place for a cup of coffee."

"You want something, Morris?" I asked. "My treat."

"So generous you are, Victor, but no, thank you. I can't drink now coffee with my stomach like it is."

"What's wrong with your stomach?"

"Other than that it is too big? It's begun to hurt at night, *mine boichik*, and the gas. You know what I think it is? The doctor, he tells me to eat fiber, fiber, fiber for my prostrate."

"Prostate," said Beth.

"You too are having such problems?"

"No," said Beth.

"All that fiber," said Morris with a dismissive wave of his hand. "Our stomachs weren't made for fiber. Kugel and kreplach and pastrami, yes. Fiber, no. It's like eating wood and it is probably what's wrong with everyone now. In my day there was no such thing as the prostrate, now it's everywhere. Just last week on the cover of *Time*. That's what you get from eating wood."

"Beth was just telling me, Morris, that she is having doubts about her New Age church."

"Really?" said Morris.

"It seems there is a nugget of truth surrounded by a lot of nonsense," said Beth.

"A nugget of truth is not so bad," said Morris. "How easy do you want it to be? Tell me how you eat a piece of corn. You take off the husk, you clean off the silk, you ignore the cob, and then, if it is cooked just right, a few minutes in boiling water, not too much, not too long, just right, there are a few perfect kernels. In the end, that's a lot of garbage for so few kernels, but they are sweet as sugar, a *mechaieh*."

"How do you know what's real and what's not?" asked Beth.

"If it was so easy, we would all be *tzaddiks*. Miss Beth, please, don't give up. As Rebbe Tarfon, the great colleague of Akiba, said, 'The day is short, the task is great, the workmen are lazy, the reward is great, and the Master is insistent.'"

"Are you calling me lazy?" I said.

"Spiritually, Victor, you are a couch potato, but I come here not to talk of the divine. Quite the opposite. The old books and ledgers your friend, Miss Caroline, she found. I was in your office, Victor, looking through them and I confess they are more *ongepotchket* than I could ever have thought. Normally with numbers I am pretty good, but these books, it is too much for a *Kuni Lemmel* like me. I need, I think, an accountant to review them for us. The accounting firm of Pearlman and Rabbinowitz, maybe you heard them? I want to hire Rabbinowitz."

"Sure," I said, "but tell him to keep his fees down. Without a contract I'm still springing for expenses and it is starting to add up. Any luck with finding what happened to the Poole daughter?"

"Such a thing is not so easy, Victor. Back then there were special places for pregnant women without husbands to go and I have Sheldon looking into that, but the records, they are either old or destroyed so don't you now be expecting much."

"I've learned not to," I said. Morris's face took on a pained expression and he was about to launch into a ringing defense of his work when he saw my smile. He sighed wearily.

"Sheldon also, I have him searching the whole of the country for persons named Wergeld. They have these computer directories on the Internet, places that have every phone number in all of America, which is astonishing, really. Everyone is in there, Victor. Everyone. Pretty soon they won't be needing people like me anymore."

"Isn't technology grand?"

"Insulting me like you are, Victor, you must be in a very good mood."

"He's in love," said Beth, "with a guiding light."

I shrugged and ignored her smirk. "What has Sheldon found?"

"A few Wergelds scattered about." He reached into his jacket pocket and pulled out his small notebook, crowded with disparate scraps of paper, the whole thing bound with a rubber band. He slipped off the rubber band and opened the book carefully, licking his thumb as he paged through until he found what he was looking for. "One Wergeld in Phoenix, one in a place called Pittsfield in Massachusetts, one in Milwaukee. Nothing yet about connecting them to your Reddmans. We're still looking. And I was right about those numbers we found on the card, thank you, they are account numbers, for banks that hold much secret money. My friend he recognized some and verified others. But still, before we can learn any more, we must know the code words and get the proper signatures."

"Which is unlikely."

"I am not a miracle worker all the time, Victor, just some of the times."

"I'm not getting very far myself," I said. "I'm still

looking for that doctor to check the medical invoice we found."

"Who is the Master?" asked Beth. "In that quote from that rabbi you said the Master is insistent. Who is he?"

"For Victor and me, as Jews, such a question is easy. The master is *Ha Shem*, the Glorious One, King of the Universe, praised be He."

"And for me?" asked Beth.

"That, Miss Beth, is for you to discover. But my guess, after all is said and done, after all your searching and questioning, my guess is your answer, it will be exactly the same."

39

THERE WAS NO DR. KARPAS listed in the Philadelphia
white pages, nor in the white pages for Eastern Montgomery
County or the Main Line or Delaware County, all of which
was not much of a surprise. The Dr. Karpas I was looking
for, Dr. Wesley Karpas, performed some sort of procedure
on Faith Reddman Shaw in 1966 and thirty years later I
didn't quite expect he'd still be practicing. Faith Reddman
Shaw, I was sure, was not the type to let any but the most
experienced slip a knife into her. Even in 1966 Dr. Wesley
Karpas most likely had a fine gray head of hair and by now
was probably long retired to some golf community in
Arizona. There wasn't much hope I'd ever discover for what
Grammy Shaw had paid the $638.90. Still, I couldn't help
but wonder why an old lady would have retained an invoice
for a medical procedure performed on her more than a quarter century before her death.

I had spent an hour calling every Karpas I could find in
Philadelphia and the suburbs and getting nowhere. *"Hello,
Mrs. Karpas? Mrs. Adrian Karpas?"* I figured my best
chance at finding Dr. Karpas was to grab hold of a son or a
cousin or some relative who might be able to give me even a
clue as to where he might be. *"Hello, is this Mr. Bruce
Karpas?"* The only problem then would be hoping the doctor remembered the procedure and would somehow be willing to tell me about it, all long shots, for sure. *"Hello, I'm
looking for a Mrs. Colleen Karpas."* You would have

thought Karpas to be a fairly unique name. *"Mrs. Kenneth Karpas?"* You would have thought that all the different Karpases in the phone book would have belonged to one extended family and known each other well. *"Miss Gwenneth Karpas?"* You would have thought. *"Hello, Mr. Angelo Karpas?"*

"Don't get your hopes up, pally," said the voice on the other end of the line, "because I'm not buying nothing."

"That's good, Mr. Karpas, because I'm not selling anything. I just have a few questions."

"You want my answers? Here. The country's going to hell in a hand basket. They're sticking it to us seniors, cutting our benefits, raising our premiums, just because we're too old to kick their butts. You want to know who I'm for? I'm for Perot."

"Perot?"

"That's right. You got a problem with that?"

"Why Perot?"

"Because he's rich."

"Don't you think he's a little crazy?"

"Sure, but who cares, he's rich."

"You don't mind that he bailed last election?"

"He's rich."

"Don't you think his solutions are overly simplistic?"

"Rich."

"Don't you think he's a little too funny-looking with those ears and all?"

"Rich, rich, rich, rich, rich."

"I get the idea, Mr. Karpas, but I didn't call to ask about politics."

"No?"

"No."

Pause.

"Well then what the hell do you want?"

"I'm looking for a Dr. Wesley Karpas. Is he by chance a relative?"

"What do you want with him for?" said Angelo Karpas.

"I just have a few questions."

"Well, if you got questions you're better off asking me."

"Why is that, Mr. Karpas?"

"Because the son-of-a-bitch is dead. Dead, dead, dead. He was my brother. He died five or six years ago."

"Did he have a son or a daughter by any chance? Someone I could talk to?"

"There's a son, big-time lawyer somewheres downtown."

"Karpas?"

"Nah, Wes changed his name a while ago when he started rubbing in better circles. He wanted a name with a little more class. He wanted to swim with society, so he changed it to the name of a fish."

"A fish?"

"Yeah, Carp, with a 'C.' I always got a laugh out of that, trying to move up in class by calling yourself after some bottom-feeding scavenger."

"Seems appropriate, don't you think?"

"You got that, pally."

"Tell me something, Mr. Karpas. Anyone ever actually call you and ask you for your political opinion?"

"Never. But they got to be calling someone, all those polls. Might as well be me."

"Might as well. Thanks for your help."

"Hey, you want to know what I watch on television, too?"

"Sure, Mr. Karpas. What do you watch on television?"

"Nothing. It all sucks."

Angelo Karpas was wrong about one thing, his long-lost nephew wasn't some big-time lawyer downtown. Oh he was downtown all right, with an office smack in Center

City, but he wasn't big time. I could tell by the office, situated atop a clothing store on Chestnut, with diamond sellers and insurance agents and a gypsy fortune-teller for neighbors, by the secretary with the high hair, by the quiet in the grubby waiting room while I sat and paged through a six-month-old *Newsweek*. Let's just say the phone wasn't ringing off the hook in the law offices of Peter Carp.

"He'll be with yous in a minute," said the secretary, flashing the quickest smile I had ever seen, more twitch than anything else, before going back to her nails.

Thanks, doll.

It was the dust, maybe, that got me to ruminating. I remembered when my office was dusty, when the cleaning ladies knew not to care, when the quiet of my phones was loud enough to leave me shaking my head with despair at the future. There was a stretch of time in my life when I wasn't making any money as a lawyer and it had been a bad stretch. Now, with the steady stream of mob clients coming through my door and dropping on my desk their cash retainers, dirty bills bound with rubber bands, my coffers were filled, my offices were dust free, my phones rang with regularity. But what about the future? Raffaello, my patron, had given up and was selling out. I was designated to set up the meeting with Dante that would, in effect, cut me out of the loop. No more of those fat cash retainers. It was what I wanted, actually, out. The game was getting too damn dangerous for a lightweight like myself but, still, I couldn't help wondering what would it be like when the game was over. Would it be back to the old life, back to dusty offices and quiet phones and a meek desperation? Or would the grand possibilities that had opened for me in the case of the Reddman demise save me from my past? A million here, a million there, pretty soon I was dust free for life. Maybe I should stop chasing the ghost of dead doctors and get back to work.

I was thinking just that thought when Carp came out of

his office to greet me. He was short and square, with a puffy face and small eyes behind his Buddy Holly glasses. He wore gray pants and a camel's hair blazer. Here's a tip you can take to the bank: never hire a lawyer in a camel's hair blazer; all it means is he isn't billing enough to afford a new suit.

"Mr. Carl?" he asked uncertainly.

"Yes," I said, popping out of my chair and reaching for his hand. "Thank you for seeing me. Call me Victor."

"Come this way," he said and I did.

"If you'll excuse my office," said Peter Carp after he was situated in the swivel chair behind his fake wood Formica desk. He indicated the mess that had swallowed his blotter, the files strewn on the floor. "It's been a killer month."

"I know what you mean," I said, and I did, more than he could realize. This was not the desk of a lawyer overloaded with briefs and motions and trial preparations. There was something too disorderly about its disorder, too offhand in its messiness. My desk was much like this in my less prosperous times, cleared only when I actually had work that needed the space to spread itself out. One brief could take over the whole of a desktop, but the books and copied cases and documents would be in a rough order. Only when I had nothing pressing would my desktop carry the heaping uneven pile of junk paper currently carried by Peter Carp's. I had put on my sharpest suit for this meeting with what Angelo Karpas had described as a big-time lawyer and now I regretted that decision. Down and out was the way to play it with Peter Carp.

He took his glasses off, wiped them with his tie. Turning his bare and beady eyes to me, he said, "Now, what is it about my father's medical practice that you're so interested in, Vic?"

"In a case I am working on I found a receipt for a medical procedure he performed in 1966. I'd like to know what it was all about."

I reached into my briefcase and pulled out the invoice and handed it to him. He put his glasses back on and examined it.

"Mrs. Christian Shaw. I don't recognize the name."

"She recently died," I said. "I represent her granddaughter."

While continuing his examination of the receipt he said, "Medical malpractice?"

"Hardly. The old lady was almost a hundred when she died and her body just expired. I expect your father performed noble service in allowing her to live as long as she did."

"He was quite a good surgeon," said Carp. "Never once sued in his entire career." He looked nervously at me and then back at the invoice.

"Did your father sell his practice?" I asked.

"Nope. He worked until the very end, which is exactly how he wanted it."

"What became of his records, do you know?"

"Tell me what kind of case you're representing the granddaughter in."

"Nothing too extravagant."

"Lot of money at stake?"

"I wish."

"Trust and estates?"

"Something like that."

"Because that is one of my specialties. Trust and estates."

Wills for widows and orphans at a price, no doubt, with Peter Carp conveniently named as executor. I shook my head. "Nothing too complicated or lucrative, I'm afraid."

"Because if you need any help on the intricacies of Pennsylvania trusts and estates law, I'd be glad to help."

"All I really need to know, Mr. Carp, is if your father's records are still available."

He looked at me and I looked at him and then he turned his attention to the invoice and flicked it once with his finger. "I'm not sure the records that are available go this far back," he said, "and even if they did, to find something this far back would take a lot of man hours."

"I'd be willing to help you look."

"And then there is the question of confidentiality. Without a waiver it is not really proper to hand over the information. And Mrs. Shaw would appear to be in no condition to grant a waiver."

Did I have the same clever gleam in my eye, sitting in my office, plotting how to grab a few bucks here and a few bucks there whenever opportunity reared its shapely neck? If I did, I never before realized how transparent it was, and how ugly. Looking at Peter Carp for me was like looking at an unflattering snapshot and wincing. "I'm sure, Mr. Carp, that if the records are available we could work something out."

"Exactly how much are we talking about?"

"Let's find the records before we discuss details."

"I suppose there would be no harm in looking," he said with a smile. His tongue darted quickly out of his mouth, wetting his thick lower lip. "You wouldn't have any trouble, would you, in making the check out to cash?"

"None at all," I said.

"Well then, Vic," said Peter Carp. "Let's go for a ride."

The Carp estate was in Wynnewood, an old suburb not too far from the western border of the city. Old stone houses, wet basements, tall trees growing too close to the sidewalk, planted fifty years before as seedlings and now listing precariously over the street. Carp took me to a decaying dark Tudor on a nice wooded plot of land going now to seed. "This was my father's house," he said, "but I live here now."

The inside was dark and dusty, half empty of furniture. Paint peeled from the wood trim in strips and the wallpaper was faded and oily. It felt like the place had been abandoned years before. Carp's father had evidently maintained it well but after his death his son had done nothing to the place except sell off the better pieces of furniture. I wondered if this was what Dr. Wesley Karpas had in mind when he changed his name to Carp and sought to rise in society, this decrepit and rundown house, this money-sucking semifailure of a son.

He took me downstairs to a basement area and pushed open a door that was partly cobwebbed over. Inside the doorway was an old doctor's office, white metal cabinets with glass fronts, an examination table, a desk. Still scattered about were strange metal instruments sitting in stainless steel pans. In the corner were piles of medical journals. The place was full of dust and the leavings of animals and with the pointed metal instruments it looked like a discarded torture chamber.

"My father stopped his surgical practice when he turned sixty," said Carp, "but he saw patients as a GP in his home office until the final stroke."

Through the examination room was another room, a waiting room of sorts, with a door to the backyard where the patients would enter. And then, in another room, off from the waiting room, were boxes piled one atop the other and file cabinets lined up like a row of soldiers at attention.

"He kept his files religiously," said Carp, as he climbed over the boxes, heading for the file cabinets. "Every so often he would clear out the files of patients he no longer saw and put them in boxes, but he made sure to keep everything. I would tell him to throw the stuff out but he said you never know, and look how right he was."

Carp opened one of the file cabinets and searched it and shook his head.

"It's not in the cabinets," he said. "Why don't we start

looking through the boxes together? Each box should be labeled with the letters of the files and year they were taken out of the main cabinets."

I removed my suit jacket and laid it carefully over a chair and then started at the boxes, shoving cartons here and there in search of the elusive "S." We found two cartons with "S" files, one cleared from the cabinets in 1986 and one from 1978. Carp, refusing to let me so much as peek inside for what he claimed were reasons of confidentiality, examined each and declared there was no file for Mrs. Christian Shaw in either. After thirty minutes more I found a box labeled "Re–Th, 1973" and Carp told me to stand back as he took a look inside.

"I don't see anything for a Mrs. Christian Shaw here," he said.

"How about Faith Reddman Shaw?"

"Reddman, huh."

"A distant impoverished line from the Pickle baron."

"No Faith Reddman Shaw, but here's something." He took a file out and spread it open atop the box. "When exactly was the date of that invoice?"

"June 9, 1966."

"Yes that's it, and the amount?"

"Six hundred, thirty-eight dollars and ninety cents."

"All right, that's it exactly, but you had it wrong."

"Wrong?"

"The patient. It wasn't this Mrs. Christian Shaw, she was just the party billed for the service. The patient was a Kingsley Shaw."

"What was the procedure?"

"Nothing too serious," he said. "Just two minor incisions, a few snips of the vasa deferentia and then a few sutures to clean up."

"What are you talking about?"

"A vasectomy. My father gave this Kingsley Shaw a vasectomy in June of 1966. Apparently it was a clean operation with no complications. No big deal. Why, is this Kingsley Shaw anybody?"

"No," I said. "Nobody at all."

After I had written out the check to cash for a thousand dollars, I asked Carp if I could use the phone. I picked up the receiver, turned my back to the hungry eyes of Peter Carp, and called my apartment.

"Hi," I said when Caroline answered.

"That cop, McDeiss is looking for you," she said. "He called your office and he just called here."

"You didn't tell him who you were, did you?"

"No, but he says if you get a chance you should show up at Front and Ellsworth, by the hockey rink. Do you know where it is?"

"I can find it. Thanks. Let me ask you something, Caroline. What's your birthday?"

"You getting me a present?"

"Sure. Just tell me."

"June 11," she said.

"What year?"

"Nineteen sixty-eight. Why?"

"Not important. If McDeiss calls back," I said, "tell him I'm on my way."

40
===

WHEN I GOT TO THE Ralph R. Rizzo Sr. Ice Skating Rink
at Front and Ellsworth there was already a crowd behind
the yellow tape. Across the street from the tape was
Interstate 95, which hacks through the eastern edge of
Philadelphia like a blunt cleaver. The ice rink, with its
facade of blue-and-white tile, was squeezed beneath the
elevated highway and beside the tiled building was an out-
door roller rink, this too in the highway's shadow.
Between the two rinks was a wedgelike opening with a
solitary bench and in that opening five or six cops mingled
around a large black thing that sat squat and smoldering.
Parked on Front Street were two fire trucks, lights still
flashing. Firemen, in black slickers, huddled with one
another, smoking cigarettes.

The crowd behind the yellow tape held the usual crew
of wide-eyed onlookers who congregate with a sort of
muted glee at the situs of a tragedy. They shook their heads
and cracked wise out of the sides of their mouths and
shucked their weight from one foot to the other and fought
to keep from laughing because it wasn't them this time.
Along with the onlookers were a few parasitic reporters,
asking questions, and the inevitable television cameras
readying the live feed for their insatiable news machines.

"What happened?" I asked one of the onlookers, an old
man, thin and grizzled with suspenders and a black beret.

"Cain't you smell it?" said the old man.

I took a sniff. The dirty stink of burned gasoline and something sickly sweet beneath it. "I'm not sure."

"They burned a car, is what they did," he said, "and they was some fool still in it when they did it. Now he ain't but bar-be-cue."

"Pleasant," I said over the quiet guffaws that rose around us. I edged past him toward the yellow tape and called a uniformed cop over.

"I'm here to see McDeiss," I said. "He asked me to come on down."

The cop gestured his head to the group of cops under the highway and lifted the tape. Like a boxer sliding into the ring I slipped beneath the yellow ribbon and headed across Front Street.

It was clammy and cool beneath the highway and the stink I had smelled from across the street hung heavy as a fog. The smoldering shape was a car, dark and wet, with its trunk unlatched, and I could make out some red beneath the carbon black. It had been a convertible and the fire had devoured the canvas top so it looked a sporty thing, that flame-savaged car. A Porsche, a red Porsche, and I started getting some idea of who it was who might have been bar-be-cued.

McDeiss was off to the side, in front of the skating rink, interviewing a kid, taking notes as the kid talked. I waited for him to finish. When he sent the kid running off down Front Street, he turned and saw me standing there. "Carl," he said with a smile. "Glad you could make it. Welcome to the party."

"A real hot spot," I said.

"We got the call about an hour and a half ago," said McDeiss, walking back to the burned-out hulk of the Porsche. I trailed hesitantly behind him. "A car was burning underneath the highway. The uniform guys showed up and called the fire guys. The fire guys showed up and sprayed down the flames. When they popped open the trunk to make sure everything was out the fire guys saw what was inside and called us."

"And since you guys are the homicide guys, I guess we know what was in the trunk."

"You want to see?"

"I think not."

"Come on, Carl, take a look. It'll do you good."

He reached back and took hold of my arm and started pulling me toward the burned Porsche, toward the rear, with the trunk lid ominously open, toward whatever lay singed and dead inside.

"I really don't think so," I said.

"I know a great restaurant just a block up on Front," said McDeiss, pulling me ever closer. The open trunk loomed now not ten feet away. "La Vigna. Maybe after our visit you can take me out for lunch."

"I'm quickly losing my appetite."

"You should know what you're dealing with here, Carl, before we talk," said McDeiss.

We were slipping around the side of the car now, McDeiss moving quickly, yanking me along. "I get the idea."

"Take a look," he said, and then he spun me around so that I almost fell into whatever it was that was in that trunk.

"Arrgh," I let out softly, closing my eyes as my stomach heaved.

A few of the cops standing around the car laughed among themselves.

"Take a good look," said McDeiss.

I took a breath and smelled that nauseating smell and my eyes gagged open, ready to spy whatever was there in the trunk.

It was empty. Well not exactly empty. There was the charred remains of the carpet, and strange pools of incinerated liquid, and miscellaneous car-type tools lying around, and the smell, sickening and strangely sweet, like a marinated beef rib left way too long on the grill, but the main event, the body, was gone. In its place was an outline drawn in chalk, an outline of a man on his side, a somewhat corpulent man, with his arms bound behind his body and his knees drawn tight to his chest.

"The ambulance guys already took him to the morgue," said McDeiss.

"You're a bastard," I said, stepping away from the car.

He opened his pad and started reading. "Male, mid-thirties, average height, mildly obese, hair dark brown, eyes indeterminate because they burst in the heat. His hands were tied behind him, his legs were bound together, a gag was stuffed in his mouth. There were no evident wounds, so he apparently burned to death, though the coroner will be more specific. His pants were pulled down and we found the remnants of legal tender deep inside his asshole, specifically a five, a ten, and two ones." McDeiss closed his pad and looked at me. "That's seventeen dollars, Carl, a paltry sum, denoting a notable lack of respect for the victim."

"What am I doing here?"

"You ever see this Porsche before?"

I shook my head.

"It's registered to an Edward Shaw. It was Mr. Shaw who was in the trunk. And the funny thing is, this Edward Shaw is the brother of Jacqueline Shaw, the woman whose death you were asking me about just a few weeks ago. So what I want to know, Carl, is what the hell is going on here?"

I looked at McDeiss and then back at the burned wreck of a German luxury sports car. "It looks," I said slowly, "like someone is killing Reddmans."

"Who exactly?"

"If I knew that I'd already be rich."

"We notified the house but we're still looking for the

other two siblings, Robert and Caroline. Any idea where they are?"

"None."

"So, if you don't know who's going after the Shaws, what do you know?"

Normally, in my position as a criminal defense attorney, I preferred to share absolutely nothing more than I was forced to share with the cops. We're on opposite sides, with the exact opposite goals, and since knowledge is power I tried to keep as much power as I could for myself. But I wasn't facing McDeiss now as a criminal defense attorney. I was looking for a third of any recovery for wrongful death against the person responsible for Jacqueline's murder and now, most likely, for Eddie Shaw's murder too. Nothing would be better than to have the cops find the guy and convict him and leave his assets dangling for me to snatch down with my teeth. There were things he couldn't know, things about my client Peter Cressi and his boss Earl Dante, about my role as innocent bystander in the hit attempt on the Schuylkill Expressway, about Raffaello's plan to turn over the city's underworld to his nemesis. But anything I learned in my investigation of Jacqueline's death, I figured, I could turn over to him, including what I had learned from Eddie's wife. Telling all I knew to McDeiss might just make my job of getting what I could out of the Reddman fortune that much easier.

"You said that place La Vigna is pretty good," I said.

"Sure," said McDeiss, "if you like Northern Italian."

"They have veal?"

"Scallopini pounded thin as my paycheck, drenched with the first pressings of virgin olives and fresh lemon."

I wasn't really hungry for veal. In reality, at that moment, surrounded by that saccharine fog of death, I feared I couldn't keep down even a swallow of Pepto-Bismol. But McDeiss, I figured, was one to sharpen his appetite even as the fresh scent of death lingered in his nostrils. I took him for the type to eat a hoagie in the morgue while an autopsy of an old and bloated corpse was being performed and enjoy every mouthful, so long as the prosciutto was imported and the provolone fresh. It was to my advantage to talk to McDeiss and there was no better enticement for McDeiss to listen, I had learned, than a good meal. Except this time, it had to seem like he was pumping me.

"Well then, why don't we try it out?" I said. "I could go for a little veal. But if you want to hear what I've found out, let's say this time you spring for the check."

McDeiss sent me across Front Street, to the other side of the yellow tape, to wait while he delegated the remainder of the crime scene work to his partner and the uniforms. I was watching him go about his business, listening to reports, talking with other witnesses, examining the car with the forensics guys. In the middle of it all he lifted up a finger to me, telling me he'd be there in a minute, and then went on with his work. For a heavy guy he was pretty limber and I watched with growing admiration as he stretched around and under the car, picking out whatever clues remained. As I watched I felt something grab hold of the crotch of my pants.

"What the . . ." I said as I tried to whirl around and found I couldn't. A block of stone was behind my back and a steel cable was now wrapped around my chest, squeezing whatever air was left out of my lungs.

I tried to swing around again but found myself only being pulled back, away from the crowd.

"Get the hell off of me," I tried to shout, my gasping voice actually loud enough for a few of the people in front of me to turn around to see what was happening. One of them was a short gray-haired man in a black suit and as soon as he turned around I stopped shouting.

"Funny seeing you here, Victor," hissed Earl Dante through his small, even set of teeth.

It was the first time I had seen him since he had started his war. The sight of him there, that close in front of me, with some monster holding me from behind, set my knees to shaking and I sagged down for an instant before I recovered. This was exactly what Raffaello had talked about. The bastard was going through me to set up the meeting.

"Funny seeing you under the highway talking to that homicide dick," continued Dante. "Funny as hell but for some reason I'm not laughing."

Dante nodded at whoever it was who was holding me from behind. The arm around my chest loosened and the hand released its hold on my crotch. My knees sagged again but I stopped myself from falling, stood straight as I could and shucked my shoulders. The mere gesture made me feel a little harder until the reality of the situation impressed itself once again upon my nerves. I looked behind me. It was the weightlifting lug who always seemed to be around when Dante appeared. The lug nodded at me and then looked away, as if there was something more important to look at down the street.

"What were you and the dick talking about like such buddy-buddies under the highway?" said Dante.

"The weather," I said.

"I hear there was a body in the trunk. It's a shame to go like that. A tragedy."

"You talking about the body or the car," I said, "'cause if you ask me, it might be a bigger shame about the car."

The lug behind me chuckled and even Dante smiled. Over Dante's head I could see McDeiss making his way out from under the highway, walking toward us. The sight of him approaching gave me a shot of courage.

"Tell me something, Earl," I said. "Who's paying you to kill Reddmans?"

The smile disappeared and his composed mortician's

face startled for an instant. Then the smile returned, but there was an ugly darkness to it now. "I don't know what you're talking about."

"Sure you do, Earl. Is it a Poole? Did a person named Poole pay for the hits?"

"Ahh, now I get it. You dumb shit, you think I flamed that bastard over there?"

"That's exactly what I think. And I think you killed his sister in the luxury apartment and left her hanging like a coat on a rack, which is why you convinced that freak Peckworth to change his story for the cops."

"You talked to Peckworth?"

"You bet I did."

"You're a dumb shit, you know that, Carl? I would have thought your little misadventure on the expressway would have wised you up enough to keep you out of the business, but no. If you weren't such a dumb shit you wouldn't think what you're thinking."

"You mean the fact that Eddie Shaw owed you a quarter of a million dollars and it looks now like he won't ever pay?" I shook my head and looked up again. McDeiss was now in the middle of the road, about twenty yards away. "I figure you got that covered. His wife told me she had to sign something before he could get his little three-point-a-week loan from you. I figure you have a note in the full amount, for a legal rate of interest, signed by the dead man and his widow. With Eddie being the fuck-up he was, you have a better shot now at getting paid from the wife with her insurance money than you ever did from Eddie."

"You're a smart guy, Victor, oh yes you are," said Dante. "You'd think a guy as smart as you wouldn't be a lowlife shyster trying to hustle an angle into someone else's game. You would think a guy as smart as you would be rich already."

"I'm working on it."

"The cop," said the lug behind me. "He's coming right this way, chief."

"There's going to be a meeting," said Dante, talking low now, suddenly in a hurry, his words hissing out. "You've gotten the word already. Play it straight, Victor, all the way. Pretend for once you're not a dumb shit and play it straight. You try to smart it out and play it on an angle and you'll end up playing it dead."

He put his hand up to my cheek and squeezed it between his fingers, like a dowager aunt showing affection to her nephew, before he spun to his right and walked off, his bodyguard in tow. He left just as McDeiss made his way through the crowd to get to me.

"Who are your friends?" said McDeiss, nodding at the two men walking away from us.

"One's a pawnbroker I know from up on Two Street."

"Anybody I should worry about?"

"Not really," I said. "He's just a guy that the dead man owed a quarter of a million dollars."

McDeiss looked at me and then turned his head to look back at Dante, but the little man and his musclebound shadow had by now turned a corner and disappeared.

"What else do you know about this case?"

"You buying me lunch?"

"I'm buying if you're talking."

"Well then," I said as we turned in the opposite direction and started walking together up the block to La Vigna, "let me ask you. Ever hear of a man named Poole?"

41

I DIDN'T RUSH RIGHT FROM THE LUNCH with McDeiss to tell Caroline about her brother. You can't just tell a girl her brother is dead and then leave to grab a super-sized extra-value meal at McDonald's. You have to hug her tightly when you tell her and let her cry on you and stroke her hair and feed her soup and rub her leg as she keens, bending forward and back, arms crossed at the waist. You tell a girl her brother is dead you better be ready to stick around and comfort her through the long sleepless night as she shivers and sobs in bed. The whole rigmarole could chew up a lot of time and there was still something I had to do that day. So I didn't tell Caroline about her dead brother right off. What I did was ask McDeiss to refrain from announcing the name of the victim to the press and instead drove back out of the city, up from the river, into the deep dark depths of the Main Line. Along the narrow road with the bending archway of trees, down to the bridge that forded the stream, up through the gate and across the wide-open field on the long winding drive that rose to Veritas.

I parked on the part of the drive that circled the front portico. Nat was working on the hedges in front of the house, pruning off defiant shoots of green. He stood on a small stepladder. He was wearing overalls, his wide straw hat, long yellow rubber gloves that gripped a set of giant silver clippers shining in the sun. When I climbed out of the car he watched me for a moment and then stepped down the ladder. The sun was bright and the air was surprisingly clear. I imagined it was always fogged or rainy or wet at Veritas, but this was a brassy spring day.

"Howdy, Mr. Carl," said Nat. He took off his hat and wiped his forehead with his sleeve. Up close I could see the sweat dripping from his temples. The red ring around his eye was bright and proud in the sun. "Miss Caroline's not here. We don't know where she is."

"I'm not here for Caroline," I said. "I'm here to see her mother."

"Also not here, I'm afraid. Still out of the country."

"Then I'll talk to Caroline's father."

He looked at me and then turned his head to stare up at the second floor and its shuttered windows. "Not a good day for a visit, I would guess. You've heard about Master Edward?"

"I heard."

"We reached Master Robert in Mexico with the news, but we can't find Miss Caroline. Any idea where she might be, Mr. Carl?"

"I'll tell her what happened," I said, "just as soon as I talk to her father."

He lifted the long shiny shears and laid their pointed tips on his shoulder. "Like I said, not a good day for a visit."

"We all have work to do," I said, "just like you and your pruning."

He nodded at the hedges. "Mrs. Shaw wants the grounds in shape for the guests. She's arriving from Greece tonight, cutting short her vacation. It seems the brightest social occasions we have around here now are funerals."

"That's about to end."

He raised his eyebrows when I said that and smiled. There was something charismatic in Nat's smile. He didn't smile often or easily, but when he did it was bright and inviting. It bespoke something shared instead of something hostile.

"Sit down a spell with me," he said. He walked over to one of the stone benches that flanked the steps leading to the front door. I sat beside him. His head was turned to the left while he talked, as if examining the uneven hedges still to be pruned on that side of the house. I looked down the long wide expanse of green, large enough to plop in an entire housing development, and wondered, silently, at the price of real estate in that part of the Main Line.

"Mrs. Shaw, the younger Mrs. Shaw," said Nat, "she named her children after the Kennedys. Edward and Robert and Jacqueline and Caroline. She wanted the glamour, I suppose."

"I didn't know that."

"This was before all the scandals erupted, all the truths emerged about their crimes and infidelities. But still, you would have thought she'd pick a less tragic family to emulate."

"Like the Pooles?"

He reached down with his clippers and snipped at an errant leaf of grass. "Hardly less tragic."

"What's your last name, Nat?" I asked.

"You know, Mr. Carl, the strangest thing happened. I was in the elder Mrs. Shaw's garden and I couldn't help but notice that the oval plot before the statue was dug up and put back down again.

"Is that a fact?"

"I wouldn't have minded so much, but the plants were replanted poorly. You have to almost drown them in water when you put them back. If you don't the roots won't properly take. It's a damn shame to kill a good plant."

"Among other things."

"Find anything interesting down there, Mr. Carl?"

"Just some ancient history," I said.

"Yes, I suppose that's right. For your generation

ancient is anything before Reagan. And what is history, really, but the register of crimes, follies, and misfortunes of mankind?"

"Shakespeare?"

"Gibbon. Have you read *The Decline and Fall of the Roman Empire*?"

"No, actually."

"You should. Very encouraging."

"Why, Nat, I didn't know you were a closet Communist."

"What do gardeners know of politics? How'd Miss Caroline take to learning all that ancient history?"

"Not so well."

"Yep. That's what I figured. Remember what I said about some things ought to being left buried?"

"But isn't it better to know the truth, no matter how vile?"

He lifted up his head and cackled. "Whoever told you such nonsense? One kind lie is worth a thousand truths."

"How much do you know about everything that has gone on with this family?"

"I'm just the gardener."

"Who killed her, Nat? Who killed Charity?"

"Oh, Mr. Carl, you said it yourself. Ancient history. I didn't show up here until years and years after Miss Charity Reddman disappeared. How could I know a thing like that?"

"But you do, don't you?"

"I'm just the gardener," he said, standing up, putting on his hat. "I've got work still to do."

"Ever hear of a family called Wergeld?"

"Never."

"Any idea why the elder Mrs. Shaw would leave a fortune in a trust entitled Wergeld?"

"We all have our secrets, I suppose."

"You haven't told me yet your family name."

"Not too much call around here to know the last name of servants."

"I'm just a servant too, I guess. No different than you."

"Oh there's a difference," said Nat. "I may just be a servant, yes, but I care about this family and its fate more deeply than you can guess, Mr. Carl. What about you? Who are you here for? You here for Caroline or are you just here for yourself?"

"Mr. Shaw's in, I suppose."

"Always," said Nat, taking his clippers back to the ladder by the hedges and climbing the steps wearily, one after the other.

I watched him for a bit and then pushed myself off the bench and started for the steps leading to the door of the Reddman mansion.

"You don't need to drag it all up to Mr. Shaw today," said Nat as he started in again with his clipping, the blades sliding one across the other with a small shivery screech. "It's a hard enough day for him as it is."

I stopped and turned around to look at him. He was still working, still clipping the offending branches one by one.

"What's your last name, Nat?"

Without looking away from the dark green hedges that surrounded the house, without slowing the pace of his shivery clips, he said, "It's not Poole, Mr. Carl, if that's what you're wondering."

I took that in and nodded to myself. Nat kept working on the hedges, as steadily and as focused as if I weren't there watching. I spun around and headed for the house.

My shoes scraped at the granite steps as I climbed toward the heavy wooden door and pulled the knob announcing my presence. I waited a bit before the door squealed open and Consuelo, dressed all in black, faced me.

"I'm here to see Mr. Shaw," I said.

She squinted her eyes at me and gave me an up-and-down examination. "No. Mr. Shaw is not seeing anyone today."

"It's very important I talk to him," I said, sweeping past her and into the decrepit front hallway of Veritas. Even though the sun was bright outside it was still dark and damp in here, the heavy riblike beams overhead catching so little of the reflected light they seemed lost in darkness. The floor of the front hallway creaked as I passed over it and made my way around the strange circular couch and toward the formal hanging stairwell.

I could hear the slap of rubber soles as Consuelo ran to catch up. She rushed in front of me just as I started up the stairway. "Stop, please, Mr. Carl. Mr. Shaw has requested to be alone all day."

"I need to see him," I said. "Today."

"If you wait down here I will see if he will make an appointment for after the funeral."

"I can't wait that long," I said, "and I'm afraid if I don't find out what's happening as soon as possible there will be another funeral and then another."

As lightly as I could I brushed her aside and started up the steps. As she almost caught up to me I climbed faster, keeping her a few steps below. I spun around the landing and continued on until I reached the second floor. Which way was Kingsley Shaw's room? I waited for Consuelo to tell me, and she did, coming up around my side and grabbing hold of my arm, standing between me and the wing on the right.

I started toward that wing with Consuelo hanging on to me. She should have been yelling at me now, calling me unpronounceable names in her native Spanish, calling for help, but her voice was strangely quiet as she begged me, with an almost fearful tone, to please please stop and not disturb Mr. Shaw.

"I'm going to speak to him today, Consuelo," I said. "If you want you can go and call the police and they, I'm sure, would be up here in no time at all to kick me out, their sirens blasting, their lights flashing, just, I'm sure, what Mr. Shaw would like to see today. Or, on the other hand, I'm willing to wait here while you go tell him that I'm here to speak to him about the deaths of his son and his daughter and about Caroline."

She stared at me, her dark features darkening even further, and then she told me to wait right there. She turned and went to the door at the very end of the hallway, glanced at me again, knocked, waited for a moment, slowly opened the door, and disappeared inside.

The next time the door opened it opened for me. Consuelo, without lifting her gaze from the floor, said, "Mr. Shaw will see you now." I offered her a smile as I passed her, a smile she didn't accept as she maintained her stare at the floor, and then I stepped through the doorway into the room of Kingsley Shaw, the door closing quietly but firmly behind me.

42

I FOUND MYSELF ALONE in a massive, high-ceilinged room that spanned the entire width of the house. Luxuriously carpeted, luxuriously outfitted, smelling richly of smoke and seeming to have been set down in this spot from another time, the room shouted the strength of a single overwhelming personality. I spun around to see all of its strange dark grandeur.

Two chandeliers of wrought iron, hanging from an ornately patterned ceiling, sprinkled a dim light on the furnishings, complemented by the uneven glow of savage iron fixtures intermittently cleaving to the walls. There were windows on three sides of the room but they were either shuttered or draped with thick maroon velvet so the daylight that did seep through, thick with spinning motes of dust, appeared uninvited and invasive, like slashing claws. A huge telescope stood forlornly by one of the draped windows and across the room, by another draped and darkened window, was a second, and beside each telescope were astronomical charts held open on wooden racks and star globes suspended in intricate wooden stands with clawed feet. The wall behind me held the head of an antlered deer, of a buffalo, of a large, pale brown cat, and weapons were studded between the taxidermy, swords, battle-axes, a thick and ornate shotgun. Massive bookshelves were filled with leather-bound volumes, one series after another in gold and green and blue and maroon, huge epic tomes, intimidating in their size and mass. One half of the room was furnished with red leather club chairs and a long leather couch, a gentleman's club for old shipping magnates to hide from their wives and smoke cigars and peruse the papers for that day's ship arrivals. A huge bed with a wrought-iron canopy stood alone in the other half, seemingly marooned on an oriental carpet of blue. Before the wall directly in front of me was a great stone fireplace, its fire crackling but low, the flame's heat not reaching across the cold to me, and above the fireplace, dominating the whole of the room, lit by its own overhead brass lamp, was a grand portrait, ten feet high, six feet wide, a portrait of a lady.

The woman in the portrait seemed strangely familiar and I stepped toward her, almost against my will. She stood in a black dress, her hands held delicately before her, a bonnet tied tightly to her head, her chin up, her head cocked slightly to the side, her face pretty and composed and absolutely self-contained. Her eyes, of course, followed my movements as I walked toward her but she stared down at me without even the pretense of concern for my presence in that room with her, as if I were no more significant than an insect crawling about the ground beneath her feet. The closer I stepped, the larger and more ominous she became and then I stopped and felt a slight shiver. I recognized her all right, I had seen her picture in the box we had dug up from Charity Reddman's grave, a picture where she was younger, gayer, oblivious still to all her future devastation. Faith Reddman Shaw. I took one more step forward and for a moment it was as if the self-containment in her face cracked and something ugly and serpentine revealed itself. But that was just the reflection of the overhead light on the painting's varnish and when I stepped back again her face regained its composure.

I heard a rasp of breath from behind me and turned quickly. In the midst of all that baroque grandeur it took me a moment to spot the source. I had been so overwhelmed by the decor I hadn't noticed anyone in the room with me but now, focused by the sound, I saw him there in the corner. Hunched, gray, his skin pasty and smoothly pale, seated in a wooden wheelchair, a tartan rug across his legs, he all but disappeared under the power of the interior design. His face was turned away from me.

"Mr. Shaw?" I said, starting to walk toward him.

He cringed, lowering his large chin into his shoulder, preparing himself as if I were wielding a weapon in my advance. I stopped.

"Mr. Shaw?" I repeated, more loudly.

Still cringing, he nodded.

I stepped forward again. "Mr. Shaw." I raised my voice to near shouting and there was a slight echo in the enormity of the room. "I'm very sorry about your son Edward. I wouldn't disturb you on a day like this, but I believe it vital that we talk right away. My name is Victor Carl. I'm a friend of Caroline's. She asked me to look into the death of Jacqueline and now, I believe, somehow, that her death and your son's death are related. I have just a few questions to ask you. Mr. Shaw?"

He just stared at the floor, his chin remaining in his shoulder.

"Mr. Shaw? Do you understand what I just said, Mr. Shaw?"

Still cringing, he nodded.

"Can we talk?"

He stared at the floor for a moment longer before placing his hands on the wheels of his chair and, his head still tilted, rolling himself slowly across the room until his chair was fronting the fire. He leaned forward, as if to warm his face by it.

One of the leather club chairs was facing the hearth and I sat in it so that I could see his profile. He had been a handsome man once, and large too, I could see, enormous really, with broad shoulders and a huge head, but it was as if he had been crushed into the space he now occupied. There was something weak and slack about his face, a statue weathered to a bland smoothness by time, and his eyes were dull and weary beneath his overgrown eyebrows. I leaned forward and crossed my hands like a schoolmarm and explained to him what I had discovered, how Jacqueline had not killed herself but had been murdered by a professional assassin who had been well paid for his services, how Edward might have been killed by the same man, how it looked as if someone was trying to destroy the heirs to the Reddman fortune toward some, as yet unknown, purpose. As I spoke I noticed that he didn't seem surprised by what I was saying. It was hard to tell if he was getting it all but I spoke slowly and loudly and he nodded as if in comprehension throughout my little talk.

"I don't know if whoever is hiring the killers is going for money or just plain blood revenge," I said, "but I think you might have some of the answers."

When I was finished I waited for a response. He stared into the fire, remaining silent.

"Mr. Shaw?" I said.

"Sometimes it speaks to me," he said. His voice was a listless monotone, as gray and pale as his coloring.

"Who?" I asked.

He pointed at the fire. "It speaks single words directly to my thoughts. Sometimes I listen to it for hours."

All right, I thought, I'll hitch a ride on his downtown train. "What does it say?"

For the first time he turned his head and looked at me. His eyes were watery and weary. It was tiring just to look at him. "It says 'cut' or 'hammer' or 'blood' or 'freedom' or 'fly' or 'escape,' just single words over and over."

"What's it saying now?" I asked, realizing he had been nodding not at my explanation but at the voice of the fire.

"It's saying, 'Alive,'" he said. "'Alive. Alive. Alive.'"

"Who's alive, Mr. Shaw?"

"She is. Alive. Again."

"Who, Mr. Shaw?"

"My mother. Alive."

I suddenly leaned back in my chair. I couldn't help but look up at the portrait staring down at me. From this angle it almost seemed as if she were smiling.

"I thought she died just over a year ago," I said.

"No, no, she's alive," he said, his voice growing suddenly more agitated. He reached out from his chair and grabbed my sleeve. "She's alive, I know it. I've seen her."

"You've seen her? When?"

He tugged at my sleeve harder. "A week ago. Outside. Come, I'll show you."

He let go of me and spun his wheelchair away from the fire, rolling it toward one of the windows with a telescope beside it. I followed behind him. When he reached the curtain he opened it with a strong pull. An invasion of light streamed in, so bright and unhindered I had to turn my face away until my eyes adjusted. When I turned back I could see through the window's bars to the rear yard of the house, straight down the hill to the pond.

"Less than a week ago I saw her in her garden," he said.

From the window there was a clear view to the overgrown hedges and wild flowers of Faith Reddman's garden. From here the mazelike pattern was much clearer and in the center clearing I could see the shape of the bench that had been devoured by the orange flowering vines.

"I saw the light," he said. "She was there. She was digging in her garden in the middle of the night. I saw the light, I heard the clang of her shovel. I swear it."

"I believe you saw the light, Mr. Shaw."

"She's come back."

"Why has she come back, Mr. Shaw?"

"She's come back to take me away, to save me. That's why she's waiting in the house, waiting for me."

"What house is she waiting in, Mr. Shaw?"

"The old house, the old Poole house. I've seen her there, at night. I've seen the lights through the trees."

"In the house by the pond?"

"Yes, she's there, waiting." He suddenly looked away from the window and stared at me with his watery eyes. "Will you take me there? Will you? I can't go myself because of my legs. But I'm light now. You can carry me."

He reached out and gripped again at my sleeve. It was frightening to see the yearning work its way beneath his slack face. This is a man worth half a billion dollars, I thought. What happiness has it bought him? I turned my face away and looked at the garden once more and then altered my focus.

"Why are there bars on your windows, Mr. Shaw?"

He dropped his head and let go of my arm. Slowly he spun his wheelchair around and rolled back to the fire. He leaned toward the glowing heat, listening. I stared at him, his color washed completely away by the sunlight now flooding through the window.

I looked around once more. This room reeked of a single personality, yes, but if the personality that had created and maintained it once belonged to this man it had clearly fled. Nothing was left but a shell. I had intended to ask him about Caroline's paternity, about the Wergeld Trust, about the Pooles, but I would get no answers from what remained of this man. I walked over to the bookshelves and their heavy tomes. Leather-bound volumes of the great works of literature, Dickens and Hugo and Balzac and Cervantes, each spine perfectly smooth. I took out volume one of *Don Quixote*. It was a beautifully made book, the boards thick, the leather hand-tooled and leafed in gold. The binding cracked when I opened it. I remembered that Selma Shaw had told me she had been brought to Veritas because her future husband had difficulty reading. I remembered the disappointment in Faith Shaw's diary over young Kingsley's failures in his studies.

"Do you read much?" I asked.

He responded as if I were merely an inconvenient distraction pulling him away from the voice of the fire. "No."

"Don't you like books?"

"The letters mix themselves up on the page."

Dyslexia? Is that why he had so much trouble learning to read as a boy? Then why are there so many books in his room? I wondered. Why would a problem reader surround himself with such potent reminders of his failings? Was it pretension? Was it merely a facade, like Gatsby's library with its uncut pages, or was it something else? I closed the book and put it away and then looked around the room with newly opened eyes and a growing sense of horror.

"Do you hunt, Mr. Shaw?" I asked while I looked at the wall full of dead animal heads.

"Once I did," he said.

"Are these your trophies?"

"No. They were my father's."

"Even the cat?"

"It's a cougar," he said in his distracted monotone.

"Is that your father's too?"

"No," he said. "Everything but the cougar."

I stepped slowly toward the cougar head, its eyes dazed, its yellow teeth bared. There was a brass plate beneath the ruffed fur of its neck. It said something I couldn't read for the tarnish, but I could make out the date: 1923. I felt colder than before. This wasn't just any cougar, I was certain, this was the cougar that had slipped down from the mountains to terrorize the farms around Veritas in 1923. The same cougar Kingsley Shaw was aiming for in that dark rain-swept night when, with his mother by his side, he fired into his father's chest. How could he live with that cat staring at him every day of his life, taunting him with that grin? And the ornate shotgun beside it, that gun, I realized, must be the gun.

I took a photograph out of my suit pocket and walked it to the fireplace to show to the man in the wheelchair. It was a photograph, removed from the metal box, of the unattractive young woman with the long face, the beady eyes, the unruly hair. "Do you know her?" I asked.

He took the photograph into his shaking hands and examined it closely. I wondered if he recognized her at all and then realized, when I saw a tear, that he did.

"Who is she?" I asked.

"Why are you here?" he said, still staring at the photograph.

"I am trying to find out who is killing your children."

"This is Miss Poole," he said. "She was my friend from long ago. She read to me."

"Do you know where she is or where her child is?"

"Why? Do you know her?" He smiled up at me with a hope that was at odds with everything he had shown me before. "Is she alive too?"

"I don't know. Her father believed that your grandfather stole his company from him. Do you believe she could be responsible for hiring the man who killed your children?"

"She was my friend," he said. "She was lovely. She could never have hurt a soul."

"Then who do you think is killing your children?" I asked.

"I told you," he said, staring up at me. "She's alive. Didn't I tell you? She's alive." He turned his face back to the photograph. "Can I keep this?"

"Sure," I said. "I'm sorry to have disturbed you, Mr. Shaw, and I'm very sorry for your loss."

With a wan smile he waved the photograph. "She used to read to me about a pond. Such a beautiful pond it was. I forget the name of it now."

"Walden Pond," I said.

"No, that's not it, but it was so beautiful."

On my way out I stopped for a moment and stared at the cougar head mounted above the door. I turned around.

"Mr. Shaw, why are there bars on your windows?"

From across the room, still staring at the photograph, he said, "Because of the first time I heard the fire speak."

"When was that?"

"Years and years ago. When I could still walk."

"What was the word it repeated the first time?"

"'Jump,'" he said. "'Jump. Jump. Jump.'"

I think all of us in this world carry our own individual hells, like a turtle shell on our backs, hauling it about from place to place, the burden so constant we often forget how its weight is twisting our bodies and spirits into grotesquery. This hell is the cost, I believe, of being human and humane, and better that, I figure, than the oblivious, spaced-out bliss promised by places like the Church of the New Life. But never have I seen an individual's personal hell so objectively and oppressively rendered in his surroundings as I saw in the room of Kingsley Reddman Shaw. Wherever he was jumping to when he ruined his legs, he was jumping to a better place than this.

I blinked into the sunlight outside Veritas. Nat had progressed in his work to the hedges on the other side of the doorway. He saw me standing on the steps and without climbing from his ladder he shouted out, "Had a pleasant meeting, Mr. Carl?"

"How long has he been like that, Nat?"

"For as long as I've been here. But it's gotten worse over the years."

"How old was he when he jumped from the window?"

"Twenty-five or thereabouts, but by then he had not been out of the room for six or seven years."

"I've never seen such a horrible place in my life."

"N'aren't too many like it. That was his grandfather's

room until the elder Mrs. Shaw moved her son into it. Much of the furnishings were left over from Mr. Reddman's time."

"Even the cougar."

"Mr. Reddman bought it from the farmer who killed it. We've tried to remove it but Mr. Shaw won't allow us."

"And the painting of Faith Reddman Shaw?"

"Mr. Reddman commissioned it, a portrait of his only surviving daughter."

"What was he like, this Claudius Reddman?"

"A hard man, Mr. Carl. Even in his last years, when he dedicated himself fully to philanthropy, he was hard. Do you know what his last words were?"

"No."

"At the end it was his lungs that rotted out. Tumors the size of frogs, I was told. The doctors kept him delirious on morphine to hide the pain. That last night, the elder Mrs. Shaw, she made sure I was there, to run for whatever the nurses needed. He was crying and shouting out and had to be restrained with leather straps. And the final thing he said before he shivered into death was, 'It was only business.'"

Nat laughed at that, and turned back to his hedges, opening the shears and clipping off two shoots of green at once.

It was only business. I wondered if that would satisfy the Pooles for whatever injustices by Claudius Reddman they believed shattered their world. Well, whatever price was paid by the Pooles, it was being paid by the Reddmans too. After what had happened to Kingsley, it seemed like overkill to go after the heirs.

I had an uneasy feeling driving down out of the Main Line, back to the city along the expressway. Kingsley Shaw had said his mother was still alive and it was she who was killing his children, but as he said it he seemed to show no overt sadness over the death of his son, or of his daughter six months before, and he seemed to have no worries for Caroline or Bobby. He said his mother was alive and killing his children and still he was begging me to take him to her. Was her spirit still alive? Could she somehow be responsible? I remembered the way I bounced off the walls when I had first seen Hitchcock's *Psycho* and I wondered if somehow Kingsley was bringing this tragedy down around himself, all in the name of his mother. I could see him in that room, in his wheelchair, wearing a black dress and black bonnet, a knife in his hand, screeching music in the background. I resolved on the Schuylkill Expressway, passing the very spot where Raffaello's Cadillac had been ambushed with me inside, I resolved then and there to never ever take a shower at Veritas.

It was late afternoon already when I parked my car on Spruce Street and walked up the stairs to my apartment and found Caroline Shaw waiting for me. I went to her and put my arms around her and told her that her brother Edward had been murdered.

Part 4

DEAD MEN
RAINING

*Money, not morality, is the principle of
commercial nations.*

—THOMAS JEFFERSON

43

San Ignacio, Belize

SAN IGNACIO IS A BEAT OLD frontier town, the capital of Belize's wild west and the gateway to Guatemala. Its narrow streets, crowded with colorfully stuccoed buildings and lined with open sewers, wind haphazardly up the sharp hillside on which it has grown. It is a city built for logging and the gathering of the sap of the sapodilla tree, which is processed into chewing gum, and though chewing gum is now largely synthetic and logging no longer takes place, the city still has the feel of a logging town, unpredictable and good-natured.

I am staying at the San Ignacio Hotel, just down the hill from a set of Mayan ruins with the comforting name of Cahel Pech, which means the place of ticks. My hotel is an old colonial outpost with a fine swimming pool. From the balcony of my room I can see the thick jungle that chokes the hills surrounding the city. I sit on the balcony and stare at the wild green of the jungle and wonder what the man I am seeking is doing right now, wonder how much he is enjoying his wealth in this tropical swelter. He has a fortune at his disposal, the whole of the Wergeld Trust, as he so brazenly let me know by the name on his account at the Belize Bank, but instead of hiding out in Paris or Rome or on a boat docked alongside a hidden cay in the Caribbean, he has come to the jungle. It was wise of him, I guess, in planning for his infinite future, to try to grow accustomed to the heat.

I am close to him now, closer than I truly believed I would find myself when I left the United States for this country. I felt his proximity on the top of El Castillo in the ancient Mayan ruins of Xunantunich and went out to confirm it on the streets of San Ignacio. The Belize Bank branch on Burns Avenue was a whitewashed building, trimmed in turquoise, just across from the New Lucky Chinese restaurant. While Canek Panti waited outside, I spoke to the assistant branch manager on the second floor. I like assistant branch managers, they are usually so willing to please without wanting to disturb their bosses, but this one was no help. "I am unable by law to tell you anything about that account, sir," he said, and no importuning, no playacting, no flashed American dollars would change his mind. I was puzzled that no one in the bank recognized the picture, but then, I figured, he had had a servant do his banking. He must trust his servant an awful lot if he trusted his servant to do his banking.

We checked out a joint called Eva's on the main strip of the city, a blue-painted shack, where, Canek told me, foreign travelers and expatriots congregate. I sat at a table under a slowly spinning fan and ordered a black bean soup called *chilmoles* and a beer. The Belikin was good and cold and the soup was good and hot, loaded with stewed chicken, a white hard-boiled egg bobbing on the surface, and the owner of the place, an expat Englishman named Bob, was talkative. He tried to book me on a river trip or in a tourist lodge in the jungle, but all I wanted to know was if he had seen the man in the photograph. "Never," he said, "and most of the visitors who come through town end up stopping here."

"Any word," I asked, "of a foreigner who has set up a ranch in the jungles nearby?"

"Not someone who hasn't come through here. Most of the ranch owners take lodgers and use us to help book their places. But it's a big jungle, mate. If you wanted to get lost you'd have no problem getting lost here."

After Eva's, Canek left to make arrangements to stay with people he had in the area. I had hired him as my guide, at ninety-five dollars a day for as long as I was in the west, and he seemed pleased by the arrangement, as was I. A friend in foreign places is rare, and one you can trust, as I trust Canek Panti, is even rarer. And who better to guide me through these jungles than a Mayan? Alone now, I took a walk around town. There were few beggars in San Ignacio, no one on the street trying to peddle me dope, and I enjoyed the walk despite the heat. I showed my photograph to store-keepers, to passersby, to the old folk sitting in the town circle at the mouth of the bridge, but no one recognized the man I am hunting. I asked the mobs of taxi drivers I saw on every corner with no better luck. I even thought to check out the waiters at my hotel. There is a restaurant overlooking the pool and it is a rather nice place that is rumored to serve the best steaks in Belize and if someone wanted to slip out of the jungle for a cocktail and a hearty meal this is where he would slip, but they all examined the picture, one after another, and shook their heads.

While on my walk, a car with speakers on top trailed a huge colorful placard through the city's streets. The placard was advertising the Circus Suarez, in town for one night only, with its prime attraction: *"7 Osos Blancos Gigantes."* The lady at the hotel told me that people were coming from all over the Cayo to see the circus and that children were being asked to bring in stray dogs to feed the seven polar bears. The circus tent was raised just up the hill from my hotel and I walked the grounds before the circus was to start, searching the waiting mob for the face of a killer. I searched until the crowd surged madly through the tiny entrance of the tent. I didn't go in myself. I felt enough out of place in Belize as it was; I didn't need to see seven polar bears doing tricks in the heat of Central America.

As I walked back down the hill to my hotel, walking along a shallow open sewer, I saw something sitting in the thin stream of excrement. I stepped closer. It was a frog, a huge frog, muscular and still, as big as a head, sitting silent, breathing darkly, staring back at me with deep menace. I spun around quickly, filled with an urgent panic, certain I was being followed. There was no one there.

The next day was market day in San Ignacio. Canek had volunteered to go off to the outlying farms to show around the photograph, so I strolled the market alone. It was set up in the middle of a dirt plaza not far from the river. Ragged trucks from the outlying farms were displaying their fare, forming an alley in the shape of an L, and buses had come bringing shoppers from all over the Cayo. Men in hats, cowboy hats or dirty baseball hats, were sitting on the covered beds of their trucks or sitting on plastic pails or standing before sacks of rice, sacks of beans, piles of cucumbers, boxes of tubers, cartons of eggs, melons and onions, peppers and carrots, black beans, pumpkin seeds, shoes, cabbages, more shoes. Women sat on the ground in front of herbs spread out on empty canvas bags. The men and women were talking Spanish or the strange language I had heard Canek speak with the ferryman, Mayan. Across a stone wall were stretched yards and yards of used clothing. I stared at everything as if my eyes were hungry, the fruits, the people, the blazing colors, showing the photograph, getting smiles but no positive response. Until a handsome young man with a round face and a mustache nodded his head in recognition.

He wore a wrinkled white long-sleeved shirt and grayed jeans and sandals and tightly slung around his shoulder was the strap of a bag, with only a piece of sheepskin to keep it from digging into his shoulder.

"You recognize him?" I asked.

He answered in Mayan and nodded his head.

"Where did you see him?"

He answered in Mayan and nodded his head.

"Do you speak any English at all?"

He answered in Mayan and nodded his head.

"Can I buy you a Belikin?" I said, stressing the name of the beer and lifting my hand as if I was chugging.

He answered in Mayan and nodded his head and smiled warmly. He walked with me to Eva's, where the owner served us up two beers and brought his cook from the back to act as my translator. His name was Rudi, the man from the market said, and his story was intriguing as all hell.

He had been working on his family's farm when a man, not a foreigner, came up to the house in a truck and said he needed to buy a great deal of supplies. Rudi sold the man what he could from his farm and went with him in the truck to the other farms in the area to purchase the rest. For what he couldn't buy at the farms he went to the same market where I had found Rudi and bought sacks of rice, sacks of beans, crates of chickens, piles of assorted vegetables and roots. When the whole load was put into the truck the man offered Rudi one hundred Belizean dollars, about fifty dollars American, to help him deliver the produce. Together, Rudi and the man drove the truck to a spot on the Macal River, just past one of the jungle lodges, where an old wooden canoe with a motor was beached and tied to a stake. Rudi and the man loaded up what they could on the canoe and began to motor south, up the river. It was a long trip upriver and often Rudi and the man had to get into the water and walk the canoe through mild rapids. Finally, the man guided the boat to the riverbank beside a pile of big rocks and beneath a giant *kepak* tree, bigger and older than any Rudi had seen by the river before. The man told Rudi to unload the produce onto the bank while he carried it, load by load, up to the site. Rudi was ordered not to leave the river under any circumstances and when the man gave the order he fingered the intricately carved handle of his machete. The man then hefted a sack of rice and disappeared up a path into the thick jungle. He was gone for twenty minutes before he returned for another load. It took an hour to unload the first boat and three boatloads to take the entire contents of the truck up the river. On the last of the three trips upriver, when the boat was approaching the pile of rocks and the giant *kepak*, Rudi saw a man staring out at them from the jungle, a foreigner. He was there for just a moment before he disappeared but Rudi had seen him clearly. And the face he had seen peering out of the jungle, he was sure, was the face in the photograph.

Canek and I spent the next day making arrangements, finding a canoe, getting together any supplies we might need. Tomorrow we are going onto the river, searching for the pile of rocks and the great ancient *kepak* tree that will lead me to my quarry. Canek tells me that *kepak* is the Mayan word for the cottonwood tree and that the Mayans believe that when the last of the cottonwoods die, all life in the rain forest will be destroyed. The tree seems a fittingly dire symbol for the man I am hunting. He bought the destruction of Jacqueline Shaw and Edward Shaw for his own vile purposes and now it is time for me to start making him pay. He's there, I know it, on the river, and I know he knows I know it. Of the people to whom I showed the picture, someone knows someone who knew to get in touch with him, I am sure. He could have killed me had he wanted to long before I arrived in San Ignacio, but he wants me to come. Maybe his new jungle life is lonely and he wants the company. Or maybe he needs someone to whom to crow. He is expecting me and I won't disappoint him. I am very close now to collecting my fortune, I am sure. And if he has other ideas, if he intends for me to be another victim, I figure I'll be perfectly safe as long as I'm with my friend, my guide, and my protector, the honorable Canek Panti.

My arms and face are covered with mosquito bites. On the balcony of my hotel room I examine those I can closely in the sun, wondering which of the swollen swaths of flesh contain the squirming larvae of the botfly the nun had so kindly warned me about on the flight into Belize. I wonder if the man I am chasing knows how to suffocate the beef-worm with glue and Scotch tape or instead lets it grow within him, like he let the evil inside him grow and fester. I know now the root of that evil, I have seen the ledgers in which it was documented in even rows of precise numbers. Some crimes are forgotten the moment they are perpetrated and it is as if they had never occurred; some crimes live on forever. The tragedy of the Reddmans was that the crime in those ledgers was of the latter. It is still alive, still virulent, still cursing the perpetrator's heirs a century after its commission.

44

THE OLD LEDGERS WERE SPREAD out on our conference room table, cracked open and releasing a finely aged mold into the air. The numbers inside were inked by hand and showed the day-to-day operations of the E. J. Poole Preserve Co. for the years up to and beyond its purchase by Claudius Reddman and the change of its name to Reddman Foods. These were the books Caroline had found behind the secret swinging panel in the library at Veritas and the accountant was now hard at work, I expected, letting the numbers in the ledgers tell him the story of how Claudius Reddman had managed to wrest control of the company from Elisha Poole. It was the very day of Edward Shaw's funeral, a day of ostentatious mourning and the false tears of heirs. Oh, what a cheery scene that would be. With Edward dead, there was nothing for Dante to gain by killing Caroline anymore, so she had left her seclusion to attend the funeral, though I still had concerns for her safety. She asked me to join her, but I declined. I had stirred the Reddman family pot enough, I figured. Today was a time to leave them to the misery of their present while we uncovered the sins of their past.

While Yitzhak Rabbinowitz, of the accounting firm of Pearlman and Rabbinowitz, worked on the books with Morris, I occupied myself with the piles of paperwork generated by the District Attorney's relentless prosecution of *Commonwealth v. Peter Cressi*. I doubted I would still be on the case after the abdication of Enrico Raffaello, and I thought of just bagging the whole thing, but my malpractice carrier liked me to actually do the work required on my cases, so I was responding to the government's requests for discovery, the government's motions *in limine*, the government's suggested jury instructions. At the same time I was busily drafting my own motions to suppress whatever I could dream up even the flimsiest reasons for suppressing. The arguments were rather weak, I admit, but they all passed my baseline standard: the redface test. Could I stand before a judge and make the argument without my face turning red from embarrassment? Barely, but barely was enough to satisfy the ethical requirements of the Bar Association and so for suppression I moved.

At about three in the afternoon I stretched at my desk and strolled over to the conference room to check on the accountant's progress. I expected to see the two men elbow-deep in ancient volumes, following the figures in the ledgers with their fingers, tap tap tapping numbers into calculators spouting long ribbons of white awash with damning sums. What I saw instead was Yitzhak Rabbinowitz and Morris Kapustin sitting together at the end of the table, feet propped, as relaxed and carefree as a couple of cronies swapping tales over coffee at the deli.

"Victor, come over, please," said Morris, waving me in. "Yitzhak, he was just telling me about our mutual friend Herman Hopfenschmidt."

"So I tell him," said Rabbinowitz, "I say, Herman, with your business such a success and with what you have in the bank, and I know how much it is because I'm your accountant, you still throw around money like a man with no arms." Yitzhak Rabbinowitz was a tall, broadly built man, bald with a bushy gray mustache. He wore a sport coat and a short-sleeved shirt so that his hairy forearms stuck out from the sleeves, one wrist adorned by a gold

Rolex, the other by a flashy gold and diamond band. He leaned back in his chair as he told the story, gesturing wildly, his words coming out slightly wet. "Be a *tsaddik*, I say. Give a little. Beside, someone in your tax bracket, you could use the deductions. Give a little, Herman, I say, give till it hurts. So what does he do? He clutches his chest and says, 'It hurts, it hurts.'"

"That Hopfenschmidt, he's always been a *chazzer*," said Morris, nodding. "He still has the first dollar he ever stole."

"I say, Herman, that's not funny. Not funny. So how much can I put you down for? Ten thousand? Frankle, he gave ten thousand last year and you earn twice as much as Frankle. And Herman says, 'It hurts, it still hurts.' I say, five then at least. Even Hersch with his one dry cleaning store, he's giving five thousand and you earn ten times as much as Hersch. Think of all the children you'll be helping, Jewish children, who can't afford even a chicken neck on *Shabbos*. What does Herman say? 'It hurts, it hurts.' I say, all right, one thousand, but that's the minimum I'll accept and he says, 'But you don't understand, Yitzhak, it hurts, it really hurts.' Next thing I know he falls off his chair. Splat, right on the ground. He was right, it did hurt. He was having a coronary."

"For real?" said Morris.

"Of course. Would I joke about such a thing? He's at Einstein as we speak. As we speak."

"Some *chazzers*, they'll do anything to keep from giving."

"Mr. Rabbinowitz," I said, interrupting. The Reddman books were sitting at the other end of the table, forlorn and alone.

He looked up at me and smiled. "Call me Yitzhak, please, Victor, now that we are working together."

Working? "Well then, Yitzhak, I was just wondering how we are doing on the books. Have you found anything yet? I'm sort of in a hurry on this."

"It's going very well, Victor. Very well, and almost we're ready to show you some things. Not quite but almost."

"You want maybe some coffee, Yitzhak?" asked Morris.

"Yes, that would be terrific," said Rabbinowitz, smiling at me. "Cream and sugar, Victor, and don't be stingy with the sugar."

"Anything else?" I said flatly.

"A doughnut or a *pitsel* cake, would be nice. Anything for you, Morris?"

"Just a water, my stomach still is not what it should be."

"You know your problem," said Rabbinowitz to Morris. "Too much fiber. It gives gas."

"Tell me something I don't already know."

"A coffee with cream and extra sugar," I said. "A *pitsel* cake and water."

"You're very kind, Victor. Thank you," said Rabbinowitz. He turned his attention back to Morris, as if I had been dismissed. "So as soon as we're finished here I'm going over to give Herman a visit up at the hospital. Coming so close to his Maker, maybe it will have softened him up. I tell you, Morris, it was a miracle, really. I think now I can get from him the ten."

"Sit down, Victor," said Yitzhak Rabbinowitz when I came back from the Wawa with the coffee and an Entenmann's cake and a bottle of mineral water. "We'll show you now what we found."

"You're ready?"

"It was rather clever, but not so very well hidden. I'm surprised that Poole didn't catch it himself. The key was learning when it was that this Reddman started keeping the books."

"We think we have it now," said Morris. "We were forced to match the handwriting in the earlier journals with some letters we found in the books and from later journals, after he bought control."

"Kapustin here was a big help," said Rabbinowitz, "which surprised me, really, because generally he is absolutely useless."

"Don't be such the *cham*," said Morris. "You, you're less than useless. The last stock he convinced me to buy, Victor, it didn't split, it crumbled."

"Tell me something, Morris," said Rabbinowitz. "If ignorance is bliss, why aren't you ecstatic?"

"Are you guys finished with your vaudeville," I said, "because the day is short, the task is great, the workmen are lazy . . ."

Rabbinowitz looked at Morris, who looked back and shrugged.

"He doesn't find us entertaining," said Morris. "I'm surprised because I find us very entertaining."

"Sit down, Victor," said Rabbinowitz, putting on a pair of half-glasses. "Sit down and we'll show you what we found."

I sat at the conference table and Rabbinowitz placed two of the books in front of me. One was a heavy old ledger, the other was smaller, and when he opened the books an ancient scent erupted, something mildewed and rotted and rich with must. The pages in each book were yellowed and cracking in the corners, some of the numbers were obliterated by time, but the handwriting in those entries that remained legible was careful and precise.

"This is the disbursement journal and the general ledger for 1896," said Rabbinowitz. "Before Reddman started doing for himself the books." He pointed out to me the meaning of the various entries in the disbursement journal and then went to a long list of figures for January. "These are the amounts paid to specific suppliers each month. We used the amounts in this book as baseline figures. Maybe you'll notice, Victor, that the monthly amounts paid to each supplier, they stay about the same, adjusted seasonally. More produce was bought in the late summer and fall when the harvests came in so more was paid out then, but everything went up roughly proportionally with each of the farmers."

"That makes sense," I said.

"The monthly totals in the disbursement journal were posted at the end of the month to the general ledger. If you also notice, at the back of the general ledger, there is a final trial balance for the year. Assets of course equal liabilities and everything seems in order. All stock at the time, as listed in the general ledger's stock register, was owned by E. J. Poole. Stockholder equity, in less sophisticated times a rough measure of the value of the company, was surprisingly high for such a business. All in all, I would have to say that the E. J. Poole Preserve Company was well and tightly run in 1896."

Rabbinowitz took two more books from the pile, the disbursement journal and general ledger for 1897, and placed them in front of me. The same hand had made the entries in these books, though a little less precisely. Rabbinowitz again went through the monthly entries in the disbursement journal, comparing the amounts paid each supplier with that paid the year before. Everything seemed in order, the monthly totals were duly posted to the general ledger, and the trial balance at year's end again showed a healthy company, all the shares of which were still owned by Elisha Poole.

He then placed the books for 1898 in front of me. As of March of that year the handwriting of the entries changed. "This is when, as best as Morris could tell, Reddman started keeping the books."

"Any indication of why?" I asked.

"None," said Morris, "but you might have noticed that Poole's handwriting, it had started to deteriorate. We think maybe that might indicate a reason."

"Any extra monies started being paid directly to Reddman?" I asked.

"No," said Rabbinowitz. "That, of course, was the first thing we checked. Reddman, he received only modest raises all along until he finally bought the company outright. He started as an apprentice tinsmith and, even though he took on more responsibility, his pay remained rather miserly. But I want to show you something here." He pointed to an entry in the disbursement journal for payments made to a farmer named Anderson. "Notice here that shortly after Reddman started doing the books, the disbursements to Anderson jumped up slightly in proportion to the amounts paid to the other farmers, just a few hundred dollars, but still an increase."

"Maybe Anderson started expanding his output."

"That of course is possible," said Rabbinowitz, who immediately turned to the back of the general ledger. "But notice, in the trial balance sheet for that year, stockholder equity didn't rise even though sales had actually improved."

"Interesting," I said.

Rabbinowitz brought out the disbursement journal for 1899 and dropped it on top of the other books, dust rising when it fell. I sneezed and then sneezed again. Morris handed me a tissue while Rabbinowitz showed me the disbursement entries, month by month, for 1899. Everything seemed stable until we got to June. Rabbinowitz tried to turn the page to find July but I grabbed hold of his wrist.

"What's that?" I asked

"I told you he'd notice it," said Morris. "He's no *yutz*."

"An unexplained jump in the amount paid to this Anderson," said Rabbinowitz with a flourish, as if we had discovered a great scientific secret. "Fifteen hundred dollars more than you would expect to see for that month."

"Any supplier decrease its payable in a similar amount?" I asked.

"Good question," said Rabbinowitz. "And the answer, it is no." He took me through the book page by page, showing that the increase was maintained for every month through the whole of the year. "Almost ten thousand dollars by year's end. Now I want to show you two things in the general ledger." He brought out another volume and paged to the trial balance at the end of the book. "First, shareholder equity dropped by about ten thousand dollars at year's end, approximately twenty percent."

"Almost the exact amount of the unexplained bonus paid to Anderson."

"Exactly right," said Rabbinowitz. "And look at this in the stock register. Eighteen ninety-nine was the first time Reddman started buying shares of stock from Poole. He bought five shares, or five percent of the company, for six thousand dollars."

"Where did a tin cutter with a pittance of a salary get six thousand dollars?" I asked, even though by then I figured I knew the answer.

"What we guess, Victor," said Morris, "is that this Reddman, he volunteered to take control of the books so that he could slip his friend Anderson a little bonus and get for himself a kickback. For some reason he figured he could get away with even more and then he hit on the idea of using the money to buy the company outright, so he raised the payoff and started buying stock. The beauty of it for him was that while he was stealing from the company, the company was losing profits and its value was decreasing, making the price he was to pay less and less. I bet he was able to convince Poole that he was doing him such a favor because of how terrible the company, it was doing."

"So, in effect," I said, "Reddman was stealing from Poole and using the money to buy Poole's company. Very clever."

"Clever, yes," said Rabbinowitz. "For a thief."

The other volumes showed the same thing, inexplicably

large payments to Anderson, weakening shareholder equity, increasingly large purchases of stock by Reddman that would have been impossible on the salary he was listed as receiving in the books. By 1904, Reddman owned forty-five percent of the stock.

"How did he get the rest?" I asked.

"He apparently took out a loan, mortgaging his stock holdings and the stock he was going to purchase," said Morris. "He used the money to buy the remaining shares held by Poole in 1905."

"A leveraged buyout," said Rabbinowitz. "Like something out of the eighties, the nineteen-eighties. This Reddman he was a thief, yes, but a thief ahead of his time."

"And listen to this, Victor," said Morris. "Right after Reddman, he bought all the stock, the sale of pickles it went *meshugge*, more than tripling in one year. Almost as if someone was keeping production low to maintain unprofitability until the entire stock of the company could be bought at a bargain price."

"So that's it," I said. "Poole was right all along. Reddman stole the company right out from under him."

"So it would seem," said Morris.

"If it was so easy for us to see it, how come Poole didn't figure it out?"

"That's a mystery," said Morris. "To solve such a mystery it will take more than looking in books."

We sat for a moment in silence, the three of us. There were still questions to be answered, of course, and there was nothing in the books that would convince a jury of anything beyond a reasonable doubt, but it was pretty clear to me. Everything about the Reddmans was based on a crime and it was as if that crime, instead of disappearing into the mists of history, had remained alive and virulent and had infected the Reddman house and the Reddman family and the Reddman legacy with a crippling rot.

"Two more things you should know, Victor," said Morris. "First, I tried, as soon as Yitzhak started growing suspicious, I tried to find out if there might be records from this farmer Anderson for us to look at. A farm he owned, in New Jersey, in Cumberland County. Through old newspapers I had Sheldon look until he found it. Very disturbing."

"What?" I asked.

"The farmhouse it burned down in 1907, with three dead, including this Anderson."

"My God," I said.

"And something else, Victor," said Rabbinowitz. "We are not the first to go through these records and discover what it is we have discovered. I could see traces of another's journey through the same books, old pencil marks, old notations, old notes stuck in the pages. Someone else, they took the very same route we took through the numbers. Your friend Morris, he thinks he knows," said Rabbinowitz.

I turned and looked at Morris.

"One of the notes," he said. "The writing it matches."

"Matches what?"

"I'm no handwriting expert," said Morris, "but the letters 's' and 't,' they are very close and the 'g,' it is identical."

"Matches what?"

"The pages of the diary we found in the box," said Morris. "She who wrote the diary, she too knew about what this Reddman had done. He was her father, no? What it must have been like for her to find out that everything she had was purchased by a crime. I shudder, Victor, shudder to even think about it."

45

AFTER RABBINOWITZ LEFT for the hospital to visit his good friend Herman Hopfenschmidt, I decided to take a spin around Eakins Oval and along Kelly Drive, past Boathouse Row, to one of the sculpture gardens planted along the banks of the Schuylkill. It was now late afternoon and I sat on a stone bench, just in front of a statue of a massively muscled man groaning forward, a representation of the Spirit of Enterprise, and watched the scullers bend with their oars as their shells skimmed across the river's surface like the water boatmen I had seen on the pond at Veritas. I had needed to get away from the office, to sit among the silent sculptures on the river's edge and watch the sun dip into the west and think about what I had learned that day. Morris had offered to trail along and I hadn't minded. I found having Morris around made me feel better, though I couldn't really say why. But Morris knew enough to stroll quietly among the statuary for a while and let me be.

I had been told that beneath every great fortune lies a great crime but it was still a shock to be confronted with the truth of that maxim so vividly. If I had wondered before what it was that had turned the Reddman family so brutally wrong I needed only to learn the origin of its wealth and power. I didn't yet understand the instrument of the family's undoing but I had little doubt that the tragedies that erupted in its history had their root in

Claudius Reddman's deception of and thievery from Elisha Poole. And the question that inevitably sprung to mind was, in light of the fortune gained and the tragedies incurred, whether or not it was worth it.

I was hip-deep now in Reddman excretion and I couldn't help but imagine myself bobbing for my own little coins. I had been promised the five percent from Oleanna if I could clear her and her people of the murder and get the insurance death benefit paid. I had been promised a kick-back from Peckworth, the used undergarment procurer, for any reduction I could wile from his street tax. Then there was the wrongful death suit I would file on behalf of Caroline Shaw against whoever it was who had ordered the murder of her sister and probably her brother too, a suit I would bring just as soon as I determined who had hired Cressi, and as soon as Caroline signed the fee agreement I so desperately wanted her to sign. And of course, it was undeniable that I was sleeping with an heiress, even if Kingsley's vasectomy made her only an ostensible heiress. It didn't take a practiced gigolo to know where that could lead. Yes, there was a lot of coin adrift in the Reddman muck to be snatched between my teeth.

"Do you know what his last words were before he died?" I asked Morris after he wandered over to the stone bench and sat beside me.

"Who now are we talking about?" said Morris.

"Claudius Reddman. His dying words were, 'It was only business.'"

Morris sat there for a moment, shaking his head. "Such words have justified more crime than even religion."

"Did you ever want to be rich, Morris?"

"Who is rich? As the scholar Ben Zoma once said, 'He who is content with his lot.'"

I looked up at him, at the calm expression on his face, the expression of a man who seemed truly content with his life and at peace with his place in the world.

"So you never wanted to be rich?" I asked.

"What, you think I'm *meshuggener*," said Morris. "Of course I wanted to be rich. I still do. Give me a million dollars, Victor, and see if I turn it down. Give me two, maybe. Give me thirty over six years with a signing bonus like a baseball pitcher and see if I push it away. Believe you me, Victor, I won't push it away."

"That's good to know," I said, and turned back to the water. "I was getting worried. What would you buy?"

He thought on that for a moment. "There was a man in Pinsk," he said finally, "who used to make the most perfect shoes in the world. I never saw a pair mind you, but I heard of them from someone whose cousin had actually held a pair in his very hands. Soft like a woman's skin, he said, and as comfortable as a warm bath. I always wanted a pair of shoes from the man in Pinsk. Of course this was before the war. I don't know now what happened to him, he is probably dead. Pinsk was not a good place to be a Jew during the war. But I have heard rumors now of a man in Morocco whose shoes, they say, are close to those of the man in Pinsk."

"You could buy anything you want and what you'd buy is shoes?"

"Not just any shoes, Victor, not the scraps of leather you wear on your feet. These shoes are a *mechaieh*, they are the shoes of a king."

"So you want to be rich so you can buy a pair of shoes," I said, nodding to myself. "I guess that makes as much sense as anything else. At least you know."

"Yes and no. With such shoes, Victor, when could I wear them? Not every day, they are too precious for everyday. I would wear them only on the *Shabbos* maybe, and not even every *Shabbos*, because even then they would wear out too soon. I would spend more time taking care of them than wearing them, I think, waxing the leather, polishing, keeping them stretched and warm. Such shoes would be more burden than anything else. As Hillel said, 'The more flesh, the more worms. The more property, the more anxiety. The more wives, the more witchcraft.'"

"That sounds like Dylan, except for the part about the witchcraft."

"Yes, your Bobby Zimmerman, I think he read Hillel."

"I can think of lots of things to buy," I said. "A Ferrari. Armani suits. A house with skylights. A set of golf clubs, those Callaway Big Bertha irons and woods, the ones that go for over a grand and have a sweet spot the size of Montana."

"You play golf?"

"With a set of Callaways I'd maybe break a hundred. But you know what, Morris? It's not the stuff, really. I just want to be rich. I want the kids who beat me up in high school to see my picture in the paper with the caption, 'Victor Carl, millionaire.' I want all the girls who turned me down to know what they missed. Being rich is like living in a state of grace and that's what I want."

"Money can't buy that, Victor. Only righteousness. As Rebbe Yoshe ben Kisma once said . . ."

"I don't want to hear from any more dead rabbis, Morris."

He turned his head to stare. Even though he was shorter than me by a foot, it felt as if he were looking down at me. "These men were very smart, Victor. The things they could teach us both."

"No more dead rabbis. Tell me, Morris, what you think about all the money you and I don't have."

"What I think? You want to know what I think, Victor? Are you sure this is what you want to hear?"

I nodded, though something in his voice gave me pause.

"Well then. I think that money it is the goal of cowards. Money is what you end up wanting if you don't have *putz* enough to stand up and decide for yourself. Money is what they want you to want so that you will work for them every day of your life and buy what they sell and fill your house and your soul with their junk. It is for those without the courage to decide for themselves. For people like our friend Beth who are seeking truths, I have nothing but respect. But for those who are taking the easy way out and bowing down to the graven image of the dollar that they plaster on the television and the movie screen simply because that it is what they are told they want, for them I have only disgust."

I was startled by his words. I had never seen Morris so angry. Generally he was a genial guy, Morris, but it was if there was something about me that had been bugging him for a while and now he felt free to expound upon it because I had insisted. I regretted asking him but I was fascinated too, it was like a cover had been whisked off the old josher and I was seeing something ferocious inside.

"Take your thief Reddman, for example," he continued. "What kind of man would do all he did just for money? What had he become? I tell you what he became, an idolater, substituting money for the true King. What did the Lord tell Moishe on Mount Sinai when he gave him the two tablets and the commandment that thou shalt have no other gods before me. *Shmot*, Chapter Twenty, verse five. He said that those who bow down and worship a graven image, the sins of the father, it shall be visited upon the children unto the third and fourth generations of them, that is what He said. You tell me if this, it did not come true with this Reddman and his children and grandchildren and great-grandchildren."

I stared at him and felt a chill just then rippling along my spine. It was as if I were in the middle of a biblical prophecy brought to life by the crimes of Claudius Reddman. I had been shown with utter clarity the cause and I was walking through the ruin-strewn landscape of the result. All that remained in shadow was the instrument of His will.

Morris looked at me and suddenly his face eased and he smiled. With a shrug he said, "So that is what I think, Victor. But it is just one man's opinion. Alan Greenspan, he knows more than I ever will about money, maybe he thinks differently, I don't know."

A long shell with eight rowers and a coxswain slid by on the river in a smooth series of rushes. The coxswain was jerking back and forth with each stroke as she yelled and the eight rowers were following her commands with perfect timing, leaning forward as one, pulling back as one, becoming a single self under the sway of the coxswain's voice. We sat in silence for a while, Morris and I, watching the boat, listening to the uneven notes of a lonely bird somewhere in the sycamores lining the river's edge. Across the peaceful flow of the water I could see the helter-skelter madness of the Schuylkill Expressway.

"I'm in trouble, Morris," I said.

"I know."

"More trouble than you could imagine. I'm in the middle of something very dangerous that I don't understand and can't control."

"Such is life for us all. Tell me, Victor, can I help?"

"Yes, I think so," I said, and then I told him how.

It was dark when I came back to my apartment that night. First thing I did after I stripped off my jacket and tie was to place another call to the 407 area code to see if Calvi had yet come off his boat. There was no answer, there wasn't even an answering machine. I stayed on the line for a desperately long time, long enough to realize that Calvi wasn't ever going to help me, and then I hung up. The instant I replaced the handset my phone started ringing. It happened so quickly it was eerie, as if my call had been chased all the way from Florida. I let it ring for a moment and felt my heart speed its beat with fear and then I answered it.

"I have to get out of here," said Caroline.

I let relief slide through me and then asked, "How was the funeral?"

"Funereal."

"I'll bet. Didn't you drive?"

"They picked me up, but they want me to stay the night and I can't. It's unbearable."

"I'll be up in forty-five minutes," I said, "but I won't pick you up at the front of the house. Remember I told you I spoke to your father?"

"Yes," she said in a whisper, as if her conversation was being overheard.

"He said he saw a light in the garden last week."

"So?" she said. "We were there, then. Remember?"

"Yes we were. But he also said he saw a light in the house that had been deeded to the Pooles."

"Why would anyone be in that old wreck?" she asked.

"Exactly," I said.

46

I HID MY CAR IN A GROVE of bushes outside the entrance of the great Reddman estate. I took my backpack out of the trunk and made my way across the low bridge that forded the stream and through the wide-open gates with their forged vines and cucumbers and their now sardonic wrought-iron legend: MAGNA EST VERITAS. Past the two great sycamores I turned left, away from the driveway, and skirted clockwise around the hill. What remained of the moon was rather dismally lit but the big house was full of light. I could hear the tinkle of glasses and the hum of voices. It seemed rather festive at Veritas that evening, considering the circumstances. But if Edward Shaw had been a blood relative of mine I might have been rather festive too.

It was too chilly a night for the black tee shirt and jeans I was sporting and I shivered as I picked my way through sparse trees, always keeping to my right the lights of the house and to my left the quiet sluicing of the stream that surrounded the property like a noose. It was taking longer than I had expected to make my way around the grounds and I started to rush until I found myself stepping into the margin of a dense wood. Only shards of the moon's light survived the canopy above and I had a hard time seeing what was now in front of my face. I stepped away from a branch that slapped my outreached hand and walked straight into the trunk of a tree, smacking my forehead. I hadn't intended to use a light so soon, not wanting anyone to spot me prowling about the grounds, trespassing like a common thief when what I really was was a lawyer on the make, but the scrape with that malicious tree was enough to convince me to pull a flashlight out of my pack and click it on.

An animate circle of tree trunks immediately sprang into existence, surrounding me. The white light of my lamp slipped past the trees closest to me before dying in the night. I had the sensation of being in the middle of something that went on forever, only able to discern the first ring around me. I took a moment to regain my bearings, the gurgle of the stream to the left, the hill and the house to the right, and then continued on my way, my path weaving here and there to avoid the black furrowed trunks blocking my way, until I entered the clearing, thick with tall grasses, that surrounded the gray and decrepit Poole house. I quickly turned off the light and was stunned by what I encountered.

Fireflies sparked around the old ruin of a house, hundreds and hundreds of them, little fingers of light that swept low in the grass or high about the porch roof and the first-floor windows of the house, flashing in a slow seductive dance. There hadn't been any fireflies on the hill leading to Veritas, or in the woods, but here they were gathering as if for some incantatory purpose of their own.

I held my breath for a moment and listened.

Just the desperate call of crickets and the hoots of a few scattered birds.

I stepped back into the darkness of the wood, leaned against a tree trunk, and waited.

Caroline came about fifteen minutes later, scrambling around the pond through the woods and into the clearing, looking around, searching. She was chic in black—black dress, black pumps, black lipstick, black motorcycle jacket covering her shoulders like a cape. As I watched her walk up to the house I thought of all the things I hadn't told her yet, how her great-grandfather was a crook, how her grandmother knew it, how her father wasn't her father. I would tell her most of it eventually, I figured, but not all of it and not now. I pushed myself off the tree and stepped toward her. She started when she saw me emerging from the darkness of the woods.

"Oh, Victor, you scared me for a moment. What are we doing here again? God, I can't believe there's anything of interest in this old wreck. I explored it all when I was younger and it was pretty dilapidated then. It must be completely falling apart by now. What did my father say he saw here? He must have been imagining it, God knows he . . ."

I walked up to her as she spoke and put my finger to her moving lips, quieting her immediately. I leaned my mouth to her ear and whispered.

"I don't know who was here when your father saw the light but I don't think it wise we let them know we are taking a look. That's why I wanted to do this at night. Did you tell anyone you were coming here?"

She shook her head.

"Did anyone see you leave? Did Nat?"

"Nat wasn't there," she whispered. And then I smelled it.

"You've been drinking."

She leaned back and looked at me defiantly. "Family tradition at funerals."

"Another of your situations?"

"Funny how having your brother incinerated can set you back."

I looked her up and down and noticed something on the inside of her arm, a patch of white gauze. I turned the flashlight on and pointed the beam right at it. "What's that?"

"Nothing," she said.

"What the hell are you doing to yourself?" I said, certain that she had gone past alcohol into something more virulent.

She took a step back.

I followed her and reached for the gauze, ripping it off.

"Oh, Caroline," I said with a sad sigh. "What are you doing to yourself?"

"It's nothing," she said, taking the gauze with its tape back from my hand and trying to reposition it on her arm. "Everyone's doing it."

"Oh, Caroline," I said again and then I couldn't say anything more. Her arm had been branded, a circular sun with regular curved rays pouring from it had been burned into her flesh and the skin around the sun was swollen red and proud. Tattoos were no longer permanent enough for her, I supposed.

"It's my body," she said with a practiced defiance that let me know she had said those very words many times before.

"Yes it is," I said.

"Are we going in or are we just standing here all night?"

"Will you be able to handle this?"

She closed her eyes and swayed a bit before nodding.

"All right," I said, "but keep it quiet."

With the flashlight in one hand and her elbow in the other, I walked with her slowly, through the dips and turns of the fireflies, toward the house. A short flight of steps led to a sagging porch of gray timber, singed at the edges by fire, and on to the front door. These were the steps, I assumed, where Faith Reddman Shaw had first discovered the Poole daughter reading to Faith's son, Kingsley. The wood creaked and bowed beneath our feet as we climbed. Caroline tripped slightly on the steps and fell into me. I pushed her straight again.

On the porch, I flashed the light briefly to the left and the right. The porch was empty of furniture, a few of the timbers had rotted completely through. One of the upright railings was charred black. Of the window on the left side of the door, two of the panes were smashed and the others were yellowed and brittle. The window on the right was boarded with plywood. A swift motion caught my attention and I aimed the beam of light at it. First one frog leaped from the porch, and then another. Cobwebs floated like ghost streamers from the railing and the roof, but the front entrance was free of them. I pointed that out to Caroline before we stepped to the door. There was an old rusted mortise lock and when I pressed down on the latch with my thumb it wouldn't budge.

"Locked?" I said.

Caroline shrugged. I leaned my side into the door and gave a shove and quick as that it creaked open. We glanced at each other for a moment and then stepped inside.

We entered directly into a large parlor room, thick with swirls of dust, scattered dead leaves, cobwebs hanging like gauze in the corners. It was cold inside. I flashed the light on an old couch, the color of dirt, sitting across from a stone fireplace. Judging by its appearance the couch hadn't been sat upon in a decade.

"I can't believe this is still here," said Caroline, softly, stepping toward it and rubbing her hand across a filthy arm. "Franklin and I cleaned up this room a bit and made fires here sometimes. We brought a rug in and sat by the hearth."

I shined the light at the fireplace. There was a small pile of coals, gray with dust. A dead mouse nestled among the remains of a fire. There was nothing on the floor before the hearth but leaves.

"The rug's gone," I said.

She shrugged. "It was long ago."

I cast the beam around the walls. A floral print wallpaper faded almost to brown, bare except for something over the mantelpiece. I stepped closer. It was a drawing of a man, a rather primitive drawing, faded and on yellow paper, tacked to the plaster above the fireplace like an ironic family portrait. The man in the picture was bald and the lines around his mouth were evident but it was done in a young person's hand. The face of the man, I realized, was somehow familiar.

"Do you recognize him?" I asked.

She walked up to it and stared.

"I think," she said, "he looks like the man in the photograph we found, with the tense-looking wife."

"That must be Elisha Poole," I said. "Probably drawn by his daughter."

"This wasn't here before," she said.

"Are you sure?"

"Hell, I don't know," she said. "Maybe it was and I didn't notice."

Off the parlor was the kitchen, a large room with a few cabinets and a large wooden table. Two rickety chairs lay strewn upon the floor. There was an old wood-burning stove with disks of metal atop for burners, the stove where the Poole daughter stirred the broth for her mother while Faith Reddman Shaw watched, entranced, from outside. Pots and pans, blackened by fire, were scattered on the floor about the stove, covered with webs and leaves. A cement sink with one faucet stood by the wall, its weight resting on a rusted metal frame.

"Cold and cold running water," I said. I stepped to it and turned the knob. Nothing.

"What exactly are we looking for, Victor?"

"I don't know," I said softly. "But I feel something here, don't you? Something cramped and desolate."

"It just feels old and cold."

An archway from the kitchen led to another room, mostly empty, with a fireplace. It must have been the dining room but there were no tables or chairs, only a massive wooden breakfront. The upper doors of the breakfront were lined, where one would expect glass, with a pleated yellowed fabric. I tugged the doors open. The shelves, covered with a browned paper, were entirely empty. The lower part of the breakfront held three rows of drawers and the drawers I could pull open also contained nothing but the same browned paper. The top middle drawer, designed for the most valuable serving pieces, was locked, but that too was probably empty. It was doubtful the Poole daughter would have taken the china but left the silver.

"I suppose she took everything she wanted and could carry out," I said, "and abandoned the rest."

"I think she just wanted to get the hell out of here," said Caroline Shaw too loudly. "Who wouldn't?"

"Shhhhhhh," I said.

At the far end of the dining room was an entranceway that led off to a narrow set of stairs. I followed the beam of light and started climbing. Slipping slightly, I grabbed hold of the banister and it tore off in my hand with a shriek. The banister slammed into the wood flooring and slid nosily down the stairs, plaster cascading behind it. I jumped as if I had been goosed. I turned around and Caroline was smirking at me.

At the top of the stairs was a hallway. In the beam of light I could see four doorways, three of them open. Across from us was a small room with a listing wooden bed frame. When we stepped in something scurried across the floor and disappeared. On the wall were tacks, spiking remnants of yellowed paper into the plaster. The floor was filled with tumors of dust and crumpled bits of white stuff and there was trash piled in one of the corners. The window was covered with plywood.

The next room was a bathroom with a wooden floor and an old toilet. The sink was ceramic and cracked and there was one faucet. Beyond the bathroom was another room completely bare of any useful furniture, in its center a heap of broken chairs and shattered china. A doll without its head rested atop a rocking chair with only one rocker. Across the hall was the door that was closed.

Without waiting for me, Caroline went to that door and shoved it open. I followed her inside. This room too had a fireplace and there was a mattress on the floor and an old transistor radio, circa not 1923 but 1979. On the wall to the right, its sole window covered with plywood, hung a poster with a grinning, multicolored skull above the legend "*STEAL YOUR FACE!*" and another showing a leather-jacketed greaser with a pair of sneakers hanging from the neck of his guitar. Bruce Springsteen? The Grateful Dead?

"I guess old Mrs. Poole was ahead of her time," I said.

"This was our room," said Caroline softly. She picked up the small black-and-gray radio and turned it on, but nothing happened. "It's still tuned to WMMR, I'd bet. Oh God."

"What was this room before you and Harrington took it over?"

"I think it was Mrs. Poole's bedroom," she said without turning to me. "I seem to remember there was stuff in the closet."

I looked at her for a moment, standing still, with the dead radio cradled in her arms like a baby, and then I stepped quickly to the closet door and pulled at it. It was stuck at first, swollen shut, but I gave it a good yank and it opened up for me with a shriek from the hinges.

Inside, moth-eaten, shabby with age, like skeletons of their former selves, were dresses, some still hanging, some slumped to the floor, their frills darkened, their colors washed out by the white light of the flashlight and their age. Which of these dresses, I wondered, had she worn on the night of the ball when she so publicly refused Claudius Reddman's offer to dance? Well, he sure as hell deserved the rebuke.

With two fingers I lifted up the dresses from the floor, finding nothing but old shoes underneath. There was a shelf above the bar and I stood up on my tiptoes to look at it. Hats and shoes, the leather cracked, and a pile of rags in the corner. I jumped up and grabbed at the rag pile and pulled them down. Dust flew and I sneezed loudly. When I stopped sneezing I noticed now, in the corner, a little wooden box. I jumped up again and snatched it. With a little work I was able to lift off the lid.

"Photographs," I said.

Caroline emerged from her reverie and we sat down together on the mattress, their mattress, to look at the pictures.

They were old black-and-white photographs, many with curly edges. There was a pretty young woman sitting on the ground, her head tilted suggestively, a long string of pearls knotted beneath her breast, and then the same woman sitting on a stoop, her hair long and young, a sly, sensual smile.

"Any idea who she is?" I asked.

"It looks like the woman that was next to Elisha Poole in the other pictures," said Caroline.

"It does, doesn't it," I said, and it did, but it also didn't. There was nothing sour in this young woman. "It must be Mrs. Poole, you're right, but look how young she is. And in this one she's almost laughing."

There were other photographs of the woman, more formal photographs, posed in a studio, going back in time until there was one of her as a young girl, with her parents, the girl wearing a frilly dress, like an angel's, button leather shoes, the serious smile of the very young. And there were pictures of a brash young man with wavy hair, leaning dramatically against a post, or clowning at the beach. On the back of the picture at the beach was written in a fading ink, "Elisha, Atlantic City–1896."

"Look how handsome he was," said Caroline. "Who would have imagined? I guess he was something before he became a bitter old drunk."

"They're all something before they become bitter old drunks."

We kept going through the pictures, shining the light carefully on each, examining them one by one. There were pictures of the woman and the man together, laughing, in love, ready to conquer the world. In one picture there was an old man with his arm around Elisha. Elisha was leaning away, as if to gain some distance. The old man's eyes were half open, one was blackened from a brawl, his nose was large and venous, teeth were missing from his mouth. "Elisha and his father," was written on the back. And there was one that brought a gasp from Caroline.

"That's my great-grandfather," she said.

A young Claudius Reddman, in a vested suit, high collar, bowler hat cocked low over his bulging eyes, standing side by side a young Elisha Poole, their arms linked, a great blocky building behind them.

"That must be the before shot," said Caroline.

I said nothing, only stared, feeling the life and camaraderie in the picture, the linked arms, the burgeoning possibilities. They had been friends. I hadn't counted on that but here was the proof. They had been friends; did that make the betrayal any deeper? Is it more acceptable to swindle a stranger than a friend? Or can a friend more clearly understand that he is only doing to his pal, his buddy, his comrade-in-arms, what his comrade-in-arms would do to him had he half a chance? Could it have been that Elisha, in paying his friend what Yitzhak Rabbinowitz had described as a miserly wage, had a hand in his own financial destruction? "It was only business," had said Claudius Reddman and I couldn't help but wonder if he hadn't learned his business practices from his dear and valued friend Elisha Poole.

So engrossed were we in the pictures that we didn't hear the front door open or the creak of someone walking through the parlor and the kitchen and the dining room. So engrossed were we that we didn't hear a thing until we heard the soft even footfalls rising up the stairs.

47

I STUFFED THE PHOTOGRAPHS back into the box and the box into my pack and clicked off the light. Darkness covered us. And in the darkness an uneven wiggle of shadow impressed itself upon the air around the door. A candle? Yes. I grabbed hold of Caroline and whispered in her ear, "Absolute silence."

The footsteps continued to climb, step by step. The light causing the uneven shadows became ever more prominent. The intruder reached the top of the stairs and hesitated.

Slowly Caroline and I crawled together off the mattress to a corner of the room where someone glancing in the doorway wouldn't so easily spot us. I crouched into a ready position and hefted the flashlight in my hand. It was as heavy as a billy club. We waited.

Ten seconds. Twenty seconds. I heard something and was about to tell Caroline to be quiet once again when I realized it was my breath, coming out in gulps. Sweat blossomed on my forehead, sweat trickled down my sides. I couldn't stop thinking of what Kingsley Shaw had said, that his mother was alive in the Poole house and waiting for him. Was it she holding the candle, rising up the steps? Whoever it was, I was certain, whoever had climbed those stairs was the murderer who had been stalking the Reddmans. And now Caroline and I were cowering in the corner like two targets. My heart jumped in my chest. I willed whoever was coming to turn around, to step down the stairs, to just go away and leave us alive.

And then the steps began again. Toward us. The uneven flicker of light growing. The intruder stopped at one door for a moment and then moved on and stopped at another and then stopped before our own.

I grabbed tighter to Caroline and held my breath. Go away, I thought, we're not here, nobody's here.

A hand with a white candle slid through the doorway and then the arm, black-sleeved, and a man's shoe.

I clicked on the light as soon as the head appeared, aiming the beam at the figure's face. It whited out for an instant before we could recognize who it was.

"Franklin?" said Caroline.

"Get that out of my face," said a calm Franklin Harrington.

I scrambled to my feet and sent the light sprawling against the far wall. His face, now lit only by the candle held below it, flickered in ominous shadow.

"Jesus, Franklin, what are you doing here?" asked Caroline, now also standing.

"I saw you go out the back of the house and I was worried about you," said Harrington, "so I followed. Little did I know you were coming here to tryst with your new boyfriend. And in our old room, yet. Trying to bring back the magic?"

"Shut up," said Caroline. "You're being a bastard."

"So what are you two up to?" he asked.

"Archaeology," I said.

He turned his attention to me, his eyes dark sockets of shadow in the candlelight. "Digging for mummies?"

"No," I said. "Pooles."

He stared at me for a moment before smiling. "Curiosity," he said, with a lighthearted warning in his voice that wasn't lighthearted at all. "What is it about the Pooles you want to know, Victor?"

"Mostly," I said, "I want to know if there are any still alive."

"And so you came here, to their old haunt, to snag yourself a Poole. Don't you think you're a little late? Maybe seventy years too late?"

He circled around the room, examining it by candle-light.

"Ahh, the memories," said Harrington. "I can truly say some of the happiest moments of my life were spent in this room. But you knew, didn't you, Caroline, that before this became the scene of our childhood romance, long before, this was Mrs. Poole's bedchamber? After her husband hanged himself and your great-grandfather deeded her this house, which she accepted only because she had no choice, no other place to go, she spent months in bed in this room, never rising, only weeping."

"She had her reasons, I figure," I said.

"Her husband's suicide was a blow, yes," said Harrington, as surely as if he were discussing a ball game he had played in a few years back. "She would have killed herself, too, except for her daughter. But even before his death, she had given herself over to mourning. Her husband would lose himself in drink and she would spend her days castigating him or cursing Claudius Reddman to the heavens, blaming their misfortunes on him."

"How do you know all this, Franklin?" said Caroline.

"I've made a study of the Pooles. They're fascinating, really. A family cursed by luck. Did you know that the grandfather, Elisha Poole's father, lost everything he owned in the depression of 1878? Ten thousand businesses failed that year, including his. He owned three buildings on Market Street, owned them outright, but mortgaged the buildings to buy shares in a gold mine in the Black Hills of the Dakota Territory from a drinking buddy. Fortunes in gold were being dug out of the ground daily then, but not from that mine. With the depression, his tenants couldn't pay the rents and he couldn't pay his mortgages. He lost the buildings and spent the rest of his life drinking in celebration of his misfortune. Just like his son, who complained so bitterly about your great-grandfather."

"Maybe he had his reasons," I said.

"What reasons, Victor?" said Caroline. "What are you trying to say?"

"Only what you suspected, Caroline," I said. "Those records you found behind the panel in the library, the accountant looked them over today. They show pretty clearly that your grandfather stole the company right out from under Elisha Poole."

She didn't respond, she just blinked at me for a moment, as if she was having trouble processing the information.

"Should I show you the rest of the house?" said Harrington, without even a hint of surprise at what I had said. "Maybe we should start with Emma's room."

He strolled out into the hallway and back to the room with the listing bed and the tacks in the wall. Caroline and I tilted our heads uncertainly at each other and then followed. His candlelight bathed the small room in a flickering yellow.

"Emma came to this house of despair when she was five," said Harrington, the tour guide. "Walked four and a half miles to the public school each day. Cared for her mother through her long bouts of melancholia and then through her final sickness. Though rather unattractive, she idolized the famous beauties of her time, cutting their pictures from the papers and tacking them onto these very walls, Theda Bara, Lillian Gish, Irene Castle. And despite it all she remained rather cheerful and good-natured, until the end of her time here. Then even she lost her battle and turned to bitterness to keep her going."

"How do you know all this?" said Caroline.

"She moved her mother permanently down to the parlor

after a crushing stroke to make it easier to carry the old woman to the porch on warm days and allow her some fresh air. She moved herself out of this room into her mother's room, which was bigger and had better light. It was in that room, our room, Caroline, that she fell in love and then fell pregnant."

"Who was her lover?" I asked.

"Does it matter? I think she still believed in love then but just a few weeks before her delivery date her mother died, the deed to the house expired, and she moved out, deserted and alone. She had the baby in an asylum for unwed mothers outside Albany."

"How do you know all this?" said Caroline. "Tell me, how?"

He turned to look at Caroline, the shadows on his face dancing from the candlelight. "She told me so herself," he said.

"Who told you?" demanded Caroline.

"Emma," he said. "She told it all to me."

He spun around, walked out of the room, and climbed down the stairs. I started shaking from the cold as I watched him go. I turned to Caroline and we stared at each other for a moment before hustling out to follow. We caught up to him in the parlor.

"Franklin, dammit, what are you talking about?" said Caroline. "Who told you all this?"

"Mrs. Poole, Emma's mother, died right here," said Harrington. "In her last breath she cursed once again Claudius Reddman, who was still then alive in the big house on the hill. There wasn't much left to curse; his lungs were tumorous and he medicated himself into a stupor with laudanum every night to keep his whole body from shaking, but that didn't stop her. She cursed your great-grandfather, Caroline, and all his progeny, much like her husband had fifteen years before. This was just after your grandfather was shot dead by his son, just a few days after actually, and, with one Reddman daughter missing and one Reddman daughter dead, it looked like the curses were all coming true. I wonder if she died at least a little happy, seeing tragedy so visibly visited upon her enemies. Think about what it is to live a life where your only joy is someone else's tragedy, think of that, Caroline. She was ruined all right, but not by your great-grandfather, no matter how much he stole from that family."

"Stop it, Franklin," said Caroline. "Just stop it. I don't want to hear anymore. In all these years, how come you never told me any of this before?"

"I didn't think you were interested in anything but your own disasters."

"Oh, just go to hell," she said. She walked over to the fireplace and looked up at the old drawing of Elisha Poole tacked above the mantelshelf. "What do you mean she told you so herself?" she asked quietly.

"When I was eighteen," said Harrington. "It was the spring while I was waiting to hear from Princeton. Your grandmother sent me to her. Emma was living in the Cambium, in the very same apartment where Jacqueline died. Your grandmother was supporting her, paying the rent, paying for a nurse to care for her. She didn't live long after my visit, almost as if she were waiting for me to come to her before she died."

The chill I had been feeling the last few minutes grew ferocious. I couldn't tell now if it was the temperature or the dawning realization. "Why would the Poole daughter be waiting for you?" I asked.

"Because, as I found out that day, I'm her grandson," said Harrington.

Caroline spun around at that and spit out, "Fuck you!"

"Through my father," continued Harrington. "Although I didn't know it at the time, that was why Faith took me out of the orphanage and brought me to Veritas, why she provided for me and paid for my education. For the same reason she was taking care of Emma. Because we were both Pooles. It was Faith who discovered that you and I were lovers, Caroline, which is why she finally introduced me to my grandmother."

"And that's why we could never be together?" said Caroline. "Tell me, you asshole, is that why?"

"The tragedy of the Pooles," said Harrington, "was not that their business was stolen from them by your great-grandfather. The tragedy of the Pooles was that they allowed themselves to be tragic. They defined themselves by what the Reddmans had taken from them, by what the Reddmans had become. I was never going to let that happen to me."

"We were in love," groaned Caroline.

"I thought I'd leave and be done with it all when I found out," said Harrington. "But I let your grandmother put me through Princeton, sort of as a recompense. I figured why not, and then I let her put me through Wharton, and then when I was offered the job at the bank, it was naturally advantageous to have her trust accounts under my aegis, and pretty soon I was neck-deep in Reddman money, so it didn't quite work out like I had thought. But I wasn't going to join the family, Caroline, at least not that. That I would never do."

"You said you loved me."

"I did."

"And you never told me."

"I didn't know until that day."

"And you didn't tell me then."

"How could I?" said Harrington, a soft pain in his voice. "You were a Reddman and I was a Poole. How could I . . ."

"Did you ever think, Franklin, did you ever consider that by leaving me you became just as much a victim as the rest of them? Did you ever think of that, you asshole?"

He didn't have a chance to answer before she was out the door.

Harrington and I both acted as if we were going to go after her, but then our eyes met and we stopped. I felt for an instant like an old-time gunfighter, waiting for the man standing across from me to make his move.

"Did you hire Jacqueline's killers?" I asked finally.

"You didn't listen to a word, did you?"

"If you didn't, who did?"

"I don't know."

"Where's your father?"

He looked at me for a moment. "He's long gone," he said. "He passed away from us years and years ago."

"Any other Poole relatives you know about?"

"None."

"Who's Wergeld?"

"That's the name of the trust I told you about."

"Who's the beneficiary?"

"I don't know."

"You come back here often?"

He looked around and shrugged. "Not in over ten years," he said.

We stared at each other a moment more, our hands twitching as if we really did have guns on our hips. I nodded my head to the wall above the fireplace where the primitive drawing of Elisha Poole was tacked. "You put that up?"

He looked at it for a moment. "No," he said.

"You know she's right, of course. If you loved her and let her go just because she was a Reddman and you were a Poole, you've given in as badly as your grandmother and your great-grandparents."

"What the hell do you know about it?"

I thought on that for a moment. "You're right," I said. "Not a thing."

On our way to the door I stopped and told Harrington I

had left something in the house. He looked at me gratefully, as if it were a cheap ploy to allow him some time
alone with Caroline. I nodded and slipped him half a smile
and let him think what he was thinking as he walked out to
her alone.

It was a cheap ploy, yes, but not to give him time alone
with Caroline. When he left I turned and walked through
the kitchen to the dining room and the massive breakfront
with the one drawer locked. Under the beam of my flashlight I took out my wallet and extracted the ornate key with
the bit like a puzzle piece attached to the shank, the key we
had found in the metal box, in the envelope marked "The
Letters." Slowly I inserted the key into the lock in the
drawer. It slipped in as though the key and the lock were
made one for the other, which they were, because without
much effort the key turned, the bolt dropped, the drawer
slid open.

Inside were packets of letters, each yellowed and brittle, tied together with pale ribbons that had once held color
but no longer. One by one I stuffed the bundles into my
pack. Among the letters was a small book of scaling brown
leather. I opened it to the title page. *Walden* by Henry
David Thoreau. I took that too. Beneath everything was a
heavy old envelope, tied shut with a string. The words on
the outside, written with a masculine hand, read: *To My
Child on the Attainment of Majority.*

I stuffed the envelope into my pack with the rest of the
stuff and headed out the door.

48

I WANTED TO TALK on the drive home, I was so excited I was bursting with talk. The whole chilling story of the Reddmans and the Pooles was coming clear and more than ever I was certain that the sad entwining of the fates of those two families was at the heart of the plague that was presently afflicting the Reddmans. We were close, so close, to figuring it all out and to taking the first steps toward retribution, as well as toward a lucrative lawsuit. I wanted to talk it out, desperately, but just as desperately Caroline wanted silence.

"Are you all right?" I asked after three of my conversational gambits had dropped like lead weights in a pool of silent water.

"No," she said.

"What can I do?"

"Just, just shut up," she said.

Well at least she knew what she wanted.

So, as we drove in silence out of the Main Line and toward the city, I considered to myself what we knew and what we still needed to learn. Claudius Reddman had stolen the company from his friend Elisha Poole, had embezzled sums which he used to buy up a portion of the stock, and then, after reducing the company's value with his thievery and through production holdbacks, had purchased the balance of the shares for an amount far below their true value. In the process of making his fortune he had ruined his friend, driving him to drink, to poverty, to suicide, and Reddman knew all he had done, too, because right after Poole's death, either out of guilt or a misplaced magnanimity, he brought Mrs. Poole and her daughter to live in the shadow of his wealth and grandeur, in the shadow of Veritas. Is it only a coincidence that shortly thereafter tragedy began to stalk the Reddmans?

Charity Reddman was murdered and buried in the plot behind the house, alongside the statue of Aphrodite. Who killed her? Was it Christian Shaw, disposing of his inconvenient lover, as Caroline believed, or was it maybe Mrs. Poole, wreaking her husband's revenge? And the Reddman tragedies didn't stop there. Hope Reddman died of consumption, which might have been poisoning instead. Christian Shaw was killed by his son with a shotgun blast to the chest. Claudius Reddman's lungs filled with tumors and his muscles grew wild with palsy. How much of this tragedy was just the natural order of things and how much was bad karma and how much was directly caused by the Pooles? We as yet had no answer and probably would never find one, but if we only reap what we sow then Claudius Reddman's harvest was appropriately bountiful. But it hadn't ended with his death.

Somewhere along the line, it appeared, Faith Reddman Shaw sought to make amends. We knew that she had examined her father's old journals and discovered his crime. Was it after this discovery that she found Emma Poole and brought her to the luxury apartment in Philadelphia to live out her life? Was it then that she found Harrington, Emma's grandchild, lost in an orphanage, and brought him to the estate to be raised as one of her own? Was the purpose of the Wergeld Trust to ease her family's conscience? Conciliation, expiation, redemption she had said she was seeking, and it appeared she had been seeking it actively. But still all this had failed, somehow, to stem the curse, because someone had hired Cressi to kill Jacqueline and probably Edward too. Their deaths might be all tied up with Edward Shaw's gambling debts, true, both killings ordered by Dante to collect on his loan, but after visiting the house of Poole I suspected it had more to do with the ugliness of the Reddman past than anything in the present. So who was ordering the killings? Harrington, the only known surviving Poole? Robert Shaw, knocking off his siblings to increase his inheritance with which he could play the market, showing himself as ruthless in matters of business as his great-grandfather? Kingsley Shaw, carrying out the deranged commands of the voice of the fire? Or was it maybe Faith Reddman Shaw herself, coming back from the dead as her son had claimed, sacrificing her grandchildren one by one as bloody final acts of reparation for her father's crimes?

Something Caroline had said nagged at me. "Where was Nat tonight?" I asked. "You said he wasn't there."

"He wasn't. I don't know where he was."

"Was he at Jacqueline's funeral?"

"Of course."

Nat, the estate's gardener and caretaker, was missing. It was not like Nat to miss a Reddman funeral. More than anyone he seemed to know the family's secrets and I wondered if perhaps his knowledge had proved deadly. A shiver crawled through me just then and I had the urge to stop the car and spin it around and return to Veritas. He was there, I would have bet, in Faith Reddman Shaw's overrun garden, lying there now just as peacefully as Charity Reddman, the two of them stretched before the statue of Aphrodite, with the mingled ashes of Faith and Christian Shaw ensconced in its base. There was a killer on the loose and its thirst knew no bounds and I was certain now that Nat had also suffered its vengeance. I would have stopped the car and turned around and checked on my certainty myself except that whoever had done it was still there, waiting, waiting for us.

"I want to go someplace where no one has ever heard of the Reddmans," Caroline said, breaking her long quiet. "Someplace where I can drink wine all day and let my hair grow greasy and no one would ever notice because the whole countryside is full of greasy drunks. France maybe."

"Last time it was Mexico."

"Well this time I mean it." She took out a cigarette, lit it with my car's lighter; the air in my Mazda grew quickly foul. "It's all gotten way out of control. I'm through."

"What about the one good thing in the Reddman past you've been looking for? How can you give up before you find it?"

"It's not there. There's nothing but cold there. All I want is to get as far from it all as I possibly can."

"It's getting worse, Caroline. Whatever is happening to your family is growing more and more brutal."

"Let it. I'm getting out."

"So that's your answer, right, run away. Sure, why not? Running is what you're best at. Quit on our investigation just like you quit on your movie."

"Who told you that?"

"Kendall."

"She talks too much."

"You have your story pat, don't you? A happy childhood, a loving home. If something went wrong in your life then it could only be because you were a failure, unworthy of the love of your mother, your father, of Harrington. That's why you trashed your movie before it was finished, why you flit from interest to interest, from bed to bed. You do everything you can to maintain your comfortable self-image of failure. It's the one thing you truly can control. 'Look at the way I branded my flesh, Mommy. Aren't I a screw-up?'"

"France, I think. Definitely France."

"What then could be more terrifying than learning that maybe it's your family that is screwed up to hell, that maybe your home wasn't so loving, that maybe you're not to blame for everything after all. What could be more terrifying than realizing that success or even love might actually be possible for you."

"Give it a rest, Victor."

"Look, I don't want to find the answers more than you do. I was doing just fine before you came along. You're the one who says she needs saving. The answers we're finding could give you what you need to save yourself, but you have to do some of the work too. You tell me it's hard, well, sweetheart, life is hard. Grow the fuck up."

"Hide out in France with me, Victor."

I thought about it for a moment, thought about all I had wanted at the start of everything and suddenly I felt a great swelling of bitterness. "It must be nice to have enough money to run from your life."

She took a deep drag from her cigarette. "Trust me, Victor, it's no easy thing being born rich."

"Sure," I said. "It's hard work, but the pay is great."

"You don't know."

"You're right about that."

"Come to France with me."

"What about the lawsuit?"

"Screw the lawsuit."

"We're so close to figuring it out."

"Is that what it's all been about? The lawsuit? Is everything we've gone through together just that?"

I glanced at her cool face in the green glow of the dashboard's light. What I noticed just then was how childlike she was. "I like you, Caroline, I care for you and I worry about you, but neither of us ever had any illusions."

After ten minutes of silence, which is a heavy load of silence, she simply said, "I have some things to pick up at your place, Victor, and then, please, just take me home."

I parked on Spruce, not far from my apartment. I took my pack from the car and Caroline and I walked together up the dark street. In the vestibule, while I was unlocking the front door, I sniffed and raised my head and sniffed again.

"Do you smell that?"

"It smells like a garbage dump on fire," she said.

Acrid, and deep, like the foul odor of burning tires. I opened the door and stepped inside. The smell grew.

"What is that?" I said. "It's like someone forgot to turn off a stovetop."

As we climbed the stairs the stench worsened. It was strongest outside my door. I went on a bit and sniffed the next doorway.

"Dammit, it's my apartment."

With fumbling fingers I tried unsuccessfully to jam the key into my lock, tried again, finally got it in, twisted hard. I felt the bolt slide. I grabbed the knob, turned it, and threw open the door. Smoke billowed, with a fetor that turned my stomach. I flicked on the light. The air was hazy with the noxious smoke and through the haze I could see that my apartment had been trashed, tables overturned, a bureau emptied, cushions from the couch thrown about. I dropped my pack upon the mess and rushed around the room's bend to search for the fire in the kitchen. When I made it halfway through the living room and finally had a clear view of the dining room table I stopped dead.

Peter Cressi was sitting at the table, leaning back calmly in the miasma, the metal box we had exhumed from Charity Reddman's grave in front of him on the red Formica tabletop. Coiled on top of the metal box was a fat black cat. One of Cressi's hands was casually scratching the fur along the cat's back, the other was holding an absurdly large gun.

"We was wondering when you was gonna get back here, Vic. I mean what kind of host are you? No matter how hard we looked, we couldn't find yous liquor."

Caroline rushed out from behind me. "Victor," she

said, "What is it? What?" and that's all she said before she
stopped, just behind me, so that Cressi, had he wanted to,
with that gun and a half of his, could have taken us both
out with one shot.

"Well, look who's with Vic," said Cressi. "Isn't this
convenient? We was looking for you too, sweetheart."

The sight of Cressi pointing that gun at me was arrest-
ing enough, but it wasn't he alone that had chilled my
blood to viscid. Sitting next to him, elbows on the table, a
small pile of ashes resting before him on the Formica like
a charred sacrifice, was the source of the nauseating
smoke polluting my apartment. It was an old man with
clear blue eyes, hairy ears, a stogie the size of a
smokestack smoldering between his false teeth.

Calvi.

49

"CALVI," I SAID.

"Who was you expecting?" said Calvi, the cigar remaining clamped between his teeth as he spoke. "Herbert Hoover?"

He was a thin wiry man with bristly gray hair and hollowed cheeks and a bitter reputation for violence. The word on Calvi was he talked too damn much, even with that voice scarred painful and rough by decades of rancid tobacco, but Calvi didn't only talk when there was a more efficient way to communicate. Once, so the story went, he had drilled a man who was skimming off the skim, drilled him literally, with a Black & Decker and a three-quarter-inch bit, drilled him in the skull until the blood spurted and the dumb chuck admitted all and pled for mercy. The downtown boys, they laughed for weeks about that one, but after that one no one dared again to skim the skim from Calvi.

"I heard you called," said Calvi. "What was it that you wanted, Vic?"

I glanced at Cressi, pointing his gun now at my face, and realized in a flash that I had been all wrong about everything, had trusted wrong and suspected wrong and now was face to face with the man who was behind all the violence that had been unleashed in the past few weeks. Calvi had returned to Philadelphia to wrest control of the city from Raffaello and the one man who could pull me out of what it was I had fallen into, Earl Dante, knew exactly how wrong I had been.

"I just called to say hello," I said. "See how the weather was down there."

"Hot," said Calvi. "Hot as hell but hotter."

"So I guess you're up just to enjoy the beautiful Philadelphia spring?"

"I always liked you, Vic," said Calvi. "I could always trust you, and you want to know why? Because I always understood your motives. You're a simple man with a simple plan. Go for the dough. The world, it belongs to simple men. I send a guy to you I know he stays stand up and does his time with his mouth shut. No question about it because you know who is paying and it ain't him, it's me. And you know what, Vic? You done never let me down."

"How's my case going?" asked Cressi. "You got it dismissed yet?"

"That was a lot of guns you were buying, Pete," I said. "And the flamethrower doesn't help. But I'm moving to suppress the tapes and whatever else I can."

"Atta boy," said Peter.

"You know why I'm here, don't you, Vic?" said Calvi.

"I think I do."

"I want to apologize about you being in the car with that thing on the expressway. It couldn't be helped. But you understand it was only business. No hard feelings, right?"

"Could I afford hard feelings right now?"

"No," said Calvi.

A gay, friendly smile spread across my face. "Then no hard feelings."

"You're exactly what the man, he meant when he said the simple will inherit the earth," said Calvi. "Let me tell you, when my turn comes, it will be very very profitable. And you, my friend, will share in those profits. Do we understand each other?"

"Yes," I said.

"So I can count on you?"

I looked at Cressi with his gun and smiled again. "It sounds like a lucrative arrangement."

"Exactly what I thought you'd say. And I'm taking that as a commitment, so there's no going back. Now I understand you've been in touch with that snake Raffaello."

"It was only because he was checking up on me after the thing with the car," I blurted. "I don't know where he is or what he is . . ."

"Shut up, Vic," said Cressi with a wave of his gun and I shut right up.

"We need to meet, Raffaello and me," said Calvi. "We need to meet and figure this whole thing out. Can you set up this meeting for us, Vic?"

"I can try."

"Good boy, Vic," said Calvi. "We're not animals. If we can avoid a war all the better."

"I think that's what he wants too," I said. "He told me he's ready to step aside as long as there's no war and his family is guaranteed safety."

"He'll turn over everything?"

"That's what he said."

"Everything?"

"So long as you give the guarantees."

Calvi took the cigar out of his mouth for a moment and stared at it and for the first time a smile cracked his face. "You hear that, Peter," he said. "It's done."

"It's too easy," said Cressi, shaking his head.

"I told you it would be easy," said Calvi. "This never was his business. He was a cookie baker before he came into it. He never had the stomach for the rough stuff. He had the stomach he would have killed me rather then let me slink off to Florida like he did. I ain't surprised he's on his knees now. You'll set up the meeting, Vic."

"Now?"

"Not yet," said Calvi. "I'll tell you when. Sit down."

"Why don't you let her go while we talk," I said, gesturing to Caroline, still standing behind me, quiet as a leg of lamb. Her face, when I looked at her, was transfixed with fear and I couldn't tell just then if she was more terrified of the sight and size of Cressi's gun or of the cat lying atop the metal box.

"She stays," said Cressi.

"We don't need her to speak to Raffaello," I said.

"She stays," said Calvi. "No more discussion. Sit down, missy. We all got to wait here some."

Cressi gestured with the gun and I pulled out two chairs from the table, one for Caroline and one for me. Carefully I placed her in the chair to the left and sat in the chair directly across from Cressi. Calvi was to our right and the metal box from Charity Reddman's grave was on the table between us. The black cat jumped off the box and high-stepped to the end of the table, sticking its nose close to Caroline's face. Her body tense and still, Caroline shut her eyes and turned her face away.

"What, missy, you don't like my cat?"

Caroline, face still averted, shook her head.

"She has a thing about cats," I said.

"It's a good cat. Come on over, Sam." The cat sniffed a bit more around Caroline and then strolled over to Calvi, who stroked it roughly beneath its neck. "I named it after a fed prosecutor who's been chasing me for years. I named it Sam, after the fed, and then took him to the vet to get his balls cut off. Very therapeutic."

Cressi laughed.

"While we're waiting," said Calvi, "maybe we can take care of some unfinished business."

Cressi leaned forward and lifted the lid off the metal box. "Where's the rest of the shit what was supposed to be inside here?"

Caroline, her face still tense with fear, looked up with surprise. "What are you talking about?"

"Whatever it is I'm talking about I'm not talking to you," snapped Cressi. "Vic knows what I'm talking about, a smart guy like him. Where's the rest of it, Vic?"

"I don't understand."

Cressi reached into his jacket and pulled out a piece of paper. "A certain party what had been paying us for our services has requested we recover this here box and its contents, which are listed right here in black and white. The photographs and documents about some trust and old pieces of diary, they're in here, all right. But the piece of paper, it lists other stuff that ain't and so maybe you know where that other stuff, it went to, Vic."

"Who's the certain party?" I asked, wondering who would be so interested in the contents of the secret box of Faith Reddman Shaw.

"Not important."

"It's important as hell."

"Give him what he wants, Vic," said a scowling Calvi, his voice ominously soft. The cat's black fur pricked up and it jumped off the table. It hopped to one of the couch cushions on the floor and curled on top of it. When it was settled it watched us with complete dispassion. "Give him the hell he wants and be done with it."

"There's a doctor's invoice of some sort," said Cressi, reading from the list.

I looked at Cressi and his gun and nodded. "All right," I said. I stood and went over to the corner and found my briefcase among the scattered contents from the closet, the case's sides slashed, its lock battered but still in place. I opened the combination and took out the invoice and handed it over.

Cressi examined it and smiled before placing it in the box. "What about some banking papers that are also missing?"

"They're not here," I said. "But I'll get them for you."

Cressi slammed the butt of his gun on the table, the noise so loud I thought the monster had gone off. Caroline inhaled a gasp at the sound of it. "Don't dick with me, Vic."

"I don't have it here. I swear."

"Where is it?"

"I'll get it for you," I said, not wanting to tell them anything about Morris.

"Go on, Peter," said Calvi, staring hard at me through the smoke of his cigar.

"A three-by-five card with certain alphanumeric strands, whatever the fuck that is."

"Also someplace else," I said.

Cressi glared at me. "What about this key it says here?"

I reached for my wallet, took out the key that had opened the breakfront drawer at the Poole house, and handed it over. Cressi examined it for a moment.

"How the fuck I know it's the right key?"

"It's the right key," I said.

"Is that it?" said Calvi.

Cressi nodded and put the list back in his jacket.

"It's very important, Vic, now that we're partners," said Calvi, "to keep this party happy. It's not so cheap making a move like we've made here. You just can't bluff your way through. Even with a cookie baker like Raffaello, you have to be ready for war, and war's expensive. This party's been our patron and we keep our patron happy. You'll get the rest of that stuff for us after the meeting."

"No problem."

"Good," said Calvi. "I think, Vic, you and me, we're going to do just fine together. You and me, Vic, we have a future."

"That's encouraging," I said. I was referring to the fact that I might actually have a future outside the range of

Cressi's gun, but Calvi smiled as if he were a recruiting
sergeant and I had just enlisted.

"You want a cigar?" said Calvi, patting at his jacket
pocket.

"No, thank you," I said as kindly as I could.

"Now we wait," said Calvi.

"Where's yous liquor?" said Cressi. "We was looking
all over for it."

"I don't have any," I said. "Just a couple beers in the
fridge."

"We already done the beers," said Cressi. He turned to
Calvi. "You want I should maybe hit up a state store?"

"Just shut up and wait," said Calvi.

Cressi twisted his neck as if trying to fracture a verte-
brae and then leaned back in silence.

"What are we waiting for?" I asked.

"It's need to know," said Calvi. "You think you need
to know?"

I shook my head.

"You're right about that," said Cressi.

And so we sat at the table, the four of us, Calvi leaning
on his elbows, his head in his hands, sucking on his stogie,
Cressi, Caroline, and I asphyxiating on the foul second-
hand smoke, none of us talking. The cat licked its fur atop
the cushion. Every now and then Calvi sighed, an old
man's sigh, like he was sitting by the television, waiting to
be called to the nursing home's evening program rather
than waiting to set up a meeting to take control of the
Philly mob. I could feel the tension in Caroline as she sat
beside me, but she was as quiet as the rest of us. I laid a
comforting hand on her knee and gave her a smile. The
silence was interrupted only by Calvi's sighs, the scrape of
a chair as we shifted our positions, contented clicks rising
from the throat of Sam the cat, the occasional rumble from
Cressi's digestive tract.

Our situation was as bleak as Veritas. Someone had

paid Calvi to kill Jacqueline and Edward and, now, to get
the contents of the box. Who? Who else had even known
that I might have it? Nat had learned we were digging. Had
he told someone? Was that the reason he was missing?
Was that the reason he was murdered, too, because he
knew about the box and someone was determined that no
one would ever know? Whom had he told about our noc-
turnal excavations? Harrington, the last Poole? Kingsley
Shaw? Brother Bobby? Which was Calvi's patron, ordering Calvi to kill Reddmans for fun and profit while building up his war chest? And why did the patron care about a
box buried in the earth many years ago by Faith Reddman
Shaw? Unless it wasn't buried by Faith Reddman Shaw.
And whoever it was, this patron had also paid to kill
Caroline, or else why would Cressi have been searching
for her, and once the bastards killed Caroline they would
have no choice, really, but to kill me too. I was the man
who knew too much. Which was ironic, really, considering
my academic career.

A peculiar sound erupted from Cressi's stomach. "I
must have eaten something," said Cressi with a weak
smile.

"It's hot down there," said Calvi, and I thought for a
moment he was referring to Cressi's stomach but he was
off on a tangent of his own. "Hot as hell but hotter. And
muggy, so there's nothing to do but sweat. What did that
snake think I was going to do, learn canasta? What am I,
an old lady? You know when they eat dinner down there?
Four o'clock. Christ, up here I was finishing lunch at
Tosca's around four o'clock and waiting for the night to
begin. At four o'clock down there they're lining up for the
early birds. They're serving early birds till as late as six,
but they line up at four. And lime green jackets. Explain to
me, Vic, sweating in a restaurant line in lime green jackets."

"I understand Phoenix has a dry heat," I said.

"White belts, white shoes, what the hell am I supposed to do down there? Golf? I tried golf, bought a set of clubs. Pings. I liked the sound of it. Ping. Went to the course, swung, the ball went sideways. Sideways. I almost killed a priest. What the hell am I doing playing golf? I went fishing once, one of them big boats. Threw up the whole way out and the whole way back. The only thing I caught was a guy on the deck behind me when a burst of wind sent the puke right into his face. That was good for a laugh, sure, but that was it for fishing. You know, I been in this business all my life. Started as a kid running errands for Bruno when he was still an underboss. You stay alive in this business, you do a few stints in the shack, your hair turns gray, you're entitled. Up here I was respected. I was feared. Down there I was a kid again, surrounded by old men with colostomy bags on their hips and old ladies looking to get laid. I was getting high school ass up here, down there ladies ten years older than me, nothing more than bags of bones held together by tumors, they're eyeing me like I'm a side of venison. They got walkers and the itch and they want to cook for me. Pasta? Sauce Bolognese? Good Italian blood sausage? Shit no. Kreplach and kishke and brust. You ever have something called gefilte fish?"

"Sure," I said.

"What's with that fish jelly that jiggles on the plate? Whatever it is, it ain't blood sausage. I hate it down there. It's hell all right, hot and steamy and the sinners they wear lime green jackets and white belts and eat pompano every night at four o'clock and play canasta and talk about hurricanes and bet on the dogs. 'Welcome to Florida,' the sign says, but it should say 'Abandon hope all of yous who fly down here.' What the hell made Raffaello think he could send me there to sweat and die?"

"So that's why you came back?" I said.

"That's right," said Calvi. "That and the money. You sure you don't want a cigar?"

I shook my head.

"Never understood why you'd drop a fin for a cigar when you could buy a perfectly good smoke for thirty-five cents."

"You got me," I said.

"I'll be right back," said Calvi, placing the cigar on the table so the end with the ash hung over the edge. He stood and hitched up his pants. "I gotta pinch a loaf."

He ambled through the living room mess and into the bathroom. The cat followed, sneaking between his legs just as Calvi shut the door on himself. As soon as we heard the first of his loud moans, the bell to my apartment rang.

"That must be them," said Cressi. "Can I just buzz them up?"

"No," I said. "You have to go down the stairs and open the vestibule door."

"What kind of shithole is this you live in, Vic?" said Cressi as he stood up and slipped the long barrel of his gun into his pants, buttoning his jacket to hide, though not very convincingly, the bulge. "And you a lawyer and all. You expecting anyone?"

"I don't think so," I said, though I wondered if maybe Morris or Beth had come by to check on me.

"Let's hope not for their sakes," said Cressi, as he started around the table and toward the door, the pistol in his pants turning his walk into a sort of waddle. He stopped for a moment and turned to us.

"Don't either of yous move or you'll piss the hell out of me."

Then he turned again and disappeared around the bend of the living room.

50

"WHAT THE HELL IS HAPPENING?" asked a frantic Caroline as soon as we were alone.

I turned to her and put my finger on her mouth and whispered. "You came to me because of my connections with the mob. Well, there's a battle going on for control of the organization and, somehow, I'm in the middle of it."

"Who are they?" she asked, whispering back. "Those two men?"

"They're the men who killed your sister and brother."

"Oh, Jesus Jesus Jesus. I'm scared. Let's get away, please."

I took hold of her and stroked her hair. "Shhhh. I'm scared, too," I said, "but it will be all right. I took care of some things."

"They knew who I was. What do they want with me?"

"I don't know," I said, lying, because I was pretty certain that what they wanted with her was for her to be dead.

"Why did he want the stuff in my grandmother's box?"

"I don't know, except maybe it's not your grandmother's box after all."

"I thought about what you said, in the car."

"That's good, Caroline, but we have a more immediate problem. We have to get you out of here."

"I know I need to change things, but it's harder than you think. You don't reorganize your life's story like you reorganize your closets. You need something to reorganize it around. What is there for me but the horrors of our past?"

I took her face in my hands and I looked at her and saw the struggle playing out on her features, but then the toilet flushed and a terror washed the struggle away with a consuming bland fear. I jumped from my chair and went to a kitchen drawer, slid it open with a jangle of stainless steel, pulled out a small paring knife. As I slammed the drawer shut I dropped the paring knife, point first, into my pants pocket. Then I went back to the table, took hold of her shoulders, and leaned over her.

"You'll have a chance to get away," I whispered. "Sometime. Keep your eyes open. Keep alert. I'll give you the sign. When I do, run. All right?"

She was staring at me, her eyes darting with panic. The water started running in the bathroom sink as Calvi washed his hands.

"All right?" I asked again.

She nodded her head.

"Now pretend to smile and be brave."

I let go of her and turned to sit on the tabletop. I was sitting casually, an arm draped over the pocket to hide the outline of the knife, when Calvi came out of the bathroom, shaking his hands. The cat ran out of the doorway ahead of him and jumped onto a cushion. Calvi looked around with suspicion. "Where's Peter?"

"My bell rang," I said. "He went to answer it."

Calvi went back to the table, sat in his seat, picked up his cigar from the edge where he had left it. He sucked deep. "Good," he said, exhaling. "They're here."

Cressi came back, not leading Morris or Beth by gunpoint, as I had feared, but with three men, apparently allies. Two I had never seen before, they wore dark pants with bulges at the ankles and silk shirts and had sharp handsome faces and slicked hair. The third I recognized for sure. The long face, the wide ears, the crumbling teeth and bottle cap glasses and black porkpie hat. It was Anton Schmidt, the human computer, who had kept Jimmy Vig's records in his head.

Anton Schmidt, his hands in his pockets and his mouth pursed open to show his rotting teeth, stopped still when he saw me. "I didn't know you were with us, Victor."

"It looks like everything's changed," I said.

"Not everything," said Anton. "The same rules, just a different opponent."

"How's your chess?"

"I'm seeing deeper into the game every day."

"Good. Maybe your rating will rise," I said.

So Anton Schmidt was now with Calvi, and might have been all along. Of all the people in that room, me included, Anton, the chess master, was by far the smartest. Calvi was more powerful than I had thought if he had Anton doing his planning. Maybe Raffaello was right to step aside.

"Everything ready, Schmidty?" asked Calvi.

"The Cubans are in, waiting for orders. I sent them over the bridge where the bus won't attract any attention. They're at a diner in New Jersey."

"They got good diners in Jersey," said Cressi. "Tell them they should try the snapper soup."

"We'll know in a few minutes," said Calvi.

Schmidt leaned over and spoke a few lines of Spanish to the two men, who nodded grimly and shot back some words of concern. Schmidt answered their questions and then turned to Calvi.

"Let's do it," said Calvi.

I had two phones in the apartment, a portable in the bedroom and one by the couch with a cord long enough to reach the table. I sat at the table with the corded phone, the line stretched taut from the outlet. Schmidt sat next to me and next to Schmidt was Calvi with the portable handset. Cressi sat across from us, his gun out of his pants and back in his hand. Caroline was sent to the bedroom, the door guarded by one of the two Cubans. Before she shut the door, Sam the cat scampered in after her. From behind the closed door we heard a shout.

"She has a thing about cats," I said.

"Make the fucking call," said Calvi.

I dialed the number I had memorized from the Rev. Custer message.

"It's Victor Carl," I said into the phone when it was answered. "Let me talk to him."

"Who?" said the voice at the other end.

"Just shut up and put him on or I'll rip off your face."

Cressi broke into a big smile. Calvi and Schmidt remained expressionless. After a few moments of dead quiet I heard his voice.

"Hello, Victor," said Raffaello. "What have you heard?"

"I've been approached about a meeting," I said flatly.

"Who? Tell me who?"

I looked over at Calvi as he listened on the portable. He nodded.

"Walter Calvi," I said.

"That bastard, that shit-smoking bastard. Is Cressi with him like we thought?"

Calvi nodded.

"Yes," I said.

"Who else, Victor? Tell me who else."

Calvi shook his head.

I looked at Anton Schmidt and said, "I don't know who else. That's all I've seen."

"Dammit, that bastard. How strong are they, Victor, tell me."

Calvi nodded. I looked at the Cubans and thought of the bus in New Jersey. "Strong," I said. "They're ready for a war."

Raffaello sighed into the phone. "Did you tell them my offer?"

"Yes."

Calvi looked at me and mouthed, "I want full control."

"They've agreed to your proposal so long as you turn over full control," I said.

"Of course. That is what this is all about."

Calvi mouthed something else. "And you'll have to leave the city," I said.

"I understand. But he agrees no reprisals, no war, and he'll guarantee my safety and my daughter's safety?"

"Absolutely," I said.

"All right. When is this meeting to take place?"

I put my hand over the mouthpiece as Calvi conferred with Schmidt. "Tomorrow morning," said Schmidt. "Five-thirty. Before the city awakes."

I relayed the message.

"Fine," said Raffaello. "That's fine. We'll meet at Tosca's."

Calvi shook his head. "The old RCA building in Camden," said Schmidt into my ear. I repeated it into the phone.

"I'm too old to go to Camden," said Raffaello. "No. It must be on this side of the river. Packer Avenue Marine Terminal, South Gate."

Anton Schmidt shook his head and whispered in my ear. "The Naval Shipyard," I said. "Pier Four."

"That's interesting," said Raffaello. "Good neutral territory, the Naval Shipyard. But how are we going to get in? There are guards."

"The Penrose Avenue gate will be open and unguarded," said Schmidt.

"That Calvi he's a rat-fucking bastard," said Raffaello after he heard what I relayed, "but at least it's not one of those Young Turks who don't respect the traditions. Calvi I can trust to keep his word. Tell him tomorrow morning, five-thirty at the Naval Shipyard, Pier Four, is acceptable. Tell him I will leave town that afternoon. Tell him after all these years the trophy, it is finally his."

"So," said Calvi after Raffaello had hung up, "it's exactly as you said, Vic. We're all going to make so much money it will bring tears to our eyes." He turned to Schmidt. "Is that the place we wanted?"

Schmidt nodded. "Get me a piece of paper."

I found him a yellow pad and Schmidt quickly sketched a pier sticking out from a straight shoreline.

"This is Pier Four," said Anton Schmidt. "It reaches out into the Delaware River. Docked on either side of the pier are two old Navy ships, mothballed for future use. Between the two ships is a giant hammerhead crane. We'll have our men here, here, and here." He placed X's on either side of the pier, where the ships would be, and an X in the middle of the pier, where the hammerhead crane sat. "If we set up the meeting so you confront Raffaello here," he said, placing two circles on the pier between the crane and the shore, "then during the whole of the exchange you'll both be covered."

"Who will be with the Cubans?" asked Calvi.

"Domino and Sollie Wags will be on the deck of this ship here, Termini and Tony T will be on the ship there, and on the crane will be Johnny Roses, keeping an eye on everyone." These were all names of minor mobsters, generally known as the most vicious and impatient of the Young Turks, who had apparently switched allegiances to Calvi to hasten their rise. "With our men set up like I say, we'll dominate the center."

"That's good. I don't want no trouble until I get what I came for."

"Raffaello's a man of his word," I said. "There won't be trouble."

Calvi looked at me and sucked deep from his cigar and let loose a stream of smoke that billowed into my face, leaving me in a spasm of coughs. "You're dead right about that, Vic," he said. "There won't be no trouble."

"The crossfire here," said Anton, "could wipe out a division."

"There won't be no trouble at all," said Calvi. "Now we need a signal, so everyone's on board at the same instant. What's Spanish for 'now'?"

"*Ahora*," said Anton, rolling the "r" like a native.

"A-whore-a," said Calvi. "Good. That's the signal. A-whore-a. When I say a-whore-a I want all hell to break loose."

Schmidt turned to the Cubans and gave them instructions in Spanish. The only word I caught was *ahora*, a number of times, *ahora* from Schmidt and then *ahora* repeated by the Cubans with smiles on their faces.

"I'll call Johnny Roses on the cell phone," said Schmidt, "and set it all up. They'll be on site in an hour."

"Good work, Anton," said Calvi. "We're going to do great things together. You're going to be my man in Atlantic City. Together we're going to rule the boardwalk."

Schmidt nodded, a small smile breaking through those pursed lips. Then he went off to the corner with his cell phone.

"What about the girl?" I said.

"Forget about the girl," said Calvi. "We're taking care of her. She'll stay right here while we wait, what could be safer?"

What indeed? I stood up and headed away from the table.

"Where you going?" asked Cressi.

"I'm going to the pot, do you mind?"

"Well, hurry up, 'cause I gotta drop a load myself."

I walked across the living room, the dark stares of the Cubans following me, and stepped into the bathroom. As soon as I closed the door I locked it and dropped down to the seat on the toilet and shook for a bit. Then I stood and went to the sink and ran the water cold and washed my face and let it tingle for a moment before I dried it with a towel. I took the towel I had just used and stretched it across the crack at the bottom of the door. There was a window in the bathroom, and I thought for a moment of climbing out and jumping, but the window was small and the fall was three stories and Caroline was still imprisoned with Sam the cat in my bedroom. So what I did instead of climbing out the window was reach for the light switch, turn it off, and then click it on three quick times, on again for three longer times, and then three short times again. On the last short burst of light I heard a banging on the door that scared the absolute hell out of me.

"Get the fuck out of there," yelled Cressi through the door.

"What's the matter?" I shouted back.

"I told you I gotta go."

"Give me a break. I'm still on the pot."

It was a good thing just then I was already in the bathroom.

51

THE PHILADELPHIA NAVAL SHIPYARD rises rusted and desolate on the southern tip of Philadelphia, a flat slab of land that reaches out like a claw into the confluence of the Schuylkill and Delaware rivers. Surrounding the yard, like funeral pyres, refinery stacks shoot the flames of burnoff into the sky, scorching the air with the thick rotted smell of sulfur. Thirty thousand blue-collar heroes used to march to work each day into the yard, bringing their hard hats and lunch buckets and cheerful profanities, before the government closed it down and sent the work to Charleston or Norfolk or Puget Sound and the workers to unemployment. Now the furnaces are cool and the machine shops quiet and the dry docks empty of all but the pigeons, who leave their marks like avian Jackson Pollocks on the wide flat-bottomed gashes that once held the proudest ships in the fleet: the *Arizona*, the *Missouri*, the *Tennessee*. There was one last gasp for the naval yard, when a German ship-builder looked to set up shop there, but the governor played it badly and the German took his toys and went away and the shipyard now is left to rust.

We were in a black Lincoln, driving south on Penrose Avenue, toward the bridge that would take us to the airport, but instead of going straight over the bridge we turned left, onto a deserted four-lane road that I had passed a hundred times before, never knowing where it went. Well now I knew; it went to the rear entrance of the

Naval Shipyard. I was sitting in the middle on the front bench of the Lincoln, with Cressi driving and Calvi beside me. Wedged into the back were Anton and Caroline, with the two Cubans at either window. I had hoped there would be a chance for Caroline to bolt as we made our way from the apartment early in the morning but Cressi, his gun back in his pants, hovered as protectively over her as if she were his sister at a frat party, so Caroline was still with us when we reached the car. Cressi literally threw her in the backseat and put the Cubans on either side as guards.

We approached the rear gate. It was unguarded and seemingly shut tight. A sign warned against unauthorized entry and cited the applicable provisions of the Internal Security Act. Another sign warned that the site was patrolled by Military Working Dogs. Cressi stopped the car just in front of the gate and Calvi stepped out. He walked to the chain that held the gate closed and gave the chain a yank. It unraveled with a slinking hiss. Calvi slid the gate open and Cressi drove us through. While Calvi shut the gate behind us and got back in the car I looked out the side and saw the signs to the now abandoned Navy Brig.

Slowly we drove along the shipyard's deserted streets, littered with empty work sheds, unused warehouses, desolate barracks. None of us said a word as we drove. Whatever work was still being done at the yard hadn't yet begun for the day and whatever guards were supposed to have been patrolling with the Military Working Dogs had conveniently chosen some other beat to pound. We passed a tractor-trailer parked by the road, its back open, the trailer empty. We passed four garbage trucks parked one after the other, their cabs dark. We drove beneath a soaring elevated section of Interstate 95 and then over a bridge, with giant green towers to lift the span vertically and allow approaching ships to enter. As we passed over the bridge, to the left we could see the reserve basin, holding dozens of mothballed gray-painted ships, frigates and cruisers and supply ships and tankers, a veritable fleet. I felt just then as intrusive as a Soviet spy during the Cold War.

We drove straight until we reached a huge deserted dry dock, surrounded by green and yellow mobile cranes, and turned left, past a vacant parking lot, past shuttered warehouses, the streets and the lots all criss-crossed with railroad tracks. As we drove I looked to my right and saw a startling sight, battleships, a pair of battleships, huge and empty, their sixteen-inch guns lowered to horizontal. I could just make out the name of the one closest to shore: *Wisconsin*. Past still more warehouses and then another dry dock, the sides of this one not vertical but tiered and its bottom red with rust. At the edge of this dry dock we turned right and stopped the car by a long low building and waited. In the Delaware River, right in front of us, were two naval cargo ships, the sharp edges of their prows pointing straight at our car. I didn't know what we were waiting for, but I knew enough not to ask. The windshield steamed over from our breaths. We sat in silence until the cell phone in Schmidty's jacket beeped. He opened it, listened for a moment, and shut it again.

"It's all in place," he said.

"Time to claim the trophy," said Calvi.

Four car doors opened and we climbed out of the Lincoln. Cressi took his huge gun from his belt, slapped open the cylinder, closed it again with a flick of his wrist. Anton pulled a small semiautomatic from his boot and chambered a round. The two Cubans unstrapped assault weapons from beneath their pant legs, flipped opened the skeleton metal stocks, and locked them in place. They both took two long clips from their pockets, each fitting one into his weapon and the second into his belt. Calvi reached into the glove compartment of his car and took out a revolver, checking it carefully before sticking it into the pocket of his long black raincoat. The sound of oiled metal clicked about us like a wave of wasps.

"Do I get anything?" I asked.

"You ever shoot a gun before, Vic?" asked Calvi.

"No," I said.

Cressi snickered.

"Then forget about it," said Calvi. "I don't need you shooting my foot off. The girl stays in the car and I want one of the Cubans with her. She is not to leave the car under any circumstances, is that understood?"

Caroline looked at me with panic and I tried to calm her with a quiet motion of my hand. Anton gave directions in Spanish and one of the Cubans took hold of her and pushed her back into the car.

"What are you going to do with the girl?" I asked.

"We're taking care of her," said Calvi, slamming her door and shucking his shoulders.

"Maybe I should be the one to guard her," I suggested.

Cressi stared at me for a long moment. "Don't go weak on me now, Vic. You're coming. It's time for you to earn your place in the new order of things. Got it?"

I nodded sheepishly.

"Good," said Calvi. "Where or whether you stand at the end it's up to you. Got it?" He turned to face the others. "You boys ready?"

There were nods and more well-oiled clicks.

"Then let's get it done."

We stepped into the street and lined up five wide before we started walking toward the cargo ships. Anton Schmidt, with his thick glasses and his porkpie hat cocked low, then Walter Calvi, with his bristly hair and his long black coat, then me, trembling uncontrollably, then Peter Cressi, his Elvisine features tight and his eyes lethal, and then the Cuban, his face impassive and the assault rifle calmly held in front of him like a tennis racket at the ready. Side by side we walked.

"What's going to happen to the girl?" I said to Calvi as we continued to walk.

"Forget about the girl, we're taking care of her."

"It's over. You don't need to kill her any more."

"What are you, an idiot?" he said just as we were about to reach the river. "I told you we was taking care of her, not killing her. Her father is paying us to protect her, which is what the hell we're doing."

I didn't have time to respond to that revelation before we reached the wharf at the river and wheeled about in line to the left so that, still five wide, we were walking now toward Pier Four. I glanced to the side and saw the Lincoln, saw the Cuban leaning against the front fender, watching us go, saw Caroline's silhouette inside, saw it all before a wall from a warehouse blocked the view. I turned my head and all thoughts about Kingsley Shaw and his pact with Calvi fled as I saw what lay ahead of us.

Aircraft carriers. Two of them. As big and as imposing as anything I had ever seen before. Aircraft carriers. Great gray fortresses sitting heavy and still in the water, their high flat flight decks towering over the pier between them. Aircraft carriers. Jesus. When Anton Schmidt had mentioned two old ships on either side of the pier I had imagined two little gray putt-putts, not aircraft carriers. They loomed ever more huge as we walked closer to the pier and I could make out the names painted on their gray paint. *Forrestal*, read the one closest to us, its sharp prow and flat deck pointing toward the shore, and the ship docked on the far side of the pier, its bow pointing to the center of the river, was the *Saratoga*. I seemed to remember something about the supercarrier *Forrestal* burning off the coast of North Vietnam, killing more than a hundred sailors, and now here it was. The *Forrestal* and the *Saratoga*. I was still gawking when we reached the pier and wheeled around once again, this time to our right, maintaining our line as we began our walk onto Pier Four itself.

The two aircraft carriers rose huge on either side of us, their flight decks reaching beyond the cement surface of the pier, and right between them was the massive hammerhead crane, rising twice as high as the carriers' flight towers, the crane standing between them like a guard, rusted and decrepit, more than twelve stories high with a huge red-and-white trailer on top. Parked before the crane was a white Cadillac, its side turned toward us. And just in front of the car, standing in the shadows of the great naval vessels, four men all in a row, waiting.

We kept walking, straight down the pier, toward the four men and the Cadillac. I looked up at the jutting decks of the aircraft carriers on either side of us. There was nothing to see. Anton Schmidt's ambush was well hidden. As we moved closer I could identify the four figures before us. Enrico Raffaello stood at the middle of the car, a black cape around the shoulders of his tan suit, leaning on a cane gripped in his left hand, a black leather satchel in his right. On one side of him was Lenny Abromowitz, Raffaello's driver, sartorially splendid in yellow pants and a green plaid jacket. On the other side of Raffaello, in a black suit, standing erect as a pole and perfectly at ease, was Earl Dante. Beside Earl Dante was his weightlifter bodyguard.

When we were fifteen yards away from Raffaello, Anton Schmidt told us to stop and we did. We stared at them and they stared at us and something ugly hung in the air between us.

"Buon giorno, Gualtieri," said Raffaello in a voice that echoed from the gray metal hulls of the boats surrounding us. "I'm saddened that it is you, old friend, who has betrayed me."

"You should never have sent me off to Florida," said Calvi.

"I thought you'd like the ocean," said Raffaello. "I thought the salt air would act as a balm on your anger."

"It's hot. Hot as hell but hotter. And you know when

they eat dinner down there? Aaah, forget about it. Don't get me started on Florida. Is that it in the bag?"

"As I promised."

"I will care for it with honor and devotion. I want you to know, Enrico, that I have nothing but respect for you."

"That is why you shoot up my car on the Schuylkill Expressway and start a war against me?"

"It was business, Enrico, only that. Nothing more. Nothing personal."

Raffaello stared hard at him for a moment and then he shrugged. "Of course. I understand."

"I knew you would," said Calvi. "You are a man of honor. Lenny, your performance in the car after that thing on the expressway was exemplary. It would be a privilege to have you drive for me."

"Thank you, Mr. Calvi," said Lenny in his thick nasal voice, "but I got granddaughters living in California, not far from Santa Anita. If you'll allow, I'll retire along with Mr. Raffaello."

"As you wish," said Calvi. "Get the bag, Anton."

Anton, with his hands in the pockets of his long black leather jacket, walked slowly toward Raffaello. As he approached, the weightlifter, his pinched nose flaring, took a step forward. Dante put a restraining hand on the weightlifter's arm and he stepped back. Anton halted before Raffaello and stared at him for a moment. Then his gaze dropped with embarrassment. Anton reached down for the black leather satchel in Raffaello's hand. Raffaello stuck out his jaw and shook his head even as he let go. Anton Schmidt, with bag in hand, backed away a few steps before turning around. He brought the black bag straight to Calvi. Without looking inside, Anton opened it.

Calvi examined the contents for a moment before reaching into the bag and pulling out what at first looked to be a small metallic sculpture two feet high. The metal was dented and scratched but it had been cleaned and polished so that it gleamed even in the morning shadow. The dark wooden base of the object supported a large brass cup atop of which crouched the figure of a man, his front knee bent, his rear leg straight, his right arm hoisting a shiny metal ball. A bowling ball? I realized only then that this was a bowling trophy. Calvi held the trophy high, examining it as if it were a priceless jewel, and his face glowed with a satisfaction as bright as the polished brass. Then he placed the trophy back into the leather bag. Anton closed it. With the black satchel tightly in his grip, Anton regained his position at the end of our line.

Calvi took a cigar and a gold lighter from his inside jacket pocket. He flicked to life a flame and sucked it into the tobacco until a plume of smoke was born. "And so it is done," he said.

"I have a home in Cape May," said Raffaello. "I was planning to retire there and spend the last years of my life painting the ocean in all four of its seasons."

Calvi sucked on his cigar for a moment before saying, "Too close."

Raffaello nodded and gave a grudging smile. "I understand. You need freedom from my influence. You are showing your wisdom as a leader already, Gualtieri. Maybe I'll go to Boca Raton, in your blessed Florida."

"Too close," said Calvi.

"I have relatives in Sedona, Arizona. The desert too can be magnificent on canvas."

"Too close."

"Yes," said Raffaello, nodding again. "This country is maybe too small for us together. I have not been to Sicily since I was a boy. It is time I return. The light there, I remember, was unearthly beautiful."

Calvi took another suck at his cigar and let the vile smoke out slowly. "Too close."

"Tell me, Gualtieri. What about Australia?"

"Too close."

Raffaello leaned toward Calvi and squinted his eyes as if peering at a strange vision. "Yes, now I see. Now I understand fully."

"You should have killed me when you had the chance, Enrico," said Calvi. He took a step forward and raised his arms and shouted as if in invocation to the heavens, "A-whore-a!"

I cringed from the fusillade I expected to thunder down upon the four men and the Cadillac but instead of thunder there was a towering silence.

Calvi looked up to the decks of the carriers, first to his left then to his right, again raised his arms and shouted, "A-whore-a!"

Nothing.

Calvi turned to Anton, who shrugged. Peter Cressi, next to me, stepped back and stared up. The Cuban looked around, dazed.

"Now, you idiots!" shouted Calvi. "Now!"

A sound, a dragging scraping sound, came from the flight deck of the *Saratoga* to our left and when we looked up we saw someone, finally, but he wasn't standing, he was falling, slowly it seemed, twisting in the air like a drunken diver, spinning almost gracefully as he fell until his body slammed into the cement surface of the pier with a dull, lifeless thud, punctuated by the sudden cracking of bones.

Another scraping to the right and a body rolling off the deck of the *Forrestal*, like a child down a hill, rolling down down, arms flailing, legs splitting, back arching from the fall and then the cracking thud, followed by another, softer sound from the body returning to the pier after its bounce. And even before that second soft sound reached us with all its portent, another scraping and another body falling, the feet revolving slowly to the sky and the head dropping until its dive was stopped by the urgency of the pier and this time there was no bounce.

From the left another body, from the right another, this one hitting not cement but water, and from the hammerhead crane behind the Cadillac still another, all falling lifeless to the street, with thuds and cracks like chicken bones being broken and sucked of their marrow, or into the river with quiet splashes, and soon it was raining bodies on Pier Four and in the middle of this storm of the macabre, Raffaello, still leaning on his cane, said in a soft voice that cut like the tone of a triangle through the strains of death, "You're right, Gualtieri. I should have killed you."

Suddenly a pop came from the hammerhead crane behind the Cadillac and the Cuban's throat exploded in blood and he collapsed to the cement like a sack of cane sugar. Before I could recover from the sight another shot cracked through the sound of breaking bodies and Anton Schmidt lay sprawled on the pier beside Calvi, the black satchel still gripped in his pale hand.

After the two shots the sounds of falling corpses and breaking bones subsided and there was a moment of silence on Pier Four.

Calvi reached a hand into his raincoat before shrugging. "Maybe the thing on the expressway, it was a bit much, hey, Enrico?"

"You could never have handled the trophy, Gualtieri," said Raffaello. "You're too small. You're a midget. Even on top a mountain you'd still be a midget. But think of it this way, you greedy dog. Whatever hell we're sending you to, at least it's not Florida."

Before Calvi could pull the pistol out of the raincoat, gunfire erupted from the *Saratoga* and the *Forrestal* and the crane and Calvi's chest writhed red as if a horde of vile stinging insects were struggling to escape the corpse as it fell.

I couldn't even register all that was happening right next to me on the pier before I felt an arm wrap with a jerk around my throat and a gun press to my head. The arm tightened and I was pulled backward.

Peter Cressi, his breath hot and fast in my ear, shouted, "You take me then you're also taking Vic."

I was so stunned by the maneuver it took me a moment to realize I couldn't breathe. I started yanking at the arm around my throat but it was like steel.

"Pietro, Pietro," said Raffaello, shaking his head. "You never were the brightest, Pietro."

"He's a lawyer," shouted Dante. "A fucking lawyer. You think you can threaten us by taking as a hostage a lawyer?"

Cressi stopped backing up. The arm around my throat tightened. I could feel the blackness starting to expand in my brain even as the gun barrel left my temple and pointed at the Cadillac. I stopped scrabbling at the arm and went limp as I reached into my pants pocket and gripped the handle of the pairing knife. With a last burst of conscious energy I pulled it out and jabbed it as hard as I could into the forearm squeezing my neck.

There was a scream, whose I wasn't then sure, and I dropped to the pavement, grappling at my throat and letting out a constricted wheeze as the scream raced away from me. Then there were two shots and the whine of angry bees over my head. The screaming suddenly stopped. I heard still another thud of death and the scrape of Peter Cressi's monster gun skidding freely along the cement of Pier Four.

On my knees, on the cement, my hands still at my throat, I looked up and saw Earl Dante, smiling his evil smile, pointing a gun straight at my head, the smoke still curling upward from the barrel in a narrow twist. And as if that sight wasn't scary enough, from out of the corner of my eye I saw a dead man rising.

52

IT WAS ANTON SCHMIDT, rising to his knees, still holding onto the black leather bag with one hand, feeling around the cement of the pier for his glasses with the other. I stared at him in amazement, waiting for a bullet to take him down again as he found his glasses and then his hat and stood, dusting himself off. His thick glasses finally on, he looked around and saw me kneeling on the cement, with Dante's gun trained at my face. He prudently backed away.

"I received a call last night on my private number," said Raffaello. "It was from a Morris something-or-other."

I started to yammer about Calvi coming at me in my apartment and my having no choice but to go along when Raffaello silenced me with his words.

"You gave my private number to a stranger," he said softly. "You involved a stranger in our business."

I pressed my palms to the ground and pushed myself to standing. "Morris is absolutely trustworthy," I said. "I would trust him with my life."

"That's exactly what you did," said Raffaello.

I almost sagged back to the ground with fear before I saw Raffaello smile and Dante lower his gun.

"This Morris person," said Raffaello, "he told me that you had signaled him that this meeting was a betrayal. That was very brave of you to get out such a signal. As you can tell, I had matters already well in hand." He nodded toward Anton Schmidt. "But still, such loyalty as you have shown, it touches my heart. Of course Earl, he is disappointed. He so wanted to kill you."

Dante shrugged as he put away his gun.

"What happened here never happened," said Raffaello.

"It's a bit messy for that, isn't it?" I said, gesturing to the street of corpses.

"It will be taken care of. You are to leave now. Our agreement is satisfied. Simply finish what you must finish and then you and Earl will meet to settle what needs to be settled and then you are free of us. Word of this may get out, Victor, but let's hope not from you, or Earl will no longer be disappointed."

He turned weakly toward the car. I noticed now that Lenny was holding onto his arm, as if even simply standing for Raffaello was a struggle. Anton Schmidt, with the black leather bag, and Dante and the weightlifter walked around the car. The doors opened and they entered the Cadillac while Raffaello was still maneuvering toward his door. I hadn't realized before how serious his injury had been from the firefight on the Schuylkill. It wouldn't be long before the trophy passed to Dante. Well, he could have it.

Just as Raffaello was about to step into the car he stopped, and turned again toward me. "Your friend, this Morris," said Raffaello. "He seemed an interesting man. It is a precious thing to have somebody who you trust so completely. Maybe someday I will meet this friend. I suspect we have much in common. Do you know if he paints?"

"I don't, actually."

"Ask him for me," said Raffaello before dropping into his seat in the car. Lenny closed the door behind him, entered the car himself, and started the engine. The Cadillac turned toward me, wheeled past, and slowly left Pier Four.

I followed it out with my eyes and then, for the first

time since we began our walk down Pier Four, I thought
about Caroline in the car with that Cuban. I started running.

Off the pier I turned left and sprinted to the dry dock
where I turned right and ran along its edge to where we
had left the car and then bit by bit I slowed myself down
until I stopped and spun in frustration.

I spit out an obscenity.

The four garbage trucks that I had seen parked on the
side of the road with their cabs empty now passed me by
and turned left at the wharf on their way to Pier Four, their
cabs no longer empty, men in overalls hanging onto the
backs. The cleanup was about to begin, but that wasn't
what had set me to cursing.

What had set me to cursing was that the black Lincoln
that should have been parked right there where I stood was
gone.

53

"PSSSST."

I twisted around.

"Psssst. Victor. Over here."

It came from down the way a bit, from behind one of the green and yellow cranes that tended to the dry dock. I walked cautiously toward the sound.

"Victor. You can't know how relieved I am to see your *tuchis*, Victor." Morris Kapustin stepped out from behind the crane. "Such shooting I haven't heard since the war. I was so worried about you. What was it that was happening there?"

"Where's Caroline, Morris?"

"I left her with the car, of course. With Beth. How was I to know what it was that was happening, who was shooting who or what?"

When I came up to him I didn't stop to say anything more, I just reached down and gave him a huge hug.

"Couldn't you maybe just thank me instead of this hugging business," said Morris, still tight in my grip. "Me, I'm not the new man they are all talking about."

"You saved my life."

"I did, yes. But such is my job and really, really, it wasn't much. Just a phone call and following such a car as that through the gate, it really wasn't much. It was your friend, Miss Beth, who did most of it. I gave her the job of watching your apartment. It was getting late and I was tired and I needed some pudding. Rosalie, mine wife Rosalie, she made for me last night some tapioca. So Beth is the one you should be hugging. Now let go already, Victor, before I get a hernia."

I released him and looked down to the wharf, where the garbage trucks had disappeared on their way to the pier. "This is a dangerous place to stay."

"This way," he said, leading me across a street and through an alleyway between warehouses. "I hid the car as best I could."

"What about the man who was with Caroline?" I asked.

"What was I to do? I didn't know what I was to do so what I did is I put him in the trunk. I figured later we'll figure out what is to be done with him."

"But he had an automatic assault rifle."

"Yes, well, a rifle in the hand it is powerful, but not as powerful as a gun at the head, no? So the rifle, now, it is in the river and the man he is in the trunk."

"Then let's get the hell out of here," I said.

The Lincoln sat in a small parking area behind a deserted factory building, the engine still running. Morris's battered gray Honda rested beside it. Caroline and Beth were leaning together on the side of the Lincoln. When Beth saw me she ran up to me and hugged me and I hugged back.

"Are you all right?"

"I think so."

"What happened?"

"I survived is what happened. And we're going to need to find ourselves a new clientele."

I looked over to Caroline, still leaning on the car, looking at me, her arms wrapped so tight against her chest it was a wonder she could breathe.

"How is she?" I asked softly.

"Shaken," said Beth. "Tired. Mute."

I let go of Beth and walked hesitantly up to Caroline.

She looked at me for a long moment and then took two steps forward and put her arms around my neck and kissed me.

"Is it over?" she asked in a voice as soft as a whisper.

"That part at least."

"What now?"

"I have something more to show you, back at the apartment."

"I'm still shaking."

"Just this one thing more."

"I haven't slept."

"It's back at my apartment."

"Let's just pretend it's over, everything is over. Please?"

She looked at me with pleading eyes but I just shook my head. I didn't tell her just then what was most pressing on my mind, not there, in the middle of the Naval Shipyard, with the bodies being thrown into the garbage trucks from a pier just a few hundred yards away. I didn't tell her what Calvi had said about her father, how he was Calvi's patron, the one who had paid for Jacqueline's death and for Edward's death and for the retrieval of the box and for her protection. I didn't tell her that, not there, not yet, and I wasn't sure I ever would. I just told her we needed to see something at my apartment and that she should get into the car.

Morris had hot-wired the Lincoln's engine, which was why it was still running. He and Beth had followed us to the Naval Shipyard in Morris's Honda but it was Caroline and I who followed Morris and Beth out, alongside the dry docks, back across the lift bridge that forded the mouth of the reserve basin, under I-95 and through the gate to Penrose Avenue. Morris took a right onto Penrose and then another right onto Pattison and we followed that to the Spectrum, where the Flyers win and the Sixers lose. Morris stopped the Honda right in front and I stopped behind him. The sign said "TOW AWAY ZONE," which was fine by me. Let the car sit in a police lot while they tried to figure out what had happened to its owner. I pulled apart the wires to kill the engine, wiped down the steering wheel and door handles to obliterate my prints, and flipped up the inside lock of the trunk. The Cuban leaped out and, without saying a word, ran, arms pumping like an Olympic sprinter. Raffaello might have had different plans for him, but I didn't work for Raffaello anymore.

As soon as Caroline and I entered my apartment I opened all the windows to air the place out. The metal box still sat on the table. As I was putting the cushions back on the sofa, Calvi's black cat, Sam, leaped from underneath a lamp. I had forgotten it was still there. It no longer had a master, it no longer had a home. It stood between Caroline and me and inspected us, haughty, still, in its impoverishment.

"It's an orphan now," I said. "What are we going to do with it?"

She lit a cigarette and looked down at it for a while and then, giving it a wide berth, she walked around it and into my kitchen. I thought she might be looking for a cleaver to butcher it to death but what she took out instead was a can of tuna fish from my pantry and a carton of milk from the fridge. She set out two bowls onto the floor. The milk clumped like loose cottage cheese when she poured it but the cat didn't seem to mind. Caroline stood back and watched it eat from afar and I watched her watch it.

"I never thought I'd see you be nice to a cat," I said.

"After what we've just been through, the little monsters seem almost benign. Almost."

When we were both showered and dressed in fresh clothes, me in jeans and a white tee shirt, her in a pair of her leggings and one of my white work shirts, her face scrubbed clean of any makeup, we sat down together on the couch, leaning into each other, as if both of us at that moment needed the physical presence of the other. Thinking of her as she fed the cat, the first act of kindness I had ever seen from her, I wondered, maybe, if after everything, maybe, we might actually be right for each other. Maybe we could make whatever was going on between us work. We were both lonely, I knew that, and we were together now and maybe that was enough. And she was stinking rich, so maybe that was more than enough. We sat quietly together, not so much embracing as leaning one on the other, watching the cat as he sat near our feet and licked its paw. Then I reached down and pulled my pack onto my lap.

"This is what I wanted to show you," I said, drawing from the pack the bundles of letters I had found in the locked drawer of the breakfront. "I found these at the old Poole house."

"All right."

"I think we should read them."

"All right."

"We can do this later if you want."

"No, let's do it now."

"You're sure?"

"Yes."

"You don't want to run away anymore?"

"Of course I want to run away. I'm desperate to run away. But wherever I ran I'd still be a Reddman. I can't control who I am, can I?"

"No."

"And I can't control who wants to kill me because of it, can I?"

"Apparently not."

"It's funny what you learn at the wrong end of a gun. You told me the men who killed my sister and brother are dead, but we still don't know who hired them. Maybe the answer is somewhere in these letters."

"Maybe."

"And maybe the one good thing I've been looking for is in there, too."

"Maybe."

She waited a moment, looking down at Sam the cat, steeling herself. "Or maybe it's just more shit."

"Probably."

She waited a moment more and then, hesitantly, she reached for one of the bundles. She untied the old ribbon carefully and looked through the letters, one by one, before passing them, one by one, to me. "These are love letters," she said. "From an Emma."

"They must be from Emma Poole. Who are they to?"

"They are each addressed 'To My Love,' without a name," she said. "Listen to this. 'To feel your hand on my face, your lips on my cheek, to feel your warmth and your weight surround me, my darling, my love, my life can hold no more meaning than this. You swear your devotion over and over and I place my fingers on your lips because to speak of the future leaks the rapture from our present. Love me now, fully and completely, love me today, not forever, love me in this moment and let the future be damned.'"

I took one of the letters she had passed to me and began to read aloud. "'If we are cursed with this passion, then let the curse torch our souls until the fire consumes itself and is extinguished. I fall not into happiness with you, my beloved, for that is impossible for cursed souls such as we, but instead in your arms I rise to the transcendent ecstasy of which the great men sing and if it be necessarily short-lived than still I wouldn't treasure it any less or bargain even a minute's worth for something longer lasting but tepid to the touch.'"

She dropped the letter in her hand and picked up another. "'Glorious, glorious, glorious is your breath and your touch and the rich warm smell of you, your skin, your eyes, your scar, the power in your legs, the rosy warmth of your mouth. I want you to devour me, my love, every inch of me, I lie in bed at night and imagine it and only delirious joy comes from the imagining. Lie with me, now, this instant, wait no longer, come to me and lie with me, now, your arms around me, now, your mouth on my breasts, now, the wild smell of your hair, now, your teeth on my neck, now, devour me my love my love my love devour me now.'"

I stared at Caroline as she read the words and was not surprised to see a tear. At least some of what she was feeling I felt also. I moved closer to her and put my arm around her.

"Who are the letters to?" I asked.

"They don't say, as if she was purposefully hiding his identity. But whoever it was we know how it ended."

"Yes, we do," I said. Whomever Emma Poole had written these paeans of love to had been the one to impregnate her and desert her, to leave her alone as she nursed her dying mother while her stomach swelled.

"Get rid of them," she said as she grabbed the letters from my hand and threw them on the floor. The cat leaped away for a moment and then jumped onto the sofa next to Caroline, who barely flinched. "I can't bear to read them. I feel like a voyeur."

"These were written more than seventy years ago," I said. "It's like looking through a powerful telescope and seeing light that was emitted eons ago by stars that are already dead."

"It's not right," she said. "Whatever she felt for the man who deserted her it has nothing to do with us. The emotions were hers and hers alone. We're trespassing."

"There's another letter," I said. "It's not from Emma." I reached into the pack and pulled out the letter entitled: *To My Child on the Attainment of Majority*.

She hesitated for a moment and then took the envelope. She unwrapped the string that bound the envelope shut and pulled out a sheaf of pages written in a masculine hand. She quickly looked at the last page to find the signature.

"It's from my grandfather," she said. "It's written to my father. Why was this letter with the others?"

I shrugged my ignorance.

She read the first lines out loud. "April 6, 1923. To my child. By the time you read this I will be dead."

She looked at me and shook her head but even while she was shaking her head she trained her gaze back onto the letter and started reading again, though this time to herself. When she was finished with the first page she handed it to me and went onto the second. In that way I trailed behind her by a few minutes, as if my telescope was a few hundred light seconds farther away from the source of the dead star's light than hers, and my emotional response similarly lagged behind.

It is hard to describe the effect of that letter. It solved mysteries that spanned the century, resolved questions that were lingering in our minds, threw into even greater highlight the terrors that stalked the Reddmans and the Pooles. But even with our out-of-synch emotional responses a peculiar reaction took place between the two of us, Caroline and me, in our separate worlds, as we read the letter. Slowly we drifted apart, not just emotionally, but physically too. Where we had been leaning upon one another when we started reading the letter, our sides and legs melded as though we were trying to become one, as the words drifted through us we separated. First there was just a lessening of pressure, then a gap developed that turned into an inch and then into a foot and then into a yard and finally, while Caroline was sobbing quietly, Sam the cat curled in her lap, and I was reading the last lines and the bold signature of Christian Shaw, Caroline was leaning over one arm of the couch and I was leaning over the other, as far apart as two could be on one piece of furniture. Had the sofa's arms not been there I fear we would have tumbled away from each other until we slammed like rolling balls into opposite walls.

What caused this fierce magnetic repellence was not any great puzzle. What had come between Caroline and me so strongly in that moment was what had never been between us and the letter was the most vivid confirmation of that yet. Christian Shaw's letter to his child gave us something that was completely unexpected in this tale of deception and betrayal and murder and desertion and revenge, it gave us an unexpected burst of hope. The letter gave us hope because what Caroline Shaw had believed to be a fiction had been shown to be real, alive, transforming, redeeming. The hope was unexpected because who could have thought that in the middle of the cursed entwining of the Reddmans and the Pooles we would find, like a ruby in a mountain of manure, a transcendent and powerful love.

54

April 6, 1923

To My Child,

By the time you read this I will be dead. My death will have been a good thing for me and richly deserved, but doubtless hard on you. My father too died when I was young. He was a stern man, I've been told, a harsh man, prone to fits of violence. But as he died before I could remember anything about him, I imagine him as a fine and gentle man. I imagine him teaching me to ride. We would have hunted together. He would have given me his rifle to shoot. I imagine him finer and more gentle with me than the real man ever could have been. It is from this imagining that I feel the great gap in my life. I would not mourn him so keenly had he just once reached from his grave and slapped me on the face.

I have been the worst of scoundrels, the lowest of cowards. I take no pride in these facts, nor utter shame. It is simple truth and you should know the truth about your father. You may have learned that I was awarded a Distinguished Service Cross for my brief adventure in the army but do not be deceived as to any heroism on my part. The medal resides in the silt at the bottom of the pond beneath the Reddman estate, Veritas, where I threw it. It is home among the frog excrement and the rotting carcasses of fish. I joined the army to escape what I had made of my life. Do not think that war is glamorous or good, child, but I welcomed it as a friend for what it was, another way to die.

In May of 1918 I led a counterattack from a trench near a village called Cantigny. It was raining and fog was rising. The muffled sounds of war were unbearably close even before the Germans attacked. It was our first battle. The Germans advanced in a wave of ferocity and we beat them back with rapid fire. It was a magnificent and ugly thing to see. Young German men fell and cried out from the mud where they fell and we maintained our fire. Then the runner brought orders for the counterattack.

I wasted no time. I was first over the top. How many trailed my wake and died I cannot know. Shells with a soft sickly whistle dropped and fell gently to the ground. The fog rose thick and green. My eyes burned. My lungs boiled. The Germans we had shot writhed red in the sucking mud. They cried out from the vile green fog through which I charged. I charged not for honor or for Pershing or for France. I charged for death. The artillery, louder now, frightful, our own, rained down like a blessing from on high. We succeeded in running the Germans from their lines in Cantigny and I succeeded, too, in my personal mission. Scraps of metal from the great Allied guns, spinning through the air like locusts with shark's teeth, sliced their welcome way into my body. I tried to lift my arms in gratitude but only one would rise and I fell face first into the mire.

Two stretcher bearers found me. I begged them to let me sleep but they ignored me and lifted me *from the mud. The ambulance raced me to a mobile surgery unit where the doctors saved my life and took off what was left of my arm. Within half an hour they were cutting apart the next poor wretch. I was shipped off to Number 24 General Hospital, Étaples. It was in Étaples, on the northern coast of France, that I met Magee.*

Number 24 General Hospital swarmed with wounded. Germans filled whole wards, so packed even the floors were crowded with their stretchers. Cries of "Schwester, Schwester," *rushed down the hallways. Other wards were stocked with our troops, the mangled, the maimed, the sufferers of trench fever, relatively cheery despite their feverish chills. Many in my unit hadn't loused themselves, hoping a bite would send them to just such a ward. Because of the crowding, the sisters had cleared offices to hold patients and I was placed in one of those.*

The small room held beds for three soldiers. My lungs were scarred from the gas. I could barely breathe. The stitches in my shoulder had grown infected and the nurses drained pus from the swelling each day. Still, I was the healthiest of the three roommates. The man to my right was swathed in bandages and never spoke my entire time in Number 24 General Hospital. He was fed by the sisters and moaned quietly in the late of night. Every once in a while the doctors would come in and cut off more of his body and bandage him up again. The man to my left had a gut wound that oozed red and then green and then, as he shouted through the night, burst and his insides slid out of him and with a quiet relief he died. They brought a stretcher for him and covered him with a flag. I struggled to stand as they carried him out, which was the cus-

tom. That evening, in the low light of dusk, they brought in someone new.

The orderlies propped him up on five pillows in the bed. They raised him by tape and webbing, which passed under his torso and was attached to the bedposts. The orderlies didn't joke like they normally did as they worked. The patient smelled of rotting meat and rancid oil and the stench of him flooded through the room. He already seemed more dead than the soldier with the gut wound. Before they left, the orderlies placed a canvas screen between his bed and mine. For three days the sisters came and woke him to feed him soup or change his bedpans. The rest of the time he slept. The only sounds in the room were the soft moans of the soldier to my right and the creaking of the webbing beneath the new patient's torso and my own shallow wheeze.

One morning, before the sisters came into our room, I heard a soft voice. "Hey, buddy, scratch my arm, will you? My right arm." I sat up, unsure from which of my roommates the voice had come. "Scratch my arm, will you, buddy, it's itching like hell."

The voice, I realized, was coming from the new man. I tilted myself out of bed, struggled to my feet, and walked around the screen. When the soldier came into view I stopped and stared. For a moment I forgot to breathe. He was an absolute horror. The arm that he wanted me to scratch was gone, but that was not all. His head was facing the ceiling and I stared at the side of his face, but he had no profile. His nose had been shot off. The entire top part of his face, including his eyes, had been mauled. Fluid leaked clear from his bandages. Of his limbs, all that remained was his left leg. His *swollen lips shook uncontrollably as he breathed. The smell of rot rose thick and noxious about him.*

"What about it? Scratch my arm, will you?"

"The surgeons took off your arm," I said. *"Like they took off mine."*

"Then how come I still feel it?" he asked.

"I don't know. I feel mine too."

"What else did they take off me, hey, buddy?" he asked.

"Your other arm," I said. *"And your right leg."*

"I knew my eyes were gone," he said. *"But I didn't know the rest. Funny thing is the left leg is the only one I can't feel. How's the face? Do I still got my looks?"*

I examined his mangled features and knew I should feel pity but felt none. "They blew off your nose," I said.

"Ahh, Christ. No eyes, no arms, no leg, no nose. The bastards." He took a deep breath. *"Don't that beat it just to hell. Hey, buddy, can you do me a favor? Can you get me a glass of water?"*

On the windowsill a pitcher and glasses were set out. I poured water into one of the glasses. I brought the glass to his swollen lips. He choked on the water and coughed as I poured it in. Much of it ran down his chin.

"Thanks, buddy," he said. *"Hey, can you do me another favor and scratch my side, my left side? It's like I rolled around in poison ivy down there."*

I put the glass down on a table by his bed and stepped toward him to scratch his side. He gave me directions, higher or lower, and I followed them. His skin was scabby and dry.

"That feels great," he said. *"Hey, buddy, one more favor. How about it? Will you kill me, buddy? Will you, please? Anything I got is yours, buddy, if*

you'll just kill me. Please, please, buddy. Kill me kill me kill me won't you kill me, buddy?"

I backed away from him as he spoke. I backed into the wall. He kept pleading until a nurse came into the room with a pot of water and cloths.

"What are you doing?" she asked.

"Visiting," I said.

"Don't," she said. "Corporal Magee is very ill. He needs his rest."

I went back to my cot as she began to wipe down Magee's torso with a wet towel.

Corporal Magee was quiet for much of the day, sleeping. Later, when we were left alone by the sisters, he started up again. "Hey, buddy. Will you kill me, buddy, will you, please?" I told him to shut up, but he kept on begging me to kill him.

"Why should you get to die," I said, finally, "with the rest of us stuck here alive?"

"What are you missing?" he asked.

I told him.

"Just the arm, are you kidding?" he said. "I had just an arm gone I'd be dancing in the street with my girl, celebrating."

"Leave me alone," I said.

He was quiet for another day, for two maybe. I couldn't stop thinking about him lying there beside me like that. Even when they came in to cut some more off the mute soldier to my right I thought of Magee. When he started in again, begging me to kill him, I said, "Tell me about her."

"Who?"

"Your girl. You said you have a girl.

"I don't got nothing anymore. The Huns they blew her away with the rest of my body."

"But you had a girl."

"Yeah, sure."

"Tell me about her."

"Why?"

"Because I'm asking."

He was quiet for a long moment. I thought he had gone to sleep. "Her name," he said finally, "is Glennis. The prettiest girl on Price Hill." He told me about her, how pretty she was, how kind, how gay, and in the telling he also told me about his life back in Cincinnati. He worked as a typesetter on the Enquirer. He went to ball games at Redland Field and himself played second base in Cincinnati's entry in the Union Printers' International Baseball Federation. He went to church and helped with collections for the poor. Nights he spent at Weilert's Beer Garden on Vine Street or sitting with Glennis on her porch on Price Hill. As he spoke of his good and honest life before the war I felt a bitter taste. He told it all to me and then, after the telling, he complained that it was gone. Once again he asked me to kill him.

"No," I told him. "You don't deserve to die."

"I don't deserve to live like this."

"Maybe not, but I won't kill you."

"Well, the hell with you," he said.

Later that week the colonel came to give us our medals. There was a little ceremony in my room and I stood while an aide gave the colonel the box and the colonel extracted the cross with the eagle's wings reaching high and pinned it onto my pajamas. "For outstanding gallantry in the battle of Cantigny," he said. The sight of the dark metal and the red, white, and blue ribbon made me sick. Magee was given a written commendation from his commanding officer for his bravery at Cantigny. I learned there that he had been in the wave of soldiers following me in my mad counterattack.

Two nights later he began begging me again.

"No," I said. "We're all stuck here, why should you break out and not the rest of us?"

"I'd kill you if I could, buddy. I swear I would."

"But you can't, can you?"

"Blame me for that, why don't you, you son of a bitch."

"You just have to suffer then along with the rest of us."

"Tell me all about your suffering, buddy. Tell me how terrible it is to see. Tell me how repulsive it is that you have a hand to feed yourself. Tell me how horrible it is that you are free to walk the corridors whenever you want. From where I'm lying, you've got nothing to die about."

"Shut up," I said. I was angry. Bitter and angry and furious at him for his innocence. "Shut up and I'll tell you what I have to die about and you'll be glad as hell you're not me." And so I told him what I had never told another soul, and what I am telling you, my child, as a slap from the grave.

My family owned a fashionable store on Market Street in Philadelphia. We were always of money but while I was at Yale the store found itself in financial distress. My father died when I was an infant and it was up to my uncle and me to save the store. My uncle fought with the bank. I decided on an easier route and became engaged to a woman whose father was a vicious businessman but extremely wealthy. My fiancée's father agreed that after the wedding he would buy a portion of the business, satisfy the banks, and save the company. The woman I was to marry was pretty and proper and harmless enough. It seemed to be an amicable enough business transaction.

While planning for our wedding, I surprisingly

found myself in love. Unfortunately I fell in love not with my fiancée but with her younger sister and she loved me back. By then, of course, arrangements had been made and to explain my infidelity to the father would have ruined any chance for the family company to survive. I had no choice but to go through with the wedding. Even so I hadn't the strength to give up my love and, inevitably, she found herself pregnant.

In the one truly brave act of my life I determined to run off with the younger sister and endure the wrath of both our families. It was but a few days before the wedding that we arranged to meet in the back of her house. But first, she told me, she needed to tell her sister, my fiancée, to explain to her everything. It was raining that night, and dark. I waited on the porch of the old caretaker's cottage at the bottom of the hill, unoccupied that night, for my beloved to come for me with her suitcase. Finally, I saw a female figure descend the slope. My heart leaped with excitement, but it wasn't the younger sister coming for me. It wasn't the younger sister at all.

My fiancée stepped noiselessly toward me in the night. A rain cape was swept about her shoulders. She clasped her hands before her. In the darkness her face seemed to glow with an unearthly dark light.

"My darling," she said. "There has been a terrible accident."

With utter dread I followed her up the hill. The rain streamed down my face. Water soaked into my shoes. My coat was useless against the deluge. I followed my fiancée to the spot on the rear lawn, beside a statue of Aphrodite, where she had planned that we would be married. There was a

*plot of freshly dug earth to be planted with flowers
for our wedding. Atop the plot was the younger sister, my beloved, sprawled beside the suitcase she
had packed only that night for our elopement. The
blade of a shovel had sliced through her neck and
into the soft ground. The shovel's wooden handle
rose like a marker from the bloody earth.*

*I fell to my knees in the dirt and wept over her.
I reached down and hugged her bloody garment to
my chest. I placed my cheek on the dead girl's belly
and felt the cold where there had once been two
precious lives.*

*While I was weeping my pretty and proper
fiancée explained to me the scandal and the ruin
that would erupt if the world learned of my affair
with the younger sister, of her pregnancy, of the
horrible accident and the woman's death. I could
still save my family's business, she said, save
myself from the scandal, save the younger sister's
memory from disgrace. I could still save myself,
she said, from a life of poverty. It took me no more
than ten minutes to decide. I wrapped my beloved
in my coat and dug a grave with the shovel, the
shovel, the shovel, I dug a grave with the shovel
and buried the suitcase and my beloved beneath
mounds of wet black earth.*

*I was married in a ceremony I don't remember
for all the brandy. My bride and I left for Europe
the next day on a great ocean liner for a four-
month journey that I don't remember. The only
sights I sighted in Europe were the bars and the
pubs. When we returned to Philadelphia I found a
gentlemen's drinking club where I could hide from
my wife and houses where I could consort with my
fellow whores. We had a son, my wife and I, borne
of deception and anger and violence, and after that*

I had nothing to do with either. Life in Philadelphia had grown far too bleak to bear. And as a topper, as should have been expected, my dear father-in-law sold off the family business from underneath us, taking another fortune for himself and ruining my uncle in the process. When the opportunity to join the army and die in France arose I jumped for it, joining the first recruiting march with uncharacteristic gusto. In my first battle, at the first opportunity, in my first counterattack, I leaped over the trench and charged into the heat of the enemy's fire. How cursed was I to survive a hero.

I told all this to Corporal Magee at Number 24 General Hospital and he remained silent for the whole of the telling. "If I had an arm," he said finally without a hint of rancor, "just one arm, I'd do you the favor of killing you. But I wouldn't trade with you for all the eyes in China."

My fever broke the night I told my story to Magee. The infection in my stump began to subside. I could breathe more deeply, as if a dead body had been removed from my chest.

Magee and I became close friends. His wounds had stopped their slow ooze and his rotted smell had all but disappeared. He would tell me more about his good life in Cincinnati. I would read out loud to him from the newspapers, about Pershing's eastern advance, or from the occasional letter sent by his girl, Glennis. I would also faithfully transcribe his lies about his condition in his letters back to her. "The doctors expect I'll be good as new within a few months. Make sure they keep my job open for me at the Enquirer because you and I are going to celebrate my return in grand style." I read to him from the Bible. I thought the suffering of a good man would ease his torment but the Book of Job was not what he wanted to hear. He preferred a more active hero, so I read to him of Samson. "Let me die with the Philistines," Samson begged of the Lord and Magee liked that part best of all. When the sister came in with his meals, I would take his tray and, resting it on his bedside, feed him.

At odd moments we would discuss spiritual subjects. He was a lapsed Catholic, a follower of the Socialist Eugene Debs, and I was at best an agnostic, and so our discussion had no formal bounds. We talked of death, of life, of reincarnation as preached by the theosophists. He wanted to come back in his next life as the second baseman for the Cincinnati Reds. I wanted to come back as a dog. Together we fought to make sense of what had happened to us. He was a good soul with a ruined body and I was a ruined soul with a relatively healthy body. We both found in this irony much to wonder at. And through our discussions, and in our time together, I came to a strange understanding of my life.

There were moments in the night when I doubted I was still alive and only by calling out to him, and having him answer, could my corporeal existence be proven. Magee was my mirror, without him I could not be certain of my own existence. And my mirror began to show me a shocking truth. He often complained of cramping in his hands when he had no hands. He spoke of things he saw though he had no eyes. I similarly could feel my arm as solid as before even as I knew it had been cut off by the surgeons. Illusions all. I began to wonder, was the bed upon which I lay similarly an illusion, was the hospital in which I was being treated, was the war in which I was maimed, was this cursed certitude I held of my own tortured uniqueness? In the night, in the thick of the dark, as I felt my mind empty of all but the rasp of my breath, I could feel something swell and grow beneath me, something unbelievably huge, something as great as all creation. It is impossible to explain what this something was, my child, but I knew it was more than everything and that Magee and I were part of it together. We were like two leaves side by side on the branch of a great sycamore, separate and unique only if we ignored the huge mottled trunk from which our branch and a thousand like it protruded. As two leaves on the same tree, Magee and I were inextricably linked and in that I found great comfort. His goodness was part of me. My evil was shared and thereby diluted. And sometimes, at night, I could feel the linkage grow, as if my existence was flowing through my connection to Magee, reaching out to every other soul, every other thing on the earth and in the heavens. In those nights, I felt myself absolved by the totality of the universe. It was through this linkage that I came to the understanding of my life you may find so strange. Just as a sycamore thrusts out leaves, so this universe thrusts out humanity. Our individuality is mere illusion and we remain, all of us, always, part of the great tree of creation, just as it remains part of us. These are the truths I learned, my child, alongside Magee in Number 24 General Hospital, Étaples, and which I pass on, now, to you.

The doctors came in twice a week. They looked at the charts clipped to our beds and discussed our cases as if we didn't exist. One was old and tall, one was old and short. They bickered among themselves in French. After many weeks they told me my

lungs had scarred over sufficiently and my infection had subsided and it was time to send me home.
The coughing, they said, would never leave me but
would do me no harm. They assured me I would be
fine. They told Magee that there was nothing more
they could do for him and that he too would soon
be home. Our departures were scheduled for the
following month.

As soon as they left, Magee began. "Hey,
Shaw, will you do it now, please, buddy, now. I
can't have Glennis see me like this. You're all I
got. Have pity on me, Shaw, please, and kill me."

: told him to save his breath, that now that I
knew him and loved him I could never hurt him, but
he didn't stop. His begging was fierce and pathetic.
One afternoon, while he was asleep, I wrote Glennis
a letter of my own. I described to her Magee's goodness and bravery and the wisdom in his heart. I also
detailed his physical condition, his blindness, his
ruined face, the loss of his limbs, his complete physical helplessness. Money would not be a problem, I
assured her, as I had access to great sums of money
to provide for Magee's comfort, but he would need
someone to care for him exhaustively. I gave it to the
sister to mail while he remained asleep.

The days leading to our departure passed. We
kept the windows open all day because of the heat.
From outside came the sounds of a world spinning
along its busy way, disastrously unaware of our
injuries. I read the Samson story to Magee again.
From the papers I read to him of Germany's immi-
nen: collapse. Glennis's letters, the ones that
passed my own in transit, grew cheerier as the war
news brightened. His old job was waiting for him.
Christy Mathewson had lately left from managing
the Reds to join the army in France. She couldn't

wait to feel his arms around her once again.

"She's a sweet girl," said Magee. "A good girl. She deserves better than this."

"There is nothing better," I said.

Five days before they were to take us out of the hospital for transport to the boat, her response to my letter arrived.

Back from the war, a one-armed cripple, I took long lonely walks around Veritas. I taught my son how to shoot and gave him my father's gun. The gun is a wide-barreled monster and it will be many years before he can handle it properly, but he clutched it like a rare and precious thing. He once asked me about the war and I told him only that it was a thing of death, not glory. One day I caught him in my room, admiring my Distinguished Service Cross. I snatched it from his hand. I bade him to follow me down the slope to the pond. "This is what this medal is worth," I told him and then I slung it to the middle of the water. It dropped to the bottom where it deserves to remain for all eternity.

When I felt healthy enough, I took a train to Pittsburgh and then another up to Cincinnati. From the station I rode a cab to the western rise of the city, to Price Hill. Glennis was waiting for me in a trim brick house. Her parents served me a meal of schnitzel and beans and a vinegar potato salad. Her mother cut my schnitzel for me and they talked of their great admiration for Magee. After the meal I met with Glennis alone in the parlor. She was a pretty girl, freckled and red-haired, Magee had been right about that at least. I gave her his tags and his stripes and the commendation from his commanding officer for his bravery at

Cantigny. She couldn't respond, red-faced and misty-eyed from shame. The last I gave back to her was her response to my letter. "He died before it arrived," I told her. "He never knew."

At that point she broke into tears and flung her arms around my neck and wept. I patted her on the back and comforted her with false words. I had planned to confront her with her betrayal but some surprising streak of goodness caused me to reassure her instead. As she hugged my neck I realized the cause of my reversal was Magee himself. We had truly become one. He had imparted to me his goodness and had diluted my evil. Just as she cried on my shoulder at her loss, I cried from my gain. Without Magee, my child, I would never have had the capacity to love your mother.

You must be certain that I love your mother, deeply and truly and with all my body and spirit. I saw your mother for the first time in many years during one of my walks. She was standing on the very porch on which I had waited for word of my young beloved nine years before. She showed me a book I had given her when she was a girl. She read to me that day and every day thereafter. There is to her a forgiving grace that I found only in one other soul, in Magee. And, through my love for your mother, I feel the same sense of linkage with the universe that I felt lying in the bed beside his. Many times I wished death had taken me from this life but I was spared, I think, only so I could love your mother. It is the truest thing I have ever done. If I were to believe that I was born to a purpose, that purpose would be to love her fully and completely and unequivocally. If I have done it poorly then that is due to my own weakness rather than any defect of hers. To say that I would die for her is a poor hon-

orific. I would live for her, to love her, to be with her through the rest of my days. You, my child, are the noble egg of that love.

Your mother is tending to your grandmother now. Your grandmother has not long to live and when the tending is over we shall leave from Veritas, together, quickly. We shall take my son and escape from all our pasts. You will be brought into this world well away from this cursed place. The doctors were wrong, my lungs would not be fine as they had promised. I grow progressively weaker. I spit up specks of bloody tissue with each cough. I am dying. I can feel the force of death upon my face just as Magee felt the force of my pillow upon his. As I granted his last wish in Number 24 General Hospital, Étaples, it was I who was reciting Samson's last words, "Oh Lord God, remember me, I pray Thee, and strengthen me, I pray Thee, only this once." I may not live long enough to explain all this to you and so I write this letter. I would die now, willingly, were it not for your mother, whose love I cannot bear to leave, or were it not for the joy I receive from my son and from my thoughts of you.

Remember my evil so you won't mourn for me, my child. Remember my love for your mother and carry it always close to your heart. Remember the man who gave me the power to accept your mother's love, for he and I will forever be a part of you, the man for whom your mother and I both agreed you would be named, Corporal Nathaniel Magee.

With all our love,

Christian Shaw

Part 5

≡

ORCHIDS

The rich are like ravening wolves, who, having once tasted human flesh, henceforth desire and devour only men.

—JEAN-JACQUES ROUSSEAU

55

On the Macal River, Cayo, Belize

WE PUT INTO THE MACAL RIVER from a dirt landing a
few miles south of San Ignacio. We are in a wooden
canoe, rough-hewn from a single tree trunk, that Canek
rented from a Belizean who lives on the river and who
made the canoe himself. "Did he burn it out with coals
like the American Indians?" I asked when I first saw it sitting in the water, stark and dark and primitive. Canek
shook his head and said simply, "Chain saw."

The canoe is thick-sided and shallow-bottomed. I sit in
front on a rough wooden plank. I am wearing my blue suit
with a white shirt, red tie, heavy black shoes. When I step
out of the jungle to see my quarry I want to look as if I
have just stepped out of court, no matter the discomfort in
the heat, and make no mistake, it is uncomfortable,
uncomfortable as hell. My collar is undone, my tie is
loose, my shirt is already soaked with sweat. As we travel
upriver we move through pockets of shade but, with the
humidity at eighty-five percent, even the shade is no
respite. At my feet is my briefcase and over the briefcase
is my suit jacket. A paddle sits across my legs but I'm not
doing any of the work. Canek Panti is standing in the back
of the canoe, a woven cowboy hat on his head, a long
wooden pole in his hands. He presses the end of the pole

into the river bottom and pushes us forward against the slight current. He is an imposing figure standing there, poling the canoe ever south, majestic as a gondolier, his ornate machete hanging from a loop in his belt.

Every once in a while the river quickens and Canek is forced to jump out of the canoe and take hold of the front rope and drag the canoe through swift water, the rope digging into his shoulder as he struggles forward. I offer half-heartedly to help but Canek waves me off and shoulders me upstream until the river calms enough for him to jump back in and pick up once again his pole. In those moments, with my suit and dry shoes, with Canek dragging me upriver, I feel every inch the ugly colonialist. Call me Bwana. We have passed women washing clothes on rocks and children swimming. A boy riding bareback on a great black horse crossed the river in front of us a mile or so back, but now we are alone with the water.

The jungle rises about us in walls of dense green, punctuated by the yellow-tipped crimson of lobster claws or star-shaped white blossoms, and the world behind those walls is alive with the sounds of animals scurrying and birds cawing. The trees overhead are thick with hairlike growths in their crooks, which Canek tells me are wild orchids. Little yellow fish leap out of the tropical waters and flat-headed kingfishers, dark blue with bright white collars, skim across the water's surface. Something oblong and heavy slips into the river before us. Mosquitoes hum around us, as well as other bugs, thicker, hunchbacked, and black. Botlass flies, Canek tells me. One of them tears into my neck, drawing blood. The bite swells immediately.

In my briefcase, wrapped in plastic to protect it from any water that might seep into the case during the course of our journey, is the original of the letter to his child written three quarters of a century ago by Christian Shaw. As I travel through this ancient Mayan jungle I can't help but wonder if the strange sense of revelation I felt atop El

Castillo in the ruins of Xunantunich was somehow similar
to what Christian Shaw first experienced at the bedside of
the terribly wounded Corporal Magee. Beth, who has lately
made a study of these things, said that in Shaw's letter she
saw the beginnings of a spiritual ideology reminiscent of
the Vedanta, one of the classic systems of Indian philoso-
phy, which teaches that the multiplicity of objects in the
universe is merely illusory and that spiritual liberation
comes from stripping the illusion and attaining a knowledge of the self as simply another manifestation of the
whole. Beth told me the ideas in the Vedanta are not too
far removed from what Jacqueline Shaw was learning from
Oleanna at the Church of the New Life. I don't know
Vedanta from Valhalla from Valium but I think it more
than a coincidence that Christian Shaw and his granddaughter were both suicidal before finding in a nascent
spirituality something to save them. They were both
trapped by the materiality and wealth and crimes of the
Reddmans and longed for an understanding richer and
deeper than that which surrounded them as members of
that ill-fated clan. One can't help but feel that they were on
the edge of some sort of solution and Beth continues to
pursue a similar path for her answer, though I still can't
figure out what it is an answer to.

But it wasn't the change effected on Christian Shaw in
that hospital in France that was most revelatory about the
letter, nor was it his confession of his knowledge and
acquiescence in the death of Charity Reddman at the hands
of her sister Faith, though that confession answered many
question about the fate of the Reddmans. No, the most
interesting aspect of the letter was a name, the name of
Shaw's fellow patient at that hospital in France, the name
that was to be given to the bastard child of Christian Shaw
and Emma Poole, the name that pointed with clean preci-
sion to the man who had perpetrated the latter-day mas-
sacre of Reddmans. It is this man whom I am hunting,

against whom my default judgment was issued, and who is the sole beneficiary of the Wergeld Trust from which I intend to wrest my fortune. Morris found out the meaning of Wergeld for me. We had thought it was a family name, but it was something else entirely, discernible from any dictionary. In feudal times, when a man was killed, a payment was made as recompense to avoid a blood feud that would result only in more killing. This payment was called a Wergeld. Faith Reddman Shaw's attempt to pay for the crimes of her father and satisfy the blood yearnings of the sole grandson of Elisha Poole had obviously failed.

The river is peaceful now and full of beauty. We pass a tree with bright red and black berries hanging down in loops, like fine coral necklaces. Two white egrets float by; a black vulture sits above us, hunchbacked and deprived. Something like an ungainly arrow, yellow and blue, shoots across the gap in the canopy above us and I realize I have just seen a toucan. The trees here are infested with the parasitic orchids, thick as moss, a few hungry red blooms spilling down, and as I look up at them something drops loudly into the quiet of the river. I turn around, startled.

"What was that?" I ask.

"Iguana," says Canek Panti.

Above me I notice a pack of thick-bodied lizards crawling along the outstretched branch of a tree. They are playing, scampering one around the other, and suddenly another falls off, splashing into the river. As I sit in the canoe, watching the iguanas and heading ever closer to the murderous lizard I am chasing, I can't help but see the parallels in the death struggle over the Reddman fortune and the war between Raffaello and Calvi for control of the Philly mob and its river of illegal money. How much all have sacrificed to Mammon is stunning. For now the mob is at peace, the deadly battle for control fought and decided on Pier Four of the Naval Shipyard. What was surprising was that, with all the missing soldiers, there wasn't much fuss in South Philly. Oh, there was some talk about a war, and the *Inquirer's* mob correspondent raised some questions in an article, but it all subsided rather quickly and life went on as if the dead had never been born. I am out of it now, just as I wanted to be out of it, and am grateful as hell for that.

There was a final meeting with Earl Dante at Tosca's in which the rules of my separation were made clear. Files were handed over, vows of secrecy were established. We looked at each other warily. He didn't trust that I wouldn't betray him if I had a chance to make a nickel out of it and I didn't trust that he wouldn't kill me just for the sport when came his ascendance to absolute power.

"One other thing," I said, after my obligations under the separation arrangement had been made clear. "I promised Peckworth that you would reduce his street tax."

"Why did you promise such a thing to that pervert?" Dante asked.

"It was the only way to find out what I needed to find out."

"We already knew what it was you were finding out."

"But I didn't know that. Why did you get him to switch his story in the first place?"

"This was a problem for us, not for some headline-happy prosecutor. We knew how to handle it on our own."

"I promised him you'd lower his street tax."

He stared at me for a long moment. Then he dropped his eyes and shook his head. "Stay out of our business," he warned before he agreed.

My last job for the mob was an appearance as Peter Cressi's counsel at his trial for the attempted purchase of all those guns, the crime that started this story for me in the first place.

"Where is your client, Mr. Carl?" the judge asked

"I don't know, Judge," I answered and, as befits an officer of the court, my answer was perfectly truthful because as far as I knew he could be in a landfill in New Jersey or in a landfill in Chester County or on a garbage barge floating slowly south looking for a place to dump. I didn't know where he was but I did know that no matter how many bench warrants were issued in his name he wasn't going to be found. So ended my last case as a mob lawyer. In the defense bar it is considered a victory if your client is not convicted and so I guess I went out a winner.

There is a bend in the river coming up. A huge black bird with a cape of white feathers around its red face swirls above and alights on a branch overhanging the water. The branch bends from the creature's substantial weight. Canek tells me it is a king vulture and I don't like the idea of it following us like that. I yell, but it holds its place on the branch, not interested in anything I have to offer until I am dead. We are close now, I can feel it. At each spot when the river turns I look anxiously for the pile of rocks and the tall cottonwood that will tell me we have arrived. I expect I'll recognize it right off, I have imagined it in my mind ever since I heard Rudi tell of it over a Belikin in Eva's, but even if I miss it I know that my trusty guide, Canek Panti, will find it for me. He is still standing behind me, stalwart and strong and able. The carved machete rests valiantly in the loop of his pants.

"Tell me something, Canek," I say as I feel us getting ever closer. "When I was mugged in the streets of Belize City was that the real thing or had you just set that up for my benefit?"

He is quiet for a long moment. His pole in the water gives off an ominous swish as he pushes us forward.

"It was the real thing," he says, finally. "Belize City can be a dangerous place for foreigners, though if those two had not come along I would have set it up much like that the next day."

"Well, then thank you again for saving me," I say.

"It was nothing," says Canek Panti.

I'm not sure exactly when I knew about Canek. I suspected him when he seemed too perfect to be true, precisely the man I had hoped to meet in my quest through Belize. The idea grew when he stayed outside while I went into the Belize Bank branch in San Ignacio, as if he were afraid that the tellers would recognize him as the man making the withdrawals from the account I was so interested in, and it grew even more when he volunteered to be somewhere else while I made my foray into the market at San Ignacio. And when Rudi, the Mayan, spoke of the man who was not a foreigner, with the intricately carved machete, who took supplies to the distant jungle camp, I was certain. I don't mind it actually, it is comforting that I am on the right track, that I won't get lost, and that, no matter what happens, Canek will be by my side.

"He's a murderer," I say.

"What he did in a foreign land is not my concern."

"Do you know what he wants with me?"

"No, Victor."

"You're not going to let him kill me, are you, Canek?"

"Not if I can help it," he says.

Just then we round the curve of the bend and I see it, plain as a street sign, the pile of large rocks and the huge cottonwood, its thick walls of roots reaching down to the water. There is a place on the bank that appears a bit worn and Canek heads right toward it. He steps into the water and secures the canoe with the rope around a sapling and then I step out onto solid ground with my heavy black shoes. Despite the heat, I take my suit jacket out of the canoe and put it on. I button the top button of my shirt. The collar rubs against the swelling where the humpbacked botlass fly bit me, but still I tighten my tie. I intend to look as officially benign as an accountant. Is it only wishful thinking that I imagine it harder to kill a man in a suit? I lift out the briefcase and nod to Canek and then follow him as he slashes us a path up from the river and into the jungle.

Branches brush my legs and face as I climb behind Canek Panti. Birds are hooting, bugs are circling my face. Beneath our feet is a path, but the thick green leaves of the rain forest have encroached upon the space we need to move through and we have to swing the leaves away, as if we were swinging away the shutter doors of a Wild West saloon. On and on we go, forward, through the jungle. Canek hacks at vines, I protect my face. Something brutal bites my cheek. I see a small frog leap away, splay-footed, its face and torso daubed with an oxygen-rich red. Then, above the normal calls of the jungle, I hear the humming of a motor, a generator, and then another sound, rhythmic and familiar, shivery and dangerous.

Suddenly, we are at a clearing. There is a long patch of closely mowed grass and atop a slight rise is a cottage, old and wooden and not unlike the Poole house, except that the porch of this cottage is swathed in mosquito netting. It is an incongruous sight in the jungle, this lawn like in any American suburb, this house, gray and weathered, surrounded by perfectly maintained bushes bright with flowers of all different colors.

And there he is, in overalls, a straw hat, with long yellow gloves on his hands, standing in a cloud of tiny yellow butterflies as he holds a pair of clippers from which the rhythmic sound emanates, shivery and silvery, the opening and closing of his metal shears as he clips at a tall thorny bush.

He stops clipping and turns from his task and the eye within the angry red ring squints at me, but not in anger. There is on his face what appears to be a genuine smile.

"Victor," says Nat, grandson of Elisha Poole and slayer of Reddmans. "Welcome to Belize. I've been expecting you."

56

Somewhere in the jungle, Cayo, Belize

"IT'S THE FUNGUS IN THE AIR that does it," says Nat, as we walk slowly side by side in an ornamental flower garden around the rear of the cottage. There are potted flowers and flowers growing in between piles of rocks and flowers hanging down from rotting tree limbs placed strategically in the ground. "The specialized fungus that feeds the germinating seeds. It's everywhere in this jungle, in every breath. It's the life blood of the orchid. Of course, like everything else, my sweethearts need careful pruning to maintain their splendor, but I've never been afraid to prune."

Nat is showing off his collection of exotic orchids. He had grown some on the Reddman estate, he says, in the garden room, where only the most hardy hybrids prospered. But here, in this tropical fungal-infested garden, he can grow anything. His orchids are the true light of his life now, he says, his children. "My collection is priceless," he says. I don't comment on the evident ironies. As I take the tour I continue holding onto my briefcase and sweating into my suit. Canek, still with his cowboy hat and machete, trails ten feet behind us.

"The slipper orchid," Nat says, pointing to a fragile blossom with three pink drooping petals surrounding what looks to be a white lip.

"Very nice," I say.

"*Masdevallia*," he says, indicating a bright red flower with three pointed petals.

"Beautiful."

"*Rossioglossum*," he says, brushing his fingers lightly along tiger-striped petals surrounding a bright yellow middle, "and *Cattleya*," he says, stroking gently a flower with spotted pink petals surrounding a florid burst of purple, "and *Dendrobium nobile*," he says, leaning his long frame down to smell the obscenely dark center of a perfect violet bloom.

"They're all amazing," I say flatly.

"Yes, they are. Here is one of the finest. *Disa uniflora*, the pride of Table Mountain in South Africa." He caresses a large scarlet flower with a pale yellowish organ in the middle that more than vaguely resembles a penis, complete with hanging testicles.

I murmur something indicating my admiration but I am horrified by his collection. I have seen an orchid before, sure, I was as miserable as any high school kid at my prom, blowing too much money on the tickets and the limo and the plaid tux and, of course, the corsage, all without any hope of getting laid, but the orchid in my prom corsage was as prim as my date and as far removed from Nat's blooms as a kitty cat from a saber-toothed tiger. The flowers Nat is growing are beastly things rising out of wild unkempt bushes. Gaudy petals, spotted and furry, drooping arrogant postures, pouty lips, sex organs explicit enough for Larry Flynt, the whole garden is pornographic.

"Acid, Victor. They thrive on acid. Look here." He points to a tender white and pink flower pushing up from a separate plot in the ground. "This is my absolute favorite. Imported from Australia. Notice, Victor, there are no leaves. This plant stays underground, in secret, feeding only on that marvelous fungus, biding its time until the flower bursts into the open for its own reproductive purposes."

"I think it's time we got down to business," I say.

Nat stops his tour and turns to stare at me, as if I interrupted the most important thing in his world, and then he smiles. "Right you are, Victor. Time for business. I'll have tea set out for us on the veranda. Excuse me, but I should change." He abruptly turns away from me and heads into the house through a rear door.

As I start to follow, Canek comes up beside me and gently takes hold of my arm. "I'll take you around to the veranda," he says and then he guides me back around the house to the front porch. He pulls away the mosquito netting, creating a gap for us to push through. Beneath a slowly spinning fan there is a table set with plates and cookies. Two seats face each other on opposite sides of the table. Canek pulls out one of the seats for me to sit upon and then he goes into the house, leaving me alone on the porch. The breeze from the fan is refreshing. Down the manicured slope of the lawn I see a long and crowded chicken coop.

Ten minutes later, out to the porch comes Nat, looking almost dashing in white pants and a white shirt with the sleeves rolled up. "The tea will be out shortly. Iced tea. While the generator's going we can enjoy the comforts of ice and fans."

"I have some things for you," I say, opening the lock and reaching into my briefcase.

"I can barely wait," he cackles, almost joyfully.

"This is a certified copy of the default judgment I gained against you for the wrongful deaths of Jacqueline and Edward Shaw. You'll notice the amount of the judgment is one hundred million dollars."

"Well," he says, taking it and looking it over with mild interest. "What's a hundred million dollars among friends?"

"And this is a notice of deposition for the ongoing collection action. You should show up in my offices next month on the date listed at ten o'clock."

"Will you have doughnuts for me, Victor? I like doughnuts."

"And this is a summons and complaint for the collection action my lawyer in Belize City filed yesterday afternoon. If you'll notice, in the complaint we're seeking to levy on all your holdings in Belize, including all real estate and improvements, which would include this property and the house and your orchid garden. I was glad to hear that the collection was priceless."

"Because it is priceless does not mean it can fetch any price, young man. Just so you know. The land we are on is rented from the Panti family, the house is worth the price of the wood, and the orchids I will of course take with me when I slip over the border, which is just a few kilometers that way, where I have rented another piece of land and have another house."

"Then we'll do it all again in Guatemala. I have also notified the FBI of your whereabouts and extradition proceedings are already beginning."

He stares at me for a moment, the ring around his eye darkening. "Are you after me or my money?"

"Your money," I say, quickly.

"Glad to hear it's not personal."

"Not at all," I say. "It is only business."

He cackles in appreciation. "That old bastard Claudius Reddman would be proud as hell of you, Victor."

Canek Panti comes onto the veranda with a tray holding a bucket of ice, two tall glasses, and a big glass pitcher of tea. He puts a glass before each of us and fills it with tea and ice. As Canek works he has the same considerate manner as when he was guiding. I thank him and he nods and leaves. I lift up the glass and take a long drink. It is minty and marvelous. Nat reaches over and lifts up the pitcher and refills my glass.

"Nothing better than a glass of tea on a hot day," he says.

"I have something else." I reach into my briefcase and pull out the letter from Christian Shaw, still covered in plastic, and hand it to him. "It was addressed to you."

He takes it and looks at it for a moment and then tears apart the plastic and opens the envelope and reads the letter inside. He reads it slowly, as if for the first time, and after many quiet minutes I see a tear well. When he finishes reading he carefully puts it back in the envelope and unabashedly wipes the line of wet running down his cheek.

"Thank you, Victor. I am touched. Truly touched. Didn't have time to take everything with me when I left. I was in an awful hurry. Knew you'd figure it all out soon enough and wanted to be gone before the police came looking. Didn't even have time to stay for Edward's funeral, no matter how pleasant that must have been. I would have taken the time, of course, to dig up my box, but you had already beaten me to that."

"The bank numbers in it were helpful in tracing your funds."

"I hoped my friend Walter Calvi would have retrieved it for me, but he seems to have disappeared."

"Things didn't quite go his way," I say. "Why did you bury it?"

"It was appropriate for it to rest in the ground there. It contained my most precious things. My legacy really."

"I figured out who was in the pictures. What was the postcard from Yankee Stadium all about?"

"A little private joke. April 19, 1923, the birth of two great institutions, Yankee Stadium and me." He laughs his high-pitched laugh.

"Both institutions seemed to have fallen on hard times," I said. From my briefcase I pull out a photocopy of the diary pages we found in the box. "You might want these too."

He looks them over and grows pensive once again. "Yes, thank you. You've been more than considerate,

Victor, for someone hounding me like a wolf. Mrs. Shaw, she ordered me to burn her diary when she felt death approach, to burn everything, but I excised the portions that concerned my father. That, and the letters, were all I really had of him. And, of course, his blood."

"I found your father's letter very moving. He seemed to have found an inner peace after all his trials. I would have thought his example of love and spiritual understanding would have convinced you to give up your dreams of revenge."

"Well, you would have thought wrong. He wasn't a Poole, was he? And he wrote that letter before he was murdered by a Reddman."

"Kingsley was his son. He didn't know what he was doing."

"Not Kingsley, that worthless piece of scrap. He pulled the trigger, yes, but it was Mrs. Shaw that did the killing. She was spying on my mother that night and she saw my mother and my father together and she couldn't help but scream. It was such an inhuman scream that my idiot half-brother mistook it for a cougar that was loose in the countryside. He took out my father's gun and when Mrs. Shaw saw my father climb the hill she told her son to fire and he did and for the first and last time in his miserable life Kingsley actually hit what he was aiming at."

I had wondered what that wild scream was that Kingsley had heard the night he killed his father and now I know, it was Faith Reddman Shaw's agonized cry as she saw her husband embrace the pregnant Poole daughter and realize that it was he who was the girl's secret lover, the father of her child. How lost she must have been to withhold that fact from her diary, how pathetic to be unable to admit the truths of her life even in her most private world. I wonder if she learned the tools of self-deception from her father just as she learned from him to pursue any and all means to satisfy her ends.

"So your father's letter didn't mute your hatred at all?" I ask.

"Not a yard, not an inch. I don't go in for that spiritual crap. And it is not as if his paeans to love would turn me around. I found my true love and still it paled next to the ecstasies of my family's revenge. But do you know who those letters actually affected? Mrs. Shaw."

"Faith Shaw?"

"None other. Changed her life, she said. Took her years to get the courage to go into her husband's room after his death. Years. But when she finally did, there she discovered the key. Eventually she thought to fit the key into the locked breakfront drawer at the Poole house, where she found the letters. The love letters from my mother and the letter addressed to me from my father. They had an enormous effect on her. They turned her heart inside out. I can't imagine, Victor, that mere words could have such an effect on a soul. She said she saw the emptiness in all her prior yearnings and crimes and sought to live from then on a life of repentance. I suppose she was ripe for something, still mourning all she had done and all her father had done before her.

"They were a pair, the two of them, two peas in a pod. You know, it wasn't just the one sister she killed, she killed the other, too. Poisoned her, to be sure that her son would be the only heir to the Reddman fortune. She called him Kingsley, which was a joke in itself, and before his birth made sure to destroy all possible pretenders to his throne. She put the poison in the broth she cooked her dying sister each morning. She had learned her father's lessons well and so, when it was time for repentance, she had much to be forgiven for. She pursued repentance as devotedly as she pursued her husband and her son's inheritance. Conciliation, expiation, redemption: that's what she was after. How unfortunate for her that the only path to what she sought with such desperation led through me."

"I had wondered how you got onto the estate."

"Yes, it was Mrs. Shaw who brought me home to Veritas. My mother had a difficult delivery from which she never recovered. She tried to raise me but had no money and no strength and so she sent me off for adoption. She didn't know where I was when Mrs. Shaw came looking for me shortly after finding the letters. It took her detectives nine years to find me. My adoptive parents were fine people. It was as happy a home as could be expected, but their fortunes had declined and they couldn't afford to turn down Mrs. Shaw's blandishments. So I was brought to Veritas to become her ward, her gardener, her servant. That was how she made it up to me, the stealing of my birthright and the killing of my father; she made me her gardener. She thought she was doing good, and I would have thought so too, I suppose, except she made a singular mistake. She also brought back my mother and put her in that apartment on Rittenhouse Square so that I could visit her and learn the truth of what had been done to me and my family."

"I thought your mother was beyond the hatred."

"Maybe once, but not after they killed my father. When we were reunited, God bless her, there was nothing left of the woman who had loved Christian Shaw, there was only the pain in her broken body and the bitterness. She was a wicked little thing and I loved her for it. She was the one who told me exactly how to decorate my half-brother's room. He would have nothing to do with his mother and so it was left to me to be his friend and companion. I was the one who moved in that wonderful painting of his mother. He didn't have the strength to say no and so she has stared down at him every day of his life. No wonder he jumped. But that wasn't all my mother wanted; toying with Kingsley was mere sport. She told me over and over how the Poole fortune was stolen, repeating all the stories her mother had told her. About how Claudius Reddman had doctored the books to steal his fortune. About how he had turned his friend Elisha Poole into a drunkard so his treachery would go unnoticed."

"I didn't know that's how he did it."

"My great-grandfather, singed with a mark similar to mine around his eye, was a fierce alcoholic and Claudius figured it wouldn't take much to get the teetotaling Elisha off the wagon. A drink here in friendship. A drink there in celebration. A bottle late at night after all the employees had gone home. It wasn't long before my grandfather was so sodden he couldn't see what was being ripped from him, from his family, from his legacy. 'Get it back, Nat,' I remember my mother telling me from her bed, her eyes steeped with hatred. 'Get back every cent.'"

When his mother's words come from his lips they have a rasping resonance as if she is still here, the broken old woman holed up in the luxury apartment on Rittenhouse Square, mouthing commands of revenge to her son.

"I think every young person needs inspiration in his life," continues Nat. "My mother was mine. I like to think I've done amazingly well following her wishes, but it wasn't as hard as it may seem, what with Mrs. Shaw so desperate to make amends for all she had done. Step by step I took it back.

"I was just returned from the war in the Pacific when Mrs. Shaw gave me the letter from my father and told me what she would do for me. Money, she said, she would give me all the money I wanted. A half a million dollars, she said. I took it right off and left. Half a million was something then and I went through it in five years. That was living, yep. Girls in Hollywood, girls in Paris. I rented a villa in Tuscany and threw wild parties. It was right out of Fellini. When I was broke I came back and demanded more. Another half-million pissed away in less time than the first. By the time I came back it was 1952. I was broke again and half a million wasn't going to do it anymore. I

wanted the whole thing. 'Get it back, Nat.' I will, Momma,
I will. That was when I convinced Mrs. Shaw to set up the
Wergeld Trust.

"It started out modestly enough. Just a million at first,
but I kept on coming back for more and she kept on giving
it. More money, more of the Reddman fortune. I was constantly tempted to leave and live high off what was in the
trust but my mother was always there to implore me not to
take a portion when I could have it all. So I stayed by Mrs.
Shaw's side, pruning her garden, accompanying her on her
walks, telling her I needed more and more and more as recompense. And with the weakness of the redeemed she kept
giving in. But it wasn't enough. Some things can't be
bought with just money.

"There was a maid that worked the house, a sweet
thing, innocent, really, until I was through with her. She
was sent away when her pregnancy was unmistakable but I
ordered Mrs. Shaw to bring the child to the estate and raise
him to be my heir. Franklin. I didn't want him to know I
was his father but we worked together on the gardens and
though he didn't know, I knew that he was a Poole and that
he would inherit the whole of the Wergeld Trust and
become as rich as he would have been had not our fortune
been stolen from us. But it wasn't enough.

"He was still just a bastard, rich now, but not a
Reddman. So I told Mrs. Shaw I needed one more thing,
the most delicious thing of all. She said no and I insisted
and she said no and I demanded and finally she gave in.
She set it up for me, like a pimp. It wasn't so hard to
arrange, really. D. H. Lawrence did most of the work.

"Summer nights, sneaking into the Poole house, the
two of us. I'd place garlands of flowers atop her head and
drop rose petals on her sharp breasts. Now she is a pitiful
wreck, Selma Shaw, but then she was different, earnest and
beautiful. I loved those nights, our brutal strivings, loud
enough so Kingsley could hear it all from his window.

That was a gift in itself, but there was more. I loved her. Truly. Imagine that, finding love in the course of revenge. When she found herself pregnant she talked of running off with me, but then our child would have been a bastard and not an heir. I loved her, Victor, but what power does love have next to imperatives of the blood. So I turned her away and instead of running off with me she stayed at Veritas and bore Kingsley's fourth child, a miracle child considering his operation, and, finally, the Pooles had burrowed their way directly into the Reddman line."

"Caroline," I whisper.

"And still it was not enough. 'Get it back, Nat. Get back every cent.' I would have stopped there, but my mother was insistent, urging me from her bed, plotting it all with me, telling me just how to do it, so that even after she died I had no doubts. It was simply a matter of pruning, like with any plant. Cut off some of the shoots and more precious sap flows into those that remain. I had to wait for Mrs. Shaw to die so that she wouldn't upset the trust, which she still controlled, and she proved to be a hardy weed, but once she was gone I was free to prune. How fortunate that Walter Calvi came looking for Edward just when I was looking for someone like him. Jacqueline and then Edward. Paid for Robert too but Calvi disappeared before he could deliver. I am not too disappointed, Robert is such a sexual misfit that he's sure to die heirless, leaving everything to my daughter. I had hoped we could unite the fortune in one family, in one heir, the final triumph of the Pooles, but somehow Mrs. Shaw discovered the two lovebirds and put an end to the affair. Even she had her limits, I suppose."

He winks at me just then, he winks at me with the self-satisfaction of a clever boy who has just played a clever trick. "Still I figure we did pretty well, we Pooles, wouldn't you say?"

Of all the stories I had heard in the dealings with the Reddmans and the Pooles, his is the most pathetic. He wants me to smile at him, to nod and acknowledge his success, but I see nothing more before me than a horribly failed life and I won't give him what he wants.

"And now it is over?" I ask.

"Absolutely."

"And you're pleased with yourself?"

"Absolutely. More tea?"

"I intend to collect on my judgment, Nat."

"Well then, I am going to disappoint you, because I no longer have one hundred million dollars."

"The records show that more than that was channeled into the Wergeld Trust by Faith Shaw."

"Yes, it was. As I said, she was trying to make recompense, poor deluded thing, but the money is not mine anymore. Just after her death, and before either of your so-called wrongful killings, I irrevocably transferred all but a few paltry million into trust for my son. He knew nothing of my plans, knew for certain of my guilt only after I had fled. The boy doesn't even know that the Wergeld trust is his upon my death. So you see, Victor, I couldn't pay it to you even if I wanted to, which I don't."

I stare at him for a moment, wondering whether to believe him or not, and suddenly I do. We had traced money, all right, but not all of what should have been there. The amount that had been transferred from the Cayman Islands to a bank in Luxembourg to a bank in Switzerland, through Libya and Beirut and back through the Cayman Islands, had been just about ten million dollars. I had hoped, somehow, in this meeting, to smoke out the rest and that's what I have done. It is gone. To Harrington. Out of my reach. A despair falls onto my shoulders.

"There's still ten million in your control," I say, clutching at anything. "We know that."

"Yes, that's about right, maybe less. Enough to support me through my old age. I like it here, Victor. I like Canek

and the country and this jungle and this river and my
orchids. I like it here very much. It has become a home,
but if you force me to move I will. Guatemala or Paraguay
or the Seychelles if need be. Do you know the
Seychelles?"

"Off the coast of Africa?"

"That's it. They have offered a nonextraditable citizen-
ship to anyone willing to pay ten million dollars to the
government. They have some very exciting orchids in the
Seychelles from what I understand, Madagascan epiphytes
like the African leopard orchid and the spectacular
Angraecum sesquipedale. If I must I'll pay the money to
them and live quite peacefully with my orchids under their
protection. But then, of course, there'd be nothing left for
you."

"What are you proposing?"

"Stop. That's what I brought you here to tell you. Stop
your efforts to trace my money. Stop your lawyer in Belize
City from continuing his suit. Do what you can to stop the
investigation by the FBI. Tell no one you have seen me
here and stop your efforts to hound me as if I were a common criminal. I like it here. I like the jungle. Go away and
let me live here in peace and when I die I will provide that
all of what remains of my money will go to satisfy your
judgment. The interest the Swiss give is rather paltry, but I
spend very little here and the amount will grow over time.
Go away and leave me alone and someday you'll get some
money out of me."

"And you would get away with everything."

"I've already gotten away with everything."

"It's a rotten deal."

"It's the only deal I'm offering, the only way you'll
ever see a dime."

I stare at him and think it over for a moment and then I
take a long drink of tea.

"Do you know what evil is, Nat?" I ask.

He looks at me for a moment, bemusement gently creasing his face. "Failure?" he suggests.

I make a loud sound like a buzzer going off. "No, I'm sorry. Wrong answer."

57

On the Macal River, Cayo, Belize

CANEK IS PADDLING ME BACK DOWN the river, toward
San Ignacio. From there I'll take one of the ubiquitous
taxis to the airport. I'm ready to get the hell out of Belize.
My hand hurts from a bite, it is swelling with a frightening
rapidity, and I suspect the botfly larva is squirming there
beneath my skin. I wonder if I have to declare the beef-
worm to customs when I land. I scratch it and it burns and
I scratch it some more. Maybe they have some glue and
some Scotch tape at the hotel. I scratch it and think on
Caroline.

I suspected that Nat was Caroline's father before he
ever admitted it to me, the remark by Calvi before our gun-
fight on Pier Four was what clued me, but I didn't tell
Caroline about Kingsley's vasectomy or my suspicions and
I won't tell her of Nat's admission of paternity either. It is
not my place, I think, to tell her that her real father is an
evil son of a bitch.

We have ended whatever it was we had, Caroline and
I. The love expressed between Emma and Christian too
powerfully illuminated what wasn't between us to allow us
to continue as anything but friends. True to her word, after
learning from the letter why her grandfather had thrown
away his medal, she signed the contingency fee agreement.

She found something else in the letter too, the one good thing she had been looking for, the transformation of her grandfather from a coward to a man. She has taken again to wearing her grandfather's medal and she is working, along with her therapist, to re-create for herself the history of her life, building on the base of Christian Shaw's transformation and late-found love, as well as on her understanding of the crimes that so deformed her family. This exercise in self-emendation has given her an attractive tranquility. She smokes less, drinks less, has taken some of the hardware out of her body. She doesn't interrupt me anymore when I speak. She has even adopted Sam the cat. Now that she has learned her family truths, her ailurophobia seems to have receded. She has not become one of those strange cat people, she does not allow Sam to sleep in her bed nor does she talk incessantly about how cute he is, but they have reached an understanding and he seems quite content in his new home in her loft on Market Street. I guess, like his former master, he figures anything beats Florida. Caroline pines still for Harrington, I think, not knowing he is her brother and not understanding why he can't be with her anymore. I suspect he'll tell her someday.

Caroline and Beth have become fast friends. I fear they talk about me over coffee when I am not around, though they deny it. Beth left the Church of New Life a while ago, turned off finally by the avarice with which Oleanna envelops her truths, and is now trying out Buddhism. Caroline went with her on her last Zen retreat, to an ashram in New Jersey. I maintain that seeking enlightenment in New Jersey is oxymoronic but they think they are on to something. Both women seemed subtly changed by the weekend, more at peace.

"What did you talk about?" I asked.

"We didn't talk."

"What did you do?"

"We did nothing."

"What did you think about?"

"We denied ourselves the luxury of thought."

"I'm not impressed," I said. "I spent the whole week-end watching golf on television and did the exact same thing."

The most hopeful aspect of Caroline's progress is that she is devoid of the bitterness over the past that has plagued the Pooles. There is a great peril to history. As a Jew I have learned to never forget, but some history, I believe, is best left behind. History is a warning to ourselves, and only by remembering where we have been and how low we have fallen can we know to where we aspire, but we lose everything when it is history that drives us completely, as it drove Nat and his mother and her mother and her husband. If we are to be more than pigeons pecking for pellets then we must transcend the bitterest of our histories and strike out on our own. Remembrance without forgiveness is a curse and there is no better proof of that than the Reddmans and the Pooles, fighting through generations over a fortune like two dogs worrying a bone. Caroline is learning of the necessity of forgiveness, as did Christian Shaw and as did, surprisingly, his wife, Faith.

I find it difficult to reconcile the young Faith Reddman Shaw, three-time murderess, with the woman who handed over so much to Nat in vain absolution of her past and her father's past. It is touching and sad, both, to think of her acceding to Nat's vile demands one after the other in hopes that, finally, her debts and her father's debts would be paid. That she was a monster, that her attempts were flawed, that the object of her attempts was evil makes the effort no less noble. This has been a tale of the basest sort, but I think that the most interesting part remains forever hidden, and that is the story of Faith's conversion from criminal to penitent. It is a story written on the human soul, indecipherable but no less real because of it. It is the true story of redemption in the Reddman history, heroically epic because she had so far up to climb. My guess is that her transformation followed a similar path to her husband's and is a journey being embarked upon by Caroline now. Good luck to her and I hope to hell she finds whatever it is she is looking for.

As for me, I don't go in for that spiritual crap, as Nat so tactfully put it. It is just a balm, I think, to conceal the painful truths we're stuck with, like a flesh-colored zit cream. Sure it is comforting to see oneself as part of the great mystical all, destined to be reborn again and again, like it is comforting to loll about in a tub of warm water, but it strikes me as a false refuge. Maybe my near-death experiences have turned me existential, but I can't help thinking now that I was born for no reason, I live for no reason, I will die for no reason. My task now is to figure out how to deal with those ugly truths without succumbing to depression and spending the rest of my life shivering with despair beneath the covers of my bed. One thing I do know for sure is that if I'm going to contemplate my place in the universe I'd just as soon do it on a beach in Aruba with an umbrella drink in my hand.

I agreed to Nat's offer. I promised to leave him alone, to tell no one where I found him, to halt all my attempts to collect on the debt pending his death. If he dies with ten million we'd get a third, half of which goes to my partner, a third of which goes to taxes, leaving me with about a million. So sometime in the future, the far future because he seemed a healthy man despite his age, I'm going to get a million dollars. As long as Nat has told me the truth. It's not all I was hoping for, but I can live with it, I suppose. Better it goes to me than to some corrupt government on the Seychelles. I don't like the idea of leaving him alone as if he got away with it but I'm nobody's instrument of retribution. "Vengeance is Mine," sayeth the Lord, and He can have it. I'm just a lawyer trying to make the best deal I can. Besides, I figure leaving Nat alone with his beastly flowers in that mosquito-infested jungle to face the heat of the dry season and the swarms of the rainy season is as close as I can come to sending him to hell. If I can do that and still end up with a million dollars, then that's what I'm going to do.

Am I still obsessed with finding a great fortune after all I've seen of the Reddmans and the Pooles? Hell yes. Obscene wealth is the great American obsession and I am nothing if not a patriot. It's just that now I think how I make it and how I spend it is every bit as meaningful as the money itself. Someday, if luck ever finds me, I'll be graced with a child of my own. The tragedy of the Reddmans has taught me that everything we've ever done is passed to our children like an inheritance. I can live with my crimes, I think, but to curse my child with my crimes is criminal and to commit them knowing that later on I'll have to hide the truth is positively craven. I'm still chasing as hard as the next guy, sure, but from here on in I act as if a child is judging every stride.

ACKNOWLEDGMENTS

For their generous help with this manuscript, I'd like to thank Richard Goldberg, Marilyn Lashner, Carolyn Marino, Joseph R. Rackman, Pete Hendley, who handed me a shark inside Belize's barrier reef, and my medical staff of Dr. Bret Lashner, gastroenterology; Dr. Michael Lauer, cardiology; Dr. Fred Baurer, psychiatry, and Dr. Barry Fabius, putting and the short game.

I wish also to thank the United States Navy and especially Warren Christensen, Public Affairs Specialist assigned to the Naval Ship Systems Engineering Station, Carderock Division, NSWC, for providing access to and information about the Philadelphia Naval Shipyard. Guillermo Chuc, of San Jose Succotz, who guided me around the ruins of Caracol, was of immeasurable help in my understanding of the Maya. I need also mention my friend Steven Grey, not for any help he provided with the manuscript, but because he sang like Elvis at my wedding.

Judith Regan, my editor, has given me nothing but encouragement and I am forever grateful for her enthusiasm and sage advice. She is one of those rare brave souls who ask for something different and then don't flinch when they get it.

Finally, a writer's raw material is time and so for giving me the time I needed to finish this book I give hugs and kisses to Nora, Jack, and especially Michael, who waited until my revisions were completed before entering our world. My wife, Pam, of course, gave me all the time I needed years before I was getting paid and so whatever I accomplish as a writer is her accomplishment too.